SHADOWS of DEATH

David Sundstrand

·

SHADOWS

of

DEATH

MINOTAUR BOOKS

NEW YORK

A THOMAS DUNNE BOOK FOR MINOTAUR BOOKS.
An imprint of St. Martin's Publishing Group.

SHADOWS OF DEATH. Copyright © 2009 by David Sundstrand. All rights reserved. Printed in the United States of America. For information, address St. Martin's Press, 175 Fifth Avenue, New York, N.Y. 10010.

www.minotaurbooks.com
www.thomasdunnebooks.com

Library of Congress Cataloging-in-Publication Data

Sundstrand, David.
    Shadows of death : a desert sky mystery / David Sundstrand.— 1st ed.
       p. cm.
    "A Thomas Dunne book for Minotaur Books"—T.p. verso.
    ISBN-13: 978-0-312-53758-6
    ISBN-10: 0-312-53758-1
       1. Animal rights activists—Fiction.   2. Animal welfare—Fiction.
    3. Serial murder investigation—California—Fiction.   4. California,
    Southern—Fiction.   I. Title.
    PS3619.U563S55 2009
    813'.6—dc22

                                                        2008036121

First Edition: March 2009

10   9   8   7   6   5   4   3   2   1

For the people of the Owens Valley

ACKNOWLEDGMENTS

•

Many thanks to the men and women of the Bureau of Land Management. Their tasks are many, their numbers small. I am especially grateful to Ranger Ron Stormo, lately retired from the Bishop Field Office. He was kind enough to read the manuscript before it went to press. The mistakes are mine, but due to Ranger Stormo's careful reading, there are fewer of them.

Once again, my thanks to all those who sat patiently while I read passages aloud to see if they sounded right and to check for drooping eyelids and raised eyebrows. You're a tolerant lot. I owe an especial debt of gratitude to Shirley Barker, a fellow writer, who was kind enough to provide careful and candid critiques of my early efforts.

Thank you, Fred, for letting me borrow your physiognomy. Thank you, Marilyn, for reminding me about Hobbes, and thank you, dear wife, for the research and unflagging support. Finally, many thanks to Cameron McClure, for her many readings, insights, and suggestions; she is an agent with the patience of Job.

AUTHOR'S NOTE

•

On December 6, 2006, Los Angeles Mayor Antonio Villaraigosa opened a diversion dam to restore water to the lower Owens Valley. Residents of the valley and dignitaries from Southern California gathered under a bright blue sky in the warmth of the winter sun to witness the flowing of the water. After almost a hundred years, it was something to behold, much as I described it in the final chapter of this book.

The greatness of a nation and its moral progress can be judged by the way its animals are treated.

—Mahatma Gandhi

SHADOWS of DEATH

I

•

This time the dead animals were in human form. Frank Flynn stood on the side of the hill and looked across the Joshua tree flats at the place Lieutenant Dewey had described as the site of the murders. The crime scene investigators had come and gone, removing the bodies, the Jeep Wrangler, and the clues; not much in the way of clues. Dewey had said nothing had been found that pointed to the shooter or shooters. That's why he'd asked Frank to look around, that and the grudging admission that Frank was really a part of law enforcement. Asking for help was an apology of sorts for past slights.

From the way Lieutenant Dewey had described the murder scene, one poacher, the one with the rifle, had been hit in the back of the head with a high-speed round that had taken away a quarter of his face and blown out the upper cheekbone and left eye. If the forensics people were able to find anything, Flynn would bet on bits of silver or lead from an expanding round, probably the same kind of round that had killed the burros. He looked back at the road and beyond. The killer of men had hit the killer of burros in the back of the head, which meant that Frank was looking out over the part of the desert where the shooter had waited in ambush. A low outcropping of caprock ran along the crest of the far hill. It was a perfect place from which to take life without being detected, a sniper position.

Flynn picked out a high spot that was in line with where the Jeep had been and started down the slope to the road, keeping the rocks as a reference point. When he reached the outcropping, he turned to look back at the murder site. The dark volcanic ridge commanded a view of the Saline Valley Road, from where the road cut through the caprock down to the dry wash that divided the two hills and up the far side. It was about six hundred yards before the ground dropped away onto the plateau. The killer had been skillful or lucky. Frank walked the ridgeline back to the road, a distance approaching two hundred yards, without seeing so much as a footprint. Returning to the beginning of his search, he moved along the ridge away from the road. He hadn't gone more than fifty feet when he spotted an empty brass shell casing, glinting in the afternoon sun. Frank kept to the rocks so he wouldn't create tracks or disturb the scene. If there was a scene, it didn't amount to much.

Two depressions in the sandy soil at the base of a gently sloping rock face were the only telltales of human activity. At this point along the ridge, a shooter could take a prone position and be as good as invisible from the road. Frank lay down on the rock and placed his elbows as if holding a rifle. Sighting along the imaginary barrel, he found himself looking at the murder site. Only problem, he kept slipping backward down the smoothness of the rock face, until his toes dug into the sand near the cup-shaped depressions where the toes of the shooter's boots must have been. He pushed up. The shooter had to be six or seven inches taller than Frank, a very tall person. He scanned the ground. Nothing he could call footprints, but there were some foot-sized disturbances taking a path across the desert toward Hunter Mountain. A trail-wise killer. He'd wrapped his feet so there wouldn't be any identifiable tracks.

Frank examined the shell casing, a .270. One shell casing, two corpses. The killer missed picking up the empty from the first shot. Oddly careless. Frank picked up the empty shell by inserting a twig in the opening where the slug and powder had been and slid it into a plastic bag. The second casing was probably still in the rifle. Something about the killer's actions made him uneasy.

He'd have to take a run over to Hunter Mountain. Probably wouldn't find a thing. Oh yeah, and he'd better get in touch with Lieutenant Dewey and give him the empty shell casing from the .270, nice flat trajectory, perfect for popping poachers. He felt the corners of his mouth lift into a smile.

Three days earlier, Frank had discovered a wounded burro and her foal not far from the site of the murders. He had ended the jenny's suffering by putting a .45 round into her head as she struggled to lift herself from the sandy soil. His attempts to catch the orphaned foal had been futile, a circular chase; the foal had kept a fixed distance between Frank and the lifeless jenny. There was no way to catch it by himself. He'd had to temporarily abandon the foal until he could come back.

He'd returned the following day with Molly Shannon, a BLM biologist who shared Frank's affection for the clever creatures, hoping that the foal would still be alive. It had worked out about the way things work out—without resolution. He and the biologist had found no sign of the burro foal. They assumed it was probably dead. Wandered off to be eaten by your neighborhood coyotes.

Later a spiraling column of vultures had shown them where another adult burro lay decomposing in the summer heat. Frank was somehow relieved by this animal's death because it meant the foal might still be alive. There was still a chance to save it. If he couldn't save the foal, he was determined to catch the poachers.

The burro killings in the Mojave triggered a burning anger. Frank hated the mindless cruelty. The gun nuts were on a rampage, coming into the desert for a weekend of random slaughter, killing things for the pure joy of it. If there were a way to run the poachers down, he would spare no effort. He'd returned later with a metal detector to see if he could find the spent slugs in the corpse, something tangible he could send to the forensics lab in Ashland, Oregon, that would make him feel better. He had met with no success.

As he made his way back to the road with his bagged .270 brass, he considered the death of the two poachers with grim satisfaction. Someone had decided to even things out. The late afternoon sun was approaching the back wall of the Sierra Nevada. Soon the high plateau country would be washed in shades of flaming gold before plunging into the deep blues of night. A line of poetry ran through his head, "Though every prospect pleases and only man is vile." He was angrier than he knew.

2

•

The suits stood in front of the chairs guarding the chief ranger's desk. The presence of federal authority hung in the air like cigarette smoke, thick and unpleasant. The FBI had arrived to direct the efforts of the Bureau of Land Management rangers. Frank Flynn lounged against the wall, his eyes wandering to the window.

Dave Meecham looked around the room. "Special Agent in Charge Peter Novak." Meecham gestured to the shorter of the two men in front of his desk. "And Special Agent Andrew Ellis." Ellis was tall and slim, clean-shaven, with fine blond hair, pink cheeks, and eager eyes. A tight smile flickered across his handsome features. "Make it Drew," he said.

Older than Ellis by fifteen or twenty years, Novak wore a rumpled, shiny brown suit. It was hard to imagine him in anything else. He flashed a friendly grin, crinkling sandy skin into a pattern of fine lines.

As the BLM rangers seated themselves across from the FBI agents, Meecham made an effort to catch Frank's eye. "Pull up a chair."

"Naw, that's okay, been riding around in the truck."

Meecham cleared his throat. "The FBI has a special interest in the killings up on Saline Valley Road. I told them we'd help them in every way possible."

"You weren't on the crime scene but came later, as I understand it," Ellis said, addressing Frank without looking up from the notebook he had withdrawn from his suit pocket.

"Nope, not much there by the time I showed up," Frank said.

Meecham had crammed mismatched chairs into his office. It was the best he could do. The FBI agents probably thought Ridgecrest was lizardville and the BLM lived in tents.

Ellis droned on in a professionally impersonal voice. "Lieutenant Robert Dewey, Inyo County Sheriff's Department, requested that you 'take a look around.'" Ellis's eyebrows raised. "Is that how you became involved in the investigation?" His eyes remained on the notebook.

Frank was beginning not to like Special Agent Ellis. He waited to see if he would look up from his notes. Frank was hoping for some *ojo a ojo*, eye to eye.

Novak cut in. "Dewey had good things to say about you, Flynn. Said nobody knew the country around here better than you."

Ellis shuffled some pages. "He also said that you know the people in this area, that you would be able to point out illegal or suspicious activities that might relate to acts of terrorism." He turned his head and raised a challenging glance, checking out Frank's reaction.

Frank was gratified. See if he could find this in his notebook. "Well, yeah, that's right, Drew. We've had a spate of terrorism. Back in the twenties, some ranchers tried to blow up the Los Angeles aqueduct, trying to get their water back. Then there was the Jackalope Conspiracy up in Jawbone Canyon, but I guess maybe that one slipped by you guys." He eyeballed the ceiling in thought. "Outside of that, not all that much happens." He brightened. "Unless you want to count body dumping. Desert's a great place to dump a body. If all the corpses stood up at one time, we'd need crowd control."

Meecham winced.

Ellis stared at Frank, his face expressionless. "Why didn't you report the note?"

Ellis's question caught Frank off guard. "Didn't find a note. Just the empty .270 casing."

Ellis nodded. "Spent, not quite empty. I guess you must have missed it." He passed Frank a ziplock bag with a small slip of paper in it.

Frank could feel his face reddening under the brown skin. "Can't make it out."

"It says, 'Ready on the left. Ready on the right.' Any idea as to what that might mean?"

"Yeah, sounds like range master's commands. Then it's 'Ready on the firing line.' What's it got to do with the murders up on the flats?"

"A man was killed in Long Beach, shot twice with a .22 hollow point, one in the heart and one in the eye. The killer cut his lips off, then left a note: 'An eye for an eye. Sandman.'" Ellis gave Frank a probing look. "The note was tucked into the victim's shirt pocket. He leaves notes. Long Beach PD found it. This time he left a note curled up in a .270 shell casing. Inyo sheriff's department found it in the empty you passed on to Lieutenant Dewey."

"Why would someone do something like that?" Meecham said. "Cut someone's lips off."

"The victim made the papers about a year ago for cutting the beaks off pelicans. He was a commercial fisherman. The judge gave him a nasty scolding and probation," Novak said and rolled his eyes.

Ellis continued. "The killer must have thought it didn't seem fair. So he did the same thing to the victim for an object lesson. We think this killer is the same person who shot the victims out here." Ellis looked back at Frank. "As I said, you must have missed it."

Frank didn't bother to explain about picking up the shell casing so as not to smear fingerprints.

"We should've filled you in before the meeting, Frank." Novak's square face wrinkled into a weathered smile. "You understand we're anxious to get a handle on this organization, especially now that we know, for sure, that they're killing people."

"Organization? As in more than one guy?" Frank said.

"Fill us in," Meecham said.

"You know about animal rights terrorists, right?" Novak asked.

"Some, not much. Out here it's the other way around." Meecham's smile was without humor.

"I'm talking about the groups that break into labs to rescue lab animals and ruin years of government-sponsored research. Crazies who run around throwing red paint on people with fur coats." He paused, waiting to see how Frank would respond. More stone face. Novak looked down and studied his shoes. "What I'm talking about is people who take the law into their own hands, disrupt scientific studies, disrupt agriculture, harass American citizens who don't happen to think the way they do, especially sportsmen who buy hunting licenses and engage in legal recreational hunting." He met Frank's stare. "You've heard about these people."

"Yup, I read the paper." He looked from Novak to Ellis and back again. "So what's all this got to do with the killings on the flats?"

Ellis looked past Frank to Meecham. "We have definite proof that the murder of the hunters up there is part of a conspiracy. An act carried out by a terrorist organization calling itself MDG."

"What's MDG stand for?" Meecham asked.

"We're not sure. Most likely, some terrorist acronym, like FARC or HAMAS," Ellis said.

Frank's face filled with contempt. "The men killed on the Saline Valley Road were killing for the thrill of it. A long way from hunters. In fact, they were criminals in violation of federal law, killing protected animals."

"That's not the point, Flynn. The point is two people were killed, and we know the killer or killers are connected to the MDG." Ellis leaned forward, tapping his notebook for emphasis.

"How do you happen to know all this, and who the hell is the MDG?" Frank said. "Pardon me for asking, but sometimes the dots don't connect up in the same way."

The two agents glanced at each other, then over to Dave Meecham.

"First we'd like to know what you discovered at the crime scene. Dewey showed us his report and the .270 shell casing and the note." Novak slipped back into his folksy demeanor. "We can match the casing up to the rifle, if we find the rifle. Better yet, in possession of the shooter."

Ellis picked it up. "Also, we'd like to know how you managed to discover evidence that was overlooked by"—he checked his notebook—"seven law enforcement officers from two *professional* law enforcement agencies."

"What's your point?" Frank said.

"Why *you*? Seems like the note means someone expected *you* to find the empty. You trained recruits at Fort Ord"—the notebook again—"and you were a small arms instructor at Hunter Liggett."

Frank locked eyes with Ellis. He could feel the heat in his cheeks and the smart-ass things he wanted to say struggling to get free. He drew a deep breath in through his nose and released it gradually through clenched teeth. "What're you trying to say, Agent Ellis?"

"It seems like someone might've been sending you a message."

"When the crime scene investigation didn't turn anything up, including the .270 brass, Lieutenant Dewey called and asked if I'd have a look around when it wasn't so crowded." He paused. "Check your notes there, Agent Ellis. I'm sure you must have indicated the time the *professionals* passed gas and departed for pavement and the Dairy Queen."

Ellis's pink cheeks flushed.

"God damn it, Frank," Meecham muttered, shaking his head.

He'd done it again. Making things tough for Dave Meecham was the last thing he wanted to do. He scrambled to repair the damage. "I apologize, Agent Ellis. Sometimes the coyote speaks from my mouth before I can chase him away."

Ellis frowned.

"My grandmother used to say that," Frank said. He looked at Novak. "She was Paiute. The coyote is a trickster and never very polite."

Novak nodded, his face solemn with understanding. Ellis looked from Frank to Novak, confused.

"Lieutenant Dewey and I have worked closely together in the past. He hoped I might find something that had been overlooked, and it so happened that I did." Frank told them about finding the dead burro, retracing the trajectory, and finding the empty shell casing and explained why he thought the killer had probably wrapped his feet.

"Yeah, that makes sense." Novak gave Frank an appraising look. "Nice piece of work, Flynn."

"The way I worked it out wasn't in the report I sent over to Dewey."

"Maybe you ought to keep better notes." Meecham was grinning. It broke the ice.

"While we're at it, why do you think the killer was a tall person?" Ellis again.

"I looked for a good place to take a shot, near where I found the casing. There was a natural indentation in the caprock, a perfect place to lie down and wait. Only thing is, I kept slipping backward down the rock. Then I discovered a couple of indentations in the sand. I figured they were made by feet attached to a body tall enough to fit the hollow just perfectly."

"In fact, the only physical evidence is the shell casing and the note," Ellis said.

"It's just a theory. The way I see it, the shooter was on foot. Did the killing and hiked cross-country to the pinyon pines on Hunter Mountain."

"How far would that be?" Novak wanted to know.

"Six, maybe seven miles."

"Why would he walk when he could drive?"

"You been up there?"

The agents shook their heads.

"It's open country. A car's easy to spot; the dust plume coming up from the road can be seen for miles. And as you know, driving a car's like wearing a big identification tag: make, model, color, plates, all that good stuff. A man walking cross-country doesn't throw up dust, and if he's wearing khaki or camo, he's damn near invisible."

"You're telling us that the killer escaped on foot across open country." Ellis looked skeptical.

Frank stared into the space between them, letting the silence gather. "There was a famous California road agent called Black Bart. He held up stages, took the money, and left behind poems. Frank scrunched up his eyes: " 'I've labored long and hard for bread, / For honor and for riches, / But on my corns too long you've tread / You fine-haired sons-of-bitches.' " Frank made a point of not looking at Ellis's silky blond hair. Bart didn't kill people, a major difference, but he took a lot of money.

"Wells Fargo posted big rewards, put on extra guards, but after every holdup, Bart just disappeared. Finally, Wells Fargo sent James B. Hume, their chief of detectives, to catch the man who robbed Wells Fargo and got away with it. Hume was the former sheriff of Hangtown, gave the town its name. Now you guys'll like this." Frank grinned. "Hume ran Bart down in San Francisco by tracing a Chinese laundry mark. It was a first-class piece of detective work using forensic evidence to catch a crook."

"What's the point here?" Novak looked impatient.

"Well, Bart was proud of his work. He told Hume how he'd gotten away with all those robberies. Everyone assumed he had a horse tied out of sight so it wouldn't be identified, but nobody figured a man would be fool enough to rob a stagecoach on foot. They were wrong. That's what he did. Hit the stage and then hiked cross-country over some pretty rugged terrain, places a horse couldn't go. He usually made it back to some small town where he was already a registered guest at one of the local hotels."

"So you think our man might have done the same thing?"

"Why not? Hide a vehicle in the high country and drive out after things have calmed down. There's a hell of a lot of Mojave Desert and not much in the way of manpower to patrol it."

Novak looked over at Meecham. "What do you think of Frank's theory, Dave?"

"Makes sense." He looked thoughtful. "Doesn't explain why he leaves notes, though."

'Maybe he's playing with us, like Bart," Frank said. "The 'eye for an eye' stuff was in Long Beach. The range master stuff was out here. Ready on the left for one guy. Ready on the right for the other." His mouth turned down in a perverse smile. "I imagine he caught them by surprise, though."

Ellis frowned. "You think this stuff is funny?"

Novak broke in. "Then it's 'Ready on the firing line.' Right?"

Frank nodded. "Then it's 'Commence firing.' He's letting us know he's not through."

Meecham glanced up at the clock on the opposite wall. "Let's eat." The agents nodded in agreement. "You guys like Mexican food?" They nodded again. "Great, we'll go over to Ralph's. Frank and I'll be along in a minute." The agents filed out into the hallway.

•

"What's this about the coyote speaking through your mouth?" Meecham asked.

"I made it up. I guess I was taking advantage of Novak's good nature. He seemed like a nice guy who might respect other cultures, especially Native American cultures, so I blamed my smart mouth on being part Paiute. You know, Coyote made me do it."

"I think there's more coyote in you than meets the eye." Meecham made a wry face. "We didn't look very good in there."

"You're right, Dave. Won't let it happen again."

"Take a seat." Meecham gestured vaguely at the battered chairs in front of his desk.

Frank sat.

"Next week, I'm going to Washington, D.C."

"You told me, Chief."

"There's a couple of things that need doing while I'm at the conference."

"Okay," Frank said.

"I want you to represent the BLM at the opening of the Sand Canyon Game Reserve. We've been invited along with California Fish and Game and U.S. Fish and Wildlife—and God knows who else." He rolled his eyes. "It's going to be a big event."

Frank's expression was stony.

Dave Meecham returned the expression. "I don't like these canned hunting outfits any more than you do, but people in the valley are excited. It means a few more local jobs. And it means tourists with big bucks. The Chamber of Commerce in Lone Pine is happy as hell. Same goes for Bishop."

"Right. Welcome, rich assholes. Hate your guts but love your money." Frank sneered.

"Damn it, Frank, that's what I don't want." Meecham's voice was steely. "These people are going out of their way to make sure everything is squared away with the right agencies. Our office has been invited for a tour of the facilities. I've been invited. You're going in my place. As senior ranger in Ridgecrest, you'll be representing the bureau while I'm in Washington."

Frank was swept with a wave of guilt. Dave Meecham was more than his colleague and boss; he was a friend, and he was entrusting Frank with the reputation of the BLM, the Ridgecrest office, and his own reputation as chief district ranger.

"Okay, Dave, and I'll make sure the coyote shuts up."

Dave Meecham's shoulders sagged as the tension dissipated. He leaned back in his chair, looking tired.

"Anything else?" Frank asked.

"Hold the fort. Sand Canyon is the big-ticket item. Fish and Wildlife will be on them about the introduction of exotic species. The new owners bought out the old Circle Cross ranch and arranged to take over the grazing leases for hunting."

Frank raised his eyebrows.

"Duane Marshall is the president and principal owner of Sand Canyon, and he is a big contributor to the NRA and has lots of juice, big political connections."

Frank choked the coyote into silence.

"There are two things for us to be concerned about. The lease land has abandoned mine sites, some marked, some not. There's a couple of uncovered shafts near the mouth of the canyon that I know of and a sign warning about old mines, but that's it. The Sand

Canyon people have promised to cover them. Check it out, and check on the other sites. The U.S. Geological Survey maps show three mines near the mouth of the canyon on BLM land. Making the area safe was part of the lease agreement."

Frank nodded. "Consider it done."

"Another thing. You know where the petroglyphs are up in Dead Indian Wash?"

Frank frowned in mock thought. "You mean Deceased Native American Paiute Wash?"

"That's the place." Meecham smiled. Frank's sense of the absurd never failed to amuse him. "They are to understand that the area is off-limits to shooting. The petroglyphs are not to be defaced by *chingaderos* shooting them up."

"Can I tell them that? No *chingaderos*." Frank asked, looking innocent.

Meecham cocked a warning eye.

"Okay, boss. I'll stick to the English and just say fuckers." He raised his hand in anticipation of Dave's irritation. "Not to worry. I'll deliver the message about the petroglyphs with professional discretion."

Dave Meecham considered his friend. They had worked together for eight years. Frank had been with the BLM for nine. A veteran with a degree in American studies, he'd hired on as a historian. The military background and penchant for solitude routed him into becoming a ranger. Meecham had come into the BLM from another law enforcement service, the way so many had. He'd been with the Border Patrol first, and then opted for the Bureau of Land Management when it incorporated an enforcement arm. Meecham was close to retirement, but he didn't talk about it. In many ways, Meecham and Frank were the odd couple, but the job and the love of the land had made them an effective team.

"Yeah, I know you'll handle it. Oh, and the preview is in a week, opening day three weeks after that. Most of the law enforcement types will skip the opening day shootout, unless they're carrying the flag for one of the departments. Too many people. My guess is that everything will be shipshape; otherwise, they wouldn't have invited us." He ran a hand through sandy hair. "Okay, let's eat," he said, rising from his chair. "See if those boys can take Ralph's hot sauce."

3

•

Seth Parker had lived above the Hendricksons' garage for more than two years, longer than anyplace else since taking his disability discharge from the army. The studio apartment felt like home. He would miss it, but time was running out. He wasn't going to die with soiled pants in some VA hospital. He'd go out with a bang, not a whimper—and he wasn't planning on going alone.

At first, the diagnosis had hit him hard. It came without a warning, but now he considered it liberation. Having absolutely nothing to lose enlarged his thinking and made him giddy with the freedom of possibilities. In the short space of three months, he had accumulated several Internet followers. Mostly wannabes, full of electronic chatter, unwilling to take that first irreversible step from talk to walk. The first one was always the hardest.

There were a couple of exceptions in the mix of losers and crazies, though. Ray in Texas understood exactly what was required of members in the MDG. He'd even posted a photograph of a kill he claimed was his. Thus far, Parker had been unable to verify it in the newspapers. The dead hunter, a great picture of him hanging from a barbed-wire fence, might have died as the result of a genuine accident. There were so many hunting accidents you could pick and choose.

John was another matter. He'd met John at the thousand-yard

range on Bear Valley Road, east of Victorville, and he could shoot accurately, an essential skill for unit members and not easily acquired. As yet, John knew nothing about target acquisition, evaluating the terrain, and evading detection, essentials to becoming an effective sniper, but he was an eager pupil. More important, he was the perfect disciple. John had been lost, drifting without purpose. Now he had been found—by Seth Parker. Parker had brought about John's transformation from a self-indulgent rich boy to a man who had discovered the satisfaction of a purpose-driven life. The righteousness of their cause was simple: justice for the innocent, an eye for an eye—or a lip for a beak. The removal of the commercial fisherman's lips had caused quite a stir. As he had explained to John, they were balancing the scales, taking up the slack in the cosmic justice department.

Of course, the game itself held a magnetic fascination. There was an electric thrill when the quarry could shoot back. The risk of death made for real hunting, not simple slaughter. It was also what made combat soldiers tick, the absolutes of life and death held in balance by the skill of the participants.

MDG was more than an acronym, a mere mind game. It was the word made flesh, the embodiment of purpose. Besides, the camo-clad, swaggering pseudo-men, who loved the wars they didn't fight in, needed a touch of reality, something that could shoot back. MDG would ensure that their life experiences were more inclusive.

When they first met, Parker had qualms about John's physical attributes—or lack of them. He questioned whether his new follower would be up to the demands of the game, but John succeeded in laying Parker's doubts to rest. He went on a regimen of diet and exercise, lost the puffy baby fat that clung to his short, tubular body, and achieved a modest degree of fitness.

John's money was an added asset. John had purchased a .50

caliber M107 sniper rifle. Very expensive, but with the infusion of John's money, the MDG could afford it. John thought the heavy round would do spectacular damage. Parker had reminded him the weapon was designed to take on lightly armored vehicles. John had replied that using the .50 would provide a wonderful object lesson. Under the bland exterior, John was very angry. Parker recognized the signs. He knew all about suppressed rage.

At first, they had just talked about their operation, developing a philosophy, a rationale that not only sanctioned the taking of human life but even required it. On the other hand, Parker knew that the real attraction was in the danger, the hunt for game that could shoot back. Then the diagnosis changed everything. Seth Parker had been gripped by a sense of urgency.

His first kills had been personally satisfying but relatively anonymous, providing no object lesson. The newspaper and television accounts reflected befuddlement. The killings were described as motiveless. Then the television reporters took to referring to the victims' deaths as sad, even tragic. Parker knew better.

His efforts had been misunderstood even when he killed the redneck who trained his pit bulls by tossing them litters of kittens and live puppies. The media didn't seem to get it. He was making things better, not worse. The families and neighbors of these violent men had lived in constant fear. They must have been swept with gratitude, or at least relief, at the removal of the source of brutality.

Violence done to animals was a precursor of violence done to human beings.

The fisherman had been his first signature killing. His death had made things much clearer and made the Sandman a celebrity. The lipless face of the man who had mutilated the pelicans had generated far more than a thousand words. The note had added just the right touch, "An eye for an eye." Everybody believed in revenge, and it added a hint of mystery. What had the victim done to deserve death at the hands of the Sandman?

The news anchors and anchorettes couldn't stop talking about it. The public had something new to be afraid of, a new vicarious thrill. They'd been handed a story that had universal appeal, controversy, and condemnation.

When Parker had posted the pictures of his most recent kills on the Web site under his nom de guerre of the Sandman, John had been quietly ecstatic, eager to participate. Parker suspected that John's motives were not completely pure, but he knew that his own motives were mixed. Although he thoroughly hated cruelty and the destruction of innocent things, he'd thoroughly enjoyed killing the man who'd mutilated the pelicans, especially the coup de grâce.

He replayed it in his head over and over again. *You shot me!* It always came as a surprise. Up close and personal was very different than a kill shot through a scope. Using the .22 provided maximum effect, minimum mess. Cutting the lips off the pelican man had been difficult and disgusting, but it was a stroke of genius. He was famous. His cause was becoming famous. That was the important part.

He looked over his apartment in preparation for the final tidying up. First, remove items that could lead directly to his identification. That would come soon enough, but by then, it wouldn't make any difference. Parker opened the gun safe where he kept his Model 70 Winchester Featherweight and the Colt Woodsman. He owned only two weapons, all he needed. One for distance, one for close up.

The Model 70 was pre-1964, a beautiful weapon. He loved the straight-grain walnut stock, the luster on the wood, the smoothness of the polished action. He couldn't bear to paint the stock or remove the sheen from the brilliant bluing of the metal. It had been his father's. Now it was his, the same rifle, but outfitted with a much improved telescopic sight. It was far from the very latest sniper setup but absolutely first rate. Besides, it was the shooter that counted. One shot, one kill. Uncle Sam had spent a lot of money on his training. It would be a shame to let it go to waste.

He slid the rifle into a padded case and tucked the Woodsman into a soft leather inside-the-belt holster, invisible to others while he was wearing a hangout shirt or light jacket. Time was hurrying along, and he must hurry with it.

First he had to drop off Orpheus and Eurydice with John. They were his breeding canaries. Eurydice, the female, didn't sing, but she was the cause of song in Orpheus, and she had begun to construct a second nest. Parker slipped the solid partition into place between the two sections of the breeding cage. Orpheus could be quite aggressive. Parker hoped the move wouldn't disrupt the nesting ritual. He cherished hopes for canary chicks within a month. He refused to think about his condition when he thought about the birds.

In less than four weeks, the Sand Canyon Game Reserve would be open for business. No matter what happened to him, he would have made his mark. They would know of his work, and if all went well, John and the others would be his legacy.

4

•

Rangers and agents filed back into the conference room, the damp sweat of their clothes making them shiver in the chill of an overactive air conditioner. Novak had manfully polished off one of Ralph's Super Burritos with *salsa verde*, apparently with no ill effect. Ellis clearly wasn't so fortunate. His handsome face was grim with dyspepsia. Frank was feeling a bit mean for having assured the pilgrim agents that Ralph's sauce was a tasty aphrodisiac.

"For men only!" Frank winked at Ralph's smiling face, tombstone teeth set in a field of blackened stubble.

Ellis had gone for the challenge. Macho is as macho does. Now pride was paying the price. Petty revenge was better than no revenge at all.

Dave Meecham cleared his throat. "So here's where we are. The killer took out two victims, both males in their thirties. Apparently they were shooting burros, just for the fun of it. No help from the autopsy report, but pretty obviously they died from gunshot wounds. The spent casing indicates a .270. Evidently the killer figured that someone would find the shell casing, because he left a note. Finally, Frank thinks he was tall, well over six feet."

"And that he just walked away from the scene," Ellis added.

"It's a working theory," Meecham responded.

Silence settled over the group. Meecham looked at the inert

bodies, dulled and lethargic from lunch. They should have just stayed until they finished up. He knew better than to take a lunch break, but he'd been striving to be hospitable, especially after Frank's coyote mouth.

Novak shuffled his papers in preparation to leave.

"Aren't you forgetting something?" Meecham said.

Novak spread his hands in inquiry. Ellis glanced out the window.

"Quid pro quo." Frank addressed Novak.

"What?" Ellis's head snapped around.

"Favor for favor. We showed you ours," Meecham replied.

Novak shrugged and settled back in his chair. "So what do you want to know?"

"What makes you think the killings are tied to these MDG animal rights terrorists?" Meecham queried.

Frank shook his head and mumbled something about an oxymoron.

"Pardon?" Ellis squinted at Frank.

" 'Animal rights terrorists' sounds like a contradiction in terms, that's all."

Ellis looked over at Meecham. "You're hooked up to the Web, right?"

"All the modern conveniences."

They wedged themselves around Meecham's desk.

"Punch up Google and type in MDG," Novak said.

Meecham watched the screen. "Take a look at this."

Frank leaned forward to get a better view of the screen. MDG in large bold script headed the page. Under the heading, a banner read WE HUNT THE SCUM OF THE EARTH, GENERAL ZAROV. The rest of the Web site contained various tabs and photos (click to enlarge) that clarified beyond a doubt that members of the MDG were not only being encouraged to hunt human beings but were, in fact, successful in this endeavor, if the photographs were to be believed.

"My God." Meecham whistled under his breath. "Looks like they're killing folks all over the country." He looked up. "How come we haven't heard anything about this?"

"The lipless corpse in Long Beach and the men killed here in the Mojave are the only confirmed victims firmly linked to the MDG organization with notes specifically left by the killer or killers. We haven't been able to track down all the photos, but we know two were definitely hunting accidents. Some were reported as accidents, but we're not so sure. Your victims are our first direct link since the killing in Long Beach."

Meecham scrolled down. Under the heading IMPROVING THE GENE POOL, there were newspaper clippings devoted to hunting accidents, followed by editorial comment. A deer hunter in South Carolina had dropped his rifle from a hunting blind in a tree. The rifle had discharged and struck the hunter in the buttocks. A brief commentary under the caption ASSHOLE SHOOTS ASSHOLE added an explanatory note that the Gutless Wonder (the term reserved for hunters who shot at domesticated game) was taking an original step to bringing about an end to prostate problems. Another accident the site editor found particularly amusing occurred when a wife managed to remove most of her husband's penis with a twelve-gauge shotgun while hunting pheasant on a "private preserve" in Nebraska. The caption here read POST-INFANT CIRCUMCISION PROVES PAINFUL.

"Why do you think this killer has anything to do with MDG? Where's the connection?" Frank asked, his voice subdued.

"Click on the Zarov Awards button," Ellis directed.

Three small photos filled the left-hand portion of the screen with text on the right. Each segment, photo plus text, was under the name of a state.

"Hit California."

A photograph of a red Jeep Wrangler filled a third of the screen.

A man leaned out of the driver's side at an unnatural angle. A large portion of his head appeared to be missing. A second man lay against the right front wheel. The text was concise:

A DOUBLE ZAROV AWARD TO THE SANDMAN! THIS IS A FIRST! These Gutless Wonders were taken at 300 yards with a .270 using a factory load with 130-grain silver tip. Good shooting, Sandman!

"These your dead guys?" Novak asked.

Frank nodded. "Looks like it, at least from what the Inyo sheriff's people said."

"This organization sponsors *terror*," Ellis said, staring at Frank.

"Can't you trace the site, the photos?" Meecham inquired.

Ellis thumbed through his notes. "According to our tech people, the terrorists are computer smart." He looked up from his notebook. "They borrow wireless signals and IP addresses. They drive around until they find a hot spot, and then they have access to the Net without leaving a trace."

Frank was thinking about deer season. An increase in hunting accidents seemed more than likely. Some of them might not be accidents. The killers would be dressed like deer hunters and pack high-powered rifles like deer hunters. Licensed to hunt, only they wouldn't be hunting deer.

"Anything you can do to help us catch these folks will save lives." Novak looked from Meecham to Frank. "We've been checking military records trying to track down this General Zarov. So far, no leads. We think he might be a Russian expatriate who's building an organization, but we need eyes and ears in the field, experienced eyes and ears. That's where the BLM comes in."

"It will be a top priority with this office. You can count on it," Meecham said.

Frank nodded and directed his next remark to Ellis. "You're right about General Zarov being an expatriate."

Ellis smirked. "What makes you think so?"

"General Zarov is a character in a short story by Richard Connell."

"What?"

"Only it's spelled Z-A-R-O-F-F, not with an O-V. In the story, he's a Russian expatriate who retires to an island because he's bored with hunting animals, too easy. So he decides to hunt human beings—because they can think."

They were all staring at Frank.

"Animals that can think are the most dangerous game. That's the name of the story."

"Jesus H. Christ." Novak continued to stare at Frank.

"I think MDG stands for 'Most Dangerous Game.'" Frank looked at Ellis. "Think about it. The MDG gave their shooter a double Zarov Award for two dead Gutless Wonders. I think they've read the story." Frank looked from Novak to Ellis. "I think they've been playing with you." Then he added as an afterthought, "If you guys know any deer hunters, I'd tell 'em to skip the fall season."

•

"How come you know about General Zaroff and 'The Most Dangerous Game'?" Meecham leaned back from his desk, looking at Frank.

"I majored in American studies, remember. All that time wasted reading history and literature." Frank grinned. "Anyway, Connell's story is pretty well known. They keep making bad movies of it set in different locales and time periods, but it always turns on someone or something hunting human beings. So college wasn't a complete waste of time after all."

"Un-huh." Meecham looked at Frank from under sandy eyebrows. "All right. I'll start on *War and Peace* tomorrow." He sat forward in his chair and grinned. "This time we looked a bit better—but no more coyote stuff."

5

•

Frank topped the rise at the head of Grapevine Canyon. He was on duty, so he was driving an official BLM vehicle, a lumbering Ford Expedition, not his favorite, but Dave Meecham had been very specific about not using private vehicles on duty. Frank was the principal offender because he preferred driving his restored '53 five-window Chevy pickup truck. Even Spartans had their vanities.

Four thousand feet below him, the floor of the Saline Valley stretched to the north, white and windswept. The descent into the valley followed a washboard road from the pinyon pines at the higher elevations to the mud-caked floor of the ancient lakebed. It would have been one of nature's tourist spots had it not been in such close proximity to Death Valley. To everyone except the hardy few, the Saline was just a hot hole in the ground. Fame had passed it by and saved it from paved roads and busloads of gaping tourists.

The SUV jounced over the bumps, jolting Frank's anger into flashes of rage. Ordinarily he would have stopped to look at the view over the valley below, but not today. Gore caked his arms and hands, despite his best efforts to sponge it off with his ruined shirt. The metal detector had been a good idea, but digging the spent bullets out of the dead burro carcasses had been all but impossible.

After rooting around in decaying flesh and organs, all he'd managed to do was cover himself with rot. He stank of death. More important, he didn't have a bullet to send to the federal forensics lab in Ashland, Oregon. The FBI wanted their killer. He wanted the poachers. It was something he could do something about.

The heavy SUV was barely under control as it lurched down the washboard road. He'd either have to slow down or risk damaging government property. He backed off, letting the vehicle jounce to a stop where a small spring crossed the road and disappeared into the canyon below. He switched off the ignition and listened to the ticking of the hot engine. Pinyon jays slipped silently from tree to tree. A file of chukar scurried along the side of the hill into the brush.

He was on his way to talk to Zeke Tucker, the man who scared people. Tucker lived in the heart of the Saline Valley in a corrugated iron single-wide. His tin home was perched on a shelf above the wash coming from Hunter Canyon. The Hunter Canyon spring was year-round, fed by snowmelt from the Inyo Mountains, a desert surprise that not many people saw. They had to get past Tucker.

Zeke Tucker was anything but friendly. He'd fashioned a miniature billboard from a four-by-eight piece of plywood that bore two words, KEEP OUT, and set it up at the edge of his property where the dirt track led to his dwelling. It was the only thing on his property that received fresh paint. From time to time, one of the rangers, usually Frank, paid Tucker a visit to caution him about brandishing his shotgun at weekenders.

Tucker came into town every couple of months for supplies—and some serious drinking. His visits to the Lone Pine Inn sent ripples through the drinking community. He ambled into town from the desert like an Old Testament prophet. His hair and beard, an uncut tangle of brown and gray, bushed away from a huge head set atop a six-foot-five-inch frame, but it was the mismatched eyes, one glittering blue, the other a muddy hazel, that caused most people to avert their gaze. In the summer, he wore a sleeveless Levi's jacket, minus the buttons, exposing expanses of hairy flesh. In the winter, he covered the jacket with a down parka. Jacket, parka, and jeans seemed to adhere to his body like a second skin rather than clothing.

In the wintertime, he smelled. You would think it would be the other way around, that he would stink in the summer, but the parka and the cold seemed to keep the odor in until he entered the confines of a warm space, where it oozed into the air, a rich stench of sweat, body oils, and dung. Then you could tell that he lived his life around animals and that he lived alone.

On his occasional trips to town, it was Tucker's habit to fling open the door of the Lone Pine Inn just at noon as the tavern opened. Then he and his canine companion, Jack-the-dog, claimed their place at the corner of the bar closest to the door. Here he sat drinking beer after beer until last call at two in the morning. He offered no word of greeting nor response to inquiries into the state of his health.

Now and then, some passerby, unfamiliar with Tucker's rules, or emboldened by Dutch courage, would try to engage him in conversation. "How're you doing there, big fella?" This caused Tucker to let his gaze fall full on the hapless stranger, the blue eye brighter than the hazel one, until the speaker faltered into silence.

The bartender, Dotty Hollander, had been assuring people for years that "Zeke's okay, just a loner. That's all. Leave him alone, he'll leave you alone." In fact, she wasn't quite sure herself. Her "Zeke's okay" routine was as much to reassure herself as the others. Tucker was definitely a bit strange—and very big. There was an aura of unpredictability about him. It made people nervous; it made Dotty nervous, so she bent the rules. Zeke's dog, Jack, came with Zeke.

Jack, an Australian shepherd, had mismatched eyes like his owner, one blue, the other hazel. Jack's hazel eye had a white spot, which some said, not in Tucker's hearing, made it possible to distinguish dog from master. He followed Tucker into the bar, taking his place at his master's feet with a contented sigh.

Jack was considerably more responsive to conversation than his human companion and thumped his tail when words came his way. Occasionally Tucker would accommodate Jack's urge to be social, especially when someone offered the dog a bite of leftover sandwich. Tucker would nod his dusty mane at the dog. "Okay, Jack." Then Jack would rise and take the food gently in his mouth, slowly wagging his tail in appreciation. People found Jack reassuring.

"Hey, Mr. Tucker." Frank hailed the trailer from the sign that marked the limit of Tucker's territory. He knew that the owner had seen his dust plume for the last twenty minutes, watching Frank's truck make its way up the steep ruts that led to the cluster of shacks, outbuildings, and fences that made up Tucker's place. He waited.

"It's mighty thirsty out here, Mr. Tucker." It was a matter of desert etiquette to share water with the thirsty. Plastic jugs of water were spaced along the Saline Valley Road where it crossed the playa, put there by the people who lived up the faint tracks leading back into the hills. Water was life.

Frank watched Tucker's angular mass stoop through a low door in a shed next to a pen of goats. Tucker stood glaring over at the truck, and then, as if having made up his mind, he began taking giant strides to the trailer, moving at a clip that would require an ordinary person to break into a trot. He stretched out a long arm, finger pointed in the direction of the shade porch he'd constructed of scrap lumber and canvas next to the single-wide. Frank got out of the truck and headed for the porch. He was careful to close the inner and outer gates behind him. That, too, was a matter of etiquette.

"Did you see the dead burros up the head of Grapevine Canyon, Mr. Tucker?" With Tucker, small talk was a waste of time. Jack-the-dog rose in greeting, tongue lolling in the heat.

Tucker nodded his head and fixed Frank with an intent look. The blue eye gleamed with an inner light.

"See anyone around?" Frank persisted.

Tucker turned away from Frank and spat a brown stream into the dirt, where it rolled across the dust like a legless bug. He shook his head.

"This makes four, Mr. Tucker, four that I know of. All within five miles of Grapevine Canyon. Somebody's still going up there and killing burros. Your place is a long way off, but it's the closest." Frank waited, hoping in vain the hermit would offer something. The bleating of the goats filled the silence. "You see anything at all?"

Tucker squinted one eye shut and tilted his head in thought. He turned abruptly and headed toward the goat pens. He whipped his head back. "Porch, Jack."

Frank hurried after him, feeling foolish at having to half run to keep up. Tucker stooped his frame through the door to the shed. Frank followed, bent forward, too close to Tucker's back to see much in the dim light. The goats clustered around Tucker, pushing at him, bleating for food. He pushed them aside and waved Frank forward, pointing at a stall fashioned of plywood and scrap. Frank leaned over the low plywood side and peered into the gloom. A fuzzy gray shape lay in the dirty straw where it nuzzled against an ancient nanny goat. Frank felt his throat constrict with a rush of emotions: relief, sorrow, anger.

He watched as the burro nursed, its head rhythmically moving with the effort, the nanny's eyes glazed with timeless patience. In here, Tucker didn't smell. Frank looked over at the angular giant, hairy arms resting atop the side of the stall.

The man was an enigma. People were full of surprises: secret dreams, fears, and mysteries. It made him wonder what Tucker's mystery was. The hermit moved in the world with solitary ease. What made him angry? Tucker made people afraid just by his presence, but he hadn't hurt anyone, or threatened anyone, if you didn't count the weekenders, and Frank didn't. It was display, not anger. Tucker didn't want visitors. Didn't like people? Maybe that was it. He was a misanthrope. That was something Frank could understand.

Shafts of sunlight, swimming with bright specks of dust, angled through the cracks in the wall, reminding Frank of the way the light slanted through the stained glass windows at Sacred Heart when he attended mass with his mother, so long ago.

The bleating of the goats filled the hot afternoon air. Tucker half knelt against the side of the stall, stroking the spiky coat along the burro's neck with the back of his fingers. In here, in this shed filled with the acrid smells of life, Tucker's riddle seemed less complicated. Frank tried to straighten up and bumped his head. The two of them made their way to the low door and emerged blinking into the bright sunlight.

"When did you find it?" Frank gestured over his shoulder at the goat shed. They sat cross-legged on the porch boards. Jack lay on his side against the aluminum siding, panting in the heat.

"Day after yesterday."

Frank thought about that, his smooth features drawn into a frown. "That's today, Mr. Tucker." He detected a disturbance in the facial hair that might signal a smile. Frank studied Tucker's head. For all the world it looked like a bush with eyes. The bush nodded. "Today?"

"Tried to catch him yesterday. This morning he was too worn out to run. He belonged to the one you killed." The blue eye glittered. "It's okay. She was shot up. I know." He turned away and looked out across the valley.

Frank wondered how Tucker knew he had to shoot the downed burro. Was he watching from somewhere? "I couldn't catch it." He smiled to himself. "Besides, I didn't have a goat."

"It would have probably died." Tucker spat into the dirt, creating another legless bug.

Frank sighed. He was probably right. The wild horse and burro adoption program wasn't perfect, but the BLM did its best.

"So you didn't see anyone, any vehicles?"

"Nope. Already told you that." He turned to look directly at Frank. "Damned abominations. They shall be struck down with fire and sword." The blue eye flashed from under lowered lids. Killing burros was one of the things that angered Tucker. Frank was glad he wasn't on the receiving end of the hermit's rage.

"There are people who agree with you, Mr. Tucker. A couple guys were killed up on the plateau, day *before* yesterday, that's two days ago." He smiled without mirth. "You know about that?"

Tucker nodded. "Couldn't miss it with all the cars and helicopters and planes."

"You don't miss much, Mr. Tucker."

"Don't miss much," the bush replied.

"Killing people is murder, Mr. Tucker, even if they're assholes. I don't need to tell you that." The words sounded hollow in Frank's head. "You know, some people think about you and your shotgun scaring folks, and it makes them nervous."

"You one of them?"

A faint breeze brushed against Frank's cheek. "No, it's not me that's nervous, Mr. Tucker."

Tucker's face wore the thousand-yard stare. "Then maybe the rest of them ought to read my sign." He looked at Frank. "Mind their own business and keep outta mine." The blue eye glittered.

"If you see anyone shooting up the countryside, I want to know about it—before we wind up with more killings." There was something about the way Tucker turned away that made Frank uneasy.

6

•

Eddie Laguna had acquired new teeth, and they were displayed in their bright white glory with the pride of ownership bestowed on pinky rings, pocket watches, and new automobiles. The new teeth were accompanied by a sexy girl, his client—Eddie had clients—a benefit of his friendship with Frank Flynn of the Bureau of Land Management, who was sitting at the end of the bar chatting with Linda Reyes.

Eddie's new teeth flashed in the smoky dimness of the Joshua Tree Athletic Club, the only watering hole in the not quite a ghost town of Red Mountain, in the middle of the Mojave Desert. It was Frank's home away from home. The conviviality of the owners, Jack Collins, Bill Jerome, and Ben Shaw, never failed to lift him from the doldrums of gloomy self-reflection.

"Hey, Eddie, looking good, my man." Ben Shaw's rough voice reverberated across the room. Shaw was one of the not-so-silent partners in the resurrection of the turn-of-the-century house of ill repute, bar, and hangout for miners and toughs. The three lifelong pals had pooled their money, purchased the ramshackle bar, and transformed it into a haven for locals and a passing curiosity for tourists making the trek across the Mojave Desert on Highway 395 in air-conditioned SUVs.

"Howdy, Ben." Eddie nodded, aware that Shaw's greeting was only the opening salvo in an attempt to get under Eddie's skin.

A new straw hat sat low over Eddie's forehead. A tiny silver bell, tied with rawhide, decorated the end knot of his jet black ponytail and tinkled faintly when he moved his head. It invited trouble, but Eddie's life had been filled with trouble.

"What'll it be, Eddie?" Linda Reyes was tending bar, her part-time employment when she wasn't working for the local newspaper, the *InyoKern Courier.* She gave Eddie a radiant smile, her amused hazel eyes taking in his getup. A small frown creased her forehead as she sized up Eddie's companion; trouble—trouble, trouble, right here in Red Mountain.

"Oh, uh, the usual," Eddie said, trying to sound casual. He turned to the waiflike creature perched next to him, legs dangling down into strapless sandals. "How about you, Miss Flowers? Would you like something to drink?"

"Tequila and grapefruit juice. That'd be just fine." She smiled up at Eddie from under a fall of thick blond hair that seemed to require frequent tossing of the head. "Lots of ice, please, sweetie," she said to Linda, her gaze fixed on her companion.

"I could use another beer too, *sweetie*," Frank said with a straight face.

Eddie's companion had a surprisingly husky voice for such a small person. She was tiny, maybe five feet, maybe not, and tricked out as the belle of Le Court Trailer. Loose-fitting lavender shorts exposed flashes of white thigh. A braless halter top of the same hue, tied up at the small of her back and the nape of her neck with bits of cloth, invited an exploratory tug.

Linda splashed Jose Cuervo into a sparkling glass and topped it off with grapefruit juice. "Here you are, *sweetie*." Linda slopped a little as she put the drink in front of the blond tart—definitely a tart—hoping the wet might find its way onto the purple handkerchief masquerading as a top. She turned to Eddie. "Aren't you going to introduce me to your friend?"

"Ah, yeah—sure. Linda, this here is Cecilia Flowers. I'm doing some guide work for her."

"I'm Linda Reyes, Eddie's pal." Linda's smile was predatory.

"Hi, Linda. Call me Cece, all my friends do." She met Linda's gaze, her china blue eyes intelligent and a trifle hard.

"Okay, Cece." Linda drew a breath. "Good to meet a friend of Eddie's. Where's he taking you, up in the mountains or out in the desert?"

"I have some mining property, but I've never really been in the desert before, so I thought I'd hire a guide so I could find my way around."

"Well, you picked the right guy. Eddie's the best." Linda felt herself relenting a bit. Eddie had pressed the collar and button line of his denim shirt, a first, and there was the new straw hat and the new teeth. She tried not to look at the teeth.

Eddie had come into a bit of cash a few months back and spent some of it on much needed dental work, but he'd cheaped out on the teeth. He'd been getting by on discolored stumps, which weren't a social asset, since his breath could kill flies at three feet. His new teeth were too white and too big, which caused his upper lip to hang up, giving him a periodic snarl. Linda smiled, wondering how Frank had reacted to the teeth. It would've been a test of character, candor versus tact.

"It was Frank who set me up with Cece." Eddie lacked tact.

"Oh, and how's that?" The sharpness of Linda's reply took Eddie off guard.

"Well, that is, he, uh, recommended me." Eddie glanced at Frank for confirmation.

"Oh, is that right? I didn't know the BLM was in the guide business." Linda's voice was icy.

Cece cut in. "Mr. Flynn said he couldn't officially recommend anyone for guide service, but that Mr. Laguna here knew the desert well, and sometimes took on clients. So I called Mr. Laguna—Eddie. We've made an arrangement." She rested a tiny white hand on Eddie's brown one.

"That's about it," Frank said. He grinned at Linda, shaking his head.

"Well, as I said, Eddie's the best." Linda turned to pick up a couple of mugs waiting for refills on the polished mahogany bar. *Mr.* Laguna. Eddie must be eating that up.

Eddie lowered his voice. "Miss Flowers is trying to locate a mine, used to be in the family. I'm helping her out." He winked his left eye, revealing a white scar across his eyelid, a momentary flash of lightning in a brown sky.

Linda gave Cece a knowing smile. "See those guys sitting back there against the wall? They collect lost mine stories, know 'em all." She pointed her chin toward three time-weathered characters sitting against the wall in tall, rickety, observer chairs watching a game of pool. "The one with beer in his mustache is my dad, the tall stringy one is Bill Jerome, and the one with the pipe, wearing the hat, is Ben Shaw." She moved down the bar, giving an extra swish to her hips. *Damn! Why in the hell am I swinging my ass at Eddie to impress a twit?* she wondered.

"Those are the guys I was telling you about." Eddie nodded at the far wall. "They're always out in the hills looking around at old mines and stuff."

Cece leaned into Eddie, an unfettered breast resting against his forearm. "You think they might be interested in investing?"

Eddie tried to concentrate on Cece's words. "We got to begin somewhere." He slid off the bar stool. "These guys, they like to talk, especially to a pretty woman—like you are." He grinned, pleased with his compliment. "I'll be right back." She watched as he rolled across the room on bandy legs, bent from rickets, not mustangs.

The grizzled faces turned in Eddie's direction.

"Nice-looking lady you're with." Shaw's remark was loaded with undisguised curiosity.

"Un, yeah, real nice person, too."

Shaw was a professional thorn, ever ready to probe and poke for soft spots. "Nothing the matter with squiring around a pretty woman, Eddie." He winked and laid a finger beside his nose. Bill Jerome let a thin smile break across his craggy face.

Eddie glared at Shaw. "I'm not squiring her around. She's a client." He wasn't sure what "squiring" meant.

"A client, oh yeah that's right, I forget you're in *bidness*. Doing a little taxidermy work for her?" Eddie was a first-class taxidermist. His shop was his garage. No boss, no taxes, no interference. Eddie Laguna was pretty close to self-sufficient. "Some serious mounting?" Shaw added.

The silver bell tinkled as Eddie's head snapped around. "Guide work! Guess you don't hear so good with all that hair in your ears."

Jack Collins frowned at Shaw, who was fairly bursting with gleeful malice. "Let the man talk, Ben."

Collins turned to Eddie. "Never mind this horse's ass. He's never happy unless he's under someone's skin. Just happens to be you today." Collins waited, nodding encouragement.

Eddie shifted his eyes from side to side. "Well, Miss Flowers owns an old mine, but she's never seen it. So I'm helping her to find it."

Shaw rolled his eyes, making audible sucking sounds. Jerome's mouth turned down at the corners, and he gave the piece of granite he wore for a head a nearly imperceptible shake.

"Does this mine have a name?" Collins inquired.

"The New Hope Mine, I think she said."

Eddie glanced back to where Cece sat with elbows on the bar, chatting with Frank Flynn, while Linda glowered from behind the bar. "I'll ask her." He paused in distraction. "Wait, you talk to her, okay?"

"Old Jack gets the nod, huh?" Shaw grinned. "I'd keep my eye on him if I were you."

"Well, you ain't me, are you?" Eddie shot Shaw a hard look.

Eddie brightened as he and Jack Collins approached where Cece sat in fragile splendor. "Jack, this here is Cecilia Flowers."

Linda moved down the bar and rested her elbows in front of Frank.

"Pleased to meet you, Miss Flowers." Collins wasn't immune to female charms, but he'd been around the track a few more times than Eddie Laguna, who'd never been to Los Angeles, a couple hundred miles to the south. He pulled absently at his mustache. *The woman's a force of nature,* he thought. He cocked his head to one side; their eyes met, taking each other's measure. Cece glanced downward and carefully replaced a dangling sandal on a shapely foot.

Collins sniffed at the telltale signs of trouble that wafted into the air like pheromones. A blarney smile creased his broad face. "Eddie thinks I may be able to help you locate some misplaced property or at least start you out in the right direction."

"Eddie says you know all about mining, Mr. Collins—"

"Jack."

Linda forcibly cleared her throat. Frank made an unsuccessful effort to cover his smirk.

"Okay, Jack. I just don't know where to begin." She reached into her large canvas purse and took out a soiled brown envelope. "I have a letter from my great-granduncle—and a map."

"Did he file a claim?"

"I don't think so. I'm not sure."

Jack tried another tack. "You have any clue as to where it is?" He struggled to keep the annoyance out of his voice.

"Oh, I don't know. That's why I hired Mr. Laguna." Her small face clouded with frustration. "I'm afraid I don't have the answers to these questions, Jack. Eddie asked me some of the same things."

Collins glanced over at Eddie and shrugged.

"Show him the ore."

"Eddie!" Cece crossed her arms and glowered.

"Jack's been to college. He used to be a teacher. And Bill over there knows all about mines and minerals."

Cece sighed and rummaged around in her purse and brought out a chunk of pink quartz. She laid it carefully on the bar as if it might have been an egg instead of a rock.

Jack reached out a thick hand, then hesitated and raised his graying eyebrows.

Cece nodded. "Sure, go ahead."

Jack picked up the quartz and squinted in the dim light. "'Scuse me a minute." He climbed off the bar stool and pushed through the padded leather door into the sunshine.

Frank leaned over to Linda, speaking in a hushed voice. "Your dad's gonna explode if that's the read McCoy—a dream come true."

Linda rolled her eyes.

Jack came shooting back into the interior of the Joshua Tree Athletic Club. "Well, I'm no expert, but this rock would've made Shorty Harris whoop it up and head for town. You can see the gold shining in the sunlight."

"Here we go." Frank laughed.

7

·

Linda sat on the rear platform of Frank's caboose, her hands wrapped around a cup of coffee. Wisps of steam lifted into the morning stillness.

Frank ruffled a newspaper. "Yeah, gold and greed and holes all over the land. Little ones, big ones, and great big ones full of cyanide." He shivered in the chill. Linda was tucked into one of Frank's sweatshirts, her feet and legs wrapped in a blanket. The first breeze of the morning brushed strands of dark hair from her forehead.

The caboose was Frank's patrimony. It rested on bare ground where his dad and his boozy buddies had run it off the end of the siding before the Southern Pacific had torn up the high line. He had the caboose, his dad's railroad watch, and his brass Southern Pacific keys. The long key fit the caboose. The short stubby one opened the locks on the sidings and derails. His dad's Savage .250-3000 was one of the few things that didn't get hocked during Francis Flynn's slide into oblivion. It stood in the storage locker under the cupola. A popgun by modern standards (nowadays, everything was a Magnum) but a beautiful piece of craftsmanship.

His dad's sun-wrinkled face lit up with filial pride when he discovered that his twelve-year-old son could outshoot him, outshoot most anyone. It was Frank's ironic gift. His maker had seen fit to make him a crack shot, and he hated killing things. He hated himself when the wounded creatures struggled to get away or fixed him with fear-filled eyes as he came to bring the finality of death. After the army, he never hunted again. His dad had already made that final drop between the boxcars, so there was no one to disappoint.

Frank looked out over the valley. When the air was clear, he could see Dirty Socks Springs at the south end of Owens Lake, which used to be a real lake before Los Angeles decided to water lawns and fill swimming pools. Once upon a time, steamers carried charcoal over to the smelter at Keeler and returned laden with bars of silver. There were even rumors of sunken treasure. All that was gone now. The city of Los Angeles got the water and the valley dried up. The caboose was a leftover from another time.

"Whatcha' thinking, Flynnman?"

"Need an Alka-Seltzer or a hair of the dog."

"Pretty big dog, huh?"

"Yup." Closed subject.

After Frank's mother died, the elder Flynn took to drink in a serious way. Before her death, it had just been a serious hobby. Right! Frank shook his head in silent protest. The elder Flynn's wake had lasted three years. Then, coming up out of the town of Mojave on a mile-long freight, he had fallen between the cars. When they found him, he was in three pieces. The funeral service was closed coffin. As Francis Flynn had explained to his son, "When one of those wheels passes over a man, it passes through him. If they could put him back together, he'd be a couple inches shorter." It was an image still sharp in Frank's mind.

His caboose was too close to the mountains to see the whole of the back wall of the eastern Sierra. The mountains thrust up from the floor of the desert, forming a jagged barrier between the rich farmland of the San Joaquin Valley and the arid land of the Owens Valley, the catch basin for the eastern slope. From his platform porch, he could see across the valley to the Inyo Mountains, brown and gray at midday, washed in gold, orange, and deep red before the sun disappeared behind the Sierra and the chill of evening touched the land. It was stark country, dry and sharp, all points and angles.

Linda tried again. "Looking for gold's an obsession, isn't it, especially the lost mines?" She pulled her arms in close to her body, trying to stay warm. "Hey, mister, Linda speak to Flynnman."

"Yup. Everyone's looking for the pot at the end of the rainbow." Frank nodded ever so slightly. "And out here, everyone has a story about a lost mine." He leaned against the iron railing, absently tugging at the end of his nose. "Did I tell you Tucker rescued a foal?"

"No. When did you see Tucker?"

"Tuesday. When I took the metal detector up to the plateau."

"No, you didn't mention seeing the fearsome Tucker."

"Well, I saw him on Tuesday."

"And?"

"And he rescued a burro foal." Frank looked away from Linda, out over the desert. "The one I had to finish had a foal. I tried to catch it, but I had to leave it there. Anyhow, Tucker saved it. Gave it over to a nursing nanny goat."

"He sounds like a good man."

"Umm-hmm. There used to be people like Jack Longstreet."

"Who's he?"

"He was a desert rat and gunman. No one knows for sure how many people he killed, but he put a few under."

"You think your desert rat Tucker killed those poachers?" She sipped her coffee and studied him over the rim. "I'd like to meet the infamous Tucker sometime."

"Not likely. He doesn't like people." Linda opened her mouth to speak, but Frank held up his forefinger. "You hear about Sand Canyon, the so-called game reserve?" He looked out over the valley. "This is where I grew up, and I'm watching it start to die. You know what that's like? People come up here, tear up the land, dump trash, go home, and water their lawns—with our water." He turned to Linda. "They bring their guns and act like the valley's a shooting gallery. Shoot at anything that moves. Now they're building a home base. It makes me sick."

The air was still, the sun bright above the rim of the Inyos. Yesterday's afternoon wind had swept the valley clear of the smog that rolled some two hundred miles up from the Los Angeles Basin. Linda had come to see the valley as Frank saw it, and her sense of protecting it was fierce. God, if she moved back to L.A., she'd be one of them, part of the problem.

He sighed. "You're right, though. I am thinking about Tucker. He might not have anything to do with the killings, but I wouldn't want to be the person who crosses him."

Linda raised dark eyebrows. "Why's that?"

Frank swung around. "He's big." Then he added, "You know what he says to me? 'Son of man, do you see what they are doing, the great abominations to drive me from my sanctuary?' It's from the Book of Ezekiel. I looked it up. That's his name, Zeke. There's more, too, stuff about executing judgments, setting blood upon the rock, unsheathed swords, the fury of the Lord, violent stuff."

Linda laughed. "He seems to fit right in. The land of loners: Seldom Seen Slim, Shorty Harris, the Montgomery Brothers."

"Forget it, Linda." Frank recognized the beginning of a campaign. "Tucker doesn't give interviews. He talks to me because he thinks has to."

"Come on, Frank. He talks to you because in some ways you're just like him."

"Another damned loner, huh?"

It was Linda's turn to raise a finger. "Loners living in the past." She sipped her coffee, her dark eyes catching the light.

In his mind's eye he was standing in the goat shed with Zeke Tucker watching the nanny suckling the burro foal, the sunlight filtering in through the cracks. A congregation of two.

"Maybe so."

"You're worried that it's all pointing to him, aren't you?"

Frank nodded. "It seems to fit a pattern."

"Why? Outside of the fact that both Tucker and the shooter are tall, where's the connection?"

"Well, the shooter used a .270. Tucker has a .270. The shooter knows the land, how long it takes to walk from point A to point B. Tucker knows the desert about as well as anyone. He lives in it. The shooter must've hated poachers. Tucker hates poachers—take my word for it. You should have seen his eyes. They're different colors, one a muddy hazel, the other bright blue. The blue one glittered like broken glass."

Frank could count on Linda not to gloss things over. She had an analytical mind, used to solving human puzzles, discovering the pattern in the chaos of things. "So what's your take on it?"

"I can see why Tucker looks good for it, but think about this. If you didn't know Tucker, what he hates and what he doesn't hate, and—this is a big if—and if you didn't think he might be dangerous when provoked, would you still consider him a suspect?"

"I never said he was a suspect."

"Okay, a person of interest."

Frank groaned. "I hate that crap."

Linda chuckled. "I know. Just the same, you think the killer might very well be Tucker, and you hate it because you like him. The fact that you hate it makes you bend over backward not to give him a free pass. What's there to go on, though, other than his size and the fact that most people think he's strange?"

"I wish that were it. I ran a quick check on him. He was arrested twice in protests against the Vietnam War. He was part of a group, Vietnam Veterans Against the War. Many of them had multiple arrests, some for assault. They weren't into passive demonstrations." He turned to look at Linda, his oval face sad and subdued. "He had an infantry MOS, which means he knows how to use a rifle."

"Oh." Her face lapsed into seriousness.

"Yeah, that's what I thought."

"You mind if I do some checking around?" Linda rested her hand on his shoulder.

"Of course not. Anything you come up with might help." He sighed. "Although so far, the more I know, the more it points to Tucker."

Linda changed the subject. "Speaking of interesting characters, I'm going to do a spec piece on our very own female treasure hunter, Cecelia Flowers, and her faithful Native American guide, Eddie Laguna."

Frank smiled. "Eddie breaks into print. He'll love that." He chuckled. "Be sure to get a picture of his smile. Can't miss an opportunity to catch those teeth for posterity.'

"That's mean, Flynnman. Eddie's proud of his new teeth. Besides, the article isn't about Eddie, it's about a female prospector out here in the Owens Valley. It's about history and lost mines, gold and treasure. People love that stuff."

"Of course, it doesn't hurt that she's a looker."

"Oh, you think so, huh?"

"Objectively speaking, she's sort of attractive."

"Just what objects are you speaking of?"

"Come on, give me a break here. She's cute. Besides, she's Eddie's squeeze, and"—he grinned—"I've got a cuter squeeze."

"You're so romantic, Ranger Frank. 'A cuter squeeze.' Gee, that makes my heart flutter."

"I hope so." He leaned over and kissed her softly on the mouth.

"Mmm. That makes my heart flutter—and other stuff, too."

8

•

They sat at opposite ends of the couch, watching John Gilman's fifty-two-inch TV. For the time being, Gilman's home was the MDG's base of operations. There was absolutely nothing tying Seth Parker, a.k.a. the Sandman, to John Gilman or Gilman's KwikMart, so it was a safe haven, for a while. The KwikMarts were the source of Gilman's considerable income and provided the financial underpinning for their operations. Gilman employed immigrants from India and Pakistan. He called them ragheads, but, by and large, they didn't steal and would put in long hours for short wages. Their efforts had propelled Gilman into the category of the idle rich. Although he'd graduated from college with a degree in business, Gilman had little education. If it didn't pertain to making money, he considered it useless. Thus, he suffered from boredom, the disease of a vacant mind.

When John encountered Seth Parker, whose mind was anything but vacant, his hero worship of the sophisticated soldier of fortune was instant. Gilman found himself rubbing shoulders with someone dangerous and famous—the Sandman. He couldn't believe his good luck. The talking heads on his big-screen TV were calling the MDG a vast terrorist organization and the Sandman a clever mastermind. John Gilman smiled. They had part of it right. The pundits theorized about a resurgence of the Weather Underground. What was that? Survivalists, ELF—thanks to Seth Parker, he knew what that was—even Al Qaeda. Parker had explained that news organizations liked to tie everything to Al Qaeda. He'd explained that just saying "Al Qaeda" scared the shit out of people.

As Parker had explained it to him, they really were terrorists, but terrorists on the right side of history. "History ultimately decides who's remembered as terrorists. Losers wind up as terrorists, winners as patriots. Winners write the history, John. Right now the MDG is a terrorist organization because we're so badly outnumbered. If we grow, if we prevail, history will redefine us. We'll be remembered with respect—as heroes.

"Our organization fights in a righteous cause. When there are enough people who think the way we do, we'll be remembered as soldiers in a just cause." Parker laid his hand on John's shoulder. "Numbers are the essential difference between a cult and a religious movement, between rebels and founding fathers. To the Romans, Christians were a cult. To the English, the colonists were rebels taking potshots from behind trees—wouldn't stand up and fight. Then the tables turned. That's our mission, to turn the tables." John Gilman found Parker's arguments compelling, especially about their role in changing history.

Now the television people were speculating about what kind of person would kill two people for no reason. Parker scoffed. "See, they don't get it."

The pretty-boy anchorman kept frowning and shaking his head in mock incredulity. The woman being interviewed, a former profiler from the FBI, was better—very serious, nice legs. Too bad she spouted the usual drivel: The Sandman was a person who was basically an insecure loner, probably the victim of violence in his childhood. The part that particularly irritated Parker was that this smart-ass woman was blabbing on as if she really knew who he was.

She crossed shapely legs. "The murder of the men in the

Mojave Desert was a transference of violence, a means of taking revenge on those who had made him feel impotent."

"Sexually impotent?" The anchorhead raised his eyebrows, creating a small vertical crease in the smooth expanse of unblemished forehead. John Gilman imagined the appearance of a dark spot between the anchorman's surprised eyes. Not having actually witnessed a shooting, he omitted the bone fragments, blood, hair, and brain matter erupting from the exit wound.

"Not necessarily," the profiler woman responded, recrossing her legs, "although sexual dysfunction frequently accompanies feelings of helplessness and low self-esteem. Snipers often feel empowered by playing God, giving themselves the power of life and death, deciding who lives and who dies." *You got that right*, Gilman thought.

"Certainly, social impotence played a part in the motivations of the D.C. snipers." She sipped some water. The anchorhead paused in levitated anticipation. "Each death temporarily validates the individual, who is unable to find validation in normal behavior. The power to reach out and take life temporarily pushes back the feelings of impotence and worthlessness. Of course, these feelings return with increasing frequency and strength. The subject has to purge these feelings by repeating the behavior that provided relief, destroying the *other*, who has become a representation of the forces that threaten the subject."

"Hasn't the MDG been identified as a terrorist organization and the Sandman an instrument of terrorism? Isn't that political rather than psychological?" Handsome Head wanted to know.

"All terrorists suffer incomplete personality development. It's what makes the irrationality of their acts plausible. Their willingness to destroy others, and frequently themselves, is a manifestation of a need to fill the void, become complete. Of course, any analysis is an attempt to offer a rational explanation of irrational behavior. How else to explain why a person would take the lives of two unknown strangers?"

"Unknown strangers!" Parker laughed out loud. "Redundant." He looked at his companion. "The great expert analyst doesn't have sufficient command of the English language to avoid an obvious redundancy."

"What a stupid bitch!" Gilman said. He wasn't sure what a redundancy was. The Sandman knew about so many things. "Why do people listen to this crap? Why are they on TV?"

"Why don't they just look at the Web site?" Parker shook his head, frowning in thought. "We'll have to refocus their attention." He continued his lesson. "If people want to be big game hunters, they should go hunt lions with a spear, or a grizzly bear with a Bowie knife, each other with hand grenades." He shook his head. "Not domesticated birds tossed from cages." He rose and went over to the computer station.

Gilman joined him, peering over Parker's shoulder at the computer screen. He was careful not to invade Parker's space.

"It appears somebody is trying to attract our attention," Parker said. "Someone has left a message on our site."

The so-called Sandman is a Bambi lover. Bushwhacking **AMERICAN** citizens is back shooting. Doesn't he have the guts to go one on one? We're eliminating the bunny huggers along with the burros and other invasive species crossing our borders.
NOTICE: Next time you come out to the Inyo Mountains, we'll have to meet up. Then we can leave your useless carcass rotting with the rest of the jackasses.
THE BROTHERHOOD OF AMERICAN SPORTSMEN

"It would be nice to accommodate them," Parker muttered under his breath. He would welcome the chance to introduce them to the fundamentals of sniper skills. Who could do it better? Top score in his training company. Second highest score ever at Fort Ord, trained by the best, handpicked by Sergeant Flynn, the small arms instructor at Hunter Liggett.

"We'll see how tough they are when a .50 caliber takes off the top of someone's head." John Gilman bobbed up and down, agreeing with himself.

"Shooting personnel with a .50 caliber round is overkill, John. Not to worry. Your .50 will be very useful at Sand Canyon."

They stared at the screen trying to imagine the person who had written the taunt.

"Who would send us this bullshit?" Gilman leaned forward as if to challenge the screen.

Parker stared at the message without seeing it, his mind probing the words. "Perhaps some hunting group angry about the killings in the Mojave, but it could be from law enforcement."

"What makes you think that?"

"The challenge is meant to provoke a response."

"Let's take 'em out. They won't stand a chance," John said, fishing for approval.

Parker looked at John Gilman, assessing him. "Everyone stands a chance until the kill shot. There are always surprises, the unexpected. Strategy gives way to tactics, tactics to training."

"I know. That's why we can take them. They're amateurs."

"Not if they're law enforcement."

Gilman remained silent while Parker reread the message.

"If the message actually came from a hunting group of some sort, it's an opportunity. If the message came from law enforcement, we'll have to be careful. We are not going to walk into an obvious trap," Parker said.

"This message is a public insult," Gilman said. "We can't let it stand."

"I agree," Parker responded and began typing up a response.

> Brotherhood of American Sportsmen? I think not. Shoot a speeding tortoise. Shoot eagles off the power poles and animals in cages. Hunting is a contest that requires an opponent. Now you have one. Say, next weekend. I'll be seeing you—through a scope.
> **THE SANDMAN**

"Now let's go find a signal so we can send our reply." He cuffed Gilman on the shoulder. "Come on, let's see what we stir up. This might work out. I wonder if they know about the turkey vultures?"

Gilman looked puzzled.

"Come on, I'll tell you in the van."

9

•

"Wait a minute." Linda reached for the binoculars as Frank brought the truck to a stop. They were on the Saline Valley Road where it hugged the edge of the mountain before it dropped into Grapevine Canyon. It was not a place to gawk without coming to a stop. A jiggle to the right and a person would take a four-thousand-foot shortcut down to the valley floor.

The Panamint Valley stretched away to the south as far as the eye could see. The Panamint Mountains rose up in a steep wall, forming the barrier between Death Valley and Panamint Valley, the last home of Seldom Seen Slim and Shorty Harris. The snowcap on Telescope Peak glistened bright white in the morning sun. Frank thought of all the lost souls that had looked up at the snow, parched with thirst, and cursed the day they had ventured into this forbidden land.

"God, this is a breathtaking spot." Linda put the binoculars up to her face. "Wait, there's a jackalope down there crossing the sand dunes."

"Don't start with the jackalope stuff." A while back, Jack Collins, Ben Shaw, and Bill Jerome had decided they were going to clear Jawbone Canyon of the all-terrain vehicles that were ripping up the landscape. They had designated Jawbone Canyon a jackalope preserve and proceeded to scatter caltrops, four-pronged spikes, along the ruts being carved into the desert by the machines. The septuagenarian eco-vandals—he thought of them as the Grumpy Wrench Gang—had caused Frank a problem or two.

"Well, one might be there. You never know." A pang of guilt shot through her. How could she think about leaving—Frank, her dad, his pals, and the desert she had come to love; the job of a lifetime against this magical place. What a hell of a choice. She put the binoculars on the seat and turned to Frank. "What are we looking for?"

"Nothing yet." He eased the truck forward. "The shooter's track pointed cross-country toward Hunter Mountain. He may have walked this section of the road."

"So much for tracks." Linda shrugged.

"Yeah, but where was he going? There's the problem. I think he probably hid a vehicle up in the pinyons somewhere, or someone picked him up."

"You're looking for a needle in a haystack."

"You're probably right, but I want to look around."

She knew Frank had spent his life in the desert, but she never ceased to be amazed at the way he could see things where others couldn't. It was a skill, and she admired it. Maybe more than a skill. She studied his face in profile, the dark eyes and thick lashes, the long arching nose and full lips. For a moment she experienced a temporal dislocation. It was as if he were part of the timelessness she felt in the desert.

"Gonna trade me in?"

She shook her head. "Not today, Flynnman."

Frank slowed the truck to a crawl, peering into likely sidetracks, looking for good places to hide a vehicle under the trees.

"I didn't know this road had so much use."

"It adds up. A few vehicles pulling into the same spot and you've got a side road, an already disturbed environment, which makes it officially open to off-road vehicles. It's after-the-fact road making."

"So what are we looking for?"

"Something not so obvious, a place to hide a vehicle that's not attractive to off-roaders."

Frank ran his truck up out of the ruts, which were filled with muddy ooze from a recent thundershower. "People come up thinking the desert's always dry and get stuck, and then we have to get 'em out." He brought the truck to a stop.

"What's so special here?"

"The rocks."

Linda leaned down to look out of the driver's side window. A cluster of car-sized granite rocks thrust up from the ground like large canine teeth. Frank put the truck into reverse and eased back along the side of the road, keeping out of the gooey ruts. A narrow ravine cut across the open area and wound down to the road from behind the rocks. He pulled up near the lip of the cutback and got out of the cab.

"Come on, let's take a look." He walked toward the rocks examining the rim of the cutback. "Someone dropped over this edge not too long ago." He pointed at a portion of caved-in dirt, then turned and headed back to the truck.

"What's up?"

They got into the vehicle. Frank grinned. "Hang on. If he can do it, so can I."

As he started the truck, he heard Linda's voice over the engine. "Make it *we*, Flynnman."

Frank angled the truck into the narrow arroyo. The passenger side dropped precipitously, threatening to roll the vehicle on its side. This was followed by the left rear wheel thudding down into the rocky bottom. The vehicle righted itself, and Frank goosed it enough to keep it jouncing over the rocks.

"Maybe we should've walked," Linda said.

"We don't know how far he went." Frank chuckled. "Besides, this way we can see if it can be done."

"You're enjoying yourself," Linda said.

Frank's head smacked against the driver's side window.

"Serves you right."

He slowed the truck to a crawl to ease around a huge boulder, running the right wheels up the side and tipping the vehicle to the left. Linda felt as if she were hanging from the armrest.

The floor of the wash became less rocky where the grade became less steep near the upthrust rocks. Here, where the wash widened, a stand of pinyon pines grew in a semicircle around the rocks. Frank brought the truck to a stop near the edge of the clearing. Pine needles and cones carpeted the ground, perfuming the air with their pungent fragrance.

"Now what?"

"Now we look around for clues." He opened the door quietly and stepped into the clearing.

Flights of blue-gray birds winged about in the trees, squawking with alarm.

"Pinyon jays. These trees are full of nuts."

"These trees?"

"Not all the trees have nuts every year. Different trees in different years. The jays know. When I was a kid, I used to go with my mother and grandmother and harvest the nuts. We always looked for the pinyon jays to tell us where the nuts were."

Linda looked up at the birds flying about in noisy profusion. "Frank, what's that?" She pointed up into the interior of a pinyon pine.

"Where?"

"There, about halfway up the trunk."

"Good eyes, white woman. You win the brass ring." In fact, that's what it appeared to be, a brass ring hanging from a nylon cord. He pushed past the lower branches and climbed up to where he could reach it, cutting the line with his pocketknife about an inch from the knot.

Linda examined the rope in Frank's hand. "Not much of a clue."

"Better than nothing. See the knot. It's a bowline. People use the knots they know how to tie. He knows how to tie a bowline. Who knows, maybe he was a Boy Scout."

"You're kidding, right?"

"Do you know how to tie a bowline?"

She shook her head.

"Most people don't, unless they were in the Scouts. Your dad and his pals probably do. Knowing how to tie knots was part of being a kid back in the forties and fifties. There are all kinds of knots: sheepshank, bowline, trucker's knot, half hitch, square knot."

"How come you know so much about knots?"

He grinned.

"Right, you were a Boy Scout."

She picked up the rope, dangling the ring to examine it. It was about three-quarters of an inch in diameter, made of two thin plates crimped together. Remnants of tan material poked out from one side where the two halves of the ring had been pressure clamped onto the canvas. "I think it's an eyelet from a tarp. See the brown material along the edges?"

Frank frowned in thought. "You know what I think?"

Linda shook her head. "Not unless you tell me."

"I think someone tied a tarp up in the trees, probably a camouflage tarp, and then the wind came along and ripped part of it loose."

"Okay. It could be anyone, though."

Frank nodded. "Yeah, it could, but why would someone bounce up that wash just to camp up here? We passed lots of better spots, level and easy to approach." He rubbed the bridge of his nose, then nodded his head as if coming to some conclusion. "I think this is where the shooter ducked the air cover. It's invisible from the road. The wash leading up to the rocks isn't exactly a highway, and rocks don't leave much in the way of tracks. Once he had his vehicle out of sight, he could've just waited it out under the trees, under his camo tarp."

He nodded again. "There's a hell of a lot of Hunter Mountain. The aerial search was abandoned after a couple days. The California Highway Patrol covered 395, 190, and the Panamint Valley Road. Hell, everyone covered the roads, but what were they looking for? Not a clue. Somebody suspicious." He grinned. "Maybe a Mexican wearing a wet rag on his head to cool off. Bingo! Homeland Security announces the capture of José bin Laden."

"You're feeling pretty cocky, Mr. Flynn. So if everyone was looking for someone they wouldn't recognize, he could've driven over to Lone Pine and checked into a motel."

"Yeah, but that would be running an unnecessary risk. Whoever this guy is, he's careful."

"Or whoever this woman is. Don't forget: equal opportunity killers."

Frank gave her a look. "She's a real stork, then, a lot taller than you or me."

She grinned.

"Right, a lot of people are taller than me. I'll rephrase that. The shooter had to have been well over six feet, though." He paused for a moment, looking back toward the road. "I think he waited for the planes to go away, then drove the dirt roads until he hit the north end of the Owens Valley and doubled back through the Saline Valley, or maybe he drove out through Ubehebe Crater. Hell, there are lots of dirt tracks."

He lifted the cord and the brass eyelet from Linda's hand and slipped it carefully into his shirt pocket. "I'll put this into a sandwich bag. Maybe it has prints."

Wind gusted through the pinyons, drowning the noise of the jays. The trees sighed to one another in timeless complaint. There was a sadness about it, all shadows and wind. Sometimes, especially in the late afternoons, Frank felt as if the trees and rocks were watching, expectant. He watched the high clouds move above the trees and felt a momentary chill as they cast their shadow on the land.

"What're you thinking?"

There was a muffled pop. Then the pinyon jays screamed in alarm as one of their number fluttered to the ground.

Frank leaned forward, listening, his gaze fixed toward the cluster of rocks between the small clearing and the road, the direction from which the sound of the shot had come. Linda knelt by the pinyon jay. One wing waved aimlessly and stilled as the bird's eyes glazed over. "It's dead, Frank." The softness of her voice was drowned by the screeching of the jays.

Two men in their early twenties trotted into the clearing from around the rocks. "Come on. I got one." Frank waited for them to discover they were not alone. When they saw the man and the woman standing near the dead bird, they stopped, hesitant and off guard.

Frank pointed at the still jay, the gray-blue body nearly indistinguishable from the bed of pine needles where it lay. "Nice shot."

The men relaxed in the temporary comfort of dispelled guilt. "Yeah, got him from back on the road." The speaker was the shorter of the two, carrying the rifle.

"That looks like the new Ruger K77, right?" Frank said.

The man nodded. "Yeah, the new .17 caliber Hornady Magnum." The man's voice lingered proudly on "Magnum."

Gotta have the gun with that magic word "Magnum," Frank thought. "A real bird killer." He smiled crookedly at the man.

"It's the varmint model," the man said, slightly offended.

"Oh yeah, that's right." He glanced down at the dead bird, then up into the pines. "Damn varmint jays, out here disturbing the peace. Eating up all the pine nuts."

The two shooters were suddenly conscious of the cacophony of sound surrounding them.

Frank eyed the shooter's T-shirt. It depicted a cowboy on his knees by a prairie grave. The cowboy's horse stood in the background, head turned toward the grieving cowhand in equine sympathy. The shirt bore the caption IT'S HARD TO STUMBLE WHEN YOU'RE ON YOUR KNEES.

"I see you're a practicing Christian, or is that shirt just for show?" Frank asked.

Both men stood mute, not sure where this was leading. The wearer of the shirt stepped forward. "Yeah, I'm a Christian." He glared at Frank. "So what's the point?"

Frank barely smiled. "Here's the point. Let's share some scripture. 'Bless the beasts and the children, for in this world they have no voice. They have no choice.' You think killing birds is Christian behavior?"

"The Bible says that?"

"Aphasians 12:14."

"It's just a bird."

"What kind of bird?" Frank asked.

The shooter looked down at the dead bird. "Blue jay."

"It was a pinyon jay. Now it's just dead." He let his gaze travel from the dead jay back to the two men.

"Screw this. Let's go," the taller man said.

"Hold up there for a minute." Frank reached in his pocket and flipped out his badge.

"Aw shit, don't tell me it's illegal to shoot a blue jay."

"Pinyon jay." Frank corrected. "It's illegal to shoot from a road. It's illegal to discharge a firearm where it might endanger someone. You shot from the road, in our direction."

"How're we supposed to know you were here? We didn't see you."

"That's the point. You're supposed to check it out."

The two men were silent.

"You can go. Wait! Before you go, why don't you see if you can pray the bird back to life?" Frank pointed at the lifeless jay. "Should be easy. Small bird. Small miracle."

"What the hell's the matter with you, man? All we did was shoot a bird."

"You can't bring it back to life, can you? In the future, stick with targets, tin cans, and legal game during hunting season. You read me?"

"Yeah, yeah, follow the rules. Obey the law. Do as we're told. I get it."

"A bit of advice. You're not the only ones around here who like to kill things. I'd go home."

"Is that a threat?" the man with the rifle said.

"Nope. Just letting you know there are some people who'd take exception to killing things for fun. Some of them even carry guns."

"We'll go wherever the hell we want."

"Suit yourself." Frank wanted to do something to scare the shit out of them, make them sorry they were mindless assholes. "Oh, don't forget your dead bird." It was the best he could come up with.

"Screw you," the shooter said. They disappeared around the rocks, heading back for the road.

"Couple of real winners there," Linda said.

"Yeah, Numb and Dumb. Born-again entitlement."

"You told them that 'Bless the Beasts and the Children' was from scripture. I thought it was from the Carpenters."

"One of my favorite songs."

IO

•

"Greg, you and Agent Novak will check out the Darwin Falls Wilderness Area. Lot of burros in there." Meecham pointed to the quadrangle map. "Okay with you, Pete?" Novak nodded. "Greg, use your pickup. No, not you, Frank." Meecham smiled. "We don't want anything to happen to Frank's truck, right, men?" The comment brought chuckles from the other rangers. "The point is, we're going to have to violate the regulations about the use of personal vehicles. If the shooter comes looking for the Brotherhood of American Sportsmen and finds nothing but the Bureau of Land Management, we'll have wasted a lot of time and money." They were crowded around a table in a small conference room at BLM headquarters in Ridgecrest, Dave Meecham doing the briefing.

"Jesse, you and Agent Ellis run up the east side of Cerro Gordo and check on the White Mountain Talc Road. Jesse, do you mind using your Bronco?"

"Sure. I mean I don't mind."

"That work for you guys?" Meecham shifted his attention to Ellis and Novak. "You'll be running the greater risks posing as hunters." Meecham made it a point to defer to the federal agents. It was their plan to horn in on the possible matchup between the Brotherhood of American Sportsmen and the Sandman, but it was BLM territory.

It was going to be an interesting operation. Special Agent Drew Ellis of the FBI and Jesus Sierra, ranger from the BLM, had met for the first time in Meecham's office, and that only to shake hands before the briefing. Sierra, the youngest BLM ranger working out of Ridgecrest, maybe the youngest ranger in the BLM, wore a thick, drooping Pancho Villa mustache to give him a few years. Without it, his round face and mischievous dark eyes made it difficult for him to look properly coplike. The name Jesus hadn't helped the cause much either, nor the long eyelashes, nor the fact that young women inevitably giggled and flirted in his presence. Mostly he shrugged it off. He had a comedic streak and was able to turn the cracks and jokes aside and redirect them at his colleagues. He even poked fun at the reserved Frank Flynn. This was much to the delight of Greg Wilson, who regarded Frank as too formidable to tease without some ganging up.

Special Agent Andrew Ellis wasn't all that sure about Sierra. This was Ellis's first time working with BLM law enforcement, and the BLM had some definite quirks. For one thing, it had the damnedest non-chain of command he'd ever encountered, and it seemed like they were all mavericks, off doing things on their own initiative. Meecham seemed reliable. He was a professional. He'd been eight years with the Border Patrol before coming to the BLM. Most of the rangers had come from somewhere else, city or county PD, Border Patrol, state police, but some of them didn't sound like law enforcement or look like law enforcement. Ellis found Sierra's appearance and demeanor disconcerting, but better Sierra than Flynn.

In Ellis's eyes, Flynn's attitude was definitely less than professional. Ellis frowned, remembering Flynn's crack about the Dairy Queen. Cocky smart-mouth with his stories about Black Bart and old-time detectives, but what really got to him was feeling like a fool, finding out that General Zaroff or Zarov or whoever was a fictional character. It didn't seem to bother Pete Novak, but not much seemed to get under Novak's skin. Ellis turned his head to where Flynn was standing bent over the maps next to Meecham. So far, nothing from Flynn but respectful silence. Frank lifted his head, and their eyes met. Ellis openly scrutinized the slim figure. Flynn was smart and quietly confident in a way that Ellis envied. He gave Ellis a small nod and returned to the map in front of Meecham.

"Flynn's going to check out Grapevine Canyon and the Hunter Mountain area. That'll put him on the Saline Valley Road." Meecham straightened up. "The Inyo sheriffs will take the paved roads: 395, 190 between 395 and the Panamint Valley Road, and Panamint Valley south to the Ballarat turnoff. The Park Service will keep an eye on Wildrose Canyon." He looked around. "Any questions?"

Wilson half-raised his hand. "We don't exactly know what we're looking for besides a tall guy with a .270, do we? I mean, is there anything that might help us narrow it down a bit?"

"Frank, anything to add?" Meecham said.

"Not much, except for some guesses. I think he might have hidden his vehicle out on Hunter Mountain. I found a place a couple miles beyond the turnoff where someone had parked a vehicle. A panel van would be my first choice, but only because you can't see what's in it, and it's a place to hole up in, or shoot from." Frank thought of Zeke Tucker's van with a stab of conscience. "There's something else, though. The timing for this isn't ideal."

"What's the matter with the timing?" Ellis snapped. Following up on the Web site challenge from the Brotherhood of American Sportsmen had been Ellis's idea. So far the Brotherhood hadn't shown up on the FBI's radar, but the country was sprouting self-proclaimed patriotic groups at a geometric rate, all full of self-righteousness. Most were harmless, but some were eager for something more substantial, like guarding the borders and taking potshots at illegals—brown illegals. No vigilantes on the Canadian border so far, but hell, you never know, and there were all those anti-American Frenchies who didn't like our foreign policy. The Web posting by the Brotherhood of American Sportsmen had an ominous ring to it. Frank considered the possibility of a free-for-all shootout, and he didn't like it much.

"There's an annual turkey vulture migration that will probably peak this weekend. There'll be lots of birders coming into the valley to help with the count, take pictures, love the vultures, that sort of thing. So we'll be having company. I imagine that's why the Sandman picked this coming weekend."

"Shit." Ellis snapped his notebook shut. "Why'd you wait till now to tell us?"

"Nobody asked me, Drew. I wasn't in on the planning." He met Ellis's eyes. "It's a pretty good plan, might even bring the Sandman out and give us a chance to catch him. Maybe you, Jesse, Pete, and Greg can pose as birders. That way you won't be designated targets." He paused. "We'll just have to hope this Sandman character knows the difference between a birder and a poacher," he added softly.

"I can't believe it. Birders!" Ellis muttered.

"Well, maybe they'll help us out, be extra eyes," Sierra suggested. "Besides, Frank there talks to ravens. Maybe he can chat up the buzzards." Sierra grinned over at Frank. "You talk buzzard, Frank?"

Frank shook his head. "Nope, just raven." He looked down at the table. "Buzzard talk is too difficult." He gave Sierra a time-to-cool-it look.

"What in God's name are you guys talking about?" Ellis glared at the two rangers.

"Don't let them yank your chain, Drew." Meecham cut in. "They've been out here too long. Not important." He took a deep breath. "If there are birders, then they'll just be an additional source of information." Meecham looked around the room again, making eye contact with each member of the task force. "How about you, Pete, anything to add?"

Novak grinned. "Be careful out there."

"Okay, then. That's it. Saturday morning at six in the parking lot, four days from now, which should give us time to have everything in order," Meecham said.

As they shuffled out of the room, Meecham gave Frank the high sign. "Frank, stick around a minute." He bent over the table, pretending to study the map until the room was empty except for the two of them, then straightened up and asked, "So what else don't you like?"

"Too many people, Dave. All good officers—"

"All?" Meecham raised his eyebrows. "What about Ellis?"

"Absolutely. Including Ellis. He's a pain in the ass, or to be fair, not the guy I'd pick for a roommate, but he knows his stuff."

"That's what I think, too."

Frank gave a half-smile. "He'll get even better when it isn't so hard for him to listen, like me learning to keep coyote quiet." The smile broadened.

"So go on, all good officers, but?"

"I think this Sandman guy would have to be pretty slow not to suspect a trap. He thinks ahead, makes careful plans."

Meecham nodded. "Yeah, but even if he does suspect something, he might respond to the challenge."

"That's what worries me. If he comes, he'll be gunning for the Brotherhood of American Sportsmen, for whoever called him a back shooter. I don't think he thinks of himself in that way. I'm damned glad the covert teams will be posing as birders instead of hunters. The Sandman has made his bones, so to speak, so he's probably feeling like he's not getting due respect. Maybe someone who calls himself the Sandman thinks he has a reputation to maintain."

Meecham rubbed his jaw, looking thoughtful. "Maybe so. Truth is, we know very little about him."

"Except that he's smart. I think he's been trained, too. That's what bothers me. He has the earmarks of a professional, and we have no idea how he'll react except for the response he posted on the MDG Web site, and he sounds pissed. That line about 'I'll be seeing you through a scope' gives me pause, Dave. The guy kills people, and he thinks he's doing the right thing, the definition of a fanatic."

"And?"

"Something's ringing a bell. Ellis might be right. Why'd the shooter leave the note? He must have figured someone would find it."

"Someone did."

Frank met Meecham's eyes. "Me, at least the casing, if not the note itself. Someone trained in small arms combat, someone who would know where to look. Ellis wanted to know why me. I'm beginning to wonder about the same thing."

Meecham paused. "What're you thinking?"

"Maybe he does know me from the army."

"One foot in front of the other. Let's see if we can get this vulture-watch, trap-the-shooter operation completed without anyone getting hurt."

Frank nodded. "I just hope all that anger doesn't get directed at anyone who's in his way. I hope he isn't crazy enough to think he can shoot someone in law enforcement and get away with it."

"Me, too, Frank; me, too. We'll all of us just have to be very careful. I'm too close to retirement to be taking extra chances."

Frank didn't like to think about Meecham retiring. He liked things the way they were. The idea of working under someone else set his teeth on edge. He made no move to leave Meecham's office.

"Spill it," Meecham said.

"I badged a couple of guys shooting pinyon jays from Hunter Mountain Road. The rounds went over our heads. Linda was with me. Anyhow, I almost lost it."

"How so?"

"What I wanted to do was take away the guy's rifle and smash it up."

"But you didn't."

"One of them had a T-shirt with a praying cowboy. One of those soppy sentimental pieces of crap, and all I could think about was how I wanted to punch him out."

"But you didn't," Meecham repeated.

"The long and the short of it was that I gave the guy a ration of shit. Then I turned badge-heavy and told him it was illegal to shoot from the road and near people."

"That it?"

"Yeah."

"Don't worry about it, Frank. He was breaking the law. You told him not to."

"You might get a complaint. I got on his case about being a phony Christian."

Meecham smiled without humor. "Think of it as therapy, helping them to get to know the asshole inside. Now it's off your chest. You can't worry about offending every dickhead you meet." He met Frank's eyes. "If you're worrying about the Sand Canyon thing, I know you'll handle it just fine."

"Count on it."

I I

•

Before heading out to Sand Canyon, Frank had taken extra pains with his dress. He knew that military types might be there: buzz cuts, knife-edge creases, and shiny black oxfords. So he'd ironed military creases in his shirt, and his khakis were crisp with spray starch. He'd spent close to an hour spit-shining his ankle boots, working the polish into the leather with water and a soft cotton cloth. It was something he hadn't done since leaving Seventh Army Noncommissioned Officers Academy. There was a comfortable mindlessness to it. Duties—someone else thought them up; all you had to do was carry them out. The simple life. He laughed silently to himself.

He thought about things too much. That was his problem. Analyzing everything made life too damn difficult. The unexam- ined life might not be worth living, but the carefully examined one was a definite pain in the ass.

He could see a distorted version of himself in the toes of his boots. The shine wouldn't last all that long, but the gleam would be there when he met Duane Marshall and his staff. He was flying the flag and "riding for the brand," as Ben Shaw was fond of saying. Thinking about Shaw made him smile, a man who skewered his en- emies and friends with equal relish. "Hey, Ranger Frank, if you can't talk about it, you shouldn't have done it." Words to live by, Frank thought. He reached up into the caboose's cupola and brought down his good Stetson. It was going to be too warm for a felt hat, but his best straw hat was fraying at the crown, and the gray Stetson looked right with the khaki uniform.

"Looking good, Flynnman," Linda remarked as Frank stepped onto the rear platform of the caboose. She snapped a couple of quick pictures.

"What are you doing that for?" Frank ducked his head down, blocking the upper half of his face with his hat.

"Too late. I have photographic proof that you were looking all spit-and-polish when you rode out to meet with the enemy." She gave a soft chuckle.

Linda had been doing research about canned hunts, hunting ranches, and especially the importation of exotic animals for trophy hunts. Eighty-three-year-old Daisy Marston, the principal owner of the *InyoKern Courier* and Linda's employer for the present, was an upland game hunter and reputed to be a first-class shot with her Ithaca twenty-gauge shotgun. There were old-timers that referred to her as Little Miss Sureshot, the sobriquet given to Annie Oakley in the heyday of competitive shooting. Nevertheless, despite her affection for hunting, or perhaps because of it, she hated the so-called hunting reserves, and Sand Canyon was going to be in her backyard.

Daisy Marston was from one of the early ranching families, tough, salty of mouth, and possessing a degree in history from the University of California at Berkeley. She had definite views of how things ought to be. When she first heard about the proposed conversion of the Circle Cross ranch into a hunting reserve, she made one of her rare trips down to the *Courier*'s offices in Ridgecrest to speak with her son, the paper's general manager, editor, and editorial writer, about the "shameful slaughter of domesticated livestock masquerading as game." Epithets like "cowardly wretches," "lacking the proper masculine equipment," and "wholly without courage," followed by a general assessment of postmodern society, "not a nickel's worth of grit in the whole damn country," were heard issuing forth from George Marston's office.

Daisy Marston was swimming upriver. Sand Canyon meant money. Nevertheless, she had not only given Linda the go-ahead to do an investigative piece but also made it a directive: "Find out about that place, and who's this Duane Marshall?" The Sand Canyon people were being careful, though, refusing interviews to hard-news reporters. They limited interviews and access to their facilities to friendlies who wrote articles extolling the virtues of private game reserves for the many publications devoted to guns and hunting. It was big business. Political business.

Frank had noticed there were already puff pieces with illustrations of smiley families and their "harvested" animals in the free real estate and tourist publications—but nothing about how the actual hunting was carried out. The brochures and mailers were somewhat more forthcoming:

NO KILL NO PAY!
Hunters enjoy the comfort of large enclosed blinds with sliding widows overlooking heavily used corn feeders. Each stand has mineral licks and timer-controlled feeders. We have the daytime cover and water . . . so they MUST come to us to hide and drink. Hunting is done from raised blinds overlooking feeders, which have been operating continuously since August. Any predators seen may be taken as well. We're going to do everything legally possible to make your hunt a productive, worthwhile experience!

The text was interspersed with pictures of grinning hunters holding up the heads of dead deer and antelope and the carcasses of "harvested" bobcats, mountain lions, and coyotes. Frank wondered what you did with a "harvested" bobcat or mountain lion. Bobcat stew? Most hunters used dogs with radio collars to tree mountain lions. Then they popped them out of the branches like Christmas tree ornaments. Many of the so-called game reserves tranquilized the bigger cats—African lions and tigers—and the hunters shot them as they wobbled about.

During a lifetime spent in the desert, Frank had encountered a mountain lion in the wild only once. They were solitary creatures, good at keeping out of sight. As a boy, he and Jimmy Tecopa had been following the drag marks from a recent kill, hoping to catch a glimpse of a real mountain lion. As they moved up the sandy wash, they'd been frozen in place by a deep coughing sound. The lion was crouched above them on the embankment, yellow eyes blazing. The carcass of a recently killed deer lay in the wash directly below. The cough was a warning, as were the blazing yellow eyes. He and Jimmy talked about the eyes lots of times after that. How it felt to be looked at as prey. That was the only time he'd actually encountered a mountain lion, and it had occurred because the lion refused to give up its kill. It was a moment Frank valued more and more with each passing year.

According to the brochure, Sand Canyon specialized in upland game and exotics: axis deer from the Indian subcontinent, European fallow deer, and African species including zebra and two of the Big Five—African lion and leopard. Because the animals weren't native, hunting seasons didn't apply. The so-called sports folk could shoot at animals all year round in unimpeded slaughter.

It wasn't one-stop shopping—yet. Trophy hunters still had to head for Africa to get the Cape buffalo, rhino, and elephant to round out the Big Five. Of course, as the brochure pointed out, for hunters with limited time it was convenient to take two species stateside and concentrate on the other three in Africa—or in Texas.

There were a few ranches in Texas where hunters could "harvest" Cape buffalo and the Bengal tiger. "Bringing in the sheaves, bringing in the sheaves . . ." Didn't they sing that old hymn in one of those *Texas Chainsaw Massacre* movies? Frank figured he was living in the wonderful world of George Orwell.

Now the marvels of technology made it possible to use a remote-controlled gun on a distant ranch from an apartment in New York or Los Angeles—Internet hunting for those who wanted to hunt without the inconveniences of the great outdoors. The techno-sportsperson could kill a couple of animals while enjoying a croissant and reading *USA Today* or the *National Enquirer*. On the killing end, there were people handy to finish off wounded animals, and the hunter didn't have to put up with all that messy skinning and butchering. The ranch did that for you. Mailed you the cured hide, mounted head, and packaged meat—no problems.

There had been an uproar when Internet hunting was introduced in Texas. Most states had passed laws against it, including California, but if you had money, almost anything went in Africa. Frank found the whole business of canned hunts disgusting, but his wasn't to reason why, his was but to do—do his best for Dave Meecham and the Bureau of Land Management, and that's what he was going to do.

He leveled the brim of his Stetson, straightened his shoulders, and placed his feet apart. "Can I help you, ma'am?"

Linda wrinkled her nose. "*May* I help you," she corrected, "and no, I don't think so, Officer, you have shifty eyes."

"Well, hell"—he pushed his hat back—"so much for the macho approach."

She turned her face up and kissed him. "I'll settle for the Flynnman anytime."

As Frank stepped down from the caboose, he was very careful not to scrape his boots. "Wish me luck."

"Don't forget to see if you can get me in for the opening cere-monies. So far, I haven't been able to set foot on the place. They don't like reporters."

"I'll see what I can do," Frank said as he climbed into the BLM Ford Expedition.

"Watch the coyote mouth."

" 'Into the valley of death rode the six hundred,' less five ninety-nine."

Linda watched as the big boxy BLM vehicle pulled onto the pavement and disappeared down the road. Her heart ached at the thought of being separated from this man. That she loved Frank was a given. That she was content to live in social and professional isolation was another thing. Her life in the Owens Valley had given her a freedom she had never experienced, yet at the same time it was confining. The life of the city to the south beckoned. Why was it every opportunity seemed to require sacrifice?

●

At 14,495 feet, Mount Whitney forms part of the back wall of the Sierra Nevada mountain range that towers above the west side of the Owens Valley. The combined ranges of the White Mountains and the Inyo Mountains rise along the eastern side. White Mountain reaches 14,256 feet, peak to peak with Mount Whitney, which makes the Owens Valley deeper than the Grand Canyon, the deep-est canyon on two continents. The valley floor follows the Owens River from Bishop at an elevation of 4,140 feet to Owens (dry as dust) Lake at 3,650 feet. Two active faults run a parallel course down the valley, one along the base of the Sierras, the other track-ing the base of the White and Inyo ranges. The land is still in mo-tion, marked by frequent earthquakes, recent lava flows, and a series of hot springs.

Frank took the Mazurka Canyon road toward the Inyos. The

road heads east from Independence, drops down a twenty-foot earthquake escarpment, created by the earthquake of 1872, and runs into the dry bed of the Owens River. The 1872 earthquake leveled most of Lone Pine and prompted the abandonment of Fort Independence. The town was rebuilt and survives because Independence is the Inyo county seat and shelters maintenance facilities for the Los Angeles Department of Water and Power. It's a place that people drive through but not where they stop.

Frank brought his vehicle to rest at the crest of the escarpment. It never failed to awe him. Twenty feet of vertical movement and thirty-five feet of lateral shift. The quake occurred before the development of the Richter scale, but geologists estimated that it had been an 8.0 or higher, right up there with the San Francisco earthquake of 1906. It was no wonder that Paiute legends were full of mighty creatures performing prodigious deeds, stacking up mountains on mountains, scooping out great valleys, and spewing forth lakes of fire. His mother's ancestors were witness to these upheavals that left no room for skeptics. *Envy them in their innocence,* Frank thought.

His eyes traveled along the near ridge of the Inyos, where granite monoliths were stacked along the skyline. One protruded above the others, Winnedumah, the frozen guardian warrior. In the old story, the outnumbered Paiutes had been defeated for possession of their valley by their traditional enemies from the great valley on the other side of the mountains. The Paiute medicine man, Winnedumah, fled into the Inyo mountains pursued by the victorious Waucobas, eager to exact a terrible revenge. When Winnedumah reached the crest of the mountains, he could go no farther. He turned and raised his hands to the sky and awaited his death, but Coyote, the creator of the Paiute world, appeared in flashes of lightning and turned Winnedumah into a stone giant. The Waucobas fled over the mountains to the great valley by the ocean, never to return. Winnedumah stands above the land of the Paiutes and watches his people and waits for the gods to return and free him from his stone prison.

Frank loved the story and its many variants. He found he took as much solace in the presence of the stone monolith as in the stained glass that filtered the light into colored patterns on the nave of the church where he had attended mass with his mother.

Before the Department of Water and Power had diverted the waters of the Owens River into the aqueduct destined for Los Angeles, the valley had been a series of meadows and wetlands, a virtual paradise. No wonder his ancestors had fought so fiercely for it, beating back competing tribes, only to lose to the white tribe, his father's tribe, who now possessed its lands and took its water. Now the lower valley had become part of the desert. "Dry as a popcorn fart," he heard Bill Jerome mutter in his guttural bass voice. Well, there was this. The valley had been saved from development. No endless tracts of houses, no strip malls, no traffic jams—except at the beginning of trout season, deer season, and the film festival. Okay, there were periodic traffic jams along Highway 395, but then the tourists went home.

He glanced down at his watch. Nine forty. He would hit the gates at five to ten and be at the ranch at ten sharp. He pulled the big SUV back on the road and headed across the valley. He thought he could feel the eyes of the stone giant watching his progress across the valley floor from the Inyo Mountains, the dwelling place of the Great Spirit.

12

•

A sign so new it had no bullet holes was bolted to a heavy metal gate blocking the old Circle Cross ranch road:

SAND CANYON GAME RESERVE
MEMBERS ONLY
FOR INFORMATION CALL (760) 555-HUNT

Frank got out of the BLM vehicle and entered the four-digit code he had been given into the keypad next to the gate that would permit him entry. The gate swung silently open, pushed by an invisible hand. He was by himself, but the movement of the gate was somehow unsettling. He pulled over the cattle guard and the gate swung shut, latching behind him with a clank. *Close Sesame!* He had entered the magic kingdom of money, where the sorcery of big bucks summoned sinister gatekeepers. He glanced up at the ridgeline where Winnedumah kept watch. *Wonder what he thinks about the white man's magic?*

Alfalfa lay browning out in the fall sun. Perfect for hunting upland game: pheasants, quail, chukar, and wild turkey. Must be cottontail heaven.

He was surprised to find another gate blocking the road at the mouth of Sand Canyon, complete with guard hut and visible gate-keeper. Frank pulled up in front of the dropped arm and handed the khaki uniformed attendant Dave Meecham's invitation.

"Are you Chief District Ranger David Meecham?" the guard inquired, scanning the invitation and Frank through dark sunglasses. He had an accent Frank couldn't place. The gate guard was dressed for his duties in a safari shirt belted at the waist and a khaki safari hat, the brim snapped onto the left side of the crown, sporting a red, white, and blue logo. He wore an expression of detached authority. *Bwana man!* Frank thought.

"No, I'm standing in for him. I'm Frank Flynn with the Bureau of Land Management."

"Just a moment, sir." The guard stepped back, keeping an unsmiling face on Frank, and picked up a radio. Frank waited while he checked to see if Frank was on the okay list.

"Go ahead, sir." He waved Frank forward as the barrier lifted.

What next? Frank thought. *Perhaps a phalanx of Zulu warriors to round out the African theme.* Frank's inner coyote was clearly restless.

The narrow mouth of Sand Canyon opened into a series of small meadows; the first seven or eight acres were mixed grassland and scrub, surrounding a seasonal stream lined with cottonwoods. The old ranch house and outbuildings lay tucked against the western ridge of hills, facing eastward, where they could warm in the morning sun and escape the high heat of late afternoon. The corrals out front were empty. Horses and cattle were no longer a major part of the operation. Just as well, Frank thought. Some jackass would take the cattle for "slow elk." Frank had a low opinion of most modern hunters, who had a tendency to shoot first and ask afterward. Sorta like modern politics, he thought. *Quiet, coyote. We meet the white chief.*

Another khaki-clad safari guide waved him over to a parking place in front of the ranch house. He had been headed for the larger paved parking area behind a series of low buildings fronting the canyon from the southeast. They were apparently shooters' blinds, each low building topped with a camouflage-covered framework, closed at the back. Frank guessed the upper blinds would be for bird shooting, the lower part enclosed for rifle fire. Two large towers flanking the blinds were probably for bird releases, so the hunters could take them on the wing—or as they dropped to the ground. Hey, they could toss them out already cleaned and plucked. Save time. *Quiet, coyote.*

He glanced up at the veranda surrounding the old ranch house as another figure in safari dress stepped through the door. He was followed by a shorter man in carefully fitted starched camouflage fatigues and polished jump boots, looking every bit the commanding officer, except for missing unit patches and badges of rank. Another civilian affecting warrior garb. Sunshine soldiers were the latest fashion.

The shorter man radiated ownership. The taller man, tan, lean, and at ease, appeared to be the real thing. His khakis were faded and worn, and the boots had mileage. He caught Frank's eye and nudged the man in camo and pointed at Frank. The shorter man extended a hand as Frank mounted the steps to the porch.

"I'm Duane Marshall, the new owner."

"Frank Flynn." Marshall clasped Frank's smallish hand in a viselike grip. "You must be from the Bureau of Land Management." His smile appeared genuine, but then, so did Ted Bundy's.

"This is Ewan Campbell, the operations manager of Sand Canyon. Ewan is from South Africa." That helped to explain the safari theme.

"Mr. Campbell," Frank said as they shook hands. Campbell's grip was firm, no more, but it was a large hand at the end of a muscular arm.

"Come on into the ranch house," Marshall suggested. "We can

have some coffee, and I'll show you a map of the layout. Then we can look over the grounds." He paused. "I assume you'll want to do that before making any decisions."

"Sure, I'm here to see the place," Frank replied. He caught his host's eye. "I'm also here to check out abandoned mining operations, take a few pictures of the petroglyphs up in Dead Indian Wash, and report back to the chief district ranger concerning safety issues. He makes the recommendations." He gave a slight smile. "When it's in his bailiwick. We're not policy makers at Ridgecrest, but I'm sure you know that."

Marshall nodded. "You are the boots on the ground, though, and if your superiors have any sense, they listen to you. So let me put it this way. We want you and the chief district ranger to be satisfied that we're doing things right."

Frank nodded. He was aware that Ewan Campbell was following every word.

Marshall led the way into the old ranch house. Old from the outside, but all leather and polished wood inside, a silk purse hiding in a sow's ear. The pine floor had been stripped, sealed, and waxed. It glowed with a deep richness that only comes from old wood.

Marshall noticed Frank admiring it. "We kept the original floor—and the walls." He gestured with a wave of his hand. "Had to take down most of the walls for refitting and reinstalling, but ninety percent of it is original. As you can see, that wood was milled when the trees were bigger around than a fence post."

Frank looked around the room. There were the heads of wildebeest, impala, eland, kudu, and other exotic animals Frank couldn't identify on the far wall surrounding the fieldstone fireplace. A leopard in full snarl crouched on the mantelpiece.

At the other end of the room, the ceiling had been opened up to accommodate a mountain lion crouched in the bare branches of a manzanita tree. *One of our own*, Frank thought. The deep maroon of the manzanita's trunk and branches set off the lion's tawny yellow coat. Frank looked into the lifeless glass eyes. He didn't feel like prey. He felt a sense of loss.

The low-ceilinged area in front of the fireplace was furnished with leather chairs and couch. The couch flanked a large slab of redwood cut and polished to serve as a coffee table, which rested on a zebra skin.

Frank gave a low whistle. "First cabin, Mr. Marshall."

"Thanks, Mr. . . . Flynn." Frank didn't fill in with *Make it Frank* or *Frank will do*. Hell, he didn't know Marshall well enough for easy familiarity and wasn't sure he wanted to. If Marshall wanted to be cozy, it would be up to him.

"Well, I'm glad you appreciate the place," Marshall pushed on. "We went to a lot of expense to restore it."

Well, not exactly restore, Frank thought, taking in the African theme. "I can imagine it set you back a bit," he said.

"Tell me about these petroglyphs. I didn't know we had any petroglyphs," Marshall said, sensing his guest's lack of enthusiasm.

"You do. Not far from here. The ancestors of the Paiute and Shoshone lived here for thousands of years. They hunted, too—for food."

A shadow passed over Marshall's face. "I take it you don't approve of hunting for sport."

"I used to hire out as a guide, a lot of years ago, but it's not my call."

Campbell's interest was piqued. "What was the game?"

"Mostly bighorn sheep. California bighorn sheep in the Sierras. Once in a while, desert bighorn, when someone hit the lottery. That was before they started flying hunters in. We walked." He met Campbell's gaze.

"I didn't know hunting desert bighorn was legal."

"It's not, with the exception of those few, maybe fifteen, who hit the lottery or win the bidding for the auctioned permits."

"I'd like to know more."

Duane Marshall cleared his throat.

"Maybe later, Flynn," the South African said.

"Anytime, Campbell."

The South African's face registered surprise, and then a small smile creased the tanned features.

"Let's use one of the dining tables, and we can spread out a map of our operation," Duane Marshall said, reasserting himself. "The private land is enclosed by the solid blue line. The dotted blue line indicates the boundaries of our operation."

"BLM land."

"That's right, Mr. Flynn." He paused, catching Frank's eye. "Mr. Flynn doesn't sound right. What do I call you? What's your rank? Lieutenant? Sergeant?"

Frank grinned. He'd let Marshall fumble long enough. "Make it Frank."

"Right. Okay, Frank. Call me Duane." He studied the ranger in reappraisal. "How do you want to do this? Take the tour, or are there some things you particularly want to see?"

"Both," Frank said. "Let's start with the tour."

•

They crossed the grounds to the recently constructed blinds, Campbell leading the way. "The feeders and water sources are out there at about two hundred yards." Campbell extended an arm. "From this site, all shooting will take place in a northeasterly direction. That means missed shots and spent rounds will end up in the canyon wall."

"That's right," Marshall added. "Safety is a major consideration.

Of course, the shotgunners will have greater latitude. That's why the bird blinds are on the roof. As you know, number six shot is pretty much spent at fifty yards, so we're okay there."

"What about the exotics? How do you plan to keep them in?"

"This area is completely fenced. So if an animal is wounded or makes a break for it, it's contained."

"That's one of the things I'm here for," Campbell interjected. "Sometimes the big cats are tethered," he added, his voice flat.

"Tethered?" Frank asked. He could sense Campbell's distaste.

"No loose lions or leopards running around. That wouldn't sit well with the valley residents, or the BLM, would it?" Marshall said.

Frank didn't respond. "Where are they kept?"

"Pens and cages are located behind the ranch house, where the corrals used to be. Plenty of shade in the afternoon." Duane Marshall glanced at his watch. "Perhaps you'd like to see the zebras that just arrived?"

"You shoot zebras?"

"They're an accepted game animal in Africa," Marshall said. Campbell made a face.

Frank wondered why someone would shoot a zebra. He didn't want to see them. "I'll skip the holding pens."

Marshall forged ahead. "The cages are transported to the field on trailers pulled by ATVs. The latches can be released by remote."

Frank thought of the automatic gate out in the middle of nowhere. He nodded. "Okay, let's take a look at the mine sites and Deceased Native American Wash."

Marshall's face creased in puzzlement. "What?"

Campbell laughed. "Dead Indian Wash, right?"

"Yup." He considered the big South African. Campbell might be someone he could like.

"Before we head up the canyon, I want you to see the blind we have set up for the disabled." Marshall led them through a sliding glass door to a shooter's stand set up in one of the blockhouse blinds. A rifle rested on a tripod bolted onto a shooting bench. A coaxial cable ran from a telescopic sighting mechanism mounted on the rifle to some sort of electronic device. The stock was attached to a bracket that was mounted onto a tracking arm.

"That's a digital camera attached to the back of the scope, which feeds into a computer station at the ranch. The rifle can be raised or lowered—see, here's the motorized turn screw—and windage can be adjusted by a second motor on the tracking arm." He beamed enthusiastically. "Simple as an erector set. The trigger mechanism can be released by the touch of a key on the computer."

"You online with this?" Frank inquired.

"Sad to say, online hunting is illegal in California, depriving the physically challenged of the opportunity to hunt. However, we're operating on a closed circuit." He turned to Frank. "You'll see it in action opening day. Our first official hunt will be kicked off by one of our members who is wheelchair bound. He used to be a hunter until a tragic accident injured his spine."

"What happened?" Frank inquired.

"A careless mistake on the part of a hunting companion on a game ranch in Texas. The brush was thick, and in the excitement of following a pheasant, the man discharged his shotgun without knowing precisely where his companions were." Marshall shook his head with regret. "The man is a quadriplegic."

The cloud of sorrow lifted, replaced by a sunny smile. "But now, thanks to our automated shooting station here at Sand Canyon, he's once again a hunter. He'll be using a touch wand in his mouth to sight in and fire the weapon. It only requires five keys, left and right for windage, up and down for elevation, and bang!" He grinned with enthusiasm. "Sand Canyon has provided the physically disadvantaged with the means to hunt. I think we're ahead of our time here."

Marshall turned to Ewan Campbell. "If anything goes wrong, we have Ewan to take care of it." The South African's face remained impassive.

Frank would've bet money that they were originally set up for Internet hunting and Marshall had decided to put the best face on the legal prohibition against computer room sportsmen.

•

Frank found that the mine sites had been covered with thick steel cable netting, in the recommended way. It kept things from falling in, and if there were bats, they wouldn't be trapped.

The petroglyphs in Dead Indian Wash were pristine. Too high up for the average vandal to bother with and easy to overlook. There were some early figures—bighorn sheep with differentiated hooves, two shaman figures, and a hunter grasping an atlatl and dart, unusual. Frank briefly explained how the atlatl was used, but after a few minutes, Marshall lost interest.

So Frank returned to the concerns of the BLM. "If your guests are interested in the petroglyphs, they can come up and take a look from the floor of the wash, but I'd discourage climbing up. Eventually, someone will get hurt or accidentally deface the petroglyphs."

Marshall's face read *so what*.

The South African seemed interested. "You mean they could take bighorn sheep with a throwing stick and a spear?"

"It wasn't really a spear. The dart itself was more akin to a large arrow and very limber. It bent during the throw. The stored energy in the bent shaft added to the velocity. They even added balance weights to the throwing stick. The weights transferred more energy to the dart, and thus more speed. They were powerful, but limited in range."

"We'll just make the canyon off-limits to guests. That way the problem's solved," Marshall said.

Frank's business at Sand Canyon was finished. Well, not quite. He had to return in a couple of weeks. He figured he'd make an appearance for the opening luncheon, take a phone call, and leave on pressing business. He didn't want to rub shoulders with these people, especially when the club members showed up and started shooting domesticated birds and tethered game. His inner coyote was definitely restive.

As he was leaving, Ewan Campbell made a point of asking Frank if he could buy him a pint sometime. Frank thought Campbell would fit in at the Joshua Tree Athletic Club, if the big South African could keep from punching one of the Grumpy Wrench Gang, most likely Ben Shaw, a man who never put fetters on his hostility. Shaw's inner coyote was healthy and well fed. Frank was envious.

"Sure, I know just the place," Frank responded. "I'll treat you to a Sierra Nevada." Then he remembered Linda's request to see if he could wangle an invitation to the opening. "Say, could I bring a guest to the luncheon? She's a local reporter, and a good friend of mine."

"Why not," Campbell said. "Give her name to Carl down at the gate. Tell him to check with me."

Before Frank stepped into the SUV, he glanced up at the western ridge overlooking the blinds. He had that feeling of being watched. He turned back to the ranch house. The big South African waved. *That must've been it*, he thought.

13

•

Frank and Ewan Campbell squinted into the wind coming off the Sierra as they crossed the dirt parking area adjoining the Joshua Tree Athletic Club.

"Where's the valet parking?" Campbell yelled against the blast.

Frank pushed through the heavy door into the dim interior. "This is the place." The patched-together tavern and its ragtag owners always put him in a good mood. "And here's the master of ceremonies," he said, stepping up to the bar. "Ewan Campbell, meet Jack Collins, owner and operator of the Joshua Tree Athletic Club. You might say Jack is the patron saint of desert rats." Frank's mood was buoyant. The first part of his mission to Sand Canyon for the BLM had come off without a hitch. Dave Meecham would be pleased. "So where's the rest of the team?"

"Out and about." Jack was guarded.

"Jack has a couple of partners"—Frank laughed quietly—"that require watching."

Collins ignored Frank's remark. "What brings you to the Mojave Desert, Mr. Campbell?" Jack inquired, shaking Campbell's hand.

"I'm with Sand Canyon."

Jack shot Frank a quizzical look.

"How 'bout a couple of Sierra Nevadas," Frank said, ignoring Jack's unstated question.

"That's the hunting ranch you're with?"

"The same," Campbell said.

"Ewan's from South Africa," Frank said.

"Oh, I see," Jack mumbled.

"So I thought I'd show him the hot spots and our desert hospitality." Frank's expression suggested that Collins let it slide.

"Welcome, Mr. Campbell, a friend of Frank's is a friend of mine." Jack's broad face expanded into beamish bonhomie. "This your first time in the Mojave?"

The big South African looked about, taking in the bar, the ancient gold pans against the far wall, and the snooker table opposite the bar. "*Nee und ja.*" He smiled. "I worked security for West Rand Mining. I grew up in the big dig, the Witwatersrand, South Africa. So you see, this place is familiar, even though I haven't been here before, mining camps being mining camps, wherever they are."

"That's the Rand in South Africa that this district here was named for?" Jack said. "You know, our Johannesburg borrowed its name from there in hopes of being as rich as the richest place on earth." Jack was clearly impressed.

"The very same."

"Why'd you leave, if you don't mind my asking?" Jack asked.

"They wanted me to start spending time underground." He made a sour face. "Way underground, more than a mile. I don't care for that."

Frank nodded. "Not for me either." Frank was out-and-out claustrophobic.

Eddie pushed through the leather-padded doors with Cece Flowers in tow. They stood waiting for their eyes to adjust to the soft light.

"What's up there, Redhawk?" Jack said, reaching into a refrigerator for an icy mug. "A tequila and grapefruit juice for you, Ms. Flowers?

"You look down in the mouth, my friend," Jack said, mixing her drink. He placed a beer in front of Eddie.

Eddie took a long pull from his beer and wiped his mouth on the back of his hand. "Thanks, Jack." He sighed and turned toward Frank and Ewan Campbell. "How're you doin', Frank?"

"Eddie, this is Ewan Campbell. Ewan, Eddie Laguna and Cece Flowers. Eddie's a genuine Native American guide," Jack said with a smile.

"Hello, Ms. Flowers, Eddie." Campbell nodded.

"Call me, Cece, Ewan," she said in a husky voice.

"I like your hat," Eddie said. "Never seen one like it."

"It's from South Africa," Campbell said.

"So what's been ringing your bell?" Frank asked, winking over at Jack.

"Very funny," Eddie said. The jokes about his bell were wearing thin. His face gathered into a frown. "We haven't had much luck in locating Cece's mine"—he sighed—"and now my truck's acting up."

"Acting up?" Jack said.

"Quit running."

"Eddie knows the desert better than anyone I know," Jack said, quickly changing subjects before Eddie asked to borrow his truck.

"Nothing like gold fever to concentrate a man's efforts," Campbell said.

"Ewan's from South Africa, Eddie. He used to work for a gold mine."

Eddie brightened. "Yeah?"

"I'm no expert about finding gold. That's for the geologists. So what're you trying to hunt down? I'd be interesting in hearing about it."

Eddie nodded and recapped the difficulty of trying to locate Ms. Cecilia Flowers's lost mine, given how hard it was to find benchmarks a hundred years old and the vague description of the mine's location in the letter.

"Well, it sounds like a tall order."

Eddie nodded. "Yeah, for sure."

"Nobody can find it if Eddie can't," Jack chimed in.

"Except I don't know gold ore from a rock."

"If it's knowing what's real gold and what isn't, most people can't tell the real thing from the fake," Campbell said. "The thing that separates the genuine article from the phony is the acid test. Give it the acid test, and the gold shines out like the sun on a bright morning."

"Sure." Eddie looked from Campbell to Jack Collins and back. He'd had his leg pulled once too often, especially by the owner of the Joshua Tree Athletic Club.

"Ewan's telling you the truth, Eddie. Most gold's got a mark on it to show how pure it is. Like twenty-four karat or fourteen karat." Jack tugged a ring from his finger. "See the mark here?"

Eddie peered at the inside of Jack's ring and saw *14kt.*

"That mark shows that it's gold, but not pure. Other metals have been mixed in to make it stronger. Pure gold is a very soft metal. You can dig into it with a pocketknife."

"I won't be looking for lost rings with marks on 'em, for Christ sakes."

"That's true enough, Eddie, but there is a way to tell the false from the true." Ewan Campbell's voice dropped, his expression suddenly earnest. "What they do is put nitric acid on it. If it's not gold, it turns green or brown. If it's real gold, the acid doesn't touch it. That's how they know what it's made of."

Eddie gave Jack a long look. "You guys aren't just making this up?"

"Nope, it's the truth, on my mother's grave," Jack touched his chest.

Campbell nodded gravely. "Same with people, Eddie. I've seen men turn as green as cabbages around nitric acid, but the hearts of gold just call for another drink."

Collins broke out laughing.

"I knew you guys were bullshitting me."

"Not really, Eddie," Frank said. "Just the part about the cabbages."

Eddie sighed. "Didn't know it. Didn't even know there was a test."

"Nobody said you're a mining engineer," Jack added.

"Yeah, well, we're about done looking anyway." Eddie looked glum.

"That's true, Jack." Cece said, in a whispery voice. "All I have is the map, the letter, and my dreams."

Frank thought she was laying it on pretty heavy, but the rest of the male contingent seemed to be lapping it up.

"You don't mind me saying so, Ms. Flowers, it takes a lot of money to run a mining operation," Campbell said. "The people who make the strikes rarely get rich. It's the developers who make all the money, and that requires investors. The days of picking up high-grade ore and retiring in a month are long gone; mostly they were never here."

Cece reached into her canvas bag and pulled out the pink quartz. "What about this? You think this is worth investing in?"

Campbell held the ore up to the shaft of sunshine coming in through the diamond-shaped door light. He whistled softly under his breath. "Did this come from your mine, Ms. Flowers?"

"A long time ago, yes. It's all I have."

"Well, if you can find the rest of it, I'd say it's more than worth developing. I'd say you have a real find."

Cece smiled. "Oh, thanks so much, Ewan. That makes me feel so much better. You don't know how discouraged I've been."

Campbell frowned in thought. "Tell you what, Cece. If you'll trust me with your ore, I think I know some folks I can show it to."

"Oh, do take it, Ewan. That would be just wonderful of you. I can't tell you how much I appreciate it. I was about ready to give up."

Campbell turned to Eddie, whose slight figure had receded into the gloomy light. "Find it for her, mate. You find it, and we'll dig up some investors. Now it's up to you."

Eddie's outsized teeth flashed in the gloom. "That's what we'll do, Mr. Campbell—and thanks."

"Well, I've got to be going. No rest for the wicked." Campbell smiled at Jack. "I imagine that keeps us both busy, right, Mr. Collins?"

Jack returned the smile. "The devil finds work for idle hands. It's been a pleasure, Mr. Campbell." He reached across the bar, and they shook hands.

"Good luck with your treasure hunt, Eddie."

"Thanks," Eddie said, bobbing his head, the silver bell voicing his gratitude.

As Frank and Campbell departed, Eddie leaned across the bar. "Say, Jack, you think I could borrow your truck until mine's running right?"

Jack sighed. "Yeah, but take care of it, Eddie. I've had that truck a long time."

"Thanks a lot, Jack." There was a time when most people wouldn't have trusted Eddie around the corner with a rag doll. Now he had friends who would lend him a truck. Pride washed over him in a great wave. He wasn't used to it.

•

Frank and Campbell pushed through the doors into the hot afternoon sun. The wind had died down, and the smell of creosote bush drifted into the air, sharp, dry, and acrid.

"That was a nice thing you did," Frank said.

"The Sand Canyon membership wipes their arses with banknotes. They're nothing if not rich."

"I mean Eddie."

Campbell shrugged. "Oh, *ja*, he is a good guy."

"Twenty-four karat." Frank smiled.

"Marshall asked me to keep an eye on you," Campbell said as they got into Frank's pickup.

"How come?" Frank asked.

"He has you picked out as an unfriendly." He waited for Frank to respond. "I did some checking up. I'd say he has a point."

"Why are you telling me? Seems like I would be easier to keep an eye on if I didn't know you were watching."

Campbell's laugh was humorless. "Right you are, mate. Spying's not my line of work."

"Finishing off wounded animals for rich phonies on pretend safaris doesn't seem like your line of work either." Frank pulled onto 395 and headed northwest toward the Sierra.

"It's not." He pulled sunglasses from his pocket and put them on against the afternoon sun. "My old line of work wasn't much better."

"Which part? Chief of security, West Rand Mining, or South African Defense Force? You left the SADF in 1994 when the new armed forces incorporated guerrilla units from the African National Congress and other anti-apartheid groups." Frank looked over at his passenger. "Everybody checks on everybody. Why'd you leave the army?"

Campbell laughed. "To keep from being murdered. You know all that bullshit about karma, things coming round. Well, it was my turn to be hunted. I'd been a good soldier. I took the king's shilling, so to speak, so I did my duty and killed black people for my country. Not just the guerrillas, no, no. I was with one of the special units whose job it was to suppress trouble before it happened, which meant quieting troublemakers, people who spoke up, tried to organize." His voice trailed away. "So after I got out, I did the same fucking thing for the mine owners."

He looked directly at Frank, his expression somber. "Mercenary. Gun for hire. This job for Sand Canyon is a step up." He chuckled softly. "Marshall and his investors hired me to put Sand Canyon together and make it work. They want a place where their guests can do what the hell they want in the privacy of their own club, and they want it to be secure." He stared out the window. "That's how a man winds up wiping other people's arses."

"Why don't you get out? Nobody's holding a gun to your head." Frank brought the truck to a stop where 395 joined Highway 14.

"I told them I'd see it through to opening day. Then I'm gone. That's what I signed on for. That's what I'll do." He fished a cigar out of his pocket. "Mind if I smoke?"

"Go ahead. I'll blame the stink on Jack Collins."

Campbell smiled. "Good guys. Good place."

"Yeah, the best."

"No, nobody's holding a gun to my head, but I've taken their money." He grinned. "A promise for services yet to be rendered."

Frank thought about making promises. "What if you gave your word to the wrong people? What if things changed? What if you give your word to people without honor, people who make up their own rules? You keep your word then?"

"*Ja.*"

"I'd say that makes you a fool."

Campbell gave Frank a hard look. "They're the ones paying the bill." His expression softened. "Look, when I'm finished with Sand

Canyon, I'm finished with guns. I'm a photographer. Pretty good, too. I've got my first showing down in Palm Desert in less than a month." He puffed on his cigar. "Come on down where I can keep an eye on you and I'll take your picture."

"Sounds good." Frank liked Campbell in spite of his past. *There but for the grace of God,* he thought. *Walk away, Ewan, while the walking's good.*

14

•

From his perch in the cupola, Frank watched the lightning flickering along the tops of the Inyo Mountains on the far side of the valley. The distant rumbling of thunder swelled and faded in jagged counterpoint to the flashes of blue light. He imagined sheets of rain sweeping across the high desert, the dry washes swollen with rivers of brown water. Not a good time to be in the plateau country, a good time to be in the caboose. He shivered in the damp air and pulled the tails of his shirt down over his bare legs.

He'd slipped from their bed, taking care not to wake Linda, finally asleep after a fitful night of tossing about. Her words had banished sleep, and his own words kept replaying in his head like a stuck record. He'd been caught unawares, flat-footed as a fool in motley.

They'd decided to celebrate Linda's birthday with dinner at the Seasons. She wore beige slacks, low heels—heels were a rarity—and a light blue silk blouse, looking like a million. He'd basked in the envious stares cast in his direction, more than likely curious stares—*what's a pretty woman like you doing with a guy like that?* stares—but that was fine with him.

"I'm hungry, Flynnman, and I'm not counting calories tonight. Let's splurge," she'd said, and they had: crab cakes and fumé blanc for appetizers, salmon for her main course, rack of lamb for his. For dessert they'd split bread pudding topped off with caramel sauce, followed by a good port. Wonderful!

"Do you know how old I am, Flynnman?"

He'd thought for a minute. "Thirty-two."

"Thirty-four," she'd said, her face serious.

"Her beauty untouched by time." He had smiled foolishly, pleased with his comment.

"Where do you see yourself in five years, Frank?"

"Jesus, where did that come from?" he blurted. "I've never given it much thought," he added quietly. "Why?"

"Time marches on." She made a face. "Birthday blues and all that."

"I guess I don't worry about the future all that much because right now seems okay. More than okay. Right now seems *great*." He grinned his most disarming grin. "You can't really do all that much about the future anyway." He shrugged. "It just comes and turns into the present—where we live. In the present."

"What is that, mañana, Paiute wisdom, or Irish folklore?"

Frank tried to collect his thoughts. He was being tried and convicted for something, but he wasn't sure of what.

"Common sense," he replied, his voice flat.

"Things change, Frank. Either you have a hand in them or you drift."

"What's the matter with drifting? It's better than running around chasing after a career, making bucks, and buying stuff. In my book, drifting's okay."

"Maybe for you. Planning for the future is common sense, too."

"I plan for the future every time I set my alarm clock." *Smartmouth speaks*, he thought. "Look, how'd we get from celebrating your birthday to future shock?"

Linda sighed. "Forget it, Frank. I should have expected as much."

"You get the script you write."

"I already said forget it." Her voice was hard.

"No, let's not. I take things as they come. That works for me. It beats the hell out of worrying about what's next."

"That's bullshit, Frank. You're in a funk about too many people moving into the valley, widening Highway 395 through Independence, development everywhere you look. You hate change. You want tomorrow to be yesterday."

"That's different."

"Oh, I see. Well, that's not me, Frank. I need to think about how things will work out," she said in a soft voice.

"Okay, then. What's next?"

"I've had a job offer from the *Los Angeles Times*."

"Oh." It was his turn to speak softly.

"Oh. That's it?"

"I don't know what the hell to say. I guess the main question is, are you going to take it?"

"You might have asked what kind of a job." Her expression was somber. "I told them I'd think it over." Silence settled over them. "You didn't ask, but it's an opportunity to do the kind of work I've dreamed of, writing in-depth articles, something beyond Mule Days, the Lone Pine Film Festival, and real estate shenanigans, things with a point and a purpose."

"Oh, I understand *now*, the purpose-driven life."

"Cheap shot, Frank." Her brows knit. "It's the kind of break that doesn't happen all that often, maybe once in a lifetime."

"I guess that means you'll take it."

"I don't know yet," she said, creasing her forehead. "I do know that I've topped out at the *Courier* running on idle, and tending bar at the Joshua Tree Athletic Club so Dad and his pals can play snooker and goof around in the desert isn't what you'd call fulfilling." She rose. "We'd better go. Tomorrow's a busy day for both of us."

That had been it. They'd driven home in the silence of small talk and gone to bed without making love.

He was angry because he'd been blindsided. He had never questioned whether Linda found her life in the backwaters of the Mojave Desert satisfying. He did. It was home. She was the one who had opted for change in her life. He hadn't considered that taking care of the Joshua Tree Athletic Club and reporting for the *Courier* wouldn't exactly satisfy a person with Linda's creative urges.

Damn! What they had seemed just right, close enough but not confining—which meant he could goof around in the desert and play metaphorical snooker. He felt suddenly chagrined. He was thinking about someone else's problems—for a change. "Tying thine ear to no tongue but thine own." He and Harry Hotspur. He found himself slightly, only *slightly*, despicable. He smiled in spite of himself. Can't let the prosecution get the upper hand.

He loved the life they shared. He loved Linda Reyes. Why couldn't things just stay like they were? She'd called it. He didn't like change. In his book, things usually changed for the worse, and this was another crappy example. Now what? The rain had begun to beat on the roof of the caboose. He slipped down the rungs that led up to the cupola and pulled the covers over her shoulders against the chill. Damn the *Los Angeles Times*. For now, it would have to go on hold. He had the Sandman and the FBI to worry about. That was more than enough.

15

•

Linda frowned. "Come on, Frank, you're antsy, the way you get before you're about to do something important. Give." She pinched his arm.

"Hey." He pulled away. "You see that, Ralph?" Frank gave Ralph a chummy look. "Attacking a uniformed officer. That's against the law. Now she has to pick up the tab."

Ralph presided over Ralph's Special Burritos, a cinder-block affair that used to be a gas station. He didn't look like a Ralph. He looked like Emiliano Zapata. He turned up the juice on his perpetual glower. "What I seen was a cop trying to shake down a pretty lady into buying him lunch." He made a grimace in Linda's direction, which passed for a smile.

"Well, grassy-ass for nothing." Frank shook his head, looking injured. "Here I am, your biggest supporter for miles around, bring the guys from the station for Ralph's Special Burritos, and this is the thanks I get."

Ralph's scowl darkened. "Yeah, and the gringos speak better Spanish than you do."

"Okay, okay." Frank winked at Linda. "Hey, how about some more of the ver-day sauce stuff. Hear that? Ver-day—*la lengua de mis padres.*"

Ralph's mustache twitched. He muttered, "*Indio ayer. Indio hoy.*"

They carried their plates across the cracked pavement to the decaying wooden picnic table that served as Ralph's patio.

"What was that last crack?"

"He said something about once an Indian always an Indian. Ralph's not PC."

"You get your jollies mispronouncing Spanish to tick him off, don't you?"

"Yeah, well, he gets his jollies beating me up for it. Besides, I help Ralph use up some of his mean so he's just normally surly with the rest of his customers."

"Mmmm." Linda wiped the sauce from her chin. "He doesn't have to be nice. These burritos do the job." She reached into the mini Playmate cooler. "Want a beer?"

"Make it a root beer." Frank looked mildly regretful.

"Right, on duty and all that." She smiled up at him. "Which brings me back to the subject," she said, shifting ground.

"What subject's that?" Frank raised his eyebrows.

"What's all this about having to be at the station early in the morning?"

"So who am I talking to? Linda Reyes, my beautiful girlfriend, or Linda Reyes, ace reporter for the *InyoKern Courier*?"

She smiled with pleasure. "You know how to do it, don't you, Mr. Smooth. Okay, the reporter's taking a nap. I'll let you know when she wakes up."

Her smile always made him smile. The hazel eyes, framed by soft dark curls, full of mischief. Not much makeup. Her mouth was a little too large, the lips full. With makeup she might look a bit like a tart. She pretty much stuck to slightly unkempt or opted for the professional look, minimum makeup, no-nonsense clothes. The professional Linda never failed to catch him off guard, so businesslike and serious, so different from the private woman he knew, full of laughter and delight with the things around her. He couldn't bear the thought of losing her.

"What, Frank? What is it?" She laid her hand on the back of his arm.

Frank shook his head. "Nothing, really."

Her dark eyebrows rose with skepticism.

"It's just that when things are just right, I want everything to stand still—but it won't." He smiled ruefully.

Linda's eyes drifted toward the decaying billboard on the opposite corner. The old highway had taken this route. Now the street through town was a bypass, strewn with ratty motels and boarded-up buildings. Originally the billboard space had been occupied by a figure of Jesus in conventional pose, eyes sad with suffering, arm raised in perpetual benediction, blessing the passing motorists hurrying through the desert going someplace—anyplace—else.

Now the raised arm flapped in tatters, and Christ's disembodied head floated above strips of paper fluttering aimlessly in the wind. She narrowed her eyes, trying to make out the words about the figure's head: . . . OUT OF HIS BELLY SHALL FLOW RIVERS OF LIVING WATER. What was that about? A man with a canvas knapsack climbed the abandoned structure to the catwalk fronting the ravaged sign.

A distant rumble from the storm clouds piling up against the Argus Mountains caught Frank's attention. The coming law enforcement operation was already cluttered with the vulture watch people. They didn't need a desert storm to make things worse. Late-season thunderstorms had been sweeping across the desert, bringing scattered showers to parts of the Mojave. Soon there would be flowers—and more rain. The storms were coming in from the southwest, building up earlier each day. Thunderheads of deep gray, edged in white, towered over the land.

"I thought you wanted to know what Zorro and his faithful

companions are up to." Frank said, his face turned toward the gathering storm.

"Yup, what's up, Zorro?"

"We're after the shooter, the guy who thinks he's General Zaroff."

"I thought that might be it. You think he'll show?"

"I think he'll be curious, but if he doesn't smell a trap, he's a dim bulb. Hard to say."

Another of Ralph's customers headed for the table. "Mind if I join you?" The newcomer stood hesitantly by the picnic table, balancing a steaming plate in one hand and clasping a beer in the other.

"Sure, take a seat." Frank gestured toward the end of the bench.

"Thanks." The new arrival sat on the bench opposite Linda and Frank and took a bite of burrito. "Man, these are good." A trail of sauce clung to reddish blond stubble, streaked with gray. His ears stuck out, and his boyish smile gave him a Huck Finn look. "Better than battalion mess. I can see why you eat here all the time." Pale blue eyes smiled at them from an oddly youthful face.

Frank felt the hair on the back of his neck rise. "How's that again?"

"Great burrito." The man smiled and nodded. "Even Esquival—you remember, the first cook who did Mexican food—couldn't make a burrito like this." He frowned; then his face brightened as if in sudden recall. "Oh, that's right; you took a discharge. By the time Esquival showed up, you were back in the States. Too bad. You missed some good army chow."

Frank studied the bearded man, trying to remember his face. "You have me at a disadvantage. I don't believe I know you."

The stranger chuckled. "Oh, you know me, Sergeant. You just don't recognize me. It was you who picked me for sniper school. You said I was the best damn shot in the outfit, next to you, of course. Three points off your score was the best I ever did." He nodded to himself. "But I got better. On my second tour in Iraq, I had a confirmed kill at twelve hundred and forty-seven yards." He waited. "Not bad, huh?"

"Parker," Frank said.

"Right, Parker. The candy-ass kid you turned into a soldier. When Stuller and them were making my life a hell, you kept me from going AWOL. It was you recommended me for the Tenth Mountain at Fort Drum, your old outfit. Remember that? And the cow? The cow's the main reason I left the presents."

"Presents?"

"You don't get it yet, do you? The dead poachers in the desert. They were from me. Ready on the left. Ready on the right. Ready on the firing line. I figured you'd find the empty brass because you'd know where to look."

"You're the Sandman."

"You got it. Now, before we go on, Sergeant, I remember you were always duty first, carry out the mission. I understand and respect that. Bringing me in is your job. So, knowing you'd have to try, I took some precautions." He reached up and turned the bill of his cap sideways.

"Frank!" Linda looked down at a spot of red light that had blossomed on her jacket.

"Get that off her, Parker. Put it on me."

"Can't do that, Sergeant. You might take a dive and try for your weapon. Then my spotter would have to pull the trigger. I really don't want that. This way we can have a talk, and there's no reflection on you. This way everyone stays safe." He nodded. The red spot shifted to Linda's forehead. She squinted and looked away.

"God damn it, Parker. Get it off her face."

Parker extended his arm, palm downward, and slowly lowered his hand. The red spot drifted back down to Linda's windbreaker.

"What do you want with me, Parker? All of that was a long time ago."

"I know that, Sergeant, but you're the same man. I read the papers. You still hate the bastards who kill things just for the fun of it. So taking out those poachers was a sign of good faith."

Frank shook his head. "I don't kill people, Parker. I arrest them."

Parker stared into Frank's eyes. "You mean you don't kill people anymore. It used to be 'One shot, one kill.'" Both remained silent.

The boyish smile returned. "I'm here because I need something from both of you, you and Ms. Reyes." The smile faded. "The media people keep missing the point, speculating about whether I'm crazy or not. They've got it completely wrong. It's not about me. It's about the sick bastards who kill for pleasure." Parker's voice hardened. "See, I want you to explain why I'm doing what I do, Ms. Reyes. You can get it right. I'm not some deranged psychopath." He smiled. "That's redundant, deranged psychopath is redundant." He breathed deeply, as if to summon concentration. "You ever notice the news readers are dumber than dirt?"

He shifted his attention to the stunned Frank. "You know me, Sergeant. I'm as sane as you are. I cried that day when they killed the cow. That's why the guys in Stuller's squad started on me about being a crybaby. You remember. You tried to stop them. You know what's in here." He pointed at the center of his chest.

His face tightened. "I want you to tell people what's really happening, Ms. Reyes. Maybe you could present a log of their atrocities. Let the public know that the people who harm the helpless and innocent won't get away with it." He let out a long breath. "That's what it's about." He smiled. "The Humane Society—only with teeth."

Linda squinted over Parker's shoulder at the abandoned billboard across the highway. She looked for the man with the knapsack, but there were only the sad, empty eyes of the paper Jesus staring out at the swirls of dust and bits of paper blowing across the windswept asphalt. She caught a flash of red light and turned away.

"That's not my job, Mr. Parker. I'm a reporter." She spoke with deliberate calm. "I try to keep my opinions out of it and stick with the facts."

"Facts? Okay, you want facts." His features settled into a hard mask. "In March of this year, a man threw four kittens into a barbecue because he was angry with his ex-wife. The story made the local paper, but when he went up in smoke it made national news. They kept talking about how terrible it was to burn to death. He should've thought of that." The blue eyes blazed. "A man in El Monte put his wife's puppy in the oven. He told the judge his wife paid more attention to the dog than to him, and it was to teach her a lesson. So the judge made him take the dog to the vet. Its feet were so damaged it couldn't walk. Now his feet are damaged." He gave a tight smile. "Hopalong Husband. Put one in each ankle.

"Another piece of talking excrement smashed a puppy's head in with a hammer because it kept him awake with its crying. He'd shut it outside. It was six weeks old. He's unfinished business. Same with the people who duct-taped a firecracker into a cat's mouth and blew its head off. I think my chances of finding them—it would take two to carry out that little piece of poetry—are better than the cops, who aren't taking a lot of interest in the case. Other things more pressing. One cop called it a prank gone bad. He needs some reeducation, don't you think?

"You want more facts, Ms. Reyes? If I had access to my computer, I'd give you a printout. Making my list, checking it twice." He laughed silently. "Then there's the thrill killing. Horses in Nevada. Burros in the Mojave. Sometimes people seem to care about the horses. Romance of the West and all that cowboy stuff.

Nobody gives a shit about the burros, though." He looked at Frank. "Except thee and me, Sarge, and your responses are limited. Mine aren't." He was breathing hard. "So I do what you can't."

He unfolded the newspaper he had been carrying and laid it out in front of them. MIKE TRAVIS MURDERED IN HOME, the headline proclaimed.

"Read it, Sarge. Oh, never mind, I'll tell you what it says. It says that terrible people invaded the football hero's home and murdered him. That he was eviscerated and fed to his dogs. True enough, as far as it goes. What it doesn't say is that Travis and his buddies staged regular dogfights for the pleasure of friends and family. That they cut the throats of the losing dogs on the spot. Part of the show. They skipped the part about kids watching the fights and the training sessions. How they suspend puppies in socks above the dogs' heads to teach them to kill.

"So what the hell. Me and my faithful companion across the street put on a show of our own. We woke old Travis up and staked him out in the dog pit. He figured nothing could happen to him because he was Mike Travis. Kept a real smart mouth going right up until we opened him up a bit, not enough to kill him. With the right medical attention he'd have probably made it, but some someone carelessly left the kennel gates open. Guess some of those dogs weren't man's best friend, or at least not Travis's."

There was stunned silence. Parker grinned boyishly. "What I wonder is, did he plead with the dogs? You know, come on, Rover, jeez, Lassie, gimme a break here. Stuff like that. What do you think?"

"I think you might be crazy," Linda said.

"That's another thing to consider before doing something cruel." The boyish smile returned. "Some crazy person might just hunt you down."

"You've turned it loose," Frank said.

"Not me, Sarge, them. They let it out of the cage when they harm the innocent. You really want to live on the same planet with the spiritually deformed? Not me! They gotta go."

"Stop now, Parker."

"Too late, Sarge. Too late for me." His young-old face sagged in despair. "Maybe it's too late for you, too. You'll have to wait and see, huh? How many targets did you neutralize in Mogadishu?"

"We went in to get them out." Frank's voice was barely audible.

"First time I ever heard you hedge, Sarge. Well, hell yes. I try not to think about it either. I try not to think about the man I watched for three days chat with his kids and smoke cigarettes in his patio. On the fourth I took off the top of his head. Bad guy neutralized. 'Neutralized,' what a handy word. Just part of the mission, right? I took no pleasure in it—then." Parker's breath was increasingly shallow and rapid. "To tell you the truth, now I enjoy my work. Every little bit of it. The scum I remove denigrates the human race." He paused to breathe. "Who balances it out? Who watches out for the helpless?" He gave a lopsided grin. "Me, Saint Seth, the Avenger. I figured you'd like that, Sarge, being raised with all the Catholic bullshit."

Parker grimaced and began to raise his hand to his head. "Shit." He waved his hand back and forth and closed his eyes. His breath was coming in gasps.

Frank's heart raced. Parker had almost given his spotter the wrong signal. "What's the matter, Parker?"

"Nothing, Sergeant. Not a thing. A memento mori, that's all." He smiled and came to his feet, steadying himself against the table. "I'm not alone, Sergeant. See the Jesus sign across the street? He's keeping an eye on things." He gave a dry laugh. "My disciple, that is—but it's a beginning. Which reminds me. Stay put until the laser's gone. Then we'll be gone." His face twisted into a forced smile. "Write up what I told you, Ms. Reyes. It was for the record. You'll be hearing from me, now and then."

Frank watched him cross the cracked pavement to the street and climb into a Dodge Caliber. *What a stupid, stupid name,* he thought. Probably a rental or stolen. It was too far away to make the plate. The car pulled away from the curb and disappeared down the highway.

"Frank, how long will we have to sit here?" Linda looked down at the motionless spot in the middle of her chest.

"Ease over to your right."

Linda scooted over. The spot held steady, then disappeared into the desert.

"It's okay. They're gone. They clamped the scope and left it behind."

●

Linda leaned against the window of Frank's truck. "What did Dave say?"

Frank folded the cell phone and set it on the seat, where it was sure to slide onto the floor. "The FBI guys want to stay the course. They think this is a 'window of opportunity.'" He gave a bitter laugh. "I don't think they trust me."

"Why wouldn't they trust you?"

"Too close to the target. You know, birds of a feather."

"What are you going to do?"

"Mine is not to reason why." He shook his head. "Dave says he thinks the operation will go as planned. If Parker's their man, fine. If not, it doesn't make any difference. One way or another, they think this is the time to close in."

She rested her hand on his shoulder. "At least *you* know who it is."

"Yeah."

"What's a memento mori?"

"A reminder of death, of your own mortality, so you don't forget to take care of your soul."

"You guys chat away in Latin?"

"Jesuit high school." He studied her face, the soft curls surrounding the intelligent eyes. He felt her receding into some distant place. It was as if he were drawing away into the darkness, leaving her behind in a place where life went on in a normal way.

"You know why he's a killer?" Frank asked.

She shook her head.

"He can't bear the suffering."

"He makes people suffer. He confessed to having a man eaten by his own dogs."

Frank shook his head. "That wasn't a confession. It was penance for being a part of it."

"Of what? What was he a part of?"

"You know your Yeats?"

Linda shook her head.

" 'The blood-dimmed tide is loosed, and everywhere the ceremony of innocence is drowned.' Yeats was a prophet, you know." He reached for her hand.

"Why does he call himself the Sandman?"

"It's a shooter's nickname. He puts people to sleep."

16

•

"There's a side canyon in a couple more miles and some abandoned mines. We could look around. See what's up." They were climbing up out of the Saline Valley, nearing the top of Grapevine Canyon. Last night's thundershowers had settled the dust, and the air was bright and perfumed with the scent of sage and pinyon. Shafts of golden sunlight pierced the towering thunderheads building up against the Sierra. In places the road was slippery with mud, but there hadn't been enough rain for washouts.

It was a perfect day, yet Eddie struggled with an altogether unfamiliar sense of gloom. Susan Funmaker had made his chest ache in tenth grade, and now here it was again. Only this time, it was Cece Flowers who had reawakened these feelings of longing. His usual cheerful expediency had been displaced by uncharacteristic introspection. He found the change awkward and depressing.

Cece was reaching the edge of impatience. Driving around the desert with Eddie had not been part of her original plan. She wanted to get on with it, to find some abandoned mine, something that would do as a stand-in for the New Hope Mine, get some investors, and split, but Eddie was determined to find the right spot. She desperately wanted to soak in a bathtub, remove the layers of grime, and put on some fresh clothes.

Eddie pointed up the side canyon. "See the tailings?"

Cece leaned forward and peered through the windshield. "That pile of rocks?"

"Those are tailings from a mine. Someone did some serious digging here," Eddie said in a tone that conveyed a certain level of acquired expertise.

"Why there?" She was concerned that the mine might not be truly abandoned. That someone still held the mining rights.

Eddie thrust his jaw forward, the effigy of the noble savage: simple, honest, and direct, the Iron Eyes Cody look. "There's a couple of trees up above the tailings. There's a spring running down the canyon." The recent rain had given birth to a number of ephemeral streams. "That fits the map, don't it?"

"Possibly. Let's take a look."

"Yeah, okay." Someday, he hoped, she'd see that all he was doing was for her.

"Are we north of Darwin?" she said in a matter-of-fact tone.

"Well, yeah." Eddie was surprised that Cece knew the name of the ghost town, much less its location. He'd headed for the higher country when it threatened to rain. Cece leaned forward to look out of Eddie's window again to check out the site. Sure enough, there was a resemblance to the crude drawings on the map. She'd tried to make the map vague by leaving out stuff from the original. The equipment looked old and rusted; although she didn't know all that much about mines and mining, she recognized the remains of a mine head from the pictures in the library. Judging by the tailings, it hadn't been a large or successful operation.

Eddie shifted Jack's International into four-wheel drive low-range and began grinding up the wash toward the pile of rock heaped below the dark mouth of a tunnel cut into the side of the canyon.

"Don't flip this thing." Cece breathed through clenched teeth.

"Not a problem. Trucks like this can climb right up the side of a mountain." Eddie brought the truck to a halt just below the lower edge of the tailings. "This'll do," he said, climbing out of the vehicle and scrambling for footing on the steep slope.

"If the mine's already here, maybe somebody else has claimed it." She squinted into the darkness of the tunnel.

"I don't think so. Look at this stuff. It's been lying around for a long time." Eddie pitched his voice to match the experts he'd seen on TV reality shows. "Suppose you found some gold, made a big strike, and rushed off to town to file your claim. Then suppose you couldn't find your way back to where you found it. Then suppose some other guy comes along and says, 'Hey, look at this gold ore, man. This here's my mine. Think I'll call it the Jackpot." He winked at Cece, even though she couldn't see it in the gloom. "Well, the first guy lost the mine, but the second guy found it. So the mine's lost for the first guy but not the second guy. See what I mean?"

"You're telling me someone already found my mine?" she snarled. "Shit, then what are we doing here?"

Eddie glanced at Cece. There it was again. Over the past two days, she had begun to sound more and more like someone's ex hanging around the Stage Stop bar and less and less like one of his friend's sisters. Somehow it made her more approachable.

"Naw, what I'm telling you is that maybe someone else could've found it, unless there's some sort of old claim marker, and man, that'd make you the winner." He sighed with resignation at her ignorance of mining affairs. "We'll look around at different mines that sort of fit the map and the letter. Rule 'em out or rule 'em in. See, most of these claims are abandoned. If you don't work 'em, then the claim lapses."

Eddie led them out onto the dirt apron fronting the tunnel. "On the bright side"—Eddie exposed a grubby grin—"sometimes they miss the main ore body." Man, he sounded good, the main ore body. "Besides, here's a level space, a good place to camp."

"Camping sounds good," Cece said, "and I need to wash up." She raised an arm, sniffed, and wrinkled her nose. "Well, you stink worse than I do. Check it out." She broke into a silvery peal of laughter, grinning at his reaction. Eddie thought she looked sexy as ever, but not as scary. Her coarse language had shortened the social distance, although he wouldn't have put it that way. Maybe he could make a move before meeting with Linda Reyes. They were supposed to meet her at the junction of the Talc Mine Road and the Saline Valley Road.

He began unloading the camping equipment from Jack's truck and stashing it in the mouth of the mine. "I'll set up the stove and heat up some water, so you can wash up."

"Great." She gave Eddie a knowing look. "Maybe you can go meet Linda and give me some privacy."

"Yeah, sure," Eddie said, his hopes somewhat dashed. He turned to go.

"Hey, how long will you be gone?"

"Couple hours at the most."

She frowned with concern and looked up at the sky.

"I'll set up the tent so you'll be nice and dry if it rains."

"Thanks, Eddie. I really appreciate it. I mean it." She gave his arm a squeeze.

Putting up the tent would be a good idea. He thought about all the things that could happen in the tent during a long stormy night. He set it up in the mouth of the tunnel, glancing up at the darkening sky as he worked. "What time is it?"

Cece looked at her watch. "Three fifteen."

"Okay, see you around five," he said, giving her the thumbs-up sign.

She reached up and kissed him on the cheek. "Thanks again," she said, glancing up at him from under the fall of blond hair.

Eddie got into Jack's truck with a soaring heart. Maybe she really liked him. That would be great. He pulled down the canyon and headed for the junction with the Talc Mine Road to meet with Linda Reyes. She was writing a story about Cece, a woman prospector in modern times. She said he'd be in it, too. That would be good for business, he thought.

17

•

The birds whirled in a giant vortex against a deep blue sky darkened with rising thunderheads. The southward drift of the migration was unapparent to the casual observer, but Seth Parker was far from a casual observer. Thousands of vultures would pass over the southern Sierra on their way to Mexico. He followed the flight of a single bird, waiting to see when it would flap its wings, watching it effortlessly ride the currents of air.

Sometimes it seemed as if they were swimming in an invisible sea. He pushed the button on the binoculars, capturing a vulture in flight, the flight feathers separated like fingers clasping the wind, its wings stretched out against the deep blue of the fall sky. The digital camera–binoculars combination was perfect for watching birds—and cops. He knew there were cops watching for two men, one of them a redheaded man with graying stubble. Now the Sandman was a clean-shaven dark-haired man, traveling with a fellow bird-watcher. Sergeant Flynn's warning was already dated.

As he topped the rise, he spotted another truck pulled off to the side. More law enforcement trying to look like birders. He shook his head. You didn't do bird counts sitting in the cab of a truck looking bored. You picked a good site, set things up, watched the sky, made notes. Blending into the company of bird-watchers was easy for Seth Parker; he was a bird-watcher. He'd stenciled a

sign on the side of his pristine VW van, ALTADENA AUDUBON SOCI-
ETY, but the paint was washable.

He'd risked bringing John along. This was his first mission.
John was overly enthusiastic and had a tendency to attract attention, but he was perfect as a bird-watcher, decked out in lace-up
boots, cargo pants, and wool cap. Law enforcement people
wouldn't give them a second look.

He thought he'd seen two more law enforcement types north
of Darwin. They were looking for the Sandman, and here he was,
hiding in plain sight. He resisted the urge to wave at the bored
cops sitting in the pickup. There was no point in tempting fate. Up
to this point, the taunt from the so-called Brotherhood of American Sportsmen appeared to be a trap. He had been watching it unfold and taking pictures of the cops. He'd post the pictures on the
Web site. Let them know how clumsy they'd been. So far, there was
no sign of the Brotherhood of American Sportsmen or Sergeant
Flynn.

•

The first shot almost tipped Walter Ortman over. His ears were
still ringing from the blast.

"Man, you are right," Ortman said to his companion. "That's
louder than hell." He took the huge revolver in his left hand and
shook his right, trying to shake away the pain. "Kicks like a mule."
He grinned with pleasure. He'd never been around a .44 Magnum
when it went off, much less actually shot one. So he was unpre-
pared for the recoil and noise, despite his partner's warning. He
shook his head as if he'd been struck, but he was absolutely de-
lighted with the power of the gun's discharge. Stunning. "We didn't
bring anything for our ears, did we?"

His companion shook his head. "All kinds of ear protectors
back at camp."

Ortman rooted around in his trouser pockets for something to stuff in his ears to protect himself from the blast: keys, change, comb. He checked his jacket pockets and found a couple of business cards and some ChapStick. He tore two strips from one of the cards, folded one into a small cone-shaped tube, and tried to fit it in his ear. It poked uncomfortably. He crunched it around in his hand and re-formed it. Then he got the idea of putting ChapStick around the edges. Much better. He made a second and inserted it into the other ear.

He picked up a Bud Lite can that he found lying on the ground and set it on a fist-sized rock. He trotted back about twenty feet and took a spread-eagle stance, gripping the Ruger Redhawk with both hands. He jerked on the trigger, flinching in anticipation of the noise and recoil. Nothing happened, except that the barrel of the revolver jumped away from the target. He'd forgotten to cock it. He'd have to work on that, flinching so bad you couldn't hit anything.

He took a deep breath, pulled back on the hammer, and re-sighted along the barrel. He held his breath in anticipation and had just started to squeeze the trigger when the gun discharged. Only this time he'd been almost ready, really hanging on. The can wasn't there. He hurried back to where he'd placed it. Gone. The rock was gone, too. Then he spotted the can way off to the left. Had to be thirty feet. He went over and picked it up. No bullet hole, but near the bottom there were half a dozen irregular tears in the metal. He turned it in his hand. The holes must have been made by the exploding rock.

Ortman grinned. It could kill rocks. He turned his gaze to the birds wheeling above. Some were so high they were no more than tiny specks, but some were low, just sailing lazily along in the afternoon breeze. He sighted up at one and moved his arms in a slow arc, following the path of flight. Boom! The vultures flapped their wings and continued to wheel about. He hadn't hit anything.

"Don't stop moving when you pull the trigger. Let it be part of the whole motion, following the bird and pulling the trigger," his friend advised. "Squeeze."

Ortman took a couple more shots. The vultures flapped their wings, gaining altitude. They were getting away. Shit. One swooped in low and paused on an invisible eddy in the wind. He took aim, letting his arm drift with the motion of the bird, and squeezed. He heard a thocking sound immediately following the deafening report. The bird crumpled and plunged to the ground. It was to be Ortman's first and last vulture kill.

"Whooee!" he shouted. He hopped around doing a victory jig. In his elation, he failed to see the tall man and his sidekick walking in their direction.

The vulture lay in a smashed and bloody mess, its body nearly torn in half. Ortman poked at it with his foot. Ugly thing, he thought, and a lot smaller lying here on the ground all broken up. It was a really good shot, that was for sure. What he needed was to try the gun out on something bigger.

Seth Parker and John Gilman were within hailing distance of Walter Ortman and his companion. "Keep an eye on the other one. Let me talk to the shooter," Parker intoned, as he raised his hand in greeting. "How're you doing?" he said, raising his voice.

Ortman cupped a hand to his ear, not bothering to hide his annoyance at being interrupted.

"How're you doing?" Parker shouted against the wind, the boyish smile in place.

"Fine," Ortman said. He waited. "What's on your mind?"

"Didn't I see you just kill a turkey vulture?"

"Yeah. You see that? Knocked him right out of the sky." The

wind whipped at Ortman's clothing, blowing in great damp gusts, wet with the rain that had fallen half a mile away.

"Hey, what kind of cap is that?" Parker said, suddenly changing the subject.

"Brotherhood of American Sportsmen," Ortman said, swelling with pride. He was the newest member.

"Oh," Parker said. "I'm just wondering why."

"Why what?" Ortman sneered.

"Why you killed the vulture." Parker paused, looking sort of sad. "They mate for life, you know."

"Jesus Christ, another bird hugger?" He grinned over at his companion.

"Oh you have the wrong person entirely." Parker extended an arm holding a prewar Colt Woodsman .22 automatic—a classic.

Ortman lifted the Ruger and yanked the trigger.

"You have to cock it first," Parker said. The Woodsman made a cracking sound, and the small-caliber bullet hit the frontal bone at the thickest part of the skull, traveled along the bone under the skin, and exited behind Ortman's left ear. He sat down heavily.

Gilman brought a Glock out from under his windbreaker and pointed it at the other man. "Do I take him?"

"Wait," Parker said.

Blood began pouring from the exit wound down the back of Walter Ortman's L.L.Bean flannel shirt. He looked up at Parker with disbelief.

"You shot me." Ortman touched the back of his neck and looked at his bloody hand. "You shot me," he said again, trying to get a grip on it.

"Yes, yes I did," Seth Parker replied, "and not very effectively, it seems. Now I'm going to have to do it again." He raised the pistol and shot Ortman in the corner of his left eye. The small, low-speed round never left the brain case. The round's impact forced the eyeball to one side, giving Ortman's face a final expression of extreme derangement. The right eye looked incredulous, and then it dimmed.

"Jesus Christ!" Ortman's companion raised his hands as if to ward off the coming shot. "Please don't. I have a wife and and kids."

"That's too bad, screwing up the gene pool like that." Parker paused. "But you get to live."

Gilman's head snapped around. "Why's that?"

Parker smiled. "Because he is a witness to our response. He gets to tell his brethren in the Brotherhood of American Sportsmen what comes of pulling the tiger's whiskers." Parker turned to the subject of their discussion. "You'll do that, won't you, tell your mighty comrades of your friend's derring-do?"

"Absolutely. Whatever you say." His eyes flickered back and forth between Parker and Gilman.

"The truth will be adequate. Tell them that your friend shot a *Cathartes aura* for no reason. *Cathartes* means purifier. That's what turkey vultures do. They clean up, purify the land. That's what we do. We remove human waste, such as yourself, from the land. Your friend here"—he gestured at Walter Ortman's body—"killed the vulture simply for the sake of killing, so we shot him for wantonly taking the bird's life. He can't undo it, bring the bird back to life, so we put a stop to his destructive activities. Makes sense, don't you think?"

"Yes, absolutely makes sense," he croaked.

"Loyalty is a wonderful virtue, isn't it," Parker said, looking at Gilman. "One so rarely encounters it." Parker looked up at the darkening sky. "Well, we have to be going. You have a cell phone?"

The man nodded.

"Toss it here."

Parker made a left-handed catch and slipped the phone into his jacket pocket. "I'll be taking your calls. Oh"—he turned back—"you have had a unique experience. You've met the Sandman face-to-face, and he didn't put you to sleep. Once in a lifetime." He held up his index finger, the boyish grin spread across his face. Then he turned to Gilman. "Get the late Sir Galahad's phone and put one in our friend's right kneecap. Can't have him wandering away and chatting with people before we have moved on."

As Parker turned to walk away, he heard the man pleading not to be shot. The conversation was cut short by the report of Gilman's 9 mm and a cry of pain. The up-close encounters were so different. He had never heard a target pleading before killing the pelican man. Targets in the scope were soundless, the whole thing playing out like a silent movie. He thought about it and decided it didn't make much difference—dead was dead.

Parker glanced back at the corpse of Walter Ortman. The cardboard tubes in Ortman's ears gave him the grotesque appearance of a diminished monster. Which was what he was, Parker thought. He turned his gaze to the distant vultures, wheeling south away from the approaching storm. He wondered which of them would be without a mate. There was absolutely nothing he could do about it. You just had to change what you could and live with the rest.

"Pick up the brass," he said to Gilman over his shoulder.

He took a small spiral notebook and pencil from his pocket and printed a note across the bottom edge, then carefully folded it up. He cut the folded piece away with his pocketknife, rolled it into a small scroll, and inserted it into an empty shell casing from the dead man's .44 Magnum. *And the eye of the sleeper waxed deadly and chill.* He leaned down and stuck the casing with the paper into the man's shirt pocket.

Thunder rumbled in a darkening sky. Plumes of gray feathered down from great billowing clouds tinged with coppery purple. A storm was coming fast. He would have to hurry back to his van before the rain made the dirt roads impassable.

The vultures would find him; then the rest of them would come and rescue the dead man's partner. They would probably bring Sergeant Flynn as well. The first fat drops of rain dropped soundlessly into the sandy soil. Hunter Mountain was closer than the highway. It would be a safe place to wait the storm out and let things settle down. Seth Parker signaled to John Gilman, and they hurried back to his van and headed north on the Saline Valley Road.

•

Frank pushed the Ford Expedition down the dirt road, hurrying back to Highway 190 before the storm washed across the gullies, making the road all but useless. He hoped most of the birders had the good sense to head for the pavement. He wondered where the treasure hunters were. He hoped they were already on pavement headed for the Joshua Tree Athletic Club. Eddie was savvy enough to avoid serious trouble. On the other hand, the vulture count drew people from all over the country, people unfamiliar with the ferocity of desert rains.

A VW van crested the hill in front of him. Frank flashed his lights and leaned on the horn. It was headed north, away from the paved highway. He hoped the driver would take the warning. Hunting for Parker would have to wait. The main thing was making sure people were safe from the storm. For now, the weather would put the renegade sniper out of commission. The heavy vehicle lurched over a chuckhole and broached. Frank deftly corrected, steering into the skid and accelerating. It was times like this he especially loved his job. He punched the window button and let the damp air stream in over his smiling face.

18

•

Linda brought the jeep to a halt at the top of a rise to get her bearings. She'd borrowed it from an admirer, Kevin McGuire, a geologist working at the research station atop White Mountain. Kevin had been hanging around Linda hoping for a chance to make a move—not that Frank ever noticed. Despite the geologist's outdoorsy good looks, Linda had been careful not to flirt. She had hated borrowing his jeep and appearing to encourage him. It made her feel like she was trading on her feminine wiles. She frowned. She *was* trading on her feminine wiles—like Cece Flowers, Eddie's blond tart.

So who was she to be calling Cece a tart? What was the difference between toying with Kevin's emotions and leading Eddie by the nose? Nothing. Cece needed Eddie's help. She needed Kevin's jeep so she could follow up on her article without Frank having had any part of it. Kevin was more sophisticated than Eddie, but that didn't make Linda's part in using his jeep any less manipulative. Right now, she was quite pleased with herself. She knew one thing for sure, that she didn't want Frank restricting her comings and goings. He'd have argued with her about the dangers involved in being out on the desert when Parker could be on the loose. The same danger faced the vulture watch people. They just didn't know about

Parker. She did, so she was safer. Forewarned is forearmed. Sometimes Frank's concern felt confining.

She pushed away her misgivings about Cece's calculated flirtatiousness and especially her eagerness to solicit investors. That signaled trouble, but she wasn't going to convict Cecilia Flowers on qualms about her motivations. So far, all she'd done was charm Eddie—and every other male she met. If she admitted it, she was jealous, and despite Cece's overt flooziness—God, she sounded like a prig—there was something about Cece she was drawn to. Perhaps the toughness. No, the independence. She went after what she wanted, and she didn't appear to be a quitter. Cece was a bounce-backer.

Linda had yet to check out her story or even cast eyes on the famous documents, the letter and the map, but she would, especially before her dad and his pals got pulled into the venture. If Cece took some of the Sand Canyon membership for a ride, well, so be it. Someone once remarked that you can't cheat an honest man.

Linda'd been on the road for more than an hour. There were dirt tracks all over this part of the plateau, leading out onto flats and disappearing into canyons and behind hills. It was a good place to get lost. She switched off the ignition and climbed up to the crest of a low ridge that paralleled the road. She'd traveled this stretch of road several times, but Frank had been driving and she had been a passenger. It wasn't the same. None of it looked familiar, or all of it looked familiar; red dirt, black rocks, Joshua trees, and clusters of scruffy cattle. What in the hell did they eat?

She turned the key and pushed the accelerator pedal halfway down. Lots of grinding, but the engine didn't start. She waited and tried again. The starter was working, but the engine didn't even sputter. Damn, she was supposed to meet Eddie and Cece in less than an hour. This was no time for car trouble. She looked up at the swelling clouds tinged with hints of bronze. Damn. She wiped her forehead on the back of her shirtsleeve. It was hot, maybe ninety, not midsummer hot, but hot enough and humid.

She remembered that Frank's truck had acted up not too long ago, and he had cursed himself for cutting the ignition in the heat. He'd called it vapor lock. He'd explained that the truck wouldn't start because the gasoline had turned to fumes in the fuel line. The truck refused to start until Frank had built up pressure in the gas tank by blowing into it, his cheeks bulging comically around the rim of the gas spout. She had started the truck when Frank had signaled her to hit the starter.

She tried to remember what Frank had said about vapor lock. "The fuel pump won't work. You can't pump fumes. They just blow away like farts in church." Men thought farts were a lot funnier than women did. She kept pointing that out, but it didn't seem to faze him.

She hit the starter again. Nothing from the engine, just the starter grinding away, and it was starting to sound labored. She jumped out and paced back and forth, kicking at rocks. "Damn." She reached down and picked up a rock and flung it across the empty desert. She picked up another, but something about it caught her eye before she could fling it into the void. "Damn it. What in hell were you thinking, Kevin, lending me a piece of junk that won't run. This is not the way to a girl's heart."

She absently tossed the rock onto the floor of the jeep and climbed back into the driver's seat as the first fat drops of rain splattered noisily against the canvas top.

•

Lightning struck Cerro Gordo, etching the slopes in electric blue. Thunder rolled across the sky and culminated with a concussive clap that Eddie felt in the pit of his stomach as he steered Jack's truck through the torrential rain. He peered out the window into the gathering darkness. Lightning flashes whitened a lunar landscape. He gave an involuntary shudder. Out on the flats, the Joshua trees looked like spirit people moving across the desert.

Great fat drops of rain splattered against the windshield and drummed on the truck's metal roof. He thought about the tent in the mouth of the tunnel and wondered how Cece was doing. As long as she stayed in the tent and didn't go wandering around, she'd be okay.

The windshield wipers were badly worn, making it difficult to see as the rain roared against the glass. He had to keep leaning out the window, giving him the shivers in the wet wind. He flipped on the headlights and squinted into the cones of dim light. He wanted to stop, but he had to find Ms. Reyes and get back and make sure Cece was all right.

All he had to do was follow the dirt road back to the junction, but the dirt road kept on going—too far, Eddie thought. Then it narrowed as he followed it into a narrow canyon, a narrow canyon carrying a good stream of runoff from the increasing rain. He backed the truck carefully down the narrow ravine until he found a place to turn around. If he followed the road back to where he had turned off, he'd be okay. He'd eliminated the right turn, so it had to be the road on the left. Somehow, he'd missed the main road. *Some Indian guide,* he thought. For sure, he wasn't going to tell Frank about it, rainstorm or no rainstorm.

He came down a small rise where the track crossed the canyon bottom and stopped the truck where a wide stream of water rushed along the bottom of the wash. He stepped into the driving rain to take a closer look. There was no way he was going to get back across. Rocks and boulders rumbled and thudded in the dark torrent.

The water had risen perceptibly by the time Eddie stepped

back into the cab. He put the transmission into reverse, counting on the four-wheel drive to get him back up the rise. The truck slipped to the right, but he corrected in time to keep it from sliding into deeper mud. Then the wheels caught on firmer ground, and he regained the high spot. He squinted into the night where the beams from the headlights disappeared into the darkness. He made out a faint outline of a dirt track angling up the side of a low hill. At least it would take him to higher ground.

As the track neared the crest of the hill, the path widened. The headlights picked up some timber framing disappearing upward into the night. Eddie had just enough time to realize that it was a head frame supporting the main winch of a mine before the truck plunged downward into darkness, causing him to strike his head against the windshield and knocking him unconscious.

A shuddering thump jolted Eddie into consciousness. His head banged against the windshield again, causing a sharp pain. He was oddly disoriented. Everything seemed upside down. The right side of his body lay pressed against the front of the cab, his head against the glass. For a moment he couldn't figure it out. He wiggled around and peered through the windshield. The truck lights illuminated the rocky sides of a square-cut shaft that disappeared into darkness. The sound of his breathing quickened as the truck slipped again, jerking him into the maw of the abyss. He couldn't figure out what bothered him the most, that he had done something so dumb or that he'd screwed up Jack's truck.

19

•

When Special Agent Drew Ellis discovered Zeke Tucker in his binoculars watching him watch Tucker, Ellis had taken umbrage. As Jesse Sierra later explained to his chief, Dave Meecham, "The plan worked, Chief. We got the shooter."

"Why'd you and Ellis decide to stop Tucker? What made you think he might be the shooter?" Meecham probed.

"He was out lurking around the head frame of an old talc mine."

"Lurking?"

"That's what Ellis said." Sierra looked uncomfortable.

"I see. What else aroused your suspicions?" Meecham queried.

"Well, he was in a panel van, sort of dirty brown. It would've been hard to spot from the air." He looked to Frank for confirmation. He didn't get any.

"See any other suspicious vans *lurking* about?" Meecham's tone was sarcastic.

"I get your point, Chief." He glanced out of the corner of his eye at the silent FBI agents. "We thought the shooter might be operating out of a van, so we gave vans an extra look."

"Besides the brown paint and the *lurking*, what especially suspicious behavior did you observe?"

"Why would someone prowl around an old talc mine?" Sierra sounded plaintive.

"Maybe he needed to take a leak," Wilson sniped.

Sierra looked uncomfortable. "Well, as a matter of fact, he did take a leak, but the thing that put us on to him was when we saw him watching us through his binoculars. There we were, staring at each other through binoculars."

"Lookin' back to see if he was lookin' back to see if he was lookin' back at me," Meecham muttered.

"What's that, Chief?"

"Never mind. You're too young. Then what?"

"Then he waves at us and gets back in his van." Sierra looked around the room. "Well, that got to Agent Ellis." Sierra looked to Ellis for confirmation. "So he says, 'Let's follow this one.'" Ellis gave a microscopic nod. "So we pull back onto the Talc Mine Road and start following the van."

"What did he do then?"

"As soon as he spots us following him, he pulls over and gets out of his vehicle. Have you seen this guy yet, Dave?"

Meecham shook his head. "Nope, but I hear he's big."

"Big is right. Huge hairy head. Really weird looking, like eyes staring out of a bush."

"What did he do after he stopped?"

"Well, nothing, but now we were suspicious. He was a very tall guy in a van. So Agent Ellis asks him if he's there for the vulture watch. He just shakes his head. Then Ellis asks him if he can take a look in the van. He says okay, but that Jack might not like it. Drew steps to one side, being careful. He tells Tucker to ask Jack to step out from the van with his hands in plain sight. Then Tucker goes 'Haw! Haw! Haw!' real loud, and I thought Drew was going to go for his piece." He turned to Ellis. "Right?" Another microscopic nod. "Then Tucker stares at Agent Ellis and says, 'You better be damn careful not to shoot my dog.' Then he gives a whistle and this dog comes flying out the window."

Wilson exploded with laughter. Dave Meecham smiled in spite of himself.

"Where's the dog now?" Frank wanted to know.

"We took him over to the animal shelter to be looked after. Tucker was more worried about the dog than anything else, even after we found the rifle, a .270. That's why we brought him in. Because of the rifle, not the dog." Sierra grinned.

Meecham frowned in thought. "You know Tucker, Frank. What do you think?"

"Tucker scares people, but he's not the killer. I thought he looked good for it, too. He was in Vietnam and saw a lot of combat. After he was discharged, he became a war protester."

Meecham raised his eyebrows. "How come you know so much about Tucker?"

"I did some checking, and Linda did some more."

"So he was 'a person of interest'?" Meecham's voice hardened.

"More like an interesting person, Dave."

Meecham leaned forward, his mouth opening to speak.

"Wait a minute, Chief. I know you think I should have brought this to you, but I didn't have a thing to go on besides a hunch, which turned out to be wrong." He gave the FBI agents a look. "After the killings on the flats, I checked on him. The burro slaughter made Tucker angry, very angry, and I got to thinking that a very angry Tucker would be capable of killing poachers. God knows they need thinning out," he muttered. They all stared at him.

He took a deep breath. "He could've done it, but he's not the one." Frank's expression was unwavering. "Seth Parker's our killer. I already told you that." The FBI agents were pointedly silent. Meecham grimaced. Frank pursued it. "For God's sake, Parker confessed—not just to me but to Linda Reyes as well. His partner put a rifle on her." Frank's expression was tight with anger.

"A scope, clamped to a billboard," Novak said.

"He had an accomplice."

"Did you see the accomplice?"

"Linda Reyes saw someone she thought was his partner," Frank said.

Pete Novak nodded, his expression noncommittal. "We'll be talking to her soon."

"I don't get it. You've got the name, the motive, and a confession. You do need to talk to her. She's going to do a piece on him for the *Times*. Look, Drew speculated the shooter might be connected to me, and I didn't like it much. Well, it turns out Drew was right. What's more, Parker made it clear that he has unfinished business, the ones on his list." He waited. "Ready on the left. Ready on the right. Ready on the firing line. You know what comes next? *Commence firing*. He's not done—and he's a professional sniper. He was in the Tenth Mountain Division."

"Your old outfit, right?" Ellis said.

"That's got nothing to do with it."

"We're looking into it," Novak said.

Ellis nodded. "That's right. It's under investigation."

The FBI agents rose as one and exited the office, Novak in the lead.

•

"Shut the door, please, Frank." The rangers stood silently, contemplating their boss's grim expression. Meecham considered the dejected rangers who had been involved in what Dave Meecham thought of as the hundred-thousand-acre fiasco. As far as he was concerned, their efforts to entice the Sandman into revealing himself had turned into a farce, perhaps a disaster. It depended on the extent of the damage to equipment and to the reputation of the BLM.

"Let me sum up here," Meecham sighed. "Greg, you and Novak had to walk out to Panamint Springs when Darwin Canyon flooded."

Wilson nodded.

"How'd Novak hold up?"

"Fine. I think he was kind of enjoying himself. He kept talking about how he'd never seen a flash flood before."

Meecham nodded. "He wasn't the only one. We're missing five people and two vehicles that were part of the vulture watch." He grimaced. "Those are the ones reported." He directed his gaze at Frank.

"There's two others we haven't heard from," Frank said.

"What two others?"

"It's complicated, Dave, but the long and the short of it is that Eddie Laguna—"

"Damn!" Meecham's forehead furrowed. "I just love hearing Laguna's mixed up in something. It gives me a feeling of security, because I know it's going to be screwed up."

Frank stared at a spot on the wall.

"Go on, Flynn."

Flynn—no more Frank. Meecham was tight. "Eddie, uh, Laguna was helping this woman, Cece Flowers, locate an old mine."

Meecham removed his glasses and rubbed the bridge of his nose. "So that makes two more unaccounted for. Laguna and the Flowers woman."

Frank nodded.

Meecham glowered down at his hands. The silence was heavy.

"Okay," Meecham finally said. "Find the missing folks. That's our job until everyone's accounted for, even Laguna. Finding the shooter will have to wait."

The rangers rose and headed for the door, relieved to be doing something.

"Hang on for a minute, Frank." Meecham waited till the others had cleared his office.

"I guess you know Novak and Ellis don't buy the stuff about Parker."

"Why the hell not? What more do they want?"

"For one, they think you're protecting Tucker." He held up his hand. "Let me finish. You and Tucker are birds of a feather. That's how they see it."

Linda had said pretty much the same thing, Frank thought. "What about Parker?"

"They figure him to be a wannabe nutcase. It doesn't help that he knows you and talks about the killings as a present to an old army buddy."

"Okay, Dave. How do they account for the Web site, the notes, his knowledge of the murder of Mike Travis?"

"It's a Web site, Frank. Anyone can put up a Web site. Anyone can read it. Travis's murder is all over the papers. He showed you his newspaper, right? The notes could be from Tucker. He's a vet, a vet with a violent history. The Dynamic Duo even considered the possibility you could've planted the notes yourself. For what reason, God only knows."

Frank shook his head in bewilderment. "We're lucky Parker didn't fall for the trap and show up. He's an absolute professional with two tours in Iraq. Combat snipers kill a lot of people. They disassociate from it. If Parker takes it in his mind to do something newsworthy, as they say, a lot of people are going to die."

"For the record, Frank, I think Parker's our man. The problem is that finding the sniper's the FBI's case."

"Thanks for the vote of confidence, Dave. Now I'll see if I can find Eddie Laguna for you. I know you're worried."

"Why not wait a couple years? Naw, he fills in the dry spots.

Besides, he's your Paiute brother. Gotta look out for endangered species."

"He's Shoshone," Frank corrected, "and I'm beginning to think we're all endangered."

Meecham's phone rang. He held up his hand and took the call. "Dave Meecham, district ranger. Yeah, he's right here." He transferred his glance to Frank and placed his hand over the mouthpiece. "Some guy named Kevin McGuire for you."

Frank reached for the phone. "Frank Flynn here. No, I don't." His face clouded over. "Did she say where she was going?" He listened for a few moments more. "I'm headed out there right now. Thanks for calling. I will." Frank passed Meecham the phone.

"What's wrong, Frank?"

"Linda's missing. She borrowed Kevin McGuire's jeep, and someone reported it abandoned near the Talc Mine Road."

20

•

Linda knew she should stay with the jeep. If the vehicle breaks down, stick with the machinery—the cardinal rule of survival in the Mojave Desert, in any desert. Finding a stationary vehicle was a lot easier than finding a moving person in the immensity of muted colors and volcanic outcroppings that made up the northern Mojave. More important, a car or truck offered protection against the ever present sun, blistering winds, and bone-chilling cold. People usually died from dehydration, sunstroke, and exposure because they panicked and tried to walk back to civilization. So Linda waited, but she found the waiting difficult. Doing nothing was exasperating.

So far, her effort to chronicle the first woman treasure hunter in the Mojave had been ridiculous. She had been frustrated at every turn. She had yet to know whether the hunt for the lost mine was legitimate or a scam to attract investors. In the morning light, she was leaning toward scam, and if Cece Flowers turned out to be a con artist, she would have been going in circles. Now her effort to meet Cece and Eddie in the desert had ended up with her spending the night in a drafty jeep that had decided to quit running, to say nothing of the fact she was hungry—not thirsty. She knew better than to go out into the desert without plenty of water.

Linda sat on the hood of the jeep and waited for the eventual vehicle to pass by. If Cece proved to be a hustler, maybe she could write about Cece Flowers, Flimflam Woman of the Mojave. She sighed. Old news that. The Mojave Desert already had famous madams who had flimflammed their way into the history books. Cece wasn't even a call girl—as far as she knew. How judgmental could she get!

She just wished whoever was coming along the Saline Valley Road would hurry up—as long as it wasn't Frank. She couldn't bear the *What are you doing here? Whose jeep?* etc. She looked up the road at the distant sound of an approaching engine. She hopped down and eagerly searched for the vehicle on the other side of the curve sweeping down from the north. Now she could let herself feel relief and finally admit that she had been feeling spooked. Yesterday, just before the storm, she had heard distant gunshots. Somebody was always shooting at something, but still, it made her uneasy.

The approaching vehicle was a VW van coming down the long grade from the pinyon pine country. Apparently she wasn't the only one who had spent the night in rain. The intense storm must have trapped others—all the bird-watchers who didn't make it back to the paved road, for a starter. The BLM would have its hands full doing search and rescue. Thank God she wasn't being rescued by Frank or one of the BLM guys. She would have died of permanent chagrin.

The van rolled to a stop opposite the jeep. "Hi there. Looks like trouble," the driver offered from under a floppy canvas hat, mirror sunglasses reflecting the morning light. Why couldn't nature people find decent hats to wear, she wondered? The bad boy sunglasses were different, though.

"Yeah, it just quit," she responded. "I thought it might be vapor locked, but it wouldn't start this morning either, so I guess that rules that out." She hoped she didn't sound like a damsel in distress. She hated the idea of sounding wimpy.

"We're headed back to the highway. At least we can get you to a gas station."

Linda went around to the passenger's side and paused momentarily to read the sign, ALTADENA AUDUBON SOCIETY. It was an old-time VW van with the little skylight windows running along the top.

The man in the passenger's side stepped out, opened the slider, and climbed in back. "There you go," he said, smiling at her as if he knew something she didn't. Something about the way he looked at her made her uncomfortable.

The driver spoke reassuringly. "Hop in. Hey, I'll bet you're hungry. We haven't got much food left, but there's this." He rummaged around in a paper bag on the floor between the seats and brought out a Reese's Peanut Butter Cup.

"Oh, God, I can't resist those when I'm full, and I'm not full." She laughed. "I'm starved." Linda got into the front seat and eagerly opened the peanut butter cup, carefully pushing the paper away from the chocolate edge so as not to break any onto the floor.

The driver put the van in gear and headed down the road. "The desert is at its best just after a rain," he said.

Linda gazed up at the cloud-shrouded peaks of the Sierra and the crisp blueness of the morning sky. "Yes, it's very beautiful." She looked over at her companion. "So you like birds, huh?"

"I raise canaries," the driver said.

She could tell he was tall. The dark glasses and floppy hat made it difficult to see him, but there was something about him that struck her as familiar.

"So how's the article about the Sandman coming along, Ms. Reyes?" He pulled away the sunglasses, revealing a smattering of freckles across his boyish features. "Meeting up with you like this affords the opportunity to give you a firsthand account of the latest chapter." The man in the back chuckled appreciatively. The half-eaten Reese's slipped to the floor. Linda smiled vaguely. She was remembering her mother's warning about taking candy from strangers.

•

"So that's about it, Ms. Reyes," Parker said, as he finished up the narrative about killing the man who shot the vulture and leaving his partner to bear witness. "You know the saying about he who lives by the sword dies by the sword." He smiled. "Same for people who slaughter defenseless creatures."

"Same for you," she said. "That's the way you'll go. Some cop will shoot you."

His smile dimmed. "I don't think so." Then the smile broadened. "But you never know. Maybe I'll get lucky."

Linda wondered at the slip of the tongue. Or was it a slip of the tongue? She cast a covert look in Parker's direction. The hat and glasses—he had put them back on—made it difficult to penetrate the surface. Besides, she had only encountered him that once at Ralph's picnic table. Yet there was something different. He seemed subdued, despite the fact he'd triumphantly recounted the brutal murder of another human being.

The man in the backseat barked out a mocking laugh. "Not likely," he said. "Tell her how many confirmed kills you have." He shifted his gaze to Linda. "Just army kills. What do you think? More than ten?" He nodded his head. "More than twenty-five? Yup. More than fifty? Yup."

"Forget it!" Parker snapped, turning to look at his partner.

"I just wanted her to know that there's no one who could take you, that's all," he said in an injured tone.

Parker shook his head in silent refutation. "There's always bad luck," he said quietly. "Bad luck can take you down. Bragging draws attention from the celestial thug." He gestured skyward.

Was Parker thinking of hubris, Linda wondered? Frank had told her Parker was a literate man. What a waste.

"Don't worry, Ms. Reyes, no harm will come to you."

"Why? Was I looking worried?"

"I would say yes."

"I was thinking about my cat. Who would take care of my cat if something happened to me." She wondered if Parker had an affection for cats. Maybe that could work in her favor.

"Um-hmm. I know there are lots of people who like cats, but I can't help but think of all the birds they kill. You have no idea how many wild birds fall prey to domestic cats." He smiled. "Besides, think about it, I raise canaries, so I tend to favor Tweety over Sylvester."

"I suppose you would." Damn, people wouldn't stay in their boxes. Parker was good company. Nothing like reality to come along and ruin your preconceptions. "Well, Hobbes, that's my cat, lives indoors. It's that or wind up a meal for a coyote. The world's full of predators," she added in a matter-of-fact tone. She glanced into the backseat at the bland features of Parker's companion. "If you're not planning on harming me, why not drop me off at the highway. I'll be okay."

"Sure you would, but there's a story I want to tell you. Seeing you standing there by your busted-down jeep, I thought to myself, nothing happens without a reason—and if you believe that crap, good luck. Anyhow, your difficulties provided me with an opportunity to tell you a couple things about your Sergeant Flynn you might not know."

"What's that?" She raised her eyebrows.

Parker took his time to respond. They were jouncing along a particularly rough section of the Saline Valley Road, where it ran over pink and gray caprock before emerging onto the broad plateau.

A field of Joshua trees stretched in front of them as the VW van began pulling through the damp earth of the desert floor.

"Why are we slowing down?"

Parker raised a slender hand and pointed toward a cluster of Joshua trees. "See the burros." Linda saw the burros standing among the Joshua trees. They had been grazing on the grasses growing under the scant protection the spiny trees offered from the desert sun. Now they were alert, ears forward, ready to bolt. The harsh sound of distant braying shattered the midday silence, and the family of burros turned and trotted away into the flats.

Parker laughed. "He was warning them that they'd seen the devil."

"How do you mean?" Linda said.

"The Qu'ran warns believers to take refuge at the braying of the donkey, for it means he's seen the devil. I suspect it turns out be us." He removed the dark glasses. "What do you think, Ms. Reyes? Those burros know better than to stick around, because they've been shot at, so seeing us is like seeing the devil, right? Of course, being a friend of Sergeant Flynn, you know all about the burro killings."

"It's disgusting."

"See, there you go in support of your local vigilante for justice."

"I didn't say that."

"Sergeant Flynn ever tell you about the cow on the Hunter Liggett shooting range?"

"He doesn't talk about his experiences in the army."

Parker gave a soft chuckle. "Yeah, I imagine not. Well, Flynn was my training sergeant, what they call a tactical noncommissioned officer. He trained recruits in combat arms, meaning how to shoot. He was damn good, too, but not just at shooting. He knew his recruits, tried to bring them along, make them into soldiers without losing their humanity." He gave Linda a long look. "I was one of his problem guys, a homesick kid who didn't fit in. I guess you could say the other recruits thought I was a sad sack, not up to snuff, and in a way, they were right."

He paused to look out over the stillness of the desert landscape. "One day we were on the firing line, and this cow wandered onto the range. The red flag went up for us to cease firing, but there was this guy Stuller and his pals; they kept firing. The cow went down but struggled to its feet, then went down again. It kept trying to get up, and Stuller and the boys kept shooting. Finally it quit moving. You could hear them whooping with joy about bringing the cow down. Their first kill, so to speak." Parker held Linda's gaze. "So don't you want to know what Sergeant Flynn was doing?"

"What was he doing?"

"He was trying to get them to stop. The whole time he was shouting, 'Cease fire! Cease fire!' But they were deaf with the joy of what they'd done. That was the end of the firing for the day. Flynn double-timed the company the four miles back to barracks, rifles at port arms. Then, before dismissing us, he asked the men who had continued to fire to step forward. No one moved. So he told them they were yellow. He said it real softly. He told them they were cowards and that he would be waiting at the motor pool after chow, without his stripes, for any cowards to show up.

"They showed up. The whole company showed up, wanting to see how it would turn out."

"So what happened?" Linda tried to keep the urgency out of her voice.

"Sergeant Flynn got his ass kicked. That's what happened. Stuller had been a longshoreman from San Pedro, the Port of Los Angeles. He had Sergeant Flynn by four inches and forty pounds. Flynn was fast and got in his licks, but then he started going down— and getting up. Stuller would drop him, and Sergeant Flynn would somehow manage to regain his feet. Pretty soon the men started shouting, 'Stay down, Sarge! Stay down!' Then Stuller says it, too. 'Stay down, Sarge. You're whipped.' Sergeant Flynn looks at him and says, 'Next time, you'll have to kill me, you yellow bastard.' Stuller just turned and walked away.

"After that, the men kept their shooting to the targets. Even the ground squirrels that lived on the range were safe. And our outfit had the highest average score by five points. The man knows how to soldier," Parker added in a soft voice.

"Why didn't he discipline them for disobeying an order?"

"He could have, but it didn't have to do with that. Respect for orders has to do with respect for the man who's giving them. That company would've followed Sergeant Flynn into hell. Some of them did."

Linda raised her eyebrows in query.

"You ask him. Anyhow, that's not the entire story. While Stuller and his followers were killing the cow, I lost it. The cow was struggling to get away from the pain, to stay alive, and it didn't know what was happening. That was the part that really got to me, the confusion. I started screaming at them, and I was crying, sobbing is more like it. Afterward, they thought I was pretty pathetic. Naturally they started making my life hell, calling me Crybaby Parker. Not all of them, but Stuller and his cronies. Well, the name stuck. Sergeant Flynn was watching all this, and I knew he wanted to put a stop to it, but you can't rescue people or even feel sorry for them. That would be the kiss of death, let me tell you.

"So Sergeant Flynn figures another way. I was a natural with the rifle, top score in the company. So he asks how I'd like to go to sniper school, join up with the Tenth Infantry at Fort Drum." Parker smiled. "So here I am. Now what do you think of all that?"

"It's an awful story."

"Yeah, but not all of it."

"No, not all of it," Linda said quietly.

"So we better get you back to the highway, Ms. Reyes. We'll drop you off about a half mile before the pavement. We'll need a head start, right? Oh, and I'll leave your cell phone at the base of the signpost." He held out his hand.

"Why leave her the cell phone?" Parker's companion spoke from the rear of the vehicle.

"Because Ms. Reyes understands better now how things stand." He held his finger to his lips. "Don't say anything, Ms. Reyes. We'll just have to trust to luck."

21

•

"All right now, let me see if I have this straight. You borrowed Kevin's jeep so you could meet up with Cece and Eddie Saturday afternoon."

Linda nodded. "That's right. It was for the article about Cece and hunting for lost mines in the Mojave Desert. I already told you about it."

"Then what?"

They were in Linda's cabin in back of the Joshua Tree Athletic Club. Frank sat on an antique oak rocking chair. Linda sat with her legs crossed leaning against the iron and brass frame of her bed.

"You already asked me that, Frank. The jeep quit, the storm came, so I waited with the vehicle."

"Then Parker and his accomplice show up."

"Yes, Parker shows up and gives me a ride close to the highway. I found my cell phone, just where he said he'd leave it, but there's no signal there."

"And the last time you saw him he was headed west."

"Right." She shot him a hard look. "We've been over it. God, this isn't an interrogation, is it? I got into the car with him—them—because I didn't recognize him. He looked different, no beard, dark glasses, and a stupid hat."

"What did he want? I mean, do you think he was looking for you?"

"No! It was bad luck. Bad timing. He wanted to know if I'd written up anything about the Sandman."

"Have you?"

"No, Frank, not until he's captured. I'm not going to give him what he wants."

"He won't let himself be taken. Snipers are usually tortured if they're captured alive. He'll go out taking people with him."

Linda's face was drawn. "He said he had another chapter for me. Then he told me about killing that man who shot the vulture." She let out a breath. "I think he's very angry—but not crazy." She shook her head. "He's too deliberate to be crazy, you know, out of control. The way he described it, so calm and matter-of-fact. It was as if he were giving a report." She looked up. "His friend is creepy. He told me he was the one watching me through the scope." She shuddered.

He crossed the room and touched her cheek. "It's okay. You're home. And you're right about him. He's not mentally ill, maybe sick at heart, but not unbalanced in any legal sense." He drew her to him. "Stay out of the desert for a while, okay?"

He felt her tense up.

"No, Frank, not okay. Why would you put restrictions on me? Do you think I should sit here in my cabin until he goes away? How about Cece Flowers? Did you ask her to stay out of the desert, give up looking for her mine?"

Their eyes locked. He didn't respond.

"That's what I thought. The answer is no. So does being with you mean I have to check in with you to make sure life is safe?"

Frank slowly shook his head. "No. No, it doesn't, but I think we both have to think about the other person, the consequences of what we do—both of us," he reiterated.

"That's fair. I think that's fair—both of us." She gave him a tight smile. "I'll be just as careful as you are."

"You're a difficult woman, Linda Reyes," he said, his face somber. He let out a breath. "So did he say where he left the wounded man and the man he killed?" Frank said, changing the subject.

"He said to tell you to look for a track leading off to the left about a mile before you reach the turnoff to Talc Mine Road and to watch for the purifiers." Her face pulled into a quizzical expression. Frank thought it made her look like a little girl, but now wasn't the time to say so; perhaps *never* was the time to say so.

"He meant the vultures. Their Latin name means purifier." Frank began pacing back and forth in her one-room cabin. "Anything else?"

"That's an awful story about the cow. God, people can be cruel."

Frank cut her off. "It's not important."

"He told me about it, how it wandered onto the shooting range and some of the soldiers shot it. He said it tried to get up, but they kept shooting at it, until it quit moving. He said you were very angry, especially because you were in charge of the shooting range."

"Range master," Frank said quietly.

"He said you called the men who did it cowards and offered to fight anyone who'd shot at the cow. That you told them to forget about your stripes, that you would wait for them at the motor pool, and that this very tough soldier from San Pedro, who had been a dockworker, came to fight you."

"Bob Stuller," Frank murmured.

Linda met Frank's eyes. "He said you were quick, but Stuller was too big for you. After a while, Stuller kept knocking you down, and you kept getting up. Just like the cow. Even Stuller told you to stay down, but you didn't. Parker said the others were ashamed and that after that, no one shot at anything except the targets. Why didn't you ever tell me about this?" Linda said.

"That one of my men beat the shit out of me?" Frank gave a mirthless smile. "Not a high point."

"Yes it was. You stood up for the right thing." Linda caught his hand.

Frank gave a dry laugh. "I didn't save the cow." He made a sour face. "Besides, I was training them to kill things. There's the weird part." He gave her a humorless grin. "Flynn's rule: No killing cows, just people."

"That's what Parker said, that you had killed people in combat." She gave him the quizzical look.

"Parker kills people—and not in combat," Frank replied, deflecting the question. "People he thinks deserve to die. He decides they should be killed; then he kills them. Who appointed him, damn it? He's a soldier gone bad, and I helped train him. Don't forget he has a list of people he plans to get rid of." Frank looked to Linda for confirmation. "He thought of the dead poachers as a gift to a pal for old times' sake. I'm not a bloody executioner, I'm a cop. Damn the day I met him." He stopped pacing and turned to Linda. "He's going to wind up dead, death by cop, most likely."

Linda squeezed his hand. "That's what I told him."

Frank barely smiled. "You take your chances, don't you?"

"He wasn't angry about it. He seemed sad."

Frank absently rubbed the bridge of his nose. "Maybe that's what he wants, to go out in a blaze of glory. Well, he knows better than that, better than anybody. There's no glory in dying."

22

•

"How're you doing, Mr. Tucker? They said you wanted to talk with me."

"You know where Jack's at?" Tucker's large, angular body seemed to take up most of the cell.

Frank smiled. "Matter of fact, I do. I picked him up from Animal Control on the way over here. He's in my truck."

Tucker stared at Frank, willing him to go on.

"In the cab of my truck with a bowl of water," Frank said.

Tucker nodded and relaxed his grip on the bars. "Thanks, Flynn."

Frank nodded. "Sure. He'll be okay, Mr. Tucker. Jack's doin' fine. Seems to like riding in the truck."

"Yeah, I should've called him Willie. You know, 'On the Road Again' Willie." The thick growth on Tucker's face twitched, which Frank supposed was a smile. Then Tucker's bushy brows knit together into a V-shaped hedge. "I was hoping maybe you could do me a favor." He stared out from under the hedge. "Could you take a run up to my place, throw the animals some hay, feed the chickens?"

Frank nodded. "Yeah, I think I can find a way to do that."

"Maybe you could check on the water setup, too. Make sure the rains didn't wash it out or fill it with mud." He searched Frank's face, trying to make up his mind about something. "There's a water tank behind my place with a line leading over to the sheds. Got it set up with a float valve to water the animals."

Frank smiled inwardly. Zeke Tucker had figured him for a soft touch on the first read. "I'm headed up that way tomorrow. I'll look in on your place."

Tucker's bushy head bobbed once in acknowledgment. "Thanks, Flynn. Appreciate it."

Frank waited for him to go on. "That it, Mr. Tucker?"

"Didn't shoot those assholes."

Frank tilted his head to one side. "Thing is, you had a .270 in your van. The poachers were killed with a .270."

"How'd they know that? The slug probably would have disintegrated too much to get a ballistics match."

Frank was taken aback. "You know about that stuff, Mr. Tucker?"

"Know about a lot of stuff. If it's in a book, people can know about it." He paused. "So how'd they know it was a .270?"

"The shooter left a casing behind. We can match that to the firing pin. Did you know that, Mr. Tucker?"

"Nope, but it figures. Getting harder and harder for decent criminals to prosper. Except for the suits. The suits steal us blind. Right, Mr. Flynn?"

"The pen is mightier than the firearm."

Tucker laughed. "Swords into ballpoint pens. Amen." The blue eye glittered. "Only I'd make it the computer, the computer is mightier. Dancing screens and crooked geeks run the show. For, yea, He will smite the thief, hip and thigh! Didn't He drive the moneychangers from the temple?" Tucker let go of the bars and retreated to the cement bench and thin mattress. "Good."

"Good?"

"Yeah, the casing won't match, and I'll be outta here."

Frank nodded. "Didn't think it would." He dropped his eyes. "I do wonder why you'd be fool enough to run around with a loaded .270 in your truck when you know the law is out looking for a shooter."

Tucker chuckled. "Man'd be a fool to run around with an un-loaded .270." He leaned back and closed his eyes. "First off, if I was looking for poachers carrying rifles, it'd be sorta dumb to go un-armed." His eyes popped open. "Notice you don't run around bare, right? Pack that army issue .45. Out there by yourself, hell, anything could happen. Well, I do the same. Only I haven't got a badge, so I'm more likely to get shot."

Frank didn't bother explaining how vulnerable BLM law en-forcement was, how often they were attacked, shot at, even killed.

Tucker went on. "You were the man who told me to keep a lookout."

"I didn't say anything about hunting them down. Thought I said something about keeping an eye out."

"That's what I was doing, just keeping my eye out." He closed the brown eye in a slow wink and lifted a finger to the glittering blue one. "Man needs protection out there."

"Mr. Tucker, I think you might do okay with sticks and stones."

Tucker squinted. "Break your bones. I get the point." Tucker let his eyelids droop. The hedge above his eyes parted and merged upward into the shaggy mane. "Say, when will they know about the casing?"

"That's a problem, Mr. Tucker. The FBI is handling the foren-sics, so I guess it depends on how important they think it is and how stacked up they are." Frank frowned. "And when they're willing to admit they're wrong."

"Hell's fire and damnation! Who's going to take care of my place?"

"I was just going to ask you that."

Tucker plunged a thick finger into the hair at the side of his head where an ear would probably be and twisted it back and forth. "Let me think about it." He worked at the ear some more. "Can you think of anyone who'd like to pick up a few bucks, Flynn? I can pay."

"That'll help." Frank thought about Eddie and wished he knew where he was. His watch said almost ten. Too late to drive back to the caboose. He'd give Linda a call and stay at her place in Red Mountain. "I'll be in touch and let you know how things are with your animals."

"Oh yeah, I forgot to tell you something." Tucker said.

"Yeah, what's that?"

"There's a guy in a mine shaft over the east side of Cerro Gordo."

"What do you mean, guy in a mine shaft?"

Tucker's whiskers moved around. "Drove his truck right down into a mine shaft. Must've thought he was one of the bats living down there. Stuck his truck about twenty feet down." He chuckled. "Jack found him. Started barking down the mine shaft. Jack don't bark for nothing. Don't know how long he's been down there, but he's pretty pissed off. I hollered down at him, and he started cussing up a blue streak. Never heard anything like it. I told him to take it easy, but he just got worse. Everyone uses rough language now and then, but I don't hold with taking the Lord's name in vain." Tucker nodded to himself. "So finally I told him to knock it off. Then he started cussing me. Well, I told him I didn't have to stick around and listen to that kind of language, so I left."

"Did he say his name? Was anyone with him?"

"He said his name was Eddie. I didn't get the last name. He was a mean-mouthed man. Anyway, I was gonna get ahold of you; then that FBI guy and the Jesus fella from your outfit arrested me."

"Why didn't you tell them about the man in the mine shaft?"

"That FBI guy pissed me off. Damn near took a shot at Jack." He glowered up at Frank. "Been the last thing he ever shot at."

"Tell me again where you found the truck."

"About two miles past where the White Mountain Talc Road joins the Cerro Gordo Road. You know, where the old head frame for the talc mine is. I saw where tracks were plowin' all over the hill, and Jack and me went to take a look. Like I said, Jack found him."

Frank nodded. "The Hazlitt talc mine?"

"That's the one. Big old hole in the ground there."

Frank pulled the cell phone from his belt and punched the autodial for the BLM station headquarters. "Dave. Listen, we've got a line on one of the missing people. I've been talking with Mr. Tucker. He says somebody stuck a truck down the main shaft of the Hazlitt talc mine, over on the back side of Cerro Gordo." He hesitated. "I think it's Eddie Laguna." Frank nodded. "Yeah, I will. See you in about"—he glanced at his watch—"half an hour." Frank turned back to Tucker. "Was there only one person down there?"

"That's all I saw or heard, but it was dark as hell down in that hole."

"Well, I've got to go. It appears a friend of mine is stuck down in a mine shaft, a guy named Eddie Laguna. That's the mean-mouth's last name."

"Huh, I'll be darned. Well, thanks for taking care of my place and watching out for Jack." Tucker stuck a large bony hand through the bars. Frank looked at the hand attached to the very large Zeke Tucker on the other side of the metal grating. He met Tucker's eyes and took the proffered hand. "That's okay, Mr. Tucker. Least I could do. Oh, and if I'm right, Mr. Tucker, the man in the mine shaft is the man I was going to ask to take care of your place." Frank grinned. "You two have a lot in common."

23

The Sierra loomed up out of the valley close enough to touch, made huge by the lingering moisture in the air. Frank leaned forward, squinting into the late morning light at a truck pulled off on the opposite side of the road. An eddy of vultures wheeled overhead. He brought the BLM Expedition to a slow stop, so he could approach on foot. The desert lay in front of him washed and clean from the rains. The morning air was crisp and tangy with wet creosote bush. Frank wanted to keep going.

"Why are we stopping?" Eddie wanted to know. He leaned forward to get a better look.

He glanced over at his seemingly indestructible companion; Eddie's obsidian eyes glinted out over high, dark brown cheeks. *Wovoka ready to lead the Ghost Dance,* Frank thought.

"Hey, what happened to your bell?" Frank said.

Eddie reached a hand into very grubby jeans. "Took it off when I was down in the hole. Didn't want to lose it." He extended a small brown hand, thick with dirt, and wiggled the bell back and forth, the sound bright and clear in the desert stillness.

Frank had met Dave Meecham, Jesse Sierra, and Greg Wilson at the Hazlitt talc mine. They had backed a tow truck up to the edge and lowered a cable and sling down to bring up Eddie Laguna. When Eddie told them about leaving Cece behind, Frank shifted his priorities from locating the dead man's body to rescuing Cece Flowers. Eddie had insisted on going along because, as he explained, he knew where she was. Now they were headed back with a chastened Eddie in the backseat and a peeved and grumpy Cece riding up front alongside Frank.

Frank pulled himself reluctantly from the SUV, not wanting to find what he suspected would be decaying in the truck. "Stay there, okay?" he said, not looking back at Eddie, who was already climbing out. Frank's steps made a soft crunching in the crushed rock surface of the road as he approached the pickup. He leaned forward, peering into the truck's cab, and was relieved to find it empty. Frank looked up at the wheeling vultures. Now there were more of them, a silent vortex, pointing to something dead or dying in the desert west of the truck.

"They found something," Eddie said, shading his eyes with his hand.

Frank nodded. "I better take a look." He turned to Eddie. "You didn't see anyone along this part of the road, did you?"

"Nope." Eddie scrunched up his face. "Say, did anyone check on Prowler?" Prowler was Eddie's black and white cat.

"We'll get you back as soon as we can." Frank looked out over the desert and headed through the rabbitbrush in the direction of the birds, followed by Eddie, hurrying along to catch up.

The dead man lay slumped to one side, as if he'd been sitting on the ground and then fallen over, which was what had happened after Parker shot him the second time. However, that wasn't immediately apparent because the vultures had been at his face, so most of the damage to his eye inflicted by the .22 had been eaten away. Only after the medical examiner found the spent slug in Ortman's braincase was the cause of death made official.

Frank had no doubts about what killed the dead man. He'd

been shot. While Eddie kept the vultures at bay, he made a cursory examination and discovered the exit wound behind the victim's right ear and noted the dried and caked blood on the back of his shirt. The man had been shot twice, once in the forehead and a second time in the left eye. After Frank found the lifeless form of smashed flesh and feathers that had once been a bird, he put it together. The dead man was Parker's present.

He bent down and searched the dead man's shirt pockets and discovered the note. *And the eye of the sleeper waxed deadly and chill.* " 'And their hearts but once heaved, and for ever grew still,' " Frank murmured. *I'd forgotten about the poetry,* he thought.

After he and Eddie covered the corpse with a plastic tarp weighted down with rocks, they returned to the vehicle, both of them worn down and ready to leave.

"What's that?" Eddie lifted his head.

Frank turned in the direction of Eddie's gaze. "What's what?"

Eddie put a hand to his ear, then dropped to one knee. "Over there."

He rose and trotted toward a cutbank, Frank in his wake.

They paused on the edge of the cutbank where a man lay propped against the dirt wall, the right side of his khakis soaked in blood.

"Help me," he croaked.

The man screamed before passing out as Frank put a pressure bandage on the leg to stem the flow of blood. Then Frank and Eddie fashioned a makeshift stretcher from a tarp and eased the man down the wash to the road.

•

"What took you so long?" Cece asked.

"There's a hurt guy," Eddie said. "We got to get him to the doctor's."

"Oh," she said. "Anything I can do?"

"Yeah, you and Eddie can ride in the back with him and keep him from rolling around," Frank said.

Cece climbed into the back of the vehicle, where Frank and Eddie had made a sort of bed for the injured man. "Looks awful," she said.

Frank picked up the radio to report to Dave Meecham. They needed a helicopter.

•

"Jammed in like a cork in a bottle." Greg Wilson peered into the main shaft of the Hazlitt talc mine. "Man oh man." He whistled under his teeth. "How'd you like to take a ride like that?" He grinned over at Jesse Sierra.

Dave Meecham frowned down into the shaft and then let his gaze travel up to the head frame. "Maybe we can rig a cable through the hoist wheel. Bring it straight up." He stepped back, a hand to his forehead sheltering his eyes from the light.

"That's the radio, Chief."

"Well, you might think about going on down and answering it, Greg, if you're not too tied up."

Sierra smirked. Greg was a magnet for flak, and he had a gift for getting under Meecham's skin. That meant that Sierra could duck under the radar—most of the time. Dave Meecham seemed to have eyes in the back of his head.

Greg came trotting back up the hill. One thing you could say for Greg was that he was never tired—lazy sometimes, but energy to burn. Not even Jesse Sierra could match him running up hills, or down hills, or stairways, or ladders, or doing anything that didn't have to do with labor. If it had to do with cleaning stuff up, Greg moved like molasses on a cold day. Today he was trotting effortlessly up a fifteen-degree slope.

"Hey, Dave, Frank found the dead guy, but there's an injured man, and Frank says they could use a helicopter."

Meecham walked back to the truck and picked up the mike. "Meecham here."

Frank's voice was broken by static but understandable. "Hi, Dave. The bad news is that besides the corpse, Parker forgot to mention they shot the man's partner in the leg. He's in a bad way from loss of blood. The good news is that we found Ms. Flowers. She's doing fine. Thought you'd like to know."

"That's good. We can get a medevac from Independence. Where will you be?"

"Where the Saline Valley Road connects to 190."

"Meanwhile, I've got to figure out how to get this damn truck out of the shaft."

"I think it belongs to Collins," Frank said.

"How'd his truck wind up down in a hole with Eddie Laguna?"

"A long story, but it seems Collins loaned it to Eddie so he could help Ms. Flowers look for her lost mine."

Meecham's frown deepened. "Well, Collins's got no complaint coming, then, lending his truck to Laguna." He shifted gears. "Who's the dead man?"

"Don't know. The vultures were at him, so I covered him with a tarp and weighted it down."

"How about the injured victim?"

"Haven't gone through his pockets for identification. I was too busy trying to stop the bleeding. He passed out when I put on the pressure bandage."

"Why do you suppose Parker killed this one?"

"I don't know for sure, but I can make a good guess. Linda says he killed him because he was killing vultures. There was a dead vulture nearby, damn near torn in half, and there was a Ruger Redhawk lying next to the victim."

"You're saying Parker killed the victim over a vulture?"

"That would be my guess."

They were both silent.

"I'll get the county on it," Meecham said.

"I'd like to get Eddie checked out at the medical center in Bishop. He says he's okay, but he took a pretty good ride down the mine shaft, and he's worried about his cat. Think you could send someone over to keep an eye on things while I take Eddie to Bishop?"

"His cat, huh? First Tucker's dog, now Laguna's cat. Well, it's not a problem. I've got just the right man in mind."

"Thanks. I'll be back to give you a hand with the truck after I get everyone back to town."

"That'll have to be tomorrow, Frank. Lots to set up. Maybe you could break the news to Collins about his truck."

"Actually, I plan on letting Eddie do that."

"Good plan." Meecham hung up the mike, grinning to himself. "Hey, Greg, got an important job for you."

Wilson looked crestfallen. His boss's "important" jobs were usually something he didn't want to do.

"Go on over to the Saline Valley Road and find Flynn. His vehicle is parked near a truck, about six or seven miles from 190."

"Right. Uh, what for?"

"Want you to keep an eye on a corpse. Keep the buzzards from finishing it up."

"Oh shit." Greg made an icky face. He hated dead things, especially rotted, gory dead things. All through his teens he'd avoided slasher movies, and now this.

"Don't worry, Greg," Meecham grinned. "The meat wagon should be there before dark, and I don't think the corpse is going anywhere, right?"

24

•

Frank awoke at daybreak with his motor running. He brewed a short pot of coffee and took his cup out to the rear platform of the caboose to greet the morning and get his bearings. Streaks of color suffused the scattered clouds, casting a pale rose light across the eastern sky. His mind raced ahead, making a list of the things piled up in front of him. He tried to put thinking about Linda and the impending job at the *L.A. Times* aside and concentrate on the loose ends in the wake of the failed effort to trap Parker.

Cece and Eddie were safe, but both of them had been lucky. It looked as if Jack Collins's truck was the main casualty among the good guys. The plunge down the main shaft of the Hazlitt mine had pretty much destroyed it. It was irrational the way a person could bond with something inanimate, but Jack loved his truck, and Frank knew he would miss it sorely.

From any perspective, the operation had been a disaster, and Dave Meecham was damned unhappy about it. Parker had made fools of them all. He'd wandered around under their noses and managed to kill Walter Ortman in the bargain.

Ortman's death had probably been a matter of bad timing. The so-called Brotherhood of American Sportsmen had been running an empty threat on their Web site. They weren't even a real organization, more like a drinking club. Had they had a real organization, they might have been spared the death of one of their members, that is, if the FBI had been able to find them before the Sandman.

As it turned out, they were a bunch of middle-class hotshots with too much money and not enough brains. Their grandiose image of themselves as rugged individualists protecting the American way had bumped into nasty reality in the person of a professional shooter. Now one of their number was gone, one of the two unlucky enough to actually have met the Sandman face-to-face—and one had lived to tell the tale, the lucky one.

Parker had pointed out to the dead man's partner, Preston Hill, that his experience was unique, encountering the Sandman and living to tell about it. That had been the point, carry the message, and he had, babbling out his story in a rush of fearful wonderment to his fellow club members gathered around his hospital bed. The Brotherhood was nothing if not a chastened group of wannabe warriors.

Frank reflected that so much about living and dying was a matter of chance. Time and place determined fate without forethought, without mercy. If Oedipus had stopped at a Starbucks, he wouldn't have killed his father on the road to Thebes. Ortman had been unlucky as well as bloody-minded. Frank recalled his own suggestion to the dipwads shooting the pinyon jays that they would be safer if they went home. They'd been lucky they'd crossed an off-duty ranger instead of Seth Parker. Walter Ortman's last act of random violence had been observed by the Sandman, and he had paid for it with his life. Parker planned; the rest of them reacted. He'd taken luck out of the equation, and they were falling all over themselves.

Frank sipped his coffee and breathed in the morning perfume blowing down from the high country. He had to get ahold of Eddie and see if he would take care of Tucker's place for a few days. That would mean he would probably wind up feeding Eddie's black and white cat, Prowler, while Eddie was feeding Tucker's goats. Frank scratched Jack's head. The dog seemed content to ride around with Frank, but he didn't like being left alone. Who did?

Before he started spinning his wheels thinking about Linda, he needed to check his e-mail, which had been piling up for a while, the important stuff mixed in with the garbage, and see what lay in store. He stepped into the dim light of the empty caboose and switched on the battery-powered electric light above the fold-down desk, where generations of conductors had worked out train orders by kerosene light. He opened his iBook and selected Mail. Then he scrolled down checking for names he recognized and al-most passed it. SANDMAN was on the subject line. Frank supposed it would be easy enough for Parker to find his e-mail address. The message itself posed a different problem:

Sarge, I've posted a few pictures on my Web site, so the people who planned the mission have an opportunity to debrief and do a better job next time. It wasn't very professional. Well, what can you do with the brass hats? So to keep things moving along, here's a new operational challenge. When I finish up this message, our team is headed for Barstow. Dogfights are big out that way, a magnet for maggots. We've pulled garbage detail again. You're on final cleanup. *Sandman*

He forwarded Parker's message to Dave Meecham and followed it with a phone call. Meecham immediately contacted Miles Cross, chief district ranger for the eastern Mojave, to give him a heads-up. While Cross was mobilizing law enforcement in Barstow, Meecham called Pete Novak to fill him in.

"Dogfighting is mostly gang stuff. You think there's a connec-tion there?" Novak asked.

Meecham made a grimace. "I thought it was redneck stuff, but I don't think it matters to the MDG. Taking the dogfighters out fits Parker's pattern. He claims he and his partner did in Mike Travis. If he gets there first, the people in Barstow will be picking up bodies, 'final cleanup.' Makes you want to take your time, doesn't it? Pretend I didn't say that."

"Say what?" Novak said, playing along.

Meecham returned to the problem. "I think his plan is to get there before us. He's a crafty son of a bitch, but I think he likes cutting it close, adds to the thrill."

"Yeah, I got you. Drew and I have been chasing down leads on the kids who blew up the cats. Real pieces of work, those two, felons in the making. Their attitude was 'So what, just cats, and we're just kids. Can't touch us.' I let Drew do the FBI routine and scare the crap out of them."

"I bet he's good at it," Meecham said.

"Yeah, he is. The point the kids seemed to miss is that they have every reason to be scared. Somehow they think because we know about this guy, they're safe," Novak said in a weary voice.

"I wouldn't want to be on Parker's list," Meecham observed.

"Keep us posted, Dave, and thanks. We'll be in touch with Barstow."

Meecham hung up feeling useless. He was in Ridgecrest, the FBI was in the San Joaquin Valley, and the killer was somewhere in the desert, seventy miles to the east in Barstow. *Better there than here*, he thought.

•

Frank wondered why Parker would tip him off. Did he want to get caught? Was he looking for suicide by police? Parker was what they called high-strung in World War II movies—they always bought it somewhere near the beginning of the second reel. The bad boys in the Fifth Platoon considered Parker a pathetic wimp—that is, before he learned to shoot. Parker had undergone quite an evolution, from crybaby to celebrity terrorist, given his due by press and public. Now he was all ready for interviews and the afternoon movies.

Maybe Parker supplied the tip because he thought his targets were too easy, no challenge. Maybe the dig about shooting people down without giving them a chance pricked his ego. The message the Brotherhood had posted referred to the killings up on the flats as back shooting. Maybe that was what was driving him, pride in his craft. So his new modus operandi might be to give a heads-up, then take the target out from under law enforcement's collective noses.

Parker had implied he kept a list. Was it an actual list or just in his head? Who else was on it besides the ones that had spilled out that day at Ralph's? He and Linda had been following the local papers for incidents of animal cruelty, especially the *Los Angeles Times*, but there were so many, too many to anticipate Parker's next move. When it came to inflicting pain and suffering on animals, there was no end of candidates for the Sandman's rage. Then there was the matter of timing. Careful planning meant Parker would act when it was safe, out of the public eye, unless he meant to make an immediate point. Frank's thoughts kept returning to the invisible list.

Would he find Stuller's name on Parker's list? It had been seventeen years. He wondered what had happened to Stuller and his group of thugs. Frank went to the veterans' Buddy Finder site and entered Charles Stuller's name, rank, unit, and approximate dates of service. There it was, Charles W. Stuller, E-4, 1st Infantry, Fort Lewis, Washington. Discharged, March 1994.

Stuller had been living in Bodfish, California, since 1997. Running true to form, he'd acquired two convictions, one for assault and the other for poaching. The poaching conviction had caused public outcry. According to a lengthy report in the *Kern County Clarion*, he'd killed a beloved town icon:

On a hot autumn afternoon in the Tehachapi Mountains, Fish and Game warden John Eckstrom, following up on an anonymous tip, found a badly butchered carcass dumped under a tree. Eckstrom informed his companion he was looking at the remains of a trophy bull elk. Just how big a trophy proved to be the poacher's undoing, that and a blatant contempt for the detective work of Fish and Game.

The poacher had discarded several empty aluminum beer cans and a half-eaten bag of Fritos. "There were fingerprints all over them," Eckstrom said. The fingerprints matched the prints taken from the .22 casings scattered nearby. Apparently, the poacher had brought down the elk, known to the townspeople of Bodfish as Big Daddy, by shooting it repeatedly with the small caliber weapon. Eckstrom, himself an avid hunter, was disgusted by the elk's death, "which must have been extremely cruel," he said. "This elk was practically tame and unafraid of human beings. It was like killing a pet."

Following the evidence and tips from outraged citizens, Eckstrom arrested Charles Stuller of Bodfish. The severed head in Stuller's garage provided the conclusive piece of evidence.

Over three hundred angry citizens signed a petition asking the court to "throw the book at him."

Superior Court Justice Wanda Lightfoot sentenced Stuller to 60 days in jail, fined him $1,000, and put him on probation for three years. In addition, she told Stuller that he was forbidden to go anywhere near lands where hunting is allowed.

Stuller's attorney argued that the sentence was harsh and that poachers rarely drew prison time. Judge Lightfoot said that in the future she planned on remedying that judicial shortcoming.

Frank wanted to personally congratulate Judge Lightfoot. Drive on over to Bakersfield and shake her hand.

Thinking about how easily he'd been able to find Stuller on the Net, in less than ten minutes, he reasoned Parker would be able to do the same. Three phone calls later—first to Dave Meecham, then to Pete Novak, followed by a conversation with the Kern County Sheriff's Office in Bakersfield—Frank headed for Walker Pass to try to save Stuller's life.

25

•

Mrs. Delowe lived on the very western edge of Pasadena on the other side of the Arroyo Seco, almost in Highland Park, so Seth Parker elected to take the 210 Freeway across town. It turned out not to be the best of moves. As he pulled onto the on-ramp, a pickup truck shot ahead of him and cut him off where the lanes narrowed from two to one. Ordinarily he wouldn't have paid the least bit of attention to the driver's ill-mannered conduct—he had come to expect motorized rudeness as just another indicator of things going to hell in a handcart—but as the truck lurched in front of him, a dog in the pickup bed almost spilled onto the pavement.

Parker cut in and out of the thickening traffic in an effort to overtake the pickup, a large metallic green GMC, sporting rear dual tires and a ridiculous air scoop mounted on the top of the cab. It was easy to follow. He cut into the diamond lane and shot ahead of the slower-moving traffic. Coming alongside the truck, he leaned across the seat and yelled out the passenger's side window.

"You almost lost your dog," he shouted against the noise of the traffic.

The two young men in the truck frowned over at him, unable to make him out. Parker shouted again, "Your dog. Your dog almost fell out."

The driver and passenger looked at each other and shrugged.

"Your dog almost fell out," Parker screamed.

The driver put his hand up to his head and made a twirling gesture, lolling his tongue to one side.

Parker felt the anger building. He pulled the VW in front of the truck and began slowing down. Both the driver and the passenger in the truck became instantly enraged, their mouths filled with curses, unheard in the rush of traffic. Parker watched them bob around in the rearview mirror, looking like hand puppets wearing silly backwards caps. He decreased his speed, trapping the truck between two lanes of traffic. Then the truck lurched for a gap in the right-hand lane, and he watched the dog spill onto the freeway.

The car following the truck struck the dog, knocking it down. The driver of the car pulled over to the meridian, braking hard. The dog, a medium-sized German shepherd, struggled to its feet, injured and confused. Parker watched the rest in slow motion. The next car struck the animal and passed over it without touching the brakes. The dog was still trying to regain its footing when it was struck again and ceased to move. Soon he couldn't see anything but traffic and the air scoop of the green pickup far ahead in the center lane.

He knew exactly what to do. There was intensity to his perceptions; the edges of things were distinct, colors sharp and vivid, and he seemed to move with quickening speed through a stream of time that flowed with stately deliberation. He brought the van back into the diamond lane and shot by the slowing lanes of traffic on his right. Far ahead he saw the flashing lights that indicated some sort of catastrophe, something that would cause a delay in traffic, a Sigalert broadcast by hovering aircraft to cursing motorists, something that would bring him nearer to the green truck, still there in the center lane.

He signaled for a lane change, smiling back at the driver closing up on his right, and moved out of the diamond lane and into the lane of traffic on the truck's immediate left. An overturned car on the outbound side of the freeway was causing the slowdown. Parker pulled even with the truck.

He honked his horn, and the capped heads turned toward him. Then their mouths began to move. Parker cupped his hand to his ear and shrugged. They were screaming, lips opening and closing as they delivered a stream of invective. Parker shot the driver in the mouth, a perfect shot, one-handed from a moving car into a moving mouth. The truck drifted halfway into the right lane.

The passenger, not understanding or perhaps not believing what had happened, stared at Parker, who smiled and waved. He should have taken another shot right then, but he couldn't resist the friendly gesture. The truck came to a sudden halt, and the passenger jumped out. Parker brought the van to a stop and steadied the Woodsman against the window frame and took aim as the man ran into moving traffic. The first of the two cars that struck the fleeing figure passed over his fallen body. Unlike the dog, the man was unable to regain his feet, but he did manage to sit up. Parker fired twice, both shots finding their mark, the first just forward of the ear in the left temple. The second shot was redundant, as was the second car, a Lexus SUV that dragged the corpse some fifteen feet.

He slipped the van into the diamond lane again and then, smiling and waving, crossed three lanes of traffic and exited onto Orange Grove Boulevard. He went north, cut down into the Rose Bowl area and across to Linda Vista, then went south again toward Highland Park. Twenty minutes later, he pulled the VW into Mrs. Delowe's garage, where his panel van was stored. He hated being rushed, but the impromptu on the 210 Freeway left him no choice. He had to get out of Dodge, as the saying went.

The most necessary things had been taken care of. John Gilman's housekeeper, Mrs. Hernandez, had promised to care for Orpheus and Eurydice. He'd updated the Web site, including the picture of the cops with their eyes closed. Another foolish taunt, but leadership required a certain degree of style; think of Patton's ivory-gripped .45s. Then he'd sent Sergeant Flynn the message about the dogfight near Barstow. He wished he could have taken the fight down himself, but it would be a bust for the local cops that would lead to drugs, parole violations, and other stuff. Dogfighters were scum.

It wouldn't be as good as taking it down himself, but he'd located Stuller, and that came first. Soon it would be up to John. The torch would be passed. An hour later his panel van was climbing up Angeles Crest Highway, heading for Palmdale, then north to the Tehachapi Mountains.

26

•

Charlie Stuller popped open another can of Coors Light, the Silver Bullet, and settled back in the lawn swing, waiting for something to interrupt the endless boredom. His buddies had stopped coming around since Judge Wacko Wanda had penned him up on his property, a quarter acre of live oak and digger pine on the outskirts of Bodfish in the Tehachapi Mountains. He thought about going back to Long Beach, where he hadn't pissed everyone off, at least not recently.

Charlie entertained no illusions about being misunderstood. People were assholes, so he didn't waste time pretending to be a nice guy. His strategy for successful living was to be a preemptive asshole—"right back atcha," only first. Even so, he didn't think the whole town would turn on him for helping himself to some free elk meat. What was the big deal? The Tehachapi Mountains were full of elk and deer. They wandered around eating up people's gardens like giant rabbits. Charlie didn't have a garden, but he'd heard plenty of complaints about how the deer ate up people's yards. So in his view, he'd done them a favor getting rid of a monster-sized rodent—with big, valuable horns. He shouldn't have kept the head.

Someone walking along the road turned into the dirt driveway leading back to his trailer, probably some bum looking for a handout. That was okay, too. Wacko Wanda's restrictions had cut him off, so even bums were welcome. Anything to make the time pass.

The visitor looked around Charlie's property with some distaste. The land was strewn with trash: cans, plastic, shattered glass, and piles of rotting wood, wire, and broken concrete. "Nice place," he said with obvious disgust.

Charlie's trailer rested near a stand of dusty pines interspersed with scrub oak.

"Don't read so good, do you?" Charlie countered.

Charlie's visitor looked puzzled. "How do you mean?"

"The sign says private property. What, you don't believe in signs?"

"Oh, that."

"Yeah, that. This is my property," Charlie said in a menacing growl.

The man's gaze wandered back over the accumulated trash in Charlie's yard. "You're kind of a pig, aren't you?"

"What'd you say?" Charlie leaned forward. He could hardly believe it, this asshole insulting him on his own property.

"I said, you're a pig, and this place is a sty."

Charlie sized up the newcomer. Tall and thin, wearing a straw hat and yellow glasses. Not much of a threat in Charlie's estimation. "You made a big mistake, asshole," Charlie said, getting to his feet. Something wasn't quite right. "Do I know you?"

"Not well, but I'm going to give you a chance to get reacquainted." The man smiled. "Remember Sergeant Flynn?"

Charlie hesitated. The remark had put him off balance. "So what's that got to do with anything?" Charlie eased closer, ready to move on this guy, whoever he was.

"Now how'd that happen, Stuller? I mean, why'd you want to fight a nice guy like Sergeant Flynn?"

"Whoever the fuck you are, you got it wrong. He wanted to fight me—a noncom picking a fight with a trainee. I kicked his sorry ass."

"That's right. Flynn called you out about killing a cow on the firing range at Hunter Liggett."

Charlie studied his guest. "So who the fuck are you?"

"Parker. Crybaby Parker."

Charlie examined the man more closely. "I don't think so."

"Well, think again."

Charley Stuller stared at the man before him. "You don't look the same."

"You do, except now you look flabby and soft."

"Yeah, well, you're about to find out how soft I am, when I kick your sorry ass."

The man's eyes filled with contempt. "That's it? Gonna kick my sorry ass before you know why I'm here?" He shook his head. "It adds up. Curiosity is a human trait, you know. *Homo sapiens*, the thinking ape. You're just ape, Stuller. Defective. Defective and destructive." He seemed to be talking to himself. "You're like a giant cockroach, Charlie—I seem to remember your Christian name is Charles—living here in your own garbage heap."

"That's it, asshole." Charlie Stuller lunged, but his opponent stepped easily to one side and hit Charlie behind his ear, driving him to the ground. While Charlie was trying to get up, the man shot him in the side of his knee. Despite numerous bar fights, usually with victims for opponents, Charlie had had little experience with real pain. The knee wound caused an immediate flash of paralyzing agony. He dropped on his back, clutched his leg, and screamed.

"Don't be a crybaby," Parker said. "You've still got one good leg. I knew a guy made it back to his unit with most of his leg blown away."

Charlie stared at the man with a dawning realization. "It's

really you—fucking Parker," he moaned through clenched teeth. "Why the fuck did you shoot me?"

"Listen carefully, and I might not kill you."

Charlie stared at his tormenter.

"We're going to play the cow game. You get to be the cow. I get to be you. The cow's mission is to clear the field of fire before Stuller and the boys bring it down. That's me. I'm you and the boys. So think about what you need to say to get me to keep from killing you."

Parker looked around. "Let's say that pile of crap over there is out of the firing line." He pointed over to a jumble of weathered scrap wood mixed in with broken cement and a tangle of rebar. "If the cow clears the firing line, makes it to home base, well, then it lives."

"I can't make it over there. This hurts like you can't believe." Charlie was clutching his knee with bloodied hands.

"Well, that's too bad. I guess the cow dies." Parker pointed the gun at Charlie's head.

"You're not going to kill me over a fucking cow." Charlie Stuller's voice quavered.

Parker aimed the gun at Charlie's foot and shot into the top of the dirty tennis shoe. Charlie screeched and rocked back and forth, his hands shuffling from his knee to his foot and back again.

"Better get moving, cow. Whoop-ee-ti-yi-o! Get along, little dogie, get along. 'It's your misfortune and none of my own.'" He sang the last part under his breath. Then he shot into the dirt near Charlie's good foot.

Charlie began dragging himself over the ground toward the trash pile that signaled safety. It was only about fifty feet away, but to Charlie it seemed like a million miles. Every foot he gained was agony. Behind him, he heard Parker breaking into song.

" 'Their tails are all matted, their backs are all raw.' You're doin' good, cow."

"Fuck you. You asshole."

Parker lifted the gun again and shot Charlie in the thigh.

"Oh, shit." Charlie started to cry. "You're gonna kill me, aren't ya?" Charlie's voice was plaintive. Blood was soaking his pant leg. "I'm bleeding to death. Help me here, please. I'm begging you."

"Cease fire! Cease fire! God damn it, stop shooting," Parker shouted. "You know who said that, Stuller? Well, I can see you're having difficulty playing the game, so I'll tell you. It was Sergeant Flynn, trying to get you and your fucked-up buddies to quit shooting at the cow, but you guys couldn't hear him, tone deaf and brain dead. You just kept on pumping rounds into the cow. Remember how it bellowed? Wait. I got it. You ask Stuller and the boys to stop shooting in cow talk. Maybe he'll be able to hear you."

"What?"

"Like this. Mooooo. Mooooo. You know, moo like a cow."

Charlie dragged himself over the broken glass and trash, groaning and mooing. He only had a few more feet to go before reaching the trash pile. He raised himself up on one elbow and stretched out his hand and touched a chunk of broken concrete. He tried to talk, but it came out in a sob.

Parker sauntered over and squatted next to Charlie. "What's that? Can't hear you, cow."

"Free," Charlie gasped. "I'm home free."

Parker shook his head. "This isn't hide-and-seek, Stuller." He smiled. "It's kick the can, you useless piece of shit. Get it, you're kicking the can."

Charlie stared at him, not understanding.

Parker stood up, shaking his head. " 'Kick the can' is slang for dead. Like the cow, you hopeless moron. You're an ignorant man, Stuller."

"Please don't. I'm sorry I shot the cow, really, really sorry. Please, don't let me bleed to death."

"Okay," Parker said and shot Charlie in the left eye. He was thinking that it might be his signature shot, the Sandman's coup de grâce. He took out a small spiral notebook, jotted down a message, and tucked it in Charlie Stuller's shirt pocket.

He crossed Stuller's yard behind the trailer and disappeared into the woods.

•

Frank arrived at the scene of the killing before the Kern County sheriffs had an opportunity to respond to his original call. The patrol car dispatched by Bakersfield had been delayed by a car accident on the Kern River Road. No crime had been committed or was in progress, as far as they knew, so they were moving with the traffic, following up on Frank's tip.

As soon as Frank discovered Stuller's corpse, he called it in and waited for the deputies to arrive. Frank showed them the dead man and assured them the crime scene was pristine. "You could do me a favor, though," he said.

"What's that, Flynn?" Deputy Eugene Bohannon didn't like Frank. Despite the fact that the deputy was nearly ten years younger than Linda Reyes, he had been smitten and made no secret of it. When Frank and Linda became an item, Bohannon didn't take it that well.

"Would you check his shirt pocket for a note?"

"Why would I do that?"

"If the killer is who I think he is, he leaves notes."

The deputy squatted next to Charlie Stuller's bloody corpse, reached into the shirt pocket, and fished out a note.

"What's it say?"

Bohannon frowned as he read the note. " 'I never saw a purple cow.' " He looked at the dark blood that filled the dead man's eye socket. "What the hell is this about?"

Frank shook his head. "Seventeen years ago, he killed a cow on the Hunter Liggett weapons range."

27

•

The lingering smell of beer and tobacco smoke permeated the Joshua Tree Athletic Club. Morning had yet to pierce the dark confines of the tavern; curtains were still drawn against the eastern light. Linda and Frank heard the faint sounds of kitchen noises as Jack Collins busied himself with breakfast preparations, bangers and bubble-and-squeak, a bit of comfort in a difficult time. At first the regulars had turned up their noses at Jack's Continental cuisine, so Jack called it sausage and hobo potatoes. They ate it up with relish.

"I'll get some coffee."

"Jack's kind of down in the mouth," Frank observed.

"That truck was his baby." She gave him a small smile. "You know what that's about, Flynnman." Linda disappeared into the kitchen.

At least she was still smiling at him, he thought.

Frank cherished his '53 Chevy pickup. He'd spent more than a year restoring it and the rest of his life guarding it. Something else from out of the past.

Frank had just missed catching up with Parker in the Tehachapis. He wondered if Parker had been aware that Frank had been thirty minutes behind him. He didn't think so. Parker had taken his time in dispatching Charlie Stuller, sure of himself, sure of his timing. Stuller's death must have been as cruel as the cow's those many years ago.

Linda came back with coffee. "Here you go." She served it at the bar from force of habit.

Frank took a surreptitious glance at the TV at the end of the bar. The screen was filled with a shot of a freeway jam-up as background for an interview with a Pasadena police detective. "Mind turning the sound up?"

Linda reached up and hit the mute button, restoring the sound.

The newscaster was going on about someone called the Freeway Shooter. In the upper right-hand corner of the screen there was a police sketch of the suspected killer.

Linda gasped. "Oh my God, that's him."

Frank nodded and held up his hand.

". . . no trace so far of the suspected assailant believed to be the man responsible for the assault on Shane Robertson of Pasadena and the death of Robertson's passenger, Orrin Dedrick, also of Pasadena. If you have any information regarding this suspect, call Secret Witness at . . ." Cindy Cho, the local news anchor, was interviewing a gawky kid standing in front of a craftsman cottage somewhere in the Linda Vista area of Pasadena. The kid was explaining about the little old lady—he waved his hand spasmodically toward the house—who had been "harboring a killer" for several years without knowing of his "homicidal killing sprees."

Then Cho shifted ground, introducing a story about the dangers of several diet products. She looked concerned. A tiny wrinkle furrowed her alabaster brow.

"After the shootings on the 210, the police will be turning Pasadena upside down," Linda said.

"They'll be too late. My guess, he's already gone to ground."

Linda started to speak. "The place up on—"

"Hunter Mountain." Frank finished her thought. "Where we

found the brass ring." His face hardened. "This time we're going to stop him, just the guys from the BLM. No FBI, no county cops. I think Dave will go for it, after this last fiasco."

"And no reporters who just happen to be driving around up in the pinyon country," she said

Frank gave Linda a meaningful look. "Parker is too good at killing people, and now he's got a short circuit. The shootings on the freeway were different from the others, spur of the moment, reckless. He's taking more chances. He must have been at Stuller's place for fifteen or twenty minutes."

She looked at him from under dark brows. "Okay."

"Okay what?"

"Okay, I'll stay in town with Cece. We'll crochet some doilies."

"I didn't mean it like that."

She sighed. "I know, Flynnman. It's the job."

Jack came out of the kitchen and opened the curtains, spilling morning light into the tavern. "You want something to eat?"

"Oh yeah, huevos rancheros, and don't spare the salsa," Frank said.

"Bangers and mash, coming up." Jack looked over his shoulder at Linda. "Daughter, can you spare a little time for business?" He shoved through the kitchen door as Ben Shaw, Bill Jerome, Eddie, and the others came in from outside, drawn by the smell of potatoes, cabbage, and onions frying in butter.

Linda raised her eyebrows at Frank. "Gotta go." She came around from behind the bar and headed for the kitchen.

"Me, too." Frank exchanged good-byes with the others. "Say, Eddie. Could you maybe do me a favor?"

"Sure." Eddie nodded, looking pleased.

"Maybe you could take a run up to Zeke Tucker's place, check on the water and feed the animals. You know where it is?"

"Sure, up in the Saline. That's Shoshone country." Eddie frowned. "You'll take care of Prowler, okay?"

"I can look in on Prowler, Eddie," Linda said smiling. She loved Eddie for worrying about his cat. Her own, Hobbes, had migrated to the bar during the day since Ben and Bill had rescued a kitten someone had dumped along the highway near Lake Diaz. Bill had dubbed it 395, but Ben called it the Kid. The boys were hugely entertained by the kitten's antics. She watched Hobbes march around with the kitten in tow, taking swipes at his tail.

Eddie interrupted her thoughts. "Thanks, Linda. I really appreciate it." He shifted his attention to Frank, keeping his voice low. "Uh, Frank, could I use your truck? Mine don't run right now, and . . ." His voice trailed off.

Frank felt his stomach tighten. Then he looked at Eddie's face. "Yeah. Don't pound her too hard on the chatter bumps." Frank paused, thinking about his truck. "Take care of her, podner."

Eddie beamed. "I'll bring her back good as new."

Frank hoped so. Jack's truck hadn't fared so well in Eddie's hands. There was something of the Joe Bfstplk about Eddie, a good guy who brought along his own bad weather and everyone else got rained on.

•

Jack slipped out the back door, leaving the rest of the breakfast chores to Linda. He walked around his damaged truck, trying to make up his mind whether it was worth keeping or not. He'd owned the old monster for sixteen years, knew all its idiosyncrasies. Though the original blue paint had long ago faded to blotchy turquoise and the black fenders to dirty gray, he still thought of it as Big Blue. He'd even planned to have it repainted. He looked inside the familiar cab. It was in pretty good shape, except for where the back window had been broken out. That could be fixed easy enough. Maybe it wasn't a total loss.

28

•

"Frank has a hunch where Parker might be holed up." Dave Meecham stood facing the three rangers in the small conference room at the BLM headquarters in Ridgecrest. "If he's right and we bring him in, then we wipe the egg off our face." The rangers nodded. They'd been made to look like fools. Nobody liked it.

"Here's the way it'll work. We'll drop off Greg and the pickup a couple hundred yards before the place where Frank thinks Parker might have gone to ground." He turned to Greg Wilson. "It'll be your job to keep him from bolting back to the turnoff. I know you know what to do, Greg, but let me make it clear. Pull the truck across the road and get in position behind it with the twelve-gauge. Don't take chances."

Greg nodded. "Right."

"It's as important to see that no one goes up the road as it is to keep Parker from coming down it. We don't want some civilian in jeopardy or getting in the way." Meecham looked at each of them. "Jesse, Frank, and I will drive on past the place and set up a roadblock at the other end. That'll be you, Jesse. Frank and I will backtrack and come in through the trees to the place where we think he is. If Frank is right about this being his hiding place, he'll be boxed in, and we'll have a good chance of taking him by surprise. That'd be good." He paused, staring down at the ground for a few moments.

"Like I said, don't take chances if he decides to shoot it out. We're all competent with firearms, but he's a pro, trained courtesy of Uncle Sam."

Frank nodded in affirmation. "Sniper training and ranger school. He'll be thinking combat, not like a civilian."

"What if he gets nervous and takes off and tries to crash through?" Greg wanted to know.

"Take out his vehicle if you can, but don't get in a duel. I don't want anyone hurt or killed, God forbid." Meecham's jaw tightened. "According to Pasadena PD, he's driving a late-model Dodge panel van, brown." Meecham smiled. "You were right, Jesse, brown's a suspicious color. Just be sure you don't blast some camper's van that we missed in the aerial sweep. If you're not sure, get out of the way. It's possible we missed someone already in the area, some family parked under the pines, and we don't know about it. We didn't see Parker's van on the flyover, but that doesn't mean he isn't there. We didn't want the plane buzzing in low and scaring him off." Meecham glanced over at Frank. "Anything else?"

"Don't forget the pictures he posted of Jesse and Ellis sitting in the truck." Frank smiled. "No shame there, Jesse. It was worth it. Ellis had his eyes closed, looked like he was asleep." They all grinned. "Remember, though, we *all* missed him. Parker knows how to hide in plain sight. He wandered around the whole area, chatting with people, watching the vultures, and giving us the laugh. Then we didn't have much to go on. Now we do. He looks harmless enough, tall, sort of gawky, a freckled redhead—but he kills people without giving it a lot of thought." Of course, he may have altered his looks. When Linda saw him, he was wearing mirror sunglasses, and she couldn't see his hair under his hat."

"He's not to be underestimated," Meecham added.

"What's he gonna think if he sees three guys in a BLM Expedition drive by?" Greg's forehead wrinkled with the question.

"Jesse and Frank will be scrunched down in the back, pretty much out of sight. A BLM vehicle with one man in it might make him alert, but this is BLM territory. He knows that, so seeing a BLM vehicle wouldn't be out of the way. Besides, he has no reason to suspect that we know about his hidey-hole. My guess is he might not see it go by, but even if he does, I don't think it'll spook him. At least I hope not," Meecham finished up.

Greg nodded.

"Okay, then." Meecham shifted gears. "We'll pull over at the point where you set up, Greg. We'll do a radio check. When Jesse's set, we'll do another. Both Frank and I will have radios, but it'll be me keeping you posted." Meecham allowed himself a small smile. "This time, there won't be FBI, county cops, or birders stepping all over each other—just us professionals." His face turned serious. "So if it falls apart, it's on us."

29

•

Seth Parker had pulled his working van under the pines, where it couldn't be seen from the air. From where he sat on the top of the hill, just above the trees, he had visual command of a quarter-mile stretch of the road from the point where it topped the rise to where it dropped out of sight behind the grade that climbed up from the meadows in the west. His view to the east was more restricted. The road turned to the left and disappeared into pinyon pines less than a hundred yards from his position. On the other hand, he could hear vehicles coming from either direction before they came into sight. He heard one now, pulling up the grade from the west.

A late-model Ford Expedition topped the rise. He studied it through the binoculars: white, with a light bar, Bureau of Land Management. The morning sun glinted off the windshield, making it impossible to see the driver. He tracked it eastward until it disappeared around the bend into the pines. He placed the binoculars on his overshirt, which he had spread on the ground, and poured some trail mix into the palm of his slender hand. Lunch: trail mix and apple juice. Maintaining energy was important. Otherwise, eating was low on Parker's priorities.

He munched slowly, listening to the stillness. Why didn't he hear the vehicle? He should still be able to hear it. He stood up, cocked his head to one side, and listened. Nothing, not even a breath of air. Earlier this morning there had been a light plane. It crisscrossed the area a couple of times and then disappeared to the north. The plane made him feel uneasy, and now the BLM. He put the binoculars in their case, picked up the shirt and the daypack, and headed for his van. It was time to move. No point in taking unnecessary risks. Maybe he could find a place up around Jackass Flats. Less chance of wandering vehicles up there, at least until deer season opened. He started the van and eased it over the rocks toward the road.

•

So far, Greg Wilson had turned back two vehicles. He'd had to take an official stance with the hotshots in the red pickup. They had come up with the usual stuff about being taxpayers and their right to use the road whenever they felt like it. Greg had listened to them complain without expression. Frank had taught him that. *Make your face hard to read, amigo. I'm not exactly an Indian, Frank. I'm not exactly an Indian either, Greg.* He'd grinned at him. *Just don't tip your hand. Give 'em something to think about, nothing to react to.* Man, it worked, too. He'd practiced in the mirror, the no-expression I-know-what-I'm-doing cop look. It even made him feel like he knew what he was doing.

The men in the pickup kept on pushing, acting tough. "Hey, man, it's our land. You work for us. We pay your salary."

"The road is temporarily closed. Turn your vehicle around and leave the area."

"Government rent-a-cops. You've got no right to push us around."

Greg had given them a steady look and then taken out his notebook and jotted down their license plate.

"What're you doing?"

"Leave now, or face arrest for interfering with federal law en-forcement." Greg straightened up to his full six-two, broad shoul-ders, narrow waist. It was one of his strong suits. He looked like an arm of the law. He was an arm of the law. Jesse Sierra looked like a Latin lover, and Frank looked like he ought to be running a leaf blower, except for his eyes and the way he moved.

Greg had held up his hand. "No more discussion. Get in the truck and leave the area or get ready to be cuffed." He said it very quietly, matter-of-fact.

The yokels got into their truck and pulled back down the road, macho images intact. They'd told him off, talked back to the cop. Greg knew they were mostly talk, knowing they were safe precisely because he was a cop. He grinned to himself. Sometimes it was fun putting the butthooks in their places. He'd done it just right, too. Writing stuff in his notebook made them think twice, made them realize they weren't invisible. He'd written down their license plate and under it added the word "assholes." Even Dave Meecham would have approved of the way he'd handled the situation, cool, calm, and restrained. He looked up to his boss. He wanted the chief ranger to trust him in the same way he did Frank.

Greg saw the van before he heard it, resting at the top of the rise. The adrenaline kicked in before his mind told him this was the guy, the van he had to stop. The van didn't move. It was about a hundred yards away, just sitting there idling quietly as if it were watching him. He couldn't see into the cab all that well, but there appeared to be just one person in it. He waited, listening to the blood thump in his ears. It had turned hot again, and the desert was still damp from the rains, strangely humid in the heat of the morn-ing sun. Wisps of moisture rose from the road into the soundless air. He took some deep breaths. He had to do something, but he didn't want to expose himself. He stepped to the front of the truck, keeping behind the hood, and waved the driver to come forward. He held the shotgun out of sight.

The driver's door opened, and the driver stepped onto the road behind the open door, reached into the front seat of the van, and rested a rifle on the window frame. Greg dove behind the truck as the rifle cracked into the stillness. He curled himself up behind the front wheel, the shotgun clutched at the ready. The rifle cracked twice more, and then he heard the van coming—coming fast. Fear turned to anger. The son of a bitch shot at him, and now he was trying to get away. Greg rose up from behind the hood and fired into the oncoming van. He kept firing, five rounds of double-aught buckshot, before the van smashed into the rear of the pickup, wrenching it around and into the softness of Greg's unprotected body.

•

Frank and Meecham had worked their way almost to the hidden clearing when they heard the first shot. They both stopped in their tracks.

"Rifle." Frank spoke in a low voice.

Meecham nodded. Two more reports came in quick succession. "Shit. Greg's in trouble."

Then they heard the steady booming of the shotgun. They both glanced back in the direction where they had left Sierra with the vehicle and realized it was too far away.

"Come on." Frank began running through the pines.

Meecham snatched the radio from his belt. "Jesse, Greg's taking fire."

"On my way."

Meecham followed in the direction Frank had taken before he

disappeared behind an outcropping of granite, gray and unmoving in the brightness of the morning light.

•

Greg lay sprawled half under the smashed-up pickup. Frank couldn't see the extent of his injuries. Jesse Sierra bent over the prostrate ranger, blocking his view.

"He crashed through." Greg's voice was surprisingly strong.

"Lie still." Jesse leaned forward to look at the lower half of Greg's body under the truck. He lifted a distraught face to Frank. Dave Meecham peered over Frank's shoulder.

"Can we get him out?" Dave's voice was tight.

Sierra looked back under the truck. Frank had shifted to the fallen ranger's other side and lowered his head down under the truck where Greg's legs extended. The left leg stuck out at an odd angle.

"He's not completely pinned." Frank looked up at Meecham. "I don't think we should wait. We need to get him out from under the truck."

Meecham nodded. "Grab the first aid kit, will you, Jesse?"

"Sorry, Dave. He just kept on coming." Greg's voice was thick with disappointment.

"You've got nothing to be sorry about." Meecham knelt, shaking his head. "A one-vehicle roadblock doesn't cut it for a psycho. My fault." He looked at Greg's face, pale with shock. "You were stand-up, Greg." He rested his hand gently on Greg's shoulder.

"His vehicle's all shot to hell." Greg's voice was trailing off. "I think I killed his van. That's something."

Meecham nodded. "You bet it is."

30

•

Parker's heart thudded. The truck blocking the road was meant for him. How did they know? Flynn! He must have done something to tip him off. The other vehicle, the one that drove past, was waiting to stop him at the other end. Trapped! Except the BLM rangers played by civilian rules, but this one had caught on fast. He'd give him that.

He'd known he'd missed the ranger as soon as he fired. Rushing the shot, he'd jerked the trigger like an amateur. It wasn't that important because he had taken out the vehicle with the next two shots. Actually, it was better this way. It looked like the ranger had been injured. It would be harder to follow him if they had to take care of casualties.

The ranger's shotgun had smashed out part of the windshield, showering him with glass. Blood trickled down his cheek. The crash into the truck had thrown him violently against the seat belt, his right thumb bent back painfully from the steering wheel. Neither injury would slow him up. After the impact, his van had careened to a forty-five-degree angle across the road, coming almost to a stop. That was when he looked back and saw the ranger wedged under the truck.

His van seemed okay; the engine was still running. He brought the van up to thirty and made himself hold it there, a safe speed for the graded dirt road, but he felt like flying. He laughed out loud, glad to be still alive. Everything was in color; bright, vivid colors, like a movie. Every time he survived a close one, it juiced him up.

He glanced down at the gauges on the dashboard. The temperature was in the red. The radiator must have been hit by the ranger's shotgun. His elation was displaced by a bad sinking feeling. It couldn't be now. He wasn't through. He'd keep going until he could find a place to pull off. Maybe they'd miss him, but he knew better. He'd have to make a stand when they caught up to him. Sergeant Flynn would probably be with them. He didn't want that. He stood a good chance of taking them, except they had Flynn. He'd have to take him first—or not at all. He wasn't sure.

He let the van coast, looking for a place to pull over. Then he saw the red pickup, facing in the opposite direction. He pulled to a stop in front of it. He needed another vehicle, and here it was. As he got out of the van, he tucked the Colt Woodsman into his belt at the small of his back. Jets of steam leaked from under the van's hood.

"Looks like you have a hot car." Two men in their early twenties sat on the tailgate of the truck drinking beer. One was shirtless and muscular, the other dark and slender, wearing a T-shirt with a picture of a praying cowboy.

Parker wasn't sure which of them had spoken, but he guessed it was the shirtless one, the one with the smirk.

"Yes, the radiator has a leak." He gave them the Huck Finn smile. "So I'm going to need your truck."

"Say what?" The one wearing the cowboy T-shirt stopped a beer in middrink.

"I said I need to use your truck." He looked from one to the other, owl-eyed behind his yellow shooting glasses.

They exchanged looks. The shirtless man turned a heavy face toward him. "What's your name, man?"

"Sandman." The smile faded. "Now please get off the truck. I'm in a hurry."

"Get fucked, Sandman." They both laughed.

Parker shot him in the chest, just to the left of the sternum, a heart shot. The man's body jerked, and he raised a hand to his heart. Bright blood pulsed from the pencil-sized puncture.

Parker looked at the man in the T-shirt. "Your friend has a hole in his chest." He glanced at the praying cowboy on the man's shirt. "Maybe a prayer or two would be in order."

The shirtless man toppled forward.

"Guess it's too late for him," Parker said.

The remaining man's face filled with horror. He slid off the truck and began backing into the trees, his eyes fixed on their assailant.

"Good move," Parker said. He retrieved his rifle and a box of cartridges from his damaged van. The other man stopped backing up near the edge of the trees, transfixed by the suddenness of the violence. He remained immobile as he watched the man with the gun calmly transfer things from the van to the truck.

Parker climbed into the truck's cab and held out his hand. "Keys?"

The man remained motionless.

"What's your name?" Parker inquired.

"Howie."

"Well, Howie. Give me the keys." He leaned forward. "It will save us both trouble."

Howie shuffled forward, slipped his hand into his pocket, and held the keys out.

"Much obliged," Parker said. He started the truck and eased it away from the side of the road. "Feel free to use my van, if you can get it running." He waved out the window as he headed north on the Saline Valley Road. His deep voice rumbled into song. "Shot him in the head and left him there for dead, left him there for dead, God damn his eyes." It was his chest, actually, but close enough, he thought.

31

•

Eddie knew mostly about Tucker from talk. Then the giant and his dog had found him and left him in a hole because Eddie had yelled at him. Now here he was taking care of his place—for Frank. He was curious to see what he would find at the big man's place, though.

He pulled Frank's truck through the gate and got out and re-latched it, slipping the wire loop over the fence post. The first thing would be to check on the water for the animals. Frank told him that Tucker had a tank up in the canyon that served as a springbox. Should be no problem.

He found that all the water troughs had water. They were pretty muddy from the storm, but the animals were okay. He adjusted the float valve on the trough supplying the nanny goat and the burro Frank had told him about. The nanny kept bleating and bumping him with her head, so he had to stop and provide feed for them all before he could finish up with fixing the float valve. It took longer than expected to feed and water the animals. Then he took the time to clean out the pens. Being around the animals made him feel good.

He stood under the low corrugated plastic overhang that shaded the animals from the desert sun. Looking into the browns, grays, and whites of the Saline Valley, no one would guess there was a hot spring up near the foothills on the east side of the valley. He used to swim there when he was a kid. Now aging hippies and bikers hung out there. He used to take care of his uncle's goats, too. He knew all about goats. He knew enough about bikers to stay out of their bars. Hippies were a mystery. He wasn't even sure what "hippie" meant or where they came from. Another weird tribe of white people, he thought.

He climbed up the slope behind Tucker's place to check on the tank. The springbox had silted up in the recent rains. The runoff had washed over the diversion ditch and poured sand and silt into the tank. Water was spilling over the top and running down the hill in muddy rivulets. The overflow must be plugged up. He stripped off his clothes and climbed into the tank's icy waters. The stream in Hunter Canyon came from snowmelt high in the Inyos. He shivered with the cold, dreading the need to submerge himself further to clear the outlet and clean the screen. He reached down and pulled up handfuls of mud and sand. The water became so clouded he couldn't see what he was doing. If only he had a shovel. He clambered out of the tank, taking care not to cut himself on the edges of the corrugated metal.

A path led from the springbox to a small shed another fifty feet up the canyon. He didn't bother with shoes or pants or shirt, just Eddie in the early afternoon sun. The lock on the door spoiled his mood, but then he noticed that the screws holding the hasp were rusted and the wood on the door frame full of dry rot. He picked up a rock, and the hasp gave way at the first blow, lock and latch hanging from the door. There were plenty of tools: sharp-nosed and flat-bladed shovels, picks, pickaxes, mattocks, sledgehammers, drill bars—and a case of 40 percent dynamite.

He loved dynamite. His uncle used to remove stumps and rocks with it, but mostly he liked to make explosions. A huge roaring boom and pieces of rock went flying everywhere. Once it broke out the windows on his aunt's house. She was mad, but his uncle didn't pay attention to what his aunt said about the dynamite, or drinking, or dynamite and drinking. If he had, then maybe his uncle would still be around, instead of scattered across his field. His aunt said the beans and peppers tasted better after the accident. Part of the big circle, she'd said, smiling contentedly. That was as close to religious teaching as Eddie came. Maybe he could take a few sticks of the dynamite in return for the extra work he was doing.

He peered into the box, almost full. Eddie looked up on the shelves and felt along the top one with his hands. There were lots of small tools and a wooden box. The box contained a coil of fuse, blasting caps, and crimping pliers. He could come back for the dynamite and caps when he finished up. He frowned. Probably old Tucker did some prospecting. Everyone seemed to be digging holes in the earth. He didn't like it. Didn't like the open pit mines. Didn't like the leaching pits. White people ruined the land, and some of the Shoshone made deals with them, the apples. A frown settled on his face when he thought of Hector Goodwater calling him an apple for hanging around white people.

He picked up a D-handle shovel and headed back to the springbox. After clearing out the muck, he figured to toss a few beers into the icy water, eat a baloney sandwich, drink a cold beer or two or three, then take a nap until the water cleared up and he could see what he was doing. Maybe he'd wait until tomorrow to head back. Frank wouldn't be back until tomorrow, out doing some kind of special bust. Being out here away from all the damn people in his life, being out here in the deep desert, he had time to think. Maybe he could figure things out about Cece. He decided to save a trip and take the dynamite, caps, and fuse now. Why wait?

He returned to Frank's truck and dumped four sticks of dynamite on the floor of the cab. Then he put the blasting caps and fuse in the glove compartment, careful to cushion the caps with a rag so they wouldn't go off. They could be tricky. He retrieved a six-pack from the now warm ice chest and headed back for the springbox.

32

•

The desk sergeant had looked at him funny when they gave him his stuff back. "Here's your property, Mr. Tucker." He pushed a large manila envelope across the desk. "Check it out and then you can sign for it."

The identification of Seth Parker as the Sandman and the shooter on the 210 Freeway in Pasadena, plus a few words from Dave Meecham, had convinced the sheriff's department and the FBI that Tucker could be "released on his own recognizance."

"Where's my rifle?"

"We're running a few tests on it. We'll let you know when we're finished."

Tucker dumped the envelope on the desk and checked it against the list: one comb, missing teeth. He put the broken comb in his pocket.

"Wait a minute, Mr. Tucker. You haven't signed for that."

Tucker glowered and took the comb back out of his pocket and put it on the counter. He continued with the list of his possessions: one Craftsman pocketknife, one Leatherman multipurpose tool; $4,367 in paper money, sixteen cents in change; one silver medal. Wasn't a silver medal, the ignorant jerks. Tucker reached for the clipboard.

"Don't you want to count your money?"

"Waste of time." He signed the receipt and pushed it across the counter. "If you stole my money, who could I complain to?" His eyebrows knit into the hedge that signaled a scowl. "This ain't a medal." He held up a silver chain attached to a silver medallion. "It's a St. Christopher."

The desk sergeant shrugged. "Okay, you've got it back."

"St. Christopher protects travelers"—Tucker paused—"and looks after fools and drunks." He squinted down at the desk sergeant. "Considering all those broken veins and the color of your nose, I think maybe you could use the help." He turned to go.

"How come you carry so much cash, Mr. Tucker?"

Tucker fixed the hefty desk sergeant with the glittering blue eye.

"Just wondering." The sergeant shrugged beefy shoulders. "Not the brightest thing to do." His face was bland. "So why don't you just hang on to your St. Christopher. You might be needing it. I'll stick with Saints Smith and Wesson."

•

Tucker picked up Jack at the Joshua Tree Athletic Club. Frank had told him they were taking care of his dog there. The caretakers turned out to be a bunch of geezers trying to get Jack to drink beer. He told them the dog wasn't a smelly drunk. They returned to playing pool and telling lies to each other.

The bar was where he found out that this Indian, Eddie Laguna, was already up at his place taking care of the animals. The woman tending bar explained it to him about Flynn having to go somewhere on official business. Damn the luck. Damn the dumb cops that had confused him with some crazy killer they were looking for.

Zeke Tucker had had second thoughts about letting anyone go poking around his place. Flynn was okay, but as soon as you told one person something, two people knew about it. He'd been in a bind, though, no damn choice. Someone had to take care of the animals. What the hell was the point in taking in the hurt and the sick if they were going to die of thirst or starve? He reached over and scratched Jack behind the ears. Flynn had sent a stranger up to his place. He didn't want that. Didn't want this Indian to figure things out.

●

He pulled the truck off to the side at the juncture where the Talc Mine Road met the Saline Valley Road. He preferred roads less traveled, not that the Saline Valley Road was a freeway, but he avoided running into people on general principles.

"Time to take a leak, huh, Jack." Tucker relieved himself on a Joshua tree. Jack preferred Great Basin sage, closer to the ground. "Now's here's what we hafta do, old boy. We hafta get back home and check on things."

He poured some water into a canteen cup, took a long drink, and set the remainder on the ground for Jack, who lapped up the water with noisy gusto. Tucker smiled down at his companion. "Truck, Jack." Jack leaped into the front of the van, and Tucker cranked it over and headed for Grapevine Canyon. The van bounced along like the pea on a roulette wheel, an empty box on overload springs chattering its way down the long washboard stretch leading to the valley floor.

"Damn." He looked in the rearview mirror. One of the rear doors had come open again. He stopped and clambered to the back of the van and reattached the baling wire from the handle to the inside of the van, making sure that it wouldn't slip loose again. He'd have to fix that for sure. Couldn't have stuff falling out of the van all the time. He grinned, his hand unconsciously rubbing the wad of bills in his pocket.

"Don't know how they could take me for a dangerous killer, Jack." Teeth showed through the shrubbery. He laughed and broke into Tennessee Ernie Ford's version of "Sixteen Tons," booming out the part about "St. Peter don'tcha call me, 'cause I can't go" and added a line of his own—"gotta have some fun and spend this dough." He scratched behind Jack's ears. "Feels good to be out, old buddy, don't it. Feels good." He smiled at the dog. "Besides, we don't a owe a damn thing to anyone." His laughter reverberated in the van. "It's the sunny side of the street for us, ol' Jack, the sunny side of the street."

33

•

Seth Parker put the truck in neutral and let it coast. The needle on the gas gauge was in the red. There was no place to buy gasoline on Saline Valley Road, and it was close to a hundred miles of dirt before the road reached the pavement at Westgard Pass. Turning around meant getting caught. Near the bottom of the long washboard grade, a dirt track led up toward the mountains on the west side of the valley. A freshly painted KEEP OUT sign stood at the foot of the track. The sign meant people, people meant another vehicle, and another vehicle meant gasoline.

He shifted the truck into low range and pulled up the dirt path, stopping at the gate. The gas gauge light flashed on momentarily. He was running on fumes. He looked down the hill at the cluster of shacks and animal pens. An old pickup truck made him reach for his binoculars. If the pickup truck had gas, he could siphon it off, or just take the truck. If he could reach the Westgard Pass road, he might make it. For sure, he had to get back up into the pinyon pine country before they spotted him from the air. The old truck appeared to be in decent shape.

He looked over the buildings for signs of life and almost missed it. There was a small brown man lying naked on the porch, right out in plain sight. He opened the gate and let the truck coast down the track. He stepped quietly out of the truck, put the Woodsman behind his back, and carefully crossed the yard.

"Are you the owner of the truck?" Parker nudged the naked figure with the toe of his boot.

The brown man's eyes popped open. "Watch where you put your fucking feet." He sat up, squinting up at a tall man standing in the dirt next to the porch.

"I said—"

"I heard what you said." The naked man picked up a grungy pair of blue jeans and put them on, hunching his butt back, pulling his penis out of sight. He grinned. "*Adios*, anteater."

"What the hell are you talking about?"

The Indian nodded in agreement with himself.

Parker heard a tinkling sound.

"That's right. Most white guys been trimmed." Eddie looked up, a thoughtful expression on his face. "I don't get it. Why the hell would a man cut part of his dick off?" He held up a hand. "No offense, man,"—the nodding head began to shake back and forth, the tinkling sound more distinct—"but it's a mystery to me." Then Parker caught the flash of the silver bell tied to the end of the man's hair.

He was wasting time. "The truck—"

The Indian interrupted again. "Yeah, it's mine." Eddie wished it were so. "Pretty fine, huh?"

"Yes, it is," Parker replied. "I'm going to have to borrow it."

"No way, man. I don't lend my vehicle to anyone." The Indian gestured toward the truck with his head. "That's a classic. Besides, why the hell would I lend my truck to someone I don't know?"

"Because I'm not giving you a choice." Parker produced the Woodsman. "If you don't make things difficult, I won't have to shoot you." He looked down at Eddie, his eyes tinged green by the yellow shooting glasses. "But I haven't time for delays."

The Indian's black eyes were bright, his face impassive. He nodded slowly, the bell tolling his understanding in a small silver voice.

"Good. Where are the keys?"

"In the truck."

"Is the truck gassed up?"

"I guess."

"How about additional gas? Cans?"

"Nope." Eddie cast a surreptitious glance at the shed.

Parker gave Eddie his boyish grin. "Don't take up poker."

"Shit." Eddie knew he'd given himself away.

"Keys?"

"In the ignition. I already said, okay? You want me to start it for you?"

Parker studied the Indian. "Is this your place?"

"I'm just here to look after the stock."

"Oh." Parker frowned. "Have you done that yet?"

"Yeah, why? What're you, my boss?"

"No, I wouldn't say that." He looked at the Indian's weathered face. There was something compelling about the small man. Maybe it was because he wasn't afraid. Maybe it was because of the bell. He wasn't sure. "Show me the telephone, please."

The Indian laughed. "You're kidding?"

"I don't kid."

The Indian gave him a sideways look. "Haven't been inside yet."

"Well, then, let's go inside." Parker gestured at the door with the Woodsman. He had to stoop as he followed the Indian through the low opening. Dim light filtered into the one large room from a single window through a draped bedsheet. As his eyes adjusted to the light, he was surprised to find the place exceptionally clean, even Spartan.

A stoneware water jug rested on the end of a long wooden kitchen table. Pots and pans and cooking utensils hung from a wire rack along the far side. The Indian gave the knives hanging from the hooks a covert glance.

Parker shook his head. "Sit on the bed. Don't move, and don't forget about not being an impediment."

The Indian gave him a quizzical look.

"Not making trouble," Parker explained. He began opening and closing drawers in a tall cabinet next to the table. "I think you'd better lie facedown on the bed."

"You've got the gun."

Parker turned to face the Indian, his eyes absent behind the reflected light on his sunglasses. The Indian sighed, flopped facedown on the bed, and spread his arms and legs. "How's this?"

"That'll do." Parker returned to opening and closing the drawers. He lifted a length of nylon clothesline from the bottom drawer. "Now's the time for you to be especially cooperative." He cut four pieces of clothesline and tied loops into each of the ends. Then he crossed the room and laid them next to the Indian. "Okay, you can sit up now."

The Indian glared at the pieces of clothesline.

"Put a loop over each wrist and ankle." He waited while the Indian slipped the loops into place. "Good. Lie back down on your stomach." Parker placed the muzzle of the Woodsman behind the Indian's ear. "Careful now." Then he secured the free end of each line to the metal bed frame. He stepped away and surveyed his efforts. "That should do it."

"Go fuck yourself."

"In your place I would be making an effort to be polite—or at least a nonirritant." Parker smiled. "That's not easy for you, is it?" He held up a hand. "Never mind. I've got to be going, no time for conversation." He turned back. "Oh, by the way, the reason I didn't shoot you is that you're taking care of the animals—and the bell. I like the bell."

They both turned toward the sound of an automobile engine. Parker stooped down to look out the window. "Are you expecting a visitor?"

"What's he driving?" The Indian's head faced the low wall.

"A large brown van."

The Indian laughed. "You bought into some trouble, asshole."

Parker swung the Woodsman around, aiming it at the Indian's head. "You need to be quiet now, or you'll be quiet permanently." His head was starting to hurt. "If the keys aren't in the truck, I'll be back to shoot you." He was at the door in two long strides. He eased it open a few inches and peered into the sunlit landscape. Then he slipped out into the shade of the porch and crossed the yard toward the stolen red truck. He needed it one more time.

•

Tucker stopped the van as soon as he saw the second truck down by the house. He recognized the BLM ranger's personal vehicle, a '53 Chevy pickup, but he didn't know anyone with a red pickup. What the hell was going on? Some jerk had left the gate open. Flynn wouldn't leave the gate open. First thing you learned living in open country was close the gate behind you, otherwise stock wandered off, got lost or stolen, or hit by automobiles. While he was looking down at his place, the door opened and a tall thin man walked across the yard toward the red truck. He looked up at Tucker and waved a long arm, got in the truck, and fired it up.

Tucker watched as the truck made its way up the grade, gathering speed as it came. Too much speed. Tucker swung around to get his rifle and remembered that it wasn't there. He scrambled toward the back of the van and was looking for a shovel, something to use as a weapon, when an impact to the side of the van drove him to the floor. He regained his feet; a second smashing blow knocked him down again. Then he realized what the skinny guy was trying to do. He was pushing him off the cutback. The third impact shoved the van over the edge. It tilted to the right, then plunged down the cutback, carrying Tucker and Jack-the-dog with it.

34

•

Frank watched the copter blow by on the way to Hunter Mountain to pick up the dead and the wounded. Dave Meecham and Jesse Sierra had elected to stay behind and wait with Greg Wilson for the helicopter to pick him up.

The cell phone had come back to life over the hill on the approach to Highway 190, and he'd called in the emergency to the BLM and then the Inyo sheriffs. The plane from the California Highway Patrol was refueling in Ridgecrest. Having alerted the county, he doubled back to go after Parker. The Inyo sheriffs were on the way to evacuate Greg Wilson, and the Highway Patrol, the Forest Service, every available agency was out looking for Parker. One of their own had been wounded.

They had a complete description of Parker and the vehicle, including the license number, which Greg Wilson had jotted down while he was backing off the unlucky men in the red pickup. The wheels were turning. Now Frank was free to reverse direction and get to Parker before he killed someone else.

The surviving victim of the hijacking, Howard Poe, said he and his friend had been sitting on the tailgate of their truck when this tall guy comes up, wants to use their truck, and when they say no way, he shoots Colin, just like that. "Then he tells me, 'There's a hole in your friend's chest,' and drives away—waves good-bye."

Frank's warning to the two men had been prophetic. Poe was lucky to be alive. Killing was coming easier to Parker. The rules were out of it. The killing in Pasadena must have been a tipping point. Doing murder had become matter-of-fact. Frank slammed over a pothole, and the heavy SUV broke into a slide. He turned into it, hitting the gas, and the vehicle straightened out, racing toward a blind curve, much too fast. He hit the brakes, slowing the vehicle down to a manageable speed. Parker had more than a two-hour head start into the Saline Valley. He didn't want to miss him again, but he didn't want to wind up over some embankment cursing himself for being a fool.

Both ends of the Saline Valley Road were plugged. If Parker tried to get out through the Westgard Pass road, a redheaded man in a red truck would be hard to miss. If he doubled back, he'd run into Frank. It was what Frank hoped. If he could stop Parker, maybe it would make up for giving him his start all those years ago.

35

●

As soon as Eddie's captor went out the door, he began working on the line holding his left wrist. It was nylon, so he knew there wasn't a ghost of a chance of breaking it, but his hands were tied to the iron bed frame with his left hand near one of the coiled springs that supplied tension to the wire net that held up the mattress of the old army cot. Where the springs attached to the frame, they bent back and ended in sharp points. Eddie dragged the cord across one of the points and snapped a couple of strands. He repeated the process until he was more than halfway through and then tried to break the rest. It wouldn't give. He went back to a few strands at a time.

The man had taken Frank's truck, and Eddie had to get it back. If he lost Frank's truck, too, he couldn't go back to the Joshua Tree Athletic Club—ever. He'd have to leave the valley. People would laugh at him. Or worse, feel sorry for him, like they used to feel sorry for dumb Doug Funmaker. He worked at the cord. Finally it gave way. It seemed like it had taken a long time, but he'd worked loose in under fifteen minutes.

He trotted up the hill to where the red pickup sat with its smashed grill pointing over the embankment and looked down on Tucker's van. It didn't look that bad. Tucker's dog was probably all right. He could hear him howling, which made Eddie wonder about the state of the owner. He scrambled down to the van at about the same time Tucker emerged from the rear doors with blood in his eye.

Zeke Tucker had returned to consciousness at the insistence of Jack-the-dog. Tucker was the source of all things good in Jack's doggy life, so he licked Tucker's face until he woke up. The big man carefully pulled himself into a sitting position, piecing together what had happened. He remembered being rammed by a red truck. He pictured a tall, thin man striding across his front yard to the truck, giving him a casual wave as if they knew each other. That had thrown him off. He didn't know him—the son of a bitch. Then the stranger had rammed his truck into the van and pushed him over the embankment.

Tucker's hand strayed absently to the side of his head—tender, and it wasn't the only place. The stranger had lifted his hand against him, and the giant meant to answer the injury. "Come on, Jack." He kicked open the rear doors that he had so recently wired shut and emerged filled with fury into the desert, where he encountered the little Indian.

"You the guy watching the animals?" he said.

"Yeah, you okay?" Eddie asked.

"Never better." Tucker strode down the hill toward one of the sheds scattered around his property with Eddie in his wake. He pulled open the door on the largest shed and yanked away a blue plastic tarp covering a Yamaha ATV. It fired up at the first touch. He thumped both gas cans strapped to the sides with his forefinger to check for content and straddled the machine. Jack jumped up on the platform behind his master. He loved going for a ride.

"Where you going?" Eddie shouted as Tucker pulled away.

" 'I will execute great vengeance upon them with furious rebukes.' " Tucker bellowed in stentorian rage.

"Wait, God damn it!" Eddie yelled. "You don't even have a gun." His voice was swallowed up in the *blat* of the ATV's exhaust.

36

•

The truck Parker had taken from the Indian had an almost full tank. Even better, it wasn't a red truck, and they would be looking for a red truck driven by a man with red hair. His hair was under a straw hat, and he was in a vintage forest green Chevy truck. It would be a while before they found the Indian. That might give him the margin of time he needed.

He thought of the man wearing the praying cowboy T-shirt, staring at him from the trees, eyes big as saucers. That one would remember him for a very long time, and he would provide a detailed description of a man with brown hair. He didn't want them to know he had dyed his hair. He probably should have killed him, too—Howie. It was harder to kill someone once you knew his name, except for that pig Stuller. That had been a pleasure. He had hesitated to kill the other man, Howie, because he was a civilian, essentially a bystander. On the other hand, the law enforcement people had their hands full and might not take a statement right away, especially since they thought they had a positive identification of the stolen truck and knew who the driver was: Seth Adrian Parker, aged thirty-seven, six feet five inches, eyes blue, hair red. They would still be looking for that man, and in a stolen red truck. All he needed was a bit of luck.

He'd been making good time on the road through the Saline

Valley, hitting fifty on the graded parts, throwing up a white plume of alkaline dust. Here, where the road climbed up out of the valley, it was slower going. The road narrowed, and the storm had turned it into a boulder-strewn washout, forcing him to slow down as he threaded his way through the debris. Rock cliffs angled up from the west side in oval slabs of the lightest gray, blending into tans and dirty yellows streaked with deep volcanic browns.

He braked sharply to avoid a jagged rock, and that was when the sticks of dynamite slid out from under the seat. He stared at the brown, paper-clad rolls on the floor of the cab, not comprehending at first. Then it fell into place. Dynamite. He stopped the truck and searched under the seat looking for caps, wondering if there was a detonator. Then he rummaged through the glove compartment and discovered the blasting caps and fusing. Old-fashioned stuff, but it would do the job. He could slow down his pursuers, at least on this end of the pursuit.

●

Except for the ticking sound of the cooling engine, the canyon was filled with an oppressive silence. The air was still and hot, humid yet from the thunderstorms. He heard the soft sound of his breath, and for a moment, he was overcome with weariness. He wanted to just sit there and wait for Flynn to show up. He knew it would be him. Who else? Who else would have laid the trap? He shouldn't have baited Sergeant Flynn about how unprofessional the Bureau of Land Management had been. Now he was probably behind him—coming fast.

He pushed down on the door handle and stepped hurriedly away from the comfort of the truck, stumbling, nearly falling down among the rocks. The canyon wall angled high above him, impassive stone monoliths, silent witnesses to his movements.

First assess the situation, he reminded himself. He had his rifle and the remainder of two boxes of ammunition. Three rounds fired at the BLM ranger left a total of thirty-seven rounds, enough to make a stand should that become necessary. There was also the Woodsman, full clip less one, plus the remainder of the box of hollow points.

Being alone in a desert was nothing new. Solitude was the sniper's ally. His lassitude was no more than an understandable reaction to the recent violence. He'd had to kill someone again and had nearly been killed himself. Now he was coming down from it, the adrenaline rush abating, the headache returning.

The man he shot in the chest really hadn't stood a chance, not with an expanding round entering resistant heart muscle. He shrugged. Somehow it seemed not to make as much difference anymore. He searched his feelings for sorrow, guilt, regret—nothing. Somewhere he'd read that an absence of guilt was the mark of a sociopath. He didn't think of himself as a sociopath. He was acting on behalf of the defenseless, bringing balance. He had spared the Indian, despite his nasty mouth—perhaps because of his nasty mouth, but more probably because the Indian had come to take care of the animals. He nodded to himself. He was letting his mind drift again.

He quickly picked up the dynamite, blasting caps, and fuse and stuffed it all in his shirt. As he stepped into the high heat of the canyon floor, he experienced a flash of pain followed by a wave of nausea. *Not yet*, he thought. He turned away from the glaring light and followed his shadow until it merged into the deeper shade of the canyon walls. He scrambled over the rocky ground into a westerly ravine, where it opened into hot shafts of afternoon sun. The heat radiated into the wash, blurring the landscape into shimmering waves. He stopped to wipe his forehead. The pain had subsided to a bearable level.

On the left, the road came from behind a large shoulder of rock where the overhanging cliff face divided into odd oval slabs stacked on edge like giant plates. At that point, the wash left the road and disappeared into a narrow gorge on the left. He worked his way up the wash and approached the overhanging rocks from the backside.

Parker stood at the summit, evaluating the position. He began to question whether the dynamite would take down enough rock to block the road. As if to confirm his doubts about the tactical disadvantages of the location, the sound of an approaching engine echoed up from the canyon below.

An ATV topped the approach leading into the narrows. He lifted his binoculars and tracked the sunlit portion of the road until the ATV jumped into view. A very large man straddled the vehicle. A gray and white dog perched on the rear platform.

Bad timing for the man and the dog, Parker thought. A small dust-colored lizard darted to the top of a nearby boulder and tilted its scaly head; a bright yellow eye glared malevolently up at him. It began pushing up and down, warning him off, protecting its territory. He glanced down at the small angry body, and a surge of unease shot through him like the onset of an illness. He had to survive. Sand Canyon was opening in less than three weeks. The man and the dog would have to be casualties. Too bad, it couldn't be helped.

He made a hole in one of the sticks of dynamite with his pocketknife and pushed a length of fuse through it. He carefully placed a cap over the end of the fuse and realized he lacked crimping pliers. That meant using his teeth. The caps were pressure sensitive and powerful. Misplaced pressure would remove his jaw. He thought of the cat that had its head blown off. He crimped down the edges with his teeth, guessing at how hard he had to bite down. Then he pushed the crimped cap and fusing into the dynamite, feeding the fuse carefully back through the hole so that its connection to the cap remained secure, leaving six inches of fuse protruding from the stick of dynamite.

That left him three minutes to get to his truck and get moving.

He'd have to scramble. He bundled the four sticks together, tying them up with a length of fusing. He lit the fuse, waited to be sure he'd done it right, then gave the dynamite an underhanded toss, lodging it between two of the rock slabs hanging over the road.

The large man had dismounted and started down the hill toward Parker's truck, followed by the dog. As he turned to go, a large white SUV roared over the grade, a BLM vehicle—Flynn.

Parker began scrambling down the gully leading back toward the road, dislodging rocks and gravel in a noisy cascade. According to his watch, he had two minutes and twenty seconds.

•

Frank had been following the ATV for some time, unable to overtake it. It was built for the terrain. After a while, he was able to make out a dog behind the rider. Tucker and his dog, and Tucker was in a hurry. Frank honked the horn, hoping to attract his attention, but no such luck. The ATV drowned his efforts in a cone of noise. Frank increased his speed. His vehicle was in a barely controlled skid as he crested the rise leading into the narrow canyon and found the ATV stopped in the middle of the road.

At the sound of the braking truck, Tucker turned. Finally something had distracted him from his single-minded course.

"Mr. Tucker. Wait a minute," Frank shouted. He threw open the door and trotted in Tucker's direction.

"Some son of a bitch wrecked my truck," Tucker bellowed.

"Wasn't the guy I sent to take care of your stock, was it?"

"Naw, he's okay. The other guy rammed me over an embankment. I'm chasing him."

"I'm chasing him, too, Mr. Tucker."

"Okay, then. Let's go," Tucker said, walking back toward the BLM vehicle.

"Can't do that, Mr. Tucker. No civilians."

Tucker's brows knit.

"It's against the rules," Frank added. "The man is very danger-ous. He kills people, Mr. Tucker. I can't put your life in danger."

Tucker threw his head back and laughed. "Too late, Ranger Flynn. Uncle Sam beat you to it."

"Look, Mr. Tucker, I have to—" His thought was cut off by a deafening roar accompanied by the pulse of a shock wave. For the briefest of moments there was silence, and then it began raining rocks, followed by a cascade of debris thundering into the ravine, filling the canyon with clouds of brown and yellow dust.

●

Parker was long gone before the dust cleared. Ahead of him, the road was empty, and there were no pursuers from behind. He re-joined Highway 168, a narrow strip of asphalt that led into the Inyo Mountains from the Owens Valley through Westgard Pass and then south into Death Valley. He encountered a lone police car speed-ing up the grade toward the pass. The driver didn't give the old green Chevy a second look. They were still looking for the man in the red truck. He turned south on 395 and picked up the road lead-ing to the Mount Whitney Fish Hatchery. He drove past the fish hatchery to the upper reaches of Oak Creek. Then he took a dim track into a cluster of pines that wound down the slope, pulled un-der the trees, and cut the engine. The end of the line—for the truck, not for the rider.

His good spirits made him smile. He had made a remarkable escape. Moved and improvised. The surprise at Sand Canyon would still be a reality. He retrieved his rifle and his daypack. The rifle was in a hard case and could easily be mistaken for fishing gear. Most likely, no one would notice the truck, thinking it be-longed to a fisherman. He hiked back down to the hatchery, fol-lowing the creek.

The Mount Whitney Fish Hatchery looked more like a medieval monastery than a fish hatchery. It was a two-story structure of native stone and huge timbers roofed in red tile. It had been built after the turn of the last century, a gift from the people of the Owens Valley to residents and visiting fishermen.

He took his phone from his daypack and punched in John's number with his thumb. "I'm at the Mount Whitney Fish Hatchery." He nodded into the phone. "Okay, I'll feed the trout while I'm waiting. See you in a few hours. I really want you to see this place. It has a tower overlooking the valley. You could hold off an army."

37

•

When the rocks began pelting the ground around Zeke Tucker and Frank Flynn, they hit the dirt, covered their heads with their arms, and waited it out. Frank was the first to get up. Tucker's ATV was farther downcanyon, under the landslide. Jack-the-dog trailed Tucker as he emerged from the swirling dust cloud. The blood running down his forehead completed the picture of Frankenstein's mad monster. Frankenstein and dog. *Frankendog* jumped into Frank's thoughts. He restrained himself from comment.

"Mr. Tucker, are you all right?"

"Yeah." He knelt beside Jack and ran his large hands over the dog's body. "Jack's good, too." He turned back and stared into the canyon. "Can't see my Yamaha."

"That's okay. I can give you a ride back to your place." Frank climbed behind the wheel of the white Expedition. "Moby Dick here seems okay."

"Wasn't your ATV that got buried," Tucker growled as he opened the passenger door. Jack hopped into the backseat, and Tucker filled the passenger side of the cab, puffs of dust flying off him in tiny cascades. *Dustyman,* Frank thought. *Dick Tracy's archenemy, or maybe Batman's nemesis, ready to gum up civilization with clouds of brown dust.* Frank realized that he had the high that followed a close call.

"What the hell you smiling about, Flynn? We almost got killed—and with my dynamite."

"Your dynamite?"

"Yeah, he must've searched the shed up by the spring."

"You're saying the man who set off the blast—his name is Seth Parker, by the way—used your dynamite."

"Yep, unless he just carries it around. Either he found it, or the Indian did, and he took it when he took the Indian's truck."

Frank's head snapped around. "How do you know he took the Indian's truck?"

"It wasn't there when I went after him, and it was there when I got there. So he must've taken it. Looked like your truck."

"Damn. That was my truck he was in, Mr. Tucker." Frank made a sour face. "I lent it to Eddie, so he could take care of your stock." He glanced over at Tucker's bloody face. "Let me clean up your wound." He reached across and opened the glovebox and took out a first aid kit.

"I can do it," Tucker said, taking the kit from Frank's hands. "Let's get going."

Frank put the SUV in drive and shot up the road, tires spitting gravel as he went. When they reached the curve leading into the long straight stretch across the bottom of the valley, Frank brought the heavy vehicle into a controlled skid and pushed it up to sixty. They were pounding up the road and bouncing around in the cab.

"You quit smiling, Ranger Flynn," Tucker remarked.

Frank gave him a sour look.

"I think your truck's probably still running. Can't say the same for my Yamaha."

"That's true, Mr. Tucker. I didn't think about your ATV." Frank sighed and eased back on the throttle. "And we're both still moving, and that's not all bad."

"Nope. Jack's okay, too." He reached back and stroked the dog's ears.

●

Eddie Laguna closed Zeke Tucker's gate and slipped the wire loop over the fence post and climbed into the Bureau of Land Management's white SUV. Frank waved from the driver's side window, and they careened down Tucker's two-track trail to the Saline Valley Road. Frank still hoped that he could report what happened in time for Parker to be apprehended. It was more than an hour back to the junction with Hunter Mountain Road and probably close to that before the damn cell phone would work. If he could get a description of his truck out—his truck, damn, how would he explain that—Parker would be easy to spot, but not easy to stop.

"Eddie, did Parker say anything to you about what he was doing? Drop any hints?"

"Nope. He was in a hurry. Told me if I was an *impediment*—what a shithead—he'd have to shoot me. He's a cold son of a bitch. Said it like, okay, if I got to kill you, I got to kill you. Ho hum."

"He's killed a lot of people, Eddie. I think he's planning on killing more."

"Who's he going to kill?"

"I'm not sure. He's got a list."

"He makes lists of people he's going to kill?"

"In a way. Yeah. He's going to kill people he thinks are cruel. Mostly people who torture animals. Like the men up on the flats. He killed them because they were killing burros."

"I got a couple names for him."

"You, too, huh?"

"What?" Eddie looked perplexed.

"You've got a list. 'They'll none of them be missed.' " He mumbled this last part.

"Yeah, probl'ly mine's not as long as his."

"He thinks he's doing the right thing. He killed those poachers up on the flats. He killed another man who was killing vultures." His face tightened up. "And he killed a man he had hated for a long time." It was hard for Frank to feel sorry for some of Parker's victims. The dead poachers were no loss, and by killing Stuller, Parker had improved the gene pool, but shooting the loudmouth kid and running down Greg Wilson was nothing but murder and mayhem. It wasn't his call, but it was hard not to make the judgments. He thought of Bill Jerome's remark about justice, "You want justice, look in the dictionary or pack a piece." That's what Parker was doing. "Where every man is a law unto himself, there is no law." He'd have to look it up.

They were about twenty minutes from Highway 190. Frank checked his phone. No signal yet. He'd been thinking that Parker took his truck to make his getaway just a step ahead of the law. He'd been a man in a hurry, so when did he have time to search the sheds and go up to the spring? Frank looked over at Eddie, slouched at ease against the door. "Okay, time to come clean, Redhawk. Where did you find the dynamite?"

"Dynamite?" Eddie tried to look guileless.

"Come on, Eddie, you didn't bring it with you. Even if Parker brought it in his van, after the roadblock, he was traveling light. So where was it?"

Eddie glanced from side to side, looking crafty. He would have made a lousy spy, Frank thought. As it was, he was an inept thief. "It was in a shed up by the spring."

Frank nodded. "That's what Tucker figured, that you took his dynamite." He raised his eyebrows. "I wouldn't screw around with Tucker, Eddie. He's not the kind of guy who strikes me as forgiving."

Eddie looked smug. "He already said it was okay."

"Don't try to tell me you asked permission to take it."

"Nope, but I told him I took it, while you were taking a leak." He grinned. "He told me not to worry about it, but not to tell people he had dynamite on his place."

Frank shifted the SUV into four-wheel as they started up Grapevine Canyon. Why wouldn't Tucker want people to know he had dynamite? More important, what was he using it for? He must be working an unregistered claim, maybe not on his property. "You see anything that might be mine tailings up in the canyon?"

"Some old stuff maybe, all covered with brush." Eddie frowned in thought. "There was some piles of dirt and rock above the springbox. The storms washed a lot of the dirt into it. Took me all day to clean it out. Why you asking?"

"No reason, just wondering."

Eddie nodded. "Okay."

Frank's questions set Eddie to thinking about Tucker. If Tucker was sitting on an old mining claim, it might be the one from Cece's map. That would be great. He could tell her he found the mine, make her dreams come true. He'd never considered being some-one's hero, but the thought of being Cece Flowers's hero made his heart race. Then he thought about Tucker and Tucker's place, a very big problem.

"Is mining in the Saline Valley still legal?" Eddie asked.

"Depends on a lot of stuff."

"Like what?"

"Whether it's in Death Valley National Park and whether it's grandfathered in under the law and whether a legal claim's been filed. Stuff like that." Frank looked over at his friend. "Why the sudden interest in the Saline Valley?"

"It's Shoshone country."

Frank suspected Eddie was feeding him a line, but that was okay. He needed to put the mine thing on the back burner anyhow.

38

•

Ralph put three paper plates weighted down with steaming burritos on the counter, and the trio adjourned to the table on the broken asphalt. Collins was glad to be away from the Joshua Tree Athletic Club and its clientele of ever curious geezers. Even the barest whiff of a treasure hunt sent them into fits of questions and stories of lost bonanzas. Old hands fished flasks of gold flakes from grubby pockets. Then the tall tales started. The fact that they authored their own fabrications didn't seem to diminish their gullibility. The richer the claim, the more credulous the audience. Jack didn't need it. He figured they really could be onto something, and they didn't want a million partners, just a million dollars.

"What's *payaso* mean?" Ben inquired, taking a seat at the sun-bleached picnic table.

"I thought you were the man who spoke the *español.*" Bill Jerome looked smug.

"I can cuss in many languages," Shaw intoned.

"Clown. He called you a clown," Collins said.

"Naw, he called you guys *payasos,* clowns. He called me a *culo,* an asshole." Shaw looked triumphant.

Collins removed a folder from a battered leather briefcase and shuffled through the papers, making a cursory examination, setting some to one side. "This is Ms. Flowers's map, the original, at least so she says." He looked at his companions and lifted a pale ivory page from the rest. "Here's the letter from her great-granduncle describing its location—sort of."

"How'd you come by Ms. Flowers's papers?" Jerome asked.

"I told you before. She gave them to Linda so she could look them over and maybe bring us along as investors."

They bent forward to read the letter over Collins's shoulders.

"Two days' travel north of Red Mountain. Hell, that doesn't do us much good. How fast would he be walking?" Shaw inquired.

"He probably had a burro. Burros don't move all that fast," Jerome added.

"Well, here's the discouraging part, boys. Linda thinks the map is a phony."

"How'd she come to that?" Shaw wanted to know.

"See how the map and letter are all discolored and wrinkled."

"Like your face, Jack. It's what happens when you're old."

Jack shook his head. "Not so, boys. If you look more closely the color's even, the same all over the page. That's not what happens when paper ages, skin either. Linda thinks the pages were soaked in tea for artificial aging." Jack paused to look into the faces of his companions. "Take a look at some old faces, gents. Some places are darker, some lighter, some mottled with liver spots. Look at Ben's nose, all broken out with tiny veins."

"Screw you, Jack. You could light your own way in the dark with that knob of yours."

"Is that conclusive?" Bill asked. "I mean, couldn't something age evenly?"

"Maybe so, but here's the final proof. Linda dug around in some old newspapers and discovered that Red Mountain used to be called Osdick, up until 1931, when they changed the name. Osdick was the superintendent of the Yellow Aster Mine in Randsburg. I guess his relatives objected to a red-light town bearing their name."

"Well, damn it all to hell," Jerome said, a mournful expression on his face.

"That's too bad. I sorta liked that girl." Shaw shook his head. "She had grit, and she was Eddie's girl . . . say, does Eddie know he's been snookered?"

"Well, that's a problem, too. Linda said she'd see if she could break it to him. My guess is that he'll take it pretty hard. You could tell he really likes her," Jack replied.

"So what do we do now?"

"Well, we'll have to see how things fall out with Eddie and Cece when Linda lets Cece know she's onto her. She told me that's where she was going to start." He reached down and took a bite of his burrito, which was well on its way to growing cold. The others temporarily dropped the conversation to follow suit.

"I was really looking forward to going on a treasure hunt," Shaw said around a mouthful of food. "I've been reading about lost mines all my life, but I've never been on a treasure hunt"—he grinned—"where you go out looking with a map and letter."

"Well, Linda did say this," Collins added. "She thinks the letter was copied from an original, and that Cece, or someone, changed it."

"Why's that?"

"The language and the information in it point to an original source. Our Ms. Flowers doesn't know the Mojave, but the letter refers to out-of-the-way locations and descriptions of stuff that match what's really there. The map might be completely phony, but she thinks there's a letter behind the letter," Jack said, washing down some burrito with a swallow of beer.

"Well, we know the name of the town wasn't Red Mountain, so the original had to refer to someplace else. It wouldn't make sense to change the name of the town from Osdick to Red Mountain because then the directions would still work," Bill Jerome put in.

"That's right, Bill. There's not that many towns out here, so all we have to do is start running them down. Follow the directions from Cerro Gordo, Darwin, or Ballarat," Shaw grinned.

"Don't forget Skidoo," Collins added.

"Let's start with Darwin." Excitement crept into Shaw's voice.

"So how big an area are we talking about?" Jerome wondered aloud.

"Well, boys, I'd say we're down to two or three hundred square miles, give or take a foot or two." Collins grinned.

"Shit," Shaw said in disgust.

"Knowing where not to look saves a lot of looking, Ben." He smiled at his comrades. "We might stand a chance."

"What makes you think so, Jack?" Jerome's voice was laden with doubt.

"Like I said, we can narrow it down. A lot of places can be eliminated. Then we search for it systematically. It'll take time, and hell, boys, that's in our favor." The expression of bonhomie had returned to Collins's wide face. "There's nothing like gold fever to keep you going. Makes the impossible possible. Shaw's still hoping to find a woman who thinks he's good-looking."

"Screw you, Jack." Shaw was smiling in anticipation.

The wind had picked up and threatened to blow away their precious forged papers. They rose, cleaned up after themselves, and crossed the blacktop toward Ben Shaw's late-model Chevy truck.

"Maybe part of the map is true," Shaw said. "Maybe it was based on an original."

"Could be. We can check it out against the directions, once we find the right town." Collins laughed

"We could ask that geologist that's sweet on Linda, Kevin McGuire, about likely spots. He used to work the Carlin Trend over in Nevada for one of the big companies."

"Why bring him into it?" Shaw grumbled.

"Well, he's been calling the bar for Linda since he lent her his jeep. I thought he just wanted to apologize, but turns out he wanted to know where she found this." Collins drew a fist-sized piece of pinkish quartz from his jacket pocket and laid it on the table.

Jerome picked up the rock with long fingers and turned it in the sunlight. His thin lips puckered into a low whistle. "Where did she get it, Jack?"

"Where the jeep broke down." His smile broadened. "Somewhere north of Darwin, boys, up by the Talc Mine Road. That might be someplace that'd fit the letter."

The storm had not been kind to the billboard of Jesus blessing the travelers. The remaining arm raised in benediction had been swept away, leaving the disembodied Savior limbless and the words of scripture reduced to . . . RIVERS OF LIVING WATER. If they had thought about it, it made better sense now, but they were thinking about rivers of gold.

39

•

Dave Meecham had left a message asking Frank to stop by his office. When Meecham abandoned the phone for face time, it usually meant something was up. A week had passed since Parker had made his third escape, if you counted Frank's near miss in Bodfish. Since then, silence. Parker hadn't bothered to post Charlie Stuller's death on the MDG Web site. Frank wondered if killing Stuller had been too personal, his death being a matter of revenge rather than an object lesson. Frank speculated that Parker was off tracking down the targets on his hit list. He wanted to be done with it, have it be someone else's worry, like Novak and Ellis, ever eager to track down an intrepid terrorist and score points with the home office.

Even though their botched effort to trap the Sandman had failed to put Parker in the hands of the law, the physical action and the aftermath had left Frank little time for brooding. After the burro killings had resumed, he had become morose, drinking too much and thinking about what a sorry lot the naked apes were, with their constant chatter and violence.

His father had drunk himself to death, unable to deal with the grief of losing Frank's mother. Frank knew he was afraid of that, of becoming a cliché: drunken Irishman or drunken Indian, take your pick. When it came to drink, genetics wasn't on his side.

One of his dad's pals, trying to jar Frank's father out of his downward slide, had called him an alcoholic. Instead of placing a fist in his pal's nose, the usual solution for the elder Flynn, his father had smiled without humor. "Never call me an alcoholic again," he'd said in a flat tone. "Alcoholics shit their pants. I don't shit my pants. I'm a drunk," he'd added with a crooked grin. They had all laughed, but the fourteen-year-old Frank, who had witnessed the exchange from the cupola of their home in the caboose, was ashamed. He never told anyone about his dad's definition of an alcoholic. He kept painful memories safely inside, where they could gnaw at his innards without interference.

He'd picked Parker for sniper training because the kid was a natural with firearms and because of the killing of the cow. When Parker had become so upset at the brutal slaughter of the poor beast that tears streamed down his cheeks, he became a target for the bullies in the training platoon.

In a world where pity and weakness were synonyms, compassion was suspect. Frank couldn't fix it, but sending Parker to sniper training was an attempt to rectify Parker's vulnerability. Frank kept his own tears inside. Indians and Irishmen didn't cry. Because he had the stripes and the skills, Frank was exempt from ridicule. What Stuller and his kind saw as pathetic weakness in Parker, Frank recognized as a tender heart. Frank had played no small part in Parker's transformation from an innocent into a professional bringer of death. Frank had thought Parker needed something to keep the bullies at bay. Now Parker, the all-American boy with the Huck Finn grin, had turned professional killer: first for his country, then in revenge for all the cruelty and horror humanity perpetrated against the innocent.

Snipers had the equivalent of a black belt in marksmanship. They were respected because they were feared. They avoided capture at all costs because they were so hated that capture often meant torture. How sweet the human condition.

In Iraq, Parker's army buddies had dubbed him the Sandman because he took out more of the enemy than an infantry platoon. The gentle heart made deadly, shrinking and dying with each killing, until it had hardened into an alien husk. There was no going back. The innocent kid was gone. What remained of Parker was without future. *I am in so far in blood that sin will pluck on sin.* Frank laughed silently. Everything was Shakespearean, if you waited long enough.

He tapped gently on Dave Meecham's door.

"Take a seat." Meecham gestured vaguely at the battered chairs in front of his desk.

Frank sat. "What's up, Dave?"

"More Sand Canyon stuff. The opening is less than two weeks away. Their operations guy, Campbell, thinks you're the man," Meecham said, getting right to the point. "You did a good job with those people, Frank, and you know the reward for good work—more work, right?" Dave smiled. "For some unaccountable reason, both Marshall and Campbell called to say how much they like you, so you're the official liaison to Sand Canyon."

Frank straightened his shoulders. "Frank Flynn, ambassador without portfolio."

"Yeah, yeah. Thanks for not griping." Meecham ran a hand through sandy hair. "If you can make some time, drop in on Greg."

"Linda and I saw him yesterday. He's got the young volunteer nursing assistants hanging around his room. I think he likes being a wounded hero."

Meecham sighed. "It's better that you hear this from me. Parker's been busy again. No red herring this time. By the way, the San Bernardino Sheriff's Department broke up a big dogfighting ring. They're still digging up dog bodies. They found a large stash of dope as well—meth, pot, and crack, one-stop shopping. So Parker wasn't blowing smoke." Meecham paused, waiting for Frank to appreciate his joke. "Get it, wasn't blowing smoke."

Frank chuckled absently. "I guess I'm slow on the uptake today."

"Hell, it was wasted, and you know how often I think of shit like that." He shook his head. "In any case, I'd say you have a first-rate informant until the FBI catches up with him. He'll use law enforcement to take down the stuff in one place while he's taking out the people on his list. His list, wish we could see that," Meecham reflected. "Unfortunately, the owner of the dog pit wasn't on hand. Maybe Parker will find him before the San Bernardino sheriffs do." Meecham's smile was grim.

"Careful what you wish for, Dave," Frank said, his voice flat.

Meecham paused. "Yeah, I know, but when the assholes kill each other off, you can't help but think it's a win-win." Meecham shook his head in silent refutation. "Anyhow, looks like he's still working on his list. A couple of high school kids in Bakersfield had their mouths blown away with blasting caps. One of them didn't make it. The other one's pretty messed up from what I gather."

"They sure it's Parker?"

"Who else? Novak called from over in Oildale. That's just north of Bakersfield. He wanted to talk to you about your conversation with Parker and the cats he told you and Ms. Reyes about." Meecham caught Frank's eyes. "They haven't a hundred percent let go of blaming you—old army buddies, guilt by association."

Frank nodded. "I can't say as I blame them." Meecham was about to speak, but Frank cut him off. "Yeah, I know. How is it my fault? I've been asking myself the same thing. Anyhow, how did he find the teenagers?" Frank said.

"When they blew the heads off the cats a couple months back, they were dumb enough to make a video of it and post it on the Net, with them in it. Their faces weren't showing, but I guess there was enough in the tape to give Parker a line on them." Meecham shook his head. "They had to have their fifteen minutes of fame." He looked up, his face filled with disgust. "God only knows what they thought was there to be proud of."

"Anyhow, Novak thinks Parker's partner picked the kids up and drove them out to an oil field, where they met Parker. They duct-taped the blasting caps into their mouths. Wrapped their whole heads in tape, lit the fuses, and turned them lose, same as the boys did to the cats. It hasn't turned up on the MDG Web site yet. If and when it does, all hell will break loose." He shook his head. "To top it off, no one knows squat about his partner." He glanced at Frank. "Except for Ms. Reyes. It turns out she's the only one who's seen him."

"That may be true. I hope he doesn't come to the same conclusion," Frank said.

"Novak says with high school kids getting blown up, the FBI is really feeling the pressure, and they're frustrated as hell. Parker seems to be invisible, and like I said, they don't know squat about his partner. Give Novak a call, fill him in again, and then let it go. He's not our problem anymore." He raised a tired face. "Who needs it?"

Between the Border Patrol and the BLM, Dave had better than twenty-five years of service. He had remarried several years ago, and his wife loved to camp and travel. She had told Linda that she and Dave planned to buy a small motor home and go gypsying around the country for a couple of years before moving up to Bishop. Frank hated to think of Dave retiring. Dave was the best boss he'd ever had, and Dave was his friend.

"You think he'd take on something like Sand Canyon?" Meecham asked.

"Do you know something I don't?" Frank said.

"It seems like the kind of thing he might go after. An attack on Sand Canyon would make the news in a big way. What do you think? Could he pull it off?" Meecham said in a soft voice.

"Once he's in position, the terrain is perfect for a sniper. On the other hand, it would be suicidal. Withdrawal would be next to impossible. Water would be a problem if he went back into the mountains. Down in the valley, he'd be too exposed. With the Inyo County sheriff's office being so close, it's unlikely he could get out before they'd be all over him."

"From what you say, Sand Canyon is an armed camp," Meecham said.

"I think that part would be appealing to Parker—the most dangerous game, and all that—and the truth of it is, I think Sand Canyon security would be overmatched. Parker's the best of the best." Frank paused in thought. "Ewan Campbell might pose a challenge. He's trained, but I doubt if he's had to deal with snipers."

"A challenge, huh?" Dave studied the man he'd worked with for eight years.

"Parker would think of it that way," Frank responded.

"Sniper training's that good, huh?"

"Yup, that good."

"Give the Sand Canyon people a heads-up and share our concern with Novak when you talk with him. I'll talk with Dewey and spare your ear."

40

•

"The big man in the safari hat is Ewan Campbell." Parker and his protégé, John Gilman, lay on the crest of the western arm of Sand Canyon, overlooking the ranch house and parking area. "See him?"

"Yeah, I see him," Gilman said. "I can see his nose hairs." He was bent over a spotting scope.

Parker was using binoculars on a small tripod. "Remember, you'll be using the scope on the .50 with a limited field of vision, and things will be busy."

"I'll be able to recognize him, no problem."

"Good. If you see him, take him out before he takes you out."

"Why him?"

"He worked with a security firm in South Africa as a private contractor. Think of it as have gun, will travel."

"Soldier of fortune," Gilman murmured in a respectful tone.

"Killer without a country," Parker said under his breath. *Like us,* he thought. "That's right, they draw good pay for putting people down, all legal at taxpayer expense." Parker rolled away from his binoculars, making eye contact with his eager pupil. "So shoot him if you see him." He pushed on the right side of his head. The pain was constant now, barely under control. The medication hadn't taken effect yet. "When Campbell hears the .50, he'll come looking for you."

He waited for the pain to subside to a bearable level. If he made it through Saturday's operation, he would have to increase the dosage, even though it tended to screw up his vision. "We'll need to make sure the canyon is blocked first. Then there will be time for taking out individuals, but only if we optimize the tactical advantage." The pain was receding. "Lay it out, John. It's what we did in the field, over and over, so we didn't have to think about it or get confused when things went chaotic. They *will* go chaotic, so we need to control first events. Lay it out."

"You'll be up here where you can cover the back area and the sheds. I'll be on the other side, overlooking the front of the ranch house and covering the gate. At twelve o'clock, I start taking out vehicles."

"And?"

"I make sure the dead cars block the exit. Absolutely sure."

"Good." Parker nodded. "That's key. Then we wait a bit. After that, the parking lot, the grounds, blinds, everything becomes the killing field." The boyish features were hard. "You take the blinds and ranch house. Ranch house first. Drive them out into the rear parking area. The incendiary rounds should do their work. Then take the blinds. At this range the armor-piercing will bounce around inside those cement boxes like killer bees. If any of them make it out, I'll be waiting." He turned and scanned the area. It looked like Campbell was heading for a vehicle. Parker returned his attention to John Gilman. "Then what?"

"We leave. Twenty minutes after the first shot, we leave. I stash the .50, in the cache by the rocks. Ride the motorcycle back to the motor home by the bass ponds and go fishing."

Parker frowned. "What about the bike?"

"I dump it in one of the pockets near the old riverbed before I get to the motor home."

"Good. Don't forget. If you get checked out, and you probably will, the engine compartment of the motor home will be cold. The refrigerator is full of beer and food for a weekend. Everything will check out. A motorcycle with a hot engine is a giveaway." He smiled. "You'll be okay. You'll be hiding in plain sight. They miss that." Parker lifted pale red eyebrows. "So have I left anything out?"

John Gilman tapped his shirt pocket. "Be sure my fishing license is where it can be seen."

Parker smiled. "Bingo."

Gilman regarded his mentor. The headaches had been coming on harder and more often. He was worried. "You going to be okay hiking out?"

"One way or another." Parker grinned. Huck Finn was back. "Yeah, I think so. Sometimes moving around eases the headache. It's only a couple miles to my motorbike. Then I'm in the clear. Dirt track to the Westgard Pass road, then 395 to the Mount Whitney Fish Hatchery. I'll call you from the picnic area. Like before." He stared down at the ranch and outbuildings. "I'm going to give Sergeant Flynn a call, see if I can draw the BLM over to the Carrizo Plain. If they think civilians are in harm's way, they'll have to check it out, even if they suspect it's another false lead."

Parker returned the binoculars to their battered leather case. "If you don't hear from me by the following morning, go home." He raised his face. "Whatever happens, we keep the MDG going. I meant to get more done, more people with us. So it's going to rest with you, John." He smiled, the young-old face looking very tired.

41

•

Frank wondered how long the call light on his phone had been flashing. He'd turned the volume off months ago. He hated the sound of a ringing phone, always intrusive and usually a prelude to bad news. It pulsed away, insistently demanding his attention.

"Frank Flynn." He spoke softly.

"Good morning, Sergeant."

Frank didn't respond.

"No more Stuller, Sarge. Ding, dong, the prick is dead, in case you didn't know."

Frank remained silent.

"We played the cow game." Parker's voice vibrated with muted triumph. "He crawled and bellowed, and I shot at him. You kept yelling for it to stop—you were there in spirit—but you remember, everyone was deaf."

"What're you doing, Parker, trying to make things right? Forget it. You killed a couple of kids. That's murder, pure and simple. What happened to all the big ideas about protecting innocent creatures?"

"Nobody's innocent except the animals, Sergeant. As for Stuller, he killed the town pet in Bodfish. The townspeople consider me a hero, or will, when they know my name."

They were both silent.

"I don't believe in hell anymore, Sergeant, but I wish it existed because there are so many people who need to be there. So just in case we end up drifting in space like Laika, you remember Laika, the dog the Russians sent up to die in space, well, I gave Stuller a taste, you know, like purgatory. He begged like a baby. He mooed and bellowed almost as good as the cow. Maybe that's what I'll hear in my head at night instead of the cow."

"Did you ever talk to anyone at the VA about it?"

"About hearing the cow in my head? Come on, Sarge, how would that sound? I've got this movie in my head, keeps playing over and over, and who would give a shit—except maybe you? Down deep, you're as glad as I am that that son of a bitch Stuller is dead. I sent him to hell, and part of you is doing a little dance. Never mind denying it. You're a lot like me, Sarge. I don't know what plays in your head at night, but I bet you see it struggling to regain its feet and hear the hoots and shooting."

Frank didn't respond. He couldn't deny Parker's words, no matter how much he wanted to erase the memory.

"Now here's the reason I called, not that it's not good talking things over with you. When I was passing through Tehachapi on my way to visit our old army buddy, I found out there's going to be a hunt for junior license holders. Start 'em young so they can find their inner Cain. You know, a family that kills together stays together, family values and all that. Hey! There're Christian hunting clubs. Did you know that?" Parker chuckled in anticipation of his next witticism. "I wonder what Jesus packs? My guess is that he just points his finger and it's zappo-deado. Like father, like son. Anyhow, Team MDG is going to sort them out. Nits make lice, Sergeant. See ya." The line went dead before Frank had a chance to respond.

He slowly put the phone down, his mind turning over Parker's warning. Why would Parker pick an organized hunt for juveniles sponsored by Fish and Game? They were children, but Parker had slipped over the edge. He hadn't hesitated to maim the high school kids who had blown up the cats. They'd have to move on it. Maybe that was the point.

42

•

Frank carried two cups of coffee out to the rear platform of the caboose, where Linda sat wrapped in a blanket against the morning chill. She was not a morning person. Frank was irritatingly cheerful and awake in the mornings, full of conversation, wisecracks, even song. He had learned to soften this congeniality until Linda had fully emerged from the arms of Morpheus. "Arms of Morpheus" was the sort of thing that came to him in the mornings and the sort of thing that she found particularly irritating. This morning was different.

The afterimages of a dream haunted his waking hours.

In the dream he scrambled up a talus-strewn slope, fleeing from a creature he could not name. Even though he knew it, he had no name for it. His legs trembled with fatigue. The thing leapt behind him with fluid ease. Above him, Winnedumah watched impassively from his stone prison.

In the way of dreams, Frank watched both his struggling doppelgänger and the dark figure in effortless pursuit. He prayed, promising to attend mass with his mother every Sunday, anything that would save him from the relentless figure, but his voice was swept away by the wind. There was only emptiness, and the sunlight was filled with darkness and the utter stillness of the void. Then a soft wind brushed the land, and Coyote trotted along the ridge of the mountains. He turned yellow eyes on Frank; his tongue lolled out of his great mouth, and he laughed a laugh like a clap of thunder. Frank awoke to the sound of rain beating on the roof of the caboose.

The dream left him feeling hollow and fearful. Long ago, he had read Erich Fromm's *The Forgotten Language,* and it was as if he'd been given a key to his dreams, but the key to this dream remained hidden. Thinking of the thing that chased him, so animated and energetic as it leapt up the slope, made him shudder with revulsion, but when he tried to look at it, remember it in his mind's eye, he couldn't see its features to know what it was. It was a thing unnamed.

"No song in your heart this morning, Flynnman." Linda pulled the blanket around her shoulders.

"Bad dream."

"What kind of a bad dream?"

"It's all mixed up. It didn't make any sense."

"Great. I tell you about my dreams, and now you hold back."

"When did you tell me about your dreams?"

"Haven't had any lately, but I would if I had them." She sipped her coffee, keeping her eyes on Frank over the rim of the cup.

"Okay, I was being chased up in the Inyo Mountains by something—I'm not sure what—but I didn't want it to catch me." He paused, making sure he had eye contact. He didn't want her to laugh. "Winnedumah was watching from his stone prison, but he couldn't do anything."

"Being a three-hundred-foot rock doesn't help."

Frank frowned and went silent.

"Okay, okay. I was enjoying the tables being turned. Cheerful Linda, crabby Frank."

He turned to her, his face solemn. "I prayed, begging for help, but there was none. Then Coyote came, looked at me, and laughed.

That's when the thunder woke us." He didn't want to tell her about being alone in the void. He felt that if he talked about it, it would come and swallow him up, swallow Linda up, everything would be gone, and he would float endlessly in the darkness.

She took his hand in hers. It was cool and dry. "What's bothering you?"

"I'm not sure. Maybe you shouldn't come to Sand Canyon on Saturday. Parker called me in Ridgecrest yesterday afternoon. He said the MDG was going to go after the junior hunting license holders that Fish and Game sponsors. They take them through safety instruction, weapons management, that sort of thing. Then they take them on a hunt. There's one in the Carrizo Plains this weekend."

Linda nodded and waited for him to continue.

"Last time he gave us a warning, he said he was going to be in Barstow. Instead, he was over in Bodfish killing Stuller."

"What's your point, Frank?"

"What if this time it's another ruse, and he's over here killing people at Sand Canyon?"

"Have you told Dave what you think?"

"Yes, Dave and the Sand Canyon people. Dave smelled a red herring, too. I talked with Duane Marshall, and he sort of chuckled about it. He said something about his security staff was second to none, trained in South Africa. He said attacking Sand Canyon would be suicide."

"What did Ewan Campbell think?"

"He took it more seriously when I filled him in on Parker's background. He said he planned to put a couple of men with binoculars and rifles up on the release platforms. He told me some of the guests would have bodyguards, but he made a face. Bodyguards aren't combat trained. He said something about thick thugs in dark glasses."

"Are you going to be there, Frank?"

"You know I am."

"Remember what we said. Equal risks." She held up her hand. "Let me finish. You know how much research I've done? The Sand Canyon people are major assholes, and I'm dropping their drawers." She drew in a breath. "They checked me out, you know that?"

"How do you mean, checked you out?"

"They called the *Courier*. Said they wanted to make sure I worked there. Considered it a matter of security because there will be some important people at the opening, all that bull."

"I can believe it. Security is a very big thing for them."

"Yeah, well, surprise, Mr. Duane Marshall and company! I'm hoping for a twofer, the *Courier* and the *L.A. Times*. Let's see how he likes them apples." Linda's eyes flashed. She was ready to take on the powers that be.

"So why are they major assholes?"

"They buy these animals at auction in Africa and other places, but mainly in Africa. Try this. At last year's auction in KwaZulu-Natal, South Africa, animals were sold from live displays and a catalog, one thousand six hundred and fifty-one from the catalog. They sell everything from white rhinos and giraffes to zebras and warthogs. The auction netted almost two million dollars. More than twenty-two thousand for a white rhino, more than two thousand for a nyala."

"Nyala?"

"It's an antelope. It has those long spiral horns that look so great on the wall. Oh, and it's endangered."

"I don't get it. Two thousand to kill an endangered animal, the price of a television set." Frank's jaw muscles clenched. He thought about Marshall wanting to show him the zebras. "Marshall's operations manager, Ewan Campbell, told me some of the animals are tethered." He shook his head. "I could tell he didn't like it much."

"He's there, isn't he? He's taking Marshall's money. He sold out." She leveled an angry gaze at Frank. "I think they're cowards, yellow through and through."

"You don't cut people much slack, do you?" Frank said, thinking of himself.

"I'm still here in Limboland, aren't I?" Her face was serious.

"Does this mean you're not taking the job?" His spirits soared.

"No, it means I haven't made up my mind."

He wished he hadn't raised the subject. She marched into the future with a confidence he'd never possessed. The passage of time didn't bring about much he cared for. Keep it like it was, that was Ed Abbey's philosophy, and it seemed okay to him.

43

•

There was rebellion in the ranks at the Joshua Tree Athletic Club, and Jack Collins's leadership of the Grumpy Wrench Gang was in jeopardy.

"He's a cop. A good guy, but a cop. Jack keeps forgetting that." Ben Shaw tamped down a recently lit pipe, hot coals flying about.

"That's not the point, Ben. It's because he's a cop that Jack doesn't want to stir up trouble and bring it down on Frank," Bill Jerome offered. They were seated in the high-backed observer chairs that ran along the far wall of the Joshua Tree Athletic Club. Morning light filtered in through elevated windows above them, filling the room with a delicate luminescence.

"Have it your way, Bill, but Jack's backed off, backed off so far we've been sitting on our hands. Hunting for gold mines we can't find is great stuff, but hunting for the people who crap on the land is righteous." Shaw tilted his head up at an unyielding angle of self-affirmation.

"Righteous? Righteous? When did you get religion?" Jerome laughed in mockery.

Shaw's expression broke into a grin. "Sounds good, though." He was clearly unashamed by Bill Jerome's unmasking. "Besides, it needs doing. Who's to do it, if we don't?'

"Jack gave Frank his word," Jerome said with finality, staring ahead.

"Okay, Bill, that's fine for Jack. Did you give *your* word?" Shaw raised his hand and pointed a couple of fingers at Jerome. "Just wait a minute." His voice had taken on an edge. "What makes Jack think he can give someone my word or yours?" Shaw shook has head, the pipe distributing hot ashes onto his shirt.

Bill Jerome remained silent. They were clearing the moral decks.

"Yeah, what I thought," Shaw said. "He can keep his word, just like the rest of us do, but that doesn't mean Jack speaks for you or me, that we have to abide by the promises he gives out in our name. Well, does it?"

Jerome stared at the sole snooker table in the room, the balls laid out on the spots, the pink ball in front of a three-ball short rack. It was ten in the morning, two hours before the doors opened. The mornings were theirs. Serious snooker and quiet conversation.

"Your break," Jerome said.

Shaw got to his feet, placed the cue ball next to the two-ball on the balk line, and bent over his cue stick, aiming for the outer edge of the red ball on the right side of the three-ball cluster of reds. Jerome watched as Shaw squinted through the smoke and then stroked the cue ball at medium speed. The cue ball struck the outer edge of the red, angled off to the bottom rail, came back on the side rail, struck the rear rail, and rolled softly forward to snuggle up behind the four-ball. Jerome was snookered.

Jerome's chiseled features darkened as he studied the table. "Okay," he said, "but Jack's not going to like it."

"He'll get over it, right?" Shaw was without remorse.

"True, Jack doesn't hold grudges, but I don't like going against him without letting him know. And I can't say as I know what Frank will do. He'll be between a rock and a hard place."

"We tell Jack, and he vetoes it. If it's after the fact, Jack's in the clear. As for Frank, he hates these assholes as much as we do. He just can't do anything about it. He's the man with the rules. That's never been our problem."

Shaw grinned, even teeth bared through the gray beard. "Can't you see it? Cars all lined up on the Circle Cross ranch road. Rich guys out there getting their camos all dusty trying to change tires. No auto club to help them out. Awww! The car fell off the jack. Awww! Took out the spare to make room for my sports goodies. Awww! Frank'd do the same thing if he wasn't a cop."

Jerome's eyes traveled about looking for a place to rest. Shaw had him. The image of the Sand Canyon crowd stacked up along a dirt road with flat tires on the day of the big opening was too appealing to pass up. He nodded in assent.

"Let's get the Injun," Shaw said.

"Jesus, Ben. Quit calling Eddie the Injun."

"Right! Let's get our red brother, Eddie Redhawk Laguna, the red man's friend, the white man's nightmare."

Jerome shook his head, but he was smiling. "Eddie might go for it. Get back at the rich white-eyes."

"Might? Hell, he'll strip to a breechclout and paint himself for war." Shaw assumed a crafty look. "Besides, he has a legitimate beef with canned hunting. He's descended from a warrior race that hunted with the wolves."

"What's this noble savage stuff you're spouting? I've heard you refer to Eddie as a digger—not to his face, I might add."

"Didn't want to hurt his feelings." Shaw's wolfish smile broadened. "Besides, this isn't about cowboys and Indians, it's about shitheads and good guys. Eddie's one of the good guys. You could say we're a rainbow coalition, a white guy"—he gestured toward Jerome—"an Indin, and a man with a tender conscience." He placed a large hand on his heart. The Joshua Tree Athletic Club rattled with their laughter.

44

•

Frank and Linda attended the early brunch for special members and the politically powerful who supported hunting and gun lobbies. Duane Marshall had signed Frank's invitation with a fountain pen and a flourish. It had been Frank's intention to skip the brunch and stick with the opening festivities in the afternoon, if you wanted to call the slaughter of cage-fed birds festive, but Linda had jumped at the opportunity to mix with the movers and shakers who pulled so many of the state's strings, especially in the rural counties of the eastern Sierra Nevada and the desert country dominated by mining interests.

"You will not skip it, even if I have to cut my hair, wear your uniform, and learn to spit."

"I don't spit much," he'd said.

"Metaphorically spit."

"Wait a minute, I can get you a real spitter. Old Tucker can hock a loogie that can crawl on its own, make turns, and travel up hill." He cracked a happy smile. "It's a wonder to behold."

"See, you've made my point. Spitting and butt humor are male provinces. I have opted for spitting. I won't have to, though, because you—*we*—are going to the brunch, where *we* will rub elbows with Darth Vader's minions, and I will be the proverbial fly on the wall."

"That'll be the day," he said.

So they had gone. There were about fifty people, Frank estimated. They were dressed in various hunting togs from Carhartt to Orvis. Frank sat next to a man who introduced himself as "Roger Whitfield, Whitfield Development, San Bernardino." Whitfield revealed that he bought all his gear at the Black Bird in Medford, Oregon, "one of the only *real* hunting and fishing stores left in the West." Frank had seen the store on a trip to the BLM offices in Medford, the largest gathering of BLM personnel west of the Mississippi.

The Black Bird was fronted by a two-story cement and papier-mâché bird that towered over the parking lot, fascinatingly obscene in its crudity. The creature looked like a cross between King Kong and a crow on steroids; huge armlike wings dangled from shoulders knotted with bulging muscles. Three fingerlike appendages curled upward into grasping claws. A genetic monstrosity devised to attract attention and alert the curious.

Originally a war surplus store, the Black Bird came to sell almost anything to do with outdoor activities, especially hunting. Y2K had been a banner year for the grotesque bird. The Apocalypse Now crowd stocked up on generators, woodstoves, canned goods, and especially guns and ammo to hold off their former neighbors soon to be transformed by computer failures into roving hordes of flesh-eating monsters. Frank could never quite figure out this connection, but many folks assured him it was there. Some of the citizenry went so far as to devise fortifications, but these folks tended to belong to the end times wackos, who predicted the arrival of the Antichrist at the drop of a computer chip.

The brunch layout was sumptuous and exotic: elk, buffalo, ostrich, alligator, sage hen, stuffed quail, and a roasted suckling pig as the centerpiece. The pig stared accusingly at Linda with cooked eyes and a decidedly unhappy expression. Linda tried to ignore it. Frank was hungry, and the piglet was already quite dead, so he helped himself. He loved roast pork.

On his father's side, Frank had grown up with such delicacies as stuffed heart, liver and onions, and corned beef. On his mother's side were fry bread, menudo (tripe stew), chicharrones (fried pork rinds), sheep's head, mutton in many forms, and unidentified meats in various red and green chili sauces. His memories were filled with the savory smells of garlic, cumin, chili, and oregano.

Linda found most of it repulsive, especially menudo. It remained one of Frank's favorite hangover cures. He had a T-shirt emblazoned with MENUDO! BREAKFAST OF CHAMPIONS, with a particularly politically incorrect cartoon of a Mexican bandido wearing crossed ammunition belts, grinning in predatory fashion, and waving a spoon. As he filled his plate, Linda gave him a disgusted look. He ignored it. Eat their food, drink their drink, listen to their talk, and go home ahead of the game. That was the plan, and he was riding for the brand.

On his right, Whitfield was explaining what a great place the Black Bird was when his monologue was interrupted by Duane Marshall's introduction of the Reverend Philip William Hardy, pastor of Holy Mount Church in North Hollywood. The Reverend Hardy rose and cleared his throat. He had none of the TV preacher about him. He was dressed in spotless khakis, with a light blue ascot tucked into the collar of a tailored safari jacket, a lesson in sartorial endeavor for aspiring pastors to the stars, Frank reflected.

Hardy's benediction was short and reaffirmed man's dominion over "all the beasts of the earth and all the birds of the air, upon every creature that moves along the ground, and upon all the fish of the sea; they are given into your hands. Everything that lives and moves will be food for you. Just as I gave you the green plants, now I give you everything." His words were definitely shooter's sentiments. Frank noted that he left out the part about "The fear and dread of you will fall upon all the beasts of the earth and all the birds of the air." The Reverend Hardy could cherry-pick with the best of them; another apostle from the Church of Selective Scripture, Frank reflected.

Following the brief benediction, Duane Marshall rose to address his guests, as they were contentedly tucking away peach cobbler topped with vanilla ice cream.

"I am not going to speak about the wonderful facilities here at Sand Canyon Game Reserve or our efforts to provide our members with only the best." He let his eyes pass over the audience in affirmation of his words. "During the course of your visit, I think Sand Canyon will speak for itself."

"Instead, I am going to introduce you to Harlan Combes, who you all know as a tireless warrior against those who would deprive Americans of their right to bear arms." Here he was interrupted by applause. He raised his voice. "Harlan and his lovely wife, Cynthia, are our guests of honor on this special day." There followed more enthusiastic applause as an elegantly beautiful woman in a muted camouflage shirt and khaki shorts rose two seats away from Marshall. She stood protectively beside her husband, her left hand resting on the back of his wheelchair. Harlan Combes sat slumped against the padded back, inert except for hooded eyes that seemed to take in the room at a glance.

"Isn't that—" Frank began

"The former assistant secretary of the interior," Linda finished under her breath. "Dysart and Combes Technologies."

"You all know Harlan Combes as one of our country's true patriots and a great American. As a consummate sportsman, Harlan is one of the principal record holders in North America." More applause from the guests interrupted the smiling Marshall. "Perhaps you may not all be aware that Cynthia Combes is a hunter par excellence in her own right. She has completed the Big Five and the Grand Slam, and her name is in both the Boone and Crockett and the Safari Club record books—many times." He paused for effect, looking at his guests gathered around in the dining area, waiting until the last clink of fork and spoon on china faded into silence.

Marshall continued in hushed tones. "I believe that most of you in this room know that Harlan suffered a tragic automobile accident in 2004, an accident that put an end to the pursuit of the sport Harlan loves most, the hunt." He turned to the figure in the wheelchair. Harlan Combes's eyes burned in features smooth and dead as melted wax. Marshall lifted his ruddy face to the audience. "As you see, Harlan is restricted to a wheelchair. I don't think he'll mind me telling you that he is a quadriplegic, unable to complete tasks you and I take for granted, much less handle a high-powered firearm. Even so, with the aid of God and a loving and devoted wife, Harlan soldiers on, steadfast, determined, and—very brave." Murmurs of approval and admiration for Harlan Combes's bravery swept the room like a soft breeze.

"Now, I have something very special to share with you, something of which we can all be proud. Here at Sand Canyon we, which includes all of you who support our right to hunt, our right to bear arms, have made it possible for Harlan to rejoin our band of hunting brothers." The brotherhood rose to their feet as one, wildly applauding Marshall's remarks.

As the luncheon guests came to their feet, Ewan Campbell slipped quietly from the room. Cynthia Combes stepped back, and Harlan Combes's wheelchair glided toward a computer station at the far end of the dining hall, his back to the gathering. From where Frank and Linda sat, they could see Combes from an angle that permitted them a side view of Combes and the computer station.

"May I call your attention to the television screen above me?" Marshall gestured to a large-screen monitor that filled with the Sand Canyon logo, a blue circle within a red circle. The white inner space contained an animation of a running deer. Crosshairs appeared dividing the smaller space neatly in quarters, centering on the running stag. The stag stopped and turned its antlered head toward the scope as a bullet emerged into view at the bottom of the screen and tracked toward the stag, striking it behind the shoulder. The stag crumpled to the ground, its image faded into the words CLEAN SHOT, CLEAN KILL. Surrounding the circular banner were the words SAND CANYON—YOUR HOME ON THE RANGE. "We're still working on the sound track." Marshall beamed at his audience. "And we're open to suggestions."

A lens-eye view of the hunting area in front of the blinds replaced the animated logo. An ATV trailing a cage emerged into view from the left side of the screen with Ewan Campbell at the wheel. Campbell brought the ATV to a stop in the center of the picture, dismounted, and moved back to the trailer and looked into the cage.

The guests sat in rapt attention watching the scene unfold. Frank couldn't make out the animal. Whatever it was, it wasn't on its feet, so it was hard to identify. Campbell thrust some sort of stick into the cage, and the animal—now Frank could see it was a mountain lion—came to its feet and slapped the stick out of Campbell's hand. Campbell turned to the camera and gave a thumbs-up and retreated from the picture. The cage gate lifted up, and the lion cautiously advanced to the opening.

The blatting sound of a horn coming from the ATV penetrated the hush of the gathering. The horn noise encouraged the animal to leave the cage. The large cat staggered forward and fell to the ground but managed to regain its feet.

"What's the matter with it?" Linda whispered.

"It's been tranquilized," Frank said. His face filled with disgust and anger.

He watched as Cynthia Combes inserted a wand into her husband's mouth so he could operate the computer.

"The honors of first blood go to Harlan Combes," Marshall boomed.

The guests watched the television screen in rapt silence, punctuated by the distant horn. The crosshairs tracked the target in spasmodic movements. They waited while Combes fumbled at the keyboard, his head bobbing up and down, sometimes missing, sometimes hitting the wrong keys. Then the crosshairs centered on the mountain lion's body. Combes bent his head forward and thrust his face downward. The lion sprang into the air and landed on its side, struggled to its feet, and lunged forward trailing intestines. Its efforts to escape were checked by a restraint not visible to the observers.

It stayed on its feet, snarling in confusion. The crosshairs made a slow and clumsy progress across the screen and momentarily rested on the animal's hindquarters. Combes again jabbed at the computer keyboard, and for a second time the mountain lion spun about. Then it lay on its side, panting from pain and exertion. Combes's head bobbed up and down, poking at the keyboard in an impotent effort to end the lion's suffering. Finally a blossom of blood exploded from the side of the cat's neck, followed by the sound of a muffled shot. Ewan Campbell had fulfilled his function.

Cloud shadow undulated across the room in the thickening silence broken only by the muted sound of the distant horn. Then Duane Marshall began to clap. An explosion of applause filled the room with relief, drowning out the witness of their collective shame.

"That was sickening," Linda murmured.

45

•

The sound of shots gave John Gilman an unwelcome jolt. He hadn't finished preparing his shooting setup. The blind was ready, but the M107 .50 wasn't in position, and he was still in a T-shirt. The padded jacket and ear protectors were in his pack. He glanced at his watch. Not yet noon. Seth had said the bird shooting wasn't scheduled until one in the afternoon. Why had they started so early? He trained his binoculars on the far field in front of the blinds. Someone on an ATV was raising dust headed out to a cage on wheels, or on a trailer. He watched as the man dragged something dead back to the cage and lifted it up onto the platform.

He shifted his attention to the gatehouse. There were three vehicles lined up. The driver of the first vehicle and the gate guard were arguing. He was supposed to start by blocking the exit at the gate. The driver got out of the truck and pointed back at the vehicles behind him. Gilman reasoned he would never have a better opportunity to block the road. That's what he was supposed to do, block the road when the shooting started. The truck was barring the entrance at the gate. Obviously the guard wouldn't let the truck in, and there was no way the driver could back up. It was a perfect setup.

Gilman scrambled down into the blind, lifted the heavy sniper rifle from its case, and pushed the front bipod into place, wiggling the spiked feet into the dirt behind the sandbag. He picked up a full magazine, shoved it in, and settled in place. He trained the .50 caliber rifle on the hood of the truck, a late-model Chevy with an extended cab. Then, he remembered the ear protectors and the padded jacket. The damn .50 kicked like a mule, and it was loud, especially with the muzzle brake. He pulled his equipment from the pack, donned the jacket, and adjusted the Slim-Line ear protectors on his head so he could wear his cap. Then he repositioned himself.

The guard and the driver, an old geezer, were still arguing. He set the scope for four hundred yards, centered the mil-dot reticle on the hood, and squeezed. The blast made him flinch, but not before the round went off. The guard and the driver had both crouched down and were looking back at the hillside. His watch said 12:00—high noon. He liked that. Then the driver jumped back into the truck with surprising agility. John squeezed off another round into the driver's side of the cab, puncturing a hole midway down the door. The geezer stayed put. He fired into the engine compartment a couple more times, just to be sure. His heart pounded with excitement.

Two sleek SUVs stacked in behind the truck had begun frantically trying to turn around, but they were too jammed up to maneuver. Unaware of what was going on, more vehicles had lined up behind them, honking their horns.

John turned his attention to the vehicle behind the truck, slamming three rounds into the engine compartment. It stopped moving. The third vehicle, a Lincoln Navigator, had managed to get into a sideways position, blocking the exit lane. He put two rounds through the windshield, then followed with another through the grille. He changed magazines—ready to rock and roll. Seth would be pleased. Cool under fire. It didn't occur to him that he was the only one doing the firing.

Where the hell was Seth? Gilman scanned the grounds. Far below him, an ATV raced across the open space next to the parking area, probably someone from security heading for the gate. He looked again. It was the security chief, the one he'd been warned about. He scrambled around trying to line up the .50 on the ATV, but it was moving too fast. Out of the corner of his eye, he noticed someone trotting toward the low hills on the left that extended back into the Inyos. The ATV disappeared under the shoulder of the hill. He lifted the binoculars for a closer look at the man on foot. It looked like Seth's old sergeant. He wondered if Seth knew that he was here. Too bad he couldn't take him out, but that was Seth's personal business. Then the former sergeant disappeared into a ravine where John couldn't see him anymore.

He knew that Seth was waiting for him to drive the people from the ranch house. It was 12:04, only sixteen minutes left. He replaced the full magazine of armor-piercing with a new magazine of incendiaries. Burn 'em out and cut 'em down. He began shooting rounds through the ranch windows. *Won't be long now,* he thought. He had never been so exhilarated and filled with such purpose in his life.

•

Seth Parker had watched the South African on the ATV trailing the cage make his way into the clearing in front of the blinds with professional curiosity. Thus he wasn't taken by surprise when shots echoed up from the floor of Sand Canyon. Dealing with the unexpected was central to his combat experience and training. By the time the shooting had ceased and one of the staff had returned to retrieve the kill—he judged it to be a mountain lion—he was fully prepared, tucked under a canvas blind. He set the scope for three hundred yards. With 130-grain rounds, there would be an additional twelve-inch drop at four hundred yards, and he could compensate for that using the mil-dot reticle without having to take time to make additional adjustments.

When Parker heard the .50 boom, he checked his watch—12:03. John had started at the gatehouse. The ATV and trailer disappeared into the barn as John crippled vehicles at the entrance to the canyon. When the first rounds smashed into the ranch house, Seth breathed deeply, emptying his mind of distractions, and waited.

46

•

The guests had begun to leave their places, milling about in search of friends and conversation. Many were clustered about Cynthia and Harlan Combes to offer their congratulations and listen to Cynthia explain the intricacies of the computer shooting system that enabled her husband, like the mythic Zeus, to strike from afar.

Frank could no longer see Harlan Combes, but he caught glimpses of the lovely Cynthia through the throng. He found it disquieting that the blond Texas beauty was such an avid trophy hunter. It was sexist, he supposed, but he didn't like it just the same. It went against the grain. He'd have to talk to Linda about it. Get her take on a woman's right to be violent. He was pretty sure she'd have an opinion on it.

He nodded in Cynthia Combes's direction. "She's killed more animals than most of the men in this room." He paused. "And that's saying something."

"What's it saying?" Linda curled her lip. "That she's acquired blood lust, has balls? Perhaps she can outspit Tucker. Fart and tell coarse jokes." She sighed. "If that were the end of it, more power to her, but killing for trophies is sick. It's like compulsive seduction, a constant need for masculine affirmation, and that's a sad pass for women's rights, don't you think?" Her smooth forehead creased slightly, giving her a feline expression. "At least, that's how I see it."

Frank thought about the types of people he'd seen hanging around gun stores, full of self-aggrandizing stories of prowess and slaughter. They were mostly pathetic, dressed for some sort of costume party, like the people here at the brunch. Only these people had the money for the right costumes and equipment.

"Yeah, maybe so," he said.

They were the last couple still seated. The noise level in the room was such that none of the guests paid attention to the distant crack and boom of the .50 caliber, except Frank. It was a familiar voice speaking out of the past. Ewan Campbell heard it as well. He lifted his head and then moved rapidly toward the kitchen area, which had a rear exit facing the outbuildings.

Frank rose to the sound of another shot, followed by two more in rapid succession.

"Where are you going?" Linda asked.

There was a shift in the conversation signaled by a sudden lowering of tone. Some of the others had noticed the sound of the shooting.

"Parker's back," Frank said, keeping his voice down. "Whatever you do, don't expose yourself. He won't be giving anyone a free pass." He laid his hand on Linda's arm. "Stay here, and don't go outside." He turned and made his way through the throng and followed Campbell's path into the kitchen.

The luncheon guests crowded around the windows overlooking the shooting blinds and field and stared toward the gatehouse. Something was going on, but they couldn't see what it was through the clouds of dust. The bleating sound of distant car horns filtered into the sudden stillness of the room.

The first shot through the dinning room window struck Roger Whitfield in the pelvis, flinging him violently to the floor. Bright blood flooded through his pants, pooling on the carefully polished wood. Whitfield seemed confused, not yet aware of what had occurred. A few minutes later he lost consciousness; his eyes glazed, and he ceased to breathe. Few were aware he was dead.

One of the men standing over his prostrate body watched as the blood spread in a widening pool. When it reached the tips of his shoes, he began to chant, "Jesus Christ! Jesus Christ! Jesus Christ!" in rising tones. People stared, but no one moved. Most of them had yet to realize what was taking place. When the second shot smashed through the window and ripped up flooring, the milling guests suddenly realized it was dangerous to be standing by the windows. They surged into the adjoining clubroom, pushing and shoving to get as far away from the dining area as possible. They wedged themselves against the far wall by the fireplace, gathering under the baleful gaze of glass eyes staring down from the dead creatures adorning the walls.

Now the shots followed in rhythmic succession, smashing through the windows and into the far wall. Some lodged in the log understructure; others buried themselves in the heavy timbers supporting the roof. They burned in the wood with a bright intensity, suffusing the gray smoke with a blue-white luminescence. Linda irrationally thought about how beautiful it was. The room filled with the acrid smell of hot metal mixed with the pungency of burning pine.

Duane Marshall stepped forward, raising his hands, and begged for their attention. "Please be calm. If we remain calm, we will be safe. Make your way into the kitchen, and one of the staff will lead you to the machine shop and the equipment sheds. These are metal buildings. I repeat, you'll be safe."

"What about that bastard who's shooting at us?" someone said.

"Good question. He's out front. He can't cover the front and the sheds in the back. And let me tell you this. He's a dead man. Our security chief and his men are already looking for him. Now, I'd like four or five volunteers to help our security staff hunt him down and take him out. We can use the hunting rifles from the gun case against the wall. We have ammunition in the tack shed by the corrals. The rest of you please follow Archie, over there." Marshall pointed to a stringy blond man in staff garb, who raised his hand.

"I'll be along in a minute." Marshall reached into the cabinet and removed a .458 Winchester Magnum, a custom-made Holland and Holland double-barrel rifle, handcrafted in London. He'd paid eighty thousand dollars for it. It was a work of art as well as a heavy-caliber hunting rifle. Unfortunately, Marshall failed to recognize that it was the wrong weapon for the task at hand. It had enormous power, meant for elephant and rhino, but the heavy bullet had a drop of close to five feet at four hundred yards. Beyond that range, it was next to useless, but the feel of it in his hands gave him misplaced confidence. The things he killed didn't shoot back.

The hastily assembled antisniper squad traipsed through the kitchen in orderly fashion. For a moment, the booming of the rifle fire had stopped. Marshall and his squad of empty weapons went out through the kitchen door and trotted toward the corrals to retrieve some ammunition.

The rest of the group crowded around Archie, who was explaining that, for safety's sake, they were to space their exits, leaving at least three yards between them. Then the heavy booming of the large weapon resumed. At that point, some of the members jammed through the doorway, drowning out Archie's call for order. "Stand back!" he shouted. "Stand back and let Mr. Combes get through, for God's sake." They stood back shamefaced, making room for Combes and his wife. Smoke drifted into the kitchen from the dining area.

Cynthia Combes led her husband to the raised threshold at the kitchen door. "I need some help here, please." Her voice was sharp but calm. Archie and three or four others stepped forward to assist Harlan Combes over the threshold onto the open cement porch and then down the two shallow steps to the ground. Combes's wheelchair was battery powered and weighed in excess of two hundred pounds; the inert form of Harlan Combes added at least another hundred and seventy. It would require two of them to get Combes through the door and down the steps, one pushing and one pulling and guiding the front wheels.

Combes anticipated their efforts and put the chair into motion before they were ready. One of the front wheels cleared the threshold, but the other went sideways, jamming the metal chair in the doorway. Combes kept pushing on the toggle switch, wedging it tighter into the door frame. Archie climbed over Combes, who swore softly under his breath. Now they would have two of them to lift the chair from the front and free the other forward wheel.

The first person in the group that had rushed out the door ahead of Combes suddenly crumpled to the ground as he reached the machine shop. This was followed by the distant sound of a discharging firearm. When the second man toppled to one side, blood splattering from his head, the rest panicked, breaking into two groups. Several ran forward toward the metal sheds. Archie shouted at them that he had the keys, but his words were drowned out in the confusion. The remainder turned back and ran for the kitchen door, where Combes and his chair blocked the way. Half a dozen guests had reached the nearest shed and began frantically pulling and banging on the corrugated iron door. Two of them went down almost simultaneously. A third fell, regained his feet, ran toward the ranch house for twenty feet, and was suddenly propelled face forward onto the ground and lay motionless, the back of his head blown away.

The others had reached the kitchen door and were attempting to climb over Harlan Combes to regain the temporary protection of the kitchen. Those trapped on the inside, which was rapidly filling with smoke, pushed in the opposite direction. Then one of the outside people flopped forward in Combes's lap. Gouts of blood and brain matter flew into the people struggling to get out. Those stranded on the open cement began screaming and swearing at Combes to get out of the way.

"Stop it, or we'll all die right here. Stop it!" Linda shouted, somehow making her voice heard. She caught Archie's eye over Combes and the body of the dead man lying in his lap. "Back them off. We'll have to pull the chair back and try again." She turned to two of the men standing near her, one large, young, and oafish, the other fortyish and fit. "Grab the chair," Linda ordered.

"Here, at the handles." Cynthia Combes indicated the rear handholds.

"We have to straighten it. You push forward," Linda said to the older man. "You pull backward and to the side," she said to the younger one, who seemed relieved that someone had taken charge. The older man gave Linda a hard look but did as she asked. The chair straightened in the opening, and they yanked it back into the kitchen, Harlan Combes's head bouncing about on still shoulders. As soon as the doorway was clear, the remainder of the group in the kitchen, including the older man who had helped free Combes, jammed through the door and ran at the locked sheds. Anything to keep from burning to death.

"I better go. I've got the keys." Archie looked at the two women and the younger man, who had helped Linda and Cynthia Combes with the chair.

"Go!" Linda nodded.

Archie sprinted through the doorway and into clean air and raced for the shed.

"Come on, if we do it right, it should be a piece of cake." Linda grinned at the young man, who smiled back. The two women positioned themselves at the back of Combes's chair. Their male counterpart stepped through the doorway and turned his back to the invisible shooter.

He may be short on brains, but he's long on courage, Linda thought.

Cynthia Combes bent over her husband. "Ease up to the sill, Harlan."

"Then hit the power on the count of three," Linda added.

Combes was coughing in the smoke. Tears ran down Linda's cheeks, blurring her vision. They would have to hurry. She could hear the fire behind them now. There was a crashing sound, and a blast of cool air swept into the kitchen through the open door. The dining room window must have gone and reversed the draft. Then she felt an explosion of heat as the fire roared to new life.

"Okay, here we go. One. Two. Three."

47

•

Seth Parker watched the struggle at the kitchen door with rising disgust. He knew the man in the wheelchair was Harlan Combes, NRA advocate, mover, shaker, and big game hunter. Right to own fully automatic weapons? Combes was for it. Fifty-caliber sniper rifles? Absolutely. Armor-piercing ammo and incendiary ammunition? Why not? How do you like the results, Mr. Secretary? He put the reticle on the doorway and waited for Combes to emerge.

Why not let him live? Parker thought. Killing Combes would be a mercy killing. Mercy killing wasn't his mission. Let him rot. Parker rested his head against his forearm, the headache insistent, just barely under control. Soon, it would be a favor if someone put him down before the pain drove him to do it himself. He had worked that out, too.

He watched listlessly as the hunt club members clustered around the machine shop door. They banged at the hasp and lock with a rock that kept disintegrating into smaller pieces. He caught the rock wielder in the reticle and squeezed, placing the round in his temple. Blood spattered against the corrugated iron door as the man slammed into the building and slid to the ground.

One of the staff members dressed in khaki came running toward them. He centered the sight on him, then hesitated. This one had courage. He'd been helping the women at the door with

Combes. He could choose who lived and who didn't. *So I choose him. How odd,* he thought. *The man has no idea I just saved his life.* He glanced at his watch. Four minutes to withdrawal. He felt oddly detached, as if none of it mattered. Perhaps it didn't.

Sand flew up into his face, and a piece of gravel pinged into his glasses from the impact of a large-caliber round that struck the rocky slope a couple of feet below him. How about that! Someone had found him. Good. There would be some challenge after all.

He searched the grounds and sheds, then the corral area. The window of the tack shed was partway up. It hadn't been before. He adjusted the scope for five hundred yards, shifted his body two yards to his left, and rested the .270 on one of the sandbags he had filled and placed when they had reconnoitered the area earlier in the week. He reached into his pocket and removed a small mirror. He angled the mirror at the sun, guided a sunspot onto the side of the tack room, and wedged the mirror in place near his previous position. He waited less than a minute for the muzzle flash. Low again. The shooter had failed to track his first shot. He put his sight just below the windowsill and fired. He worked the bolt smoothly without spoiling his sight picture and fired again. He waited. No return fire. Target neutralized and no one to report to. Okay. Good shooting, Seth. "Thank you, Sergeant," he whispered under his breath. He checked his watch again. A minute past disengagement.

He returned his attention to the ranch house. Flames were pouring from under the eaves. Seven bodies lay motionless in the early afternoon sun. " 'The Angel of Death spread his wings on the blast, / And breathed in the face of the foe as he passed,' " he murmured to himself.

Harlan Combes's wheelchair lay on its side near the edge of the steps. Parker watched as the two women who had freed Combes from the doorway dragged him toward the machine shop. He'd have to put them in for the Silver Star, and the foot soldier and the big kid who'd helped them for the Bronze Star. The rest would get the dead yellow bird. He drew back from the edge of his blind and scrambled down the hill until he hit the faint trail that would take him back to his dirt bike. He was terribly tired, and he needed to check on John.

48

•

Frank waited for the .50 to fire again. The shooter had to be somewhere along the ridge across the canyon from the ranch house, probably near the summit overlooking the floor of the canyon. His BLM vehicle with the AR-15 and the twelve-gauge pump was parked in front of the ranch house in the line of fire. Trying to approach it would be suicidal. He would be facing the shooter armed with a handgun, but it wasn't a complete disadvantage, since the big .50 caliber sniper rifle was next to useless at close quarters. That meant stealth was essential.

An ATV roared into sight from behind the ranch house. Ewan Campbell was hell-bent for the far side of the canyon, on his way to silence the sniper with the .50. Now was the time for him to make his move. He began trotting across the open area, away from the vehicles, exposed but unnoticed—he hoped. His skin prickled in anticipation of the shot that would end his life. He needed to get past the fear and clear his mind for what was coming. He had to get close enough to the shooter for the handgun to be an advantage rather than a handicap.

To his right, he heard the report of a rifle. Someone had taken up a position in one of the shooting blinds. The .50 boomed in reply. Several shots crackled in response. Campbell's security people had forted up and were returning fire. Frank headed for the low saddle between the high ridgeline and the crest of the hill over-looking Sand Canyon. The best approach would be to cross over the ridge out of the immediate line of fire and work along the back-side, staying under the shoulder of the hill. From the direction Campbell had been heading, there was a chance they could catch the shooter in a crossfire. He wished they were in communication. He was pretty sure Campbell was unaware that he was coming up the northwest slope.

If the shooter was Parker, Frank knew that he wouldn't con-sider his position as having a front line. Snipers frequently worked inside enemy lines. They were trained to think that the enemy would approach from any and all directions. No safe zone. On the other hand, Parker had his hands full, Parker or his pal, whoever was on the .50. Where was the other guy? As far as Frank could tell, there appeared to be only one shooter. If he could get within fifty feet, Frank figured he had a better than even chance.

He reached the base of the slope, checked the terrain, and readied himself to move on the shooter. He didn't have a ghillie suit, the special camouflage clothing that made snipers all but invisible, but he was wearing khakis in a country of tans and grays. He placed his Stetson carefully on its crown in the lee of a clump of sage and weighted it down with a fist-sized rock. The hat was a 10X Stetson, a gift from Linda, and he planned on coming back for it. He put his yellow shooting glasses in his shirt pocket and picked up handfuls of loose dirt, tossing dirt and dust into the air and letting it rain down on his head. He was taking a dust bath, covering himself with the color of the desert. No shiny spots. He made sure his St. Christopher, his mother's gift, was tucked inside. He reversed his belt buckle and rubbed dirt and gravel into his brightly shined ankle boots. An hour's work down the drain.

49

•

John Gilman watched the smoke billow out from under the roof. Soon the ranch would be cinder and ashes. The destruction he'd brought about made him giddy and uncertain. The rattle of rifle fire from the towers fronting the hunting blinds interrupted his moment of inaction. The rounds fell short, kicking up puffs of dust below his position. *Amateurs*, he thought. They were shooting uphill and failed to compensate.

He shifted positions, brought the heavy rifle to bear on the nearest tower, and began a steady barrage of incendiary rounds. The heavy recoil and the steady thumping of the rifle prevented him from noticing that he was taking fire from his immediate right until a round tore through the top of a sandbag in line with his head. A wave of fear wiped away his sense of invulnerability. He'd almost been hit. He hugged the ground, afraid to move.

This was no good. Eventually he'd have to move, and the invisible shooter would kill him. He reached for his spotting scope and squirmed along the ground, where the sandbags offered greater protection. He removed the tripod and wedged the scope between the sandbags and searched the slope to the south of his position. At first the hillside appeared to be absent of human activity, but then a small cloud of dust rose from behind a ridge of rock about halfway up the hill, where the ground became steep.

He adjusted the magnification on the scope and carefully examined the rock formation. The red, white, and blue of the Sand Canyon logo briefly jumped into view. The logo adorned the hats and shirts of all Sand Canyon staff members. He decreased the magnification and refocused. The logo slipped out of sight, momentarily reappeared, and then slipped away. It came and went according to the position of the person's head between the rocks either side of the narrow slot where he had set up shop.

Gilman worked the .50 into position by folding back the bipod and extending the muzzle between the sandbags. He waited for the logo to make an appearance. The rifle fire had stopped. His opponent was probably waiting for him to resume fire with the .50. This was it, the most dangerous game, and he was up for it. He tossed a rock into the sandbags nearest where the .50 had been set up, hoping to raise some dust and draw fire. A tiny puff rose into the rising breeze and disappeared. Nothing. They waited, each hoping for the other's mistake. Gilman knew that movement brought the invisible into view. He wore desert camouflage, no logo or color to give him away. If he carefully restricted his movements, he would remain unseen. Then it occurred to him to run a couple of rounds into the sandbags with his Glock .40. It was loud, and it would raise a hell of a dust cloud. The Glock wasn't as loud as the .50, but the noise and the dust might provoke fire. He extended the Glock with his left hand, maintaining a careful sight picture with the sniper rifle, the reticle fixed on the slot where he had seen the logo. He let two rounds go into his former position. A substantial cloud of dust rose into the air.

The response was almost immediate. Two rounds tore into the hillside that he had just vacated, followed hard on by the double crack of the rifle. The muzzle flash wasn't visible in the brightness of the sun. The logo failed to materialize. He fired into the sandbags again, three shots in rapid succession. He waited, trying to account for the number of rounds the other shooter had used. The logo probably appeared when the shooter turned his head to change magazines. The red, white, and blue patch popped into view. He squeezed off a round, being careful not to hurry his shot. The logo disappeared.

A round tore into the sandbag closest to his face, burying gravel into his skin. It hurt like hell, and for a moment he thought he'd been hit. His damned opponent had faked him out. He removed his goggles and wiped them free of dirt, then exchanged the incendiaries for armor-piercing and trained the .50 on the crevice. He focused the sight on the rock face and emptied the magazine. He heard the rounds ricochet as they careened away into the valley. *Now or never,* he thought. He quickly reattached the bipod and the carry handle and prepared to make a run for it.

Smoke began to rise from the nearer release tower. He watched as three men scrambled to the ground and ran for the closest blind. Then he began climbing the twenty-odd feet to the crest of the ridge. A hail of fire followed him up the hill, all of it falling short. He almost laughed at their efforts. Now he was a bona fide combat veteran. He crested the hill and dropped onto the lee side, gasping for breath and laughing with relief.

He'd done it, all of it: blocked the gate, set the ranch house on fire, and maybe taken out the security chief. He was elated. What remained should be a piece of cake.

50

•

Frank paused for breath. The physical exertion of the steep climb gave him something to think about besides a round he would never hear ending his life. He worked his way carefully along the arm of the ridge, staying just below the skyline. He assumed the shooter was positioned below the line of sight from the hill's shoulder. Behind him, wisps of smoke were rising from the ranch house. Soon it would be a heap of ashes.

Fresh rabbit droppings patterned the ground. He bent down and studied the rabbit tracks crisscrossing the dusty soil and wondered about their journeys. What random patterns brought things together in designs of life and death—*if design govern in a thing so small?*

There hadn't been any gunfire for several minutes. High above him, a red-tailed hawk cried into the still air. A barrage of gunfire from the release tower provoked a response from the .50, a steady boom, boom, boom, as the shooter sent the heavy rounds into the elevated position Campbell's men had chosen. *They're too exposed*, he thought.

He scrambled up the hillside, less concerned now about raising a dust trail. The shooter had his hands full returning fire. As he reached the ridge, he turned to look back at the ranch house. Smoke was pouring from the front porch, and tongues of flame were lifting from the roof. When the people came running out of the ranch house, they'd be in the open, sitting ducks—and they'd have to come out. What was Linda doing? He wanted to go back, but stopping the shooter *now* was more important than ever.

Rivulets of sweat ran down his chest and back. He sucked in the hot desert air. It seared his lungs, making it difficult to breathe. He hadn't heard the .50 for a while. He stopped and listened. The sound of what he was pretty sure was a heavy-caliber handgun cracked above him. What the hell was going on? He pushed on up the slope, pushing down on his knees to relieve the aching muscles in his legs. More pistol shots. After a pause, the shooters on the tower opened up with a hail of fire.

As Frank followed the slope below the crest of the ridge, he heard the sound of a motorcycle echoing up from a side canyon that ran along the base of the hills. A small man wearing a billed cap disappeared down the wash on a dirt bike. Not Parker. It had to be the other one. Frank turned back to retrace his steps down the hillside. He knew now that Parker would be on the other side of the ranch house, waiting for the fleeing luncheon guests. The open space behind the ranch house would be the principal killing field. *I'm too late,* he thought.

A warm desert wind swept up from the south. In the distance, a great dust cloud was lifting away from the dry bed of Owens Lake, the Paiute Eden blowing in the wind. He turned to look across the canyon at the jumble of rocks along the crest of the Inyos and saw the huge monolith of the stone warrior, Winnedumah. In the rising wind, he imagined he heard Coyote's voice laughing at him for being tricked. He had been reacting, doing Parker's unseen bidding. He wouldn't be tricked again.

51

•

Frank reached the canyon floor in less than half the time it had taken to ascend the ridge, his clothing and skin ripped by his headlong descent. He ran toward the burning ranch house, skirted the front, and stopped in the clearing behind the kitchen entrance. There were bodies everywhere. He bent forward, hands on knees, gasping for breath, his eyes fearfully moving from one body to the next.

"Frank. Frank."

He looked toward the corrals, where a cluster of people had gathered by the tack shed. Then he saw her near the door, arms waving above her head. He drew a breath and trotted past the dead toward those that lived, his chest aching with relief.

•

Linda's account of the events at Sand Canyon completed the picture. Parker and his partner had worked as a team driving the brunch guests out into the open and killing them at will. Frank hadn't anticipated it. For him, it had never been a game. He tried not to remember hunting human beings as anything but the nightmare of warfare. Now eight people had been killed, including the principal owner of Sand Canyon, Duane Marshall, dead beneath a window, clutching a custom hunting rifle. Ewan Campbell's right hand had been badly damaged by rock fragments torn loose by the last salvo directed at him by Parker's accomplice before he disappeared over the hill.

Linda told him about the part she and Cynthia Combes had played in freeing Combes from the doorway. She told him about the young jock, Brad "Spike" Nelson, who had stayed to help, and Archie's mad dash across the killing field to the machine shop with the keys. Frank listened to her story with bland detachment. He knew he was disengaging, stepping inside and shutting down, preparing himself for what was to follow.

Frank looked about him, at the ground strewn with the dead, at Linda and the frightened and confused faces, and knew it was spinning out of control. He watched himself as in a dream, the disembodied detachment coming on him from another place where he had been a bringer of death. He turned away and headed for his vehicle.

"Where are you going?"

"To find Parker."

"Leave it to the others, for God's sake."

"I can't do that. He'll just kill more people."

"You can't fix it, Frank. It's not your fault. These people need your help. I need your help. Besides he's already gone."

"I know where he's going." He waved distractedly as he walked away.

•

At the blocked gate, he rammed his way through the fence, pretty well smashing up the front of the BLM Explorer. He pushed past the sideways Lincoln Navigator and drove down the side of the dirt road, one wheel riding the berm, flying past the hunters jamming the road, waiting for the opening day of bird shooting at Sand Canyon. The less favored had been the lucky ones.

Once he'd had to stop and explain the situation to the first of the county deputies trotting up the road, their vehicles abandoned in the traffic jam leading to the gatehouse. He'd taken the opportunity to inquire about anyone riding a dirt bike and provided a brief description. "He's a small man wearing desert camouflage, including a billed cap."

"Yeah, we saw a guy matching that description on the road down near the river."

"This side of the river or before the ponds?" Frank asked.

"This side. We didn't pay any attention to him. Sorry, Flynn. He seemed like some kid out beating around on the dirt."

"It's okay. Just get a description out. I better get going." He could hear the sirens from the approaching emergency vehicles. He pulled away from the patrol cars and hit the accelerator. Maybe, just maybe, he could find the man behind the .50 before he hooked back up with Parker.

He cleared the road jam and raced down the dirt road doing close to sixty. He checked the side roads for dust plumes. Dirt bikes kicked up lots of dust. He glanced over at a camper pulled off on a dirt track by one of the stagnant ponds. A man sat in a folding chair holding a fishing rod. Drowning worms wasn't Frank's idea of fishing. He liked working the streams. The fishing rod was an excuse to go hiking.

He slowed to a stop by the Owens riverbed, dry as dust this time of year. He was below the intake for the Los Angeles aqueduct. He watched the fisherman, who was just sitting there, rigid and motionless. No beer, no book, just staring straight ahead. He studied the man, examining him for something he might recognize, but it wasn't there. Still, something about the man didn't sit right. That was it. The fisherman was sitting in the chair upright, posed with a rod, and he hadn't once glanced in Frank's direction.

Hiding in plain sight took practice.

Frank cupped his hands to his mouth. "Any luck?"

The man slowly turned to look at Frank, then put his hand to his ear.

"Any luck?" Frank shouted.

The man shook his head and turned again to stare at the stagnant pond.

Frank waved, got into his vehicle, and drove off. He brought the SUV to a stop where the road dipped down into a dry gully shaded by tamarisk plants and got out, carefully closing the door without slamming it. Now to work north of the man and come back through the tangle of dead willow and encroaching tamarisk. He reached into the cab and removed the Remington twelve-gauge pump and headed up the wash.

52

•

Desiccated arrowweed, saltbush, and Russian thistle danced and rattled in the erratic breeze as if possessed with repressed frenzy. Frank moved quietly through the undergrowth, pausing every so often to determine his bearings. He stopped when a bit of reflected light caught his eye from the windshield of the fisherman's camper truck.

Frank edged forward. The man was gone. The fishing pole rested against the empty chair. The truck and camper were at a forty-five-degree angle to him, the nose of the truck pointing northwest. He moved quickly now, trying to cover the open ground between himself and the truck as rapidly as possible. As he drew within seven or eight feet, the side door opened and a smallish man wearing a billed cap stopped in midstep. At first his face simply registered surprise, but when he saw the uniform and the shotgun, it filled with fear.

"Hold it right there," Frank said in a normal tone of voice.

The man stepped backward, his hand still on the door.

"Don't move. Law enforcement business." Frank raised his voice and the shotgun.

For a moment, they were both motionless. Then the man suddenly drew the door shut. "Go away," he yelped.

"You need to come out with your hands in the air. I'm with the

Bureau of Land Management. Step out of the camper, now." Frank was partially protected by his angle of approach to the door. He moved to his left, so he wouldn't be immediately vulnerable if the door opened suddenly. As Frank edged farther to his left, two shots in quick succession smashed through the small window above the door, showering him with glass. Apparently the louvered window had spoiled the man's aim. Frank fired twice. The roar of the shotgun filled the air; the rest of the glass disappeared in the blast. The second shot blew a fist-sized hole in the metal door below the window. The sound of moaning drifted into the desert. Then, "Shit! Oh, shit!"

Frank moved to the wall of the camper and used the shotgun's muzzle to open the door. The man lay on his side, his right shoulder and upper arm a bloody pulp. He regarded Frank with innocent blue eyes. "He told me not to shoot you."

"His mistake," Frank said.

"I saw you down on the ground. I didn't kill you, but I could have."

"Your mistake," Frank said. He looked at the injured man. "What's your name?"

"John Gilman."

"Looks like you're bleeding to death, John Gilman."

"Help me," Gilman said.

"I'm not so inclined," Frank said. He wasn't sure whether Gilman heard him or not. The blue eyes were glazing over.

Frank was reaching for his cell phone when he heard a tinny version of "The Ride of the Valkyries" coming from the dead man's shirt pocket. *No Valhalla for you, John Gilman*, he thought as he fished the phone from the dead man's pocket.

He pushed the talk button and breathed into the phone just loudly enough to let the caller know someone had answered.

"John?" a voice said.

"Nope, looks like I found him first." Frank waited for the question.

"Sergeant Flynn?"

"Yup. John's here, but he's not feeling talkative."

"What're you saying, Sergeant?" Parker's voice ratcheted up

"You know what I'm saying. You sent a recruit into combat." Frank waited, then filled in the silence. "Bad leadership, Parker. You didn't take care of your man. You sent him out poorly trained. Now look at him."

"Just tell me if he's okay, Flynn."

"Sergeant Flynn," Frank corrected. "Well, yeah, he's okay in a way." He paused. "You were raised Catholic, Seth. You know, God, heaven and hell, sin and redemption, all that stuff. If your John Gilman was a good man, he's okay. In a better place, they tell us. That is if he minded his P's and Q's, faced Mecca, and lit the candles in the dark with faith in his heart."

He listened to the ragged breathing on the other end.

"But you and I know no one comes back." He nodded to himself. "Just as well, too. They'd come looking for us, wouldn't they? All those people we killed doing our duty, you more than me. Better to go into the darkness alone than face all those angry dead folks, don't you think?"

Neither man spoke for a moment.

"Why'd you kill all those people at Sand Canyon, Parker?"

"Were they people? I don't remember any people. What I remember is a bunch of sickos who needed to kill things to feel alive. I balanced things out. If you don't buy that, look at it this way. The MDG put some excitement and danger in their miserable fucking existence." He laughed quietly. "You're more like me than you want to admit, Sergeant. You just wouldn't cross the imaginary line. That's all it is, a line made up by the people with power to protect themselves from people like us—the ones who do their killing for them.

You know I'm right. Christ Almighty, that place stinks to heaven, an abomination. I would have walked around it blowing a trumpet, but since God went away, I do what I can."

"What about John Gilman? Was he a person? Wait, don't answer that. You're right. He was just a simple shit, a cipher. He needed to be taken out. Bang! Bang! Gone to make room for us supermen. The deciders, deciding who lives, who dies." Frank felt as if he'd been just gliding down a river, but somewhere up ahead there was a waterfall with rocks, and the current was too strong to pull to the shore. "Where are you, Seth?"

"You coming for me, Sergeant? You knew someday it had to come down to this, didn't you?"

"It never occurred to me. I always thought you were okay."

"I'm at the Mount Whitney Fish Hatchery, Sergeant. You know the place?"

"Yes."

"We're quits, Sarge. You killed John. Now I'm going to kill you."

"One way or another, Parker."

"There're a couple of families here you might want to evacuate before we start the dance. We don't want any collateral damage, do we?" He sniggered. "That's only possible if you come alone. If you bring others along, well, I'll kill them, too. So come alone, Sarge, and we'll finally find out, huh?"

"What will we find out, Parker?" He already knew the answer.

"Which of us is best, Sarge. I'm betting on me." The line went dead.

53

•

Frank pocketed John Gilman's cell phone, reached for his own, and punched up the autodial for Dave Meecham.

"Frank, damn glad to hear your voice. What the hell is going on up there?" It was as close as Meecham came to being excited.

"Parker and his pal—John Gilman was his name—took the place apart. A real slaughter, Dave. The county's all over it."

"Was?"

"We traded shots. He lost."

"Are you okay?"

"Linda and I are both okay." He took a deep breath. "Where are you?"

"Just south of Olancha."

Meecham was about an hour away. He'd have time. "Here's the thing, Dave, I'm quitting. As of right now, I resign."

"What the hell are you talking about?"

"I'll turn in my stuff tomorrow. I quit, as of"—he looked at his watch—"one forty-two this afternoon."

"Will you tell me what the hell is going on?"

"You're breaking up, Dave. I'm losing you." He switched off the phone. He was losing them all: Dave Meecham, Jesse Sierra, Greg Wilson, all of them would be out of his life. He brought up the number of Linda's cell phone and hit the call button.

"Hi. Listen, I'm sorry I left like that."

"I know." She hesitated. "Ben's in a bad way. He was one of the first ones hit down by the gate. Bill was with him, but he's okay. Bill, I mean, he wasn't hit. Dad wasn't with them. I don't know where he is." She was running it all together.

"Where are they taking Ben?"

"They're on the way to Bishop right now. When I find Dad, I'll be driving him up. He's going to take it hard."

"How bad is it?"

"I didn't see him. From what I could find out, he was hit in the thigh and lost a lot of blood."

"Ben's a tough old guy." He was thinking of the damage a .50 caliber round could do to the human body.

"Why were they there?"

"Bill says they'd planned to throw those things on the road that give flats. Dad wasn't there because they didn't want him to know. They knew he wouldn't go for it because he had given you his word they were through with that stuff." Her voice broke, and she stopped and drew breath. "Oh, Frank, I can't think of Ben being gone." She was choking back the grief.

"I know," he said.

"You didn't find Parker?" It was a question.

"No. I found his partner, the one shooting at the ranch and the gatehouse, the one who burned you out and shot Ben." He paused. "He's dead."

"Are you okay?"

"I'm fine. Listen, I know where Parker is, but I can't bring in Dave and the others. It'll just mean putting them in certain danger if I do. I have a chance to bring it to an end, so I'm going after him."

"Don't! You can't make everything come out right. Wait for the others." Her voice was urgent.

"Dave is on his way to Sand Canyon. When he gets there, tell him what's up, okay?" He waited. "Okay?"

"I'll do that for you, Frank, and you come back here, where you're needed."

"There's another thing you should know. I just quit the BLM, so they won't be mixed up with a rogue ranger." He chuckled softly. "That could be a TV series, *The Rogue Ranger*."

"Where are you?" she asked.

"On my way to get Parker."

"Damn you, Frank Flynn. If you wind up dead, we don't have much of a future." Her voice was cracking.

"Not to worry. I have a chance to stop him before he gets anyone else, and this way it's no one's fault if he gets away again—or if he doesn't. Linda, I love you very much." He hung up before she could say anything to change his mind.

He took the Mount Whitney Fish Hatchery Road and followed it as far as the turnoff for the dirt parking lot below the hatchery. There was one car pulled up under the trees. Two young Latina women sat on one of the benches next to the lower pond keeping an eye on two six- or seven-year-old boys fooling around near the edge of the water. A school of fat dark trout trailed them near the water's edge. The fish were waiting for pellet feed from the coin dispensers spaced around the breeding pond.

The older of the two boys ran back to his mother and begged for a coin, but she shook her head. "No more. The fish will grow so big they will eat you." Her companion laughed.

"Nuh-uh," the boy said, glancing nervously back at the dark roiling bodies.

Frank approached the women. "Hi, there. I'm afraid we're temporarily closing the fish hatchery. Police business."

The women glanced at each other, unsure of what was happening.

"Nothing to worry about, but you need to round up your children and leave."

They frowned at Frank, not completely believing him.

"You need to move along. If you leave now, there's no danger." He looked around. "Just the two children?"

"Yes, just my boys." Frank could see she was the older of the two. He realized they were sisters.

"That's good."

The women called the children and climbed into an old Chevy truck, the boys crowding between them. Frank followed them out in his vehicle and locked the gate across the entrance. The hatchery no longer functioned as a breeding facility. The grounds and ponds were maintained for the tourists. He didn't want anyone to wander in and get caught up in the crossfire. He watched as the truck turned back onto Highway 395 and headed south.

Gilman's phone launched tinny Valkyries into the soft afternoon air.

"Okay, Sergeant. I make it out to be two ten. What do you say to two thirty?"

"Fine by me." Frank glanced up at the tower. "Duel in the sun, huh? Why don't we just hang it up, Parker? There's been too much killing already. Let's make it stop."

"Can't do it, Sergeant. It's gone too far. It's coming to an end, like you said, one way or another. Can't bear it anymore."

"What? What can't you bear anymore?"

He was gone.

Frank drove up the road past the hatchery and parked his vehicle under some cottonwoods lining the stream. He would approach the hatchery from Oak Creek, staying in the cover of the willows. Parker would figure him for that, so he'd have to be careful about moving the shrubbery around. He hoped the wind would pick up and make it harder for his movements to give him away. He slung the shotgun over his shoulder, picked up the AR-15 and a spare clip of ammo, and put on his shooting glasses to reduce the glare.

The south entry to the Mount Whitney Fish Hatchery was beneath a stone tower rising up three stories overlooking the grounds. The hatchery had been built from native rock with local money and local labor. In places the walls were three feet thick.

Frank knew the tower was a trap. Parker knew it, too. There was no path of retreat. On the other hand, it was close to impregnable. He made his way down the creek, the clear water softly gurgling among the rocks, forming small pools where brook trout waited for careless insects to dimple the surface of the water. He kept to the north side of the creek, placing his moving shape among the shadows, stopping in the stillness, moving with the wind as it pushed up the canyon from the valley floor.

When he was approximately even with the long cement fish runs, he stopped to look over the grounds. The tower rose above the far end of the building, not more than three hundred yards to the south. To be seen was to be dead. A bright glint of reflection caught Frank's eye. He studied the opening, fronting the north side of the tower. The glint flashed again. He smiled to himself, fumbling with Gilman's phone. He brought up the incoming calls, selected the number of the last call, and pushed the dial-up button.

"Why are you calling, Sergeant?"

"Clumsy stuff, Parker. The flasher."

"Okay." There was a pause, followed by heavy breathing. "You might have been overeager, Sergeant." This was followed by a soft groan.

"You wounded, Seth?"

"Not like you think. I'm doing fine." A round whispered by Frank's right ear, followed by the crack of the rifle. Frank dropped to the ground, behind a large boulder. Two more rounds chipped into the top of the rock, sending shards of granite flying into the stream and peppering his skin and flying up into his shooting glasses. The sound of Parker's tinny laughter rose into the air from the still open phone. "The flasher located you, Sarge, not me. When you see it, I can see you."

Frank closed the phone and stuffed it in his pocket. How had Parker missed? Frank knew he should have been dead, but here he was. Maybe Parker was playing with him. Letting him know who was best.

He worked his way downstream far enough so that the rise of the land blocked the line of sight from the tower. He trotted below a small earthen dam diverting water into one of the ponds, then worked his way toward the hatchery from the northeast. A group of teenagers on bicycles were riding along the short dirt road leading to the parking lot. Damn. Parker wouldn't shoot the boys, but he would find a way to exploit their presence. He had to warn them off. He dropped back and began working his way toward the parking lot. A white F150 pickup truck rolled up the road and came to a stop by the gate. Two men slid out the passenger's side door, away from the hatchery, Dave Meecham and Jesse Sierra. Dave and Linda must have put their heads together and figured it out. Parker would kill them as easily as blowing out a candle.

Frank rose and started walking toward the hatchery. The whoosh of a round near his head made him flinch. The sound of the shot rooted Meecham and Sierra behind the truck. It was the only warning Frank could provide. He reached the pond and took the path along the southern edge. Two more rounds struck the surface of the fishpond, raising geysers of water into the air that faded into fleeting rainbows. The trout darted away into the shadows and recesses near the shore.

As Frank reached the open lawn leading up to the entrance at the base of the tower, "The Ride of the Valkyries" jingled into the air. It lifted his heart. If Parker was using the phone, Meecham and Sierra were safe, and for the moment, so was he.

"Hi, Seth. Nice afternoon, *verdad?*"

"What the hell are you doing, Sergeant?" Parker sounded very tired.

"Coming up to have a chat."

"I said come alone. You shouldn't have brought in the others."

"I didn't, Seth. Keep it between you and me." There was no response. "Parker! Parker!"

He caught movement from the corner of his eye. Meecham and Sierra had left the cover of the truck and were trying to work their way through the trees.

He put the phone to his mouth. "I'm coming up, Seth. I know you can hear me. I'm on my way." He hurried across the lawn.

The crack of the .270 reverberated into the afternoon stillness, amplified by the confines of the stone walls. Frank turned as Dave Meecham crumpled to the ground. *God damn! God damn!* He put the assault rifle to his shoulder and ran ten rounds into the tower window, shifting the entry point from left to right, hoping the jacketed rounds would bounce around against the rocks and cement. He put in a second clip and did it again. He could hear the rounds pinging as they ricocheted inside the stone room. Then he tossed the rifle to the ground and ran for the entrance, clutching the shotgun.

He pushed through the door marked EMPLOYEES ONLY and leapt up the stairs leading to the top floor of the tower. He shouldn't have left his hat behind. Stupid thought. Then, holding the shotgun to his shoulder, he kicked the door open. Parker sat on the floor, blood leaking out from under him and spreading across his midsection.

"It was a hornet's nest in here, Sarge. It wasn't a good place to fort up." Parker's rifle lay on the cement. He nodded toward it. "It was my dad's." He looked down at the polished wood and steel. "Pre-1964." He fixed his gaze on Frank. "I've got brain cancer, Sarge. It hurts like hell." He frowned down at the growing splotch of blood on his shirt. He smiled. "I knew you'd come for me. I wish you hadn't killed John. That made me angry as hell."

"What about the people you killed, Parker? What about the man you just shot down?"

"Who was he?"

"A damned good man." Frank raised the shotgun and took up the slack.

Parker smiled. "I told you we were alike." He dabbed his hand on his bloody shirt as if not quite believing he'd been shot. "They always looked so surprised. Now I think I get it."

"Why am I alive, Seth? You could've taken me out a couple of times."

Parker smiled. "Yeah, I know, but I owed you, and you're a good man, Sarge." His voice was weak.

"You killed a better man, Parker. His name was Dave Meecham. Say it, you son of a bitch. Say his name."

"Dave Meecham," he said.

"Damn you to hell." He shot Parker in the chest. He stood for a minute, listening to the wind blowing up from the valley. Then he heard footsteps on the stairs, and in that moment, he saw the thing that chased him in his dream as clearly as if he were staring in the water.

"Frank! Frank! Are you okay?"

"Yeah, I'm fine, Jesse."

Jesse Sierra came through the door, holding a shotgun at the ready, and took in Parker's bloody body; then he turned his face to Frank. "Dave's been shot." Sierra's voice broke. "He's dead, Frank."

"Have you called it in?"

"Yes, but all the emergency services are out at Sand Canyon."

"I'll come down with you." The two rangers followed the path skirting the pond. A cloud of fine dust enveloped the valley in a murky gray.

54

•

It had been three days since the events at Sand Canyon, and Shaw had barely survived. His left leg had been shattered, almost severed above the knee by the large-caliber round. The surgeon removed the rest. Bill Jerome had pulled him out the passenger door and controlled the bleeding with an improvised tourniquet comprised of his shirt sleeve and an oval-shaped pebble clamped against the artery. Shaw complained bitterly about Jerome's ministrations, claiming the tourniquet hurt worse than being shot. Bill Jerome had strong hands.

Linda stood between her father and Jerome on the far side of Shaw's hospital bed. Eddie Laguna and Cece Flowers stood on the other side, Eddie grinning, Cece's small face grave with concern. Frank stood behind them, his smooth features expressionless.

"These two are going to harm one another if you don't get well soon," Linda said, gesturing toward her father and Bill Jerome.

"I've been thinking about that," Shaw said. "I'm going to get fixed up with a wooden leg, like old Pegleg Smith. Take it off and smack the smart-mouths when things get out of hand." The thought crossed Frank's mind that if Shaw had a pegleg and a parrot, he'd be a perfect Long John Silver.

"Yeah, a wooden leg'd go along with your hobnailed tongue," Eddie added.

Shaw's eyes were watery with weariness. "Take care, Redhawk. I'll be up on my feet—foot—before you know it."

Cece picked up Shaw's large weathered hand. "I can't believe I've been worried about you, Mr. Shaw, but I have." She smiled and squeezed his hand.

"Careful with that hand squeezing. You might bring on a case of RLS."

"RLS?"

"Restless leg syndrome." He rolled his eyes and gave Cece a lascivious look.

"What's he talking about?" Eddie queried, looking suspicious.

Collins laughed. "It's like in that song, 'Reincarnation,' when the cowboy looks down at the pile of horse shit in the road and thinks how it made the passage from grave to plant to horse and out the other end. The cowboy looks at it and thinks"—Collins leaned down close to Shaw, smiling hugely—"Ben, you ain't changed all that much."

"We have to be going, Bill. Cece is going to help me run the club while you're laid up," Linda said.

"That's great," Shaw laughed. "The boys will be lined up at the bar two deep."

Linda, Cece, and Eddie waved their good-byes at the doorway.

Frank moved closer to the side of Shaw's bed. "The wooden leg is a good idea, Ben. I can see you whipping it off and chasing the punks from the club."

"Hell, I don't need the leg. I've got crazy eyes, and without my teeth, I look like Wolfman." He grinned, exposing gums between large, pointed canines. "They took my teeth, afraid I'd choke." Shaw waited for Frank to continue.

"Just wanted to tell you I won't be around for a while."

"Where're you going?" He raised a tired arm. "Never mind, it's none of my business, Frank."

Frank smiled. "I'll be spending some time with old Tucker up in the Saline. I'm giving him a hand. He lost a big toe moving around some equipment."

Shaw gave Frank a knowing look. "Mining equipment, I'll bet."

"Yup, that's right." He studied Shaw's whiskered face. "Tucker and Rocky Surrette were moving his single stamp mill, and the shoe came off and fell on his foot. Took his big toe right off. He could've bled to death if Surrette hadn't been there. He drove him into the clinic at Lone Pine a couple days ago, but he's back at his place because of the animals. Surrette has a place of his own to keep an eye on, so I thought I'd give Tucker a hand until he gets back on his feet." Frank glanced at the depression in the bedding where Shaw's left leg would have been. "Sorry, Ben, I could've put it differently."

"It's all right. I already made that joke. I'll have to get used to it." Shaw exposed his canines through the graying beard.

Very Wolfman-like, Frank thought. "How long have you known that Tucker was sitting on the mine?"

"It started to add up after we found out the letter was a phony. We figured the town was probably Darwin, not Red Mountain. And old Tucker waving the shotgun around, scaring people away from his place. Well, that made sense, too."

"I'm glad you're sticking around, Ben. The Joshua Tree Athletic Club won't be the same till you're back."

"No, it won't, and with Cece tending bar, my return won't be greeted with enthusiasm." Shaw looked thoughtful. "How long you going to be up in the Saline Valley?"

"I'm not sure, Ben. I'm suspended with pay until they're through with the investigation." He paused. "I don't know about all that yet."

Shaw's face lapsed into seriousness. "Well, the club won't be the same without you, either. Don't forget, the Joshua Tree Athletic Club will always be your home away from home, amigo."

"Count on it, Frank." Collins put a meaty hand on Frank's shoulder.

"Yeah, we can shoot a game or two, so I can win now and then. You're the only fish I can count on."

"Thanks, Bill. Maybe I can swamp out the place for you boys and earn my keep."

The partners looked cheerfully downcast.

Frank put on a smile. "Now that you have Cece helping out, Linda won't be so tied up. Seems like she's been pretty busy between the paper and the bar." It felt lame as soon as he'd said it.

"So she told you," Collins said, raising tired eyes.

"Yeah. She didn't say it's definite, though?" Frank made it a question.

Collins nodded. "No, there's that, but she's got the bit in her teeth." The silence settled between them. "What are you going to do about it?" he said.

"I don't know, Jack. I'm not sure there's much I can do."

Collins shook his head. "For an Irish lad, sometimes you're dumb as a post."

"That's old news, Jack."

55

•

The time on Zeke Tucker's place had been oddly peaceful. After the second day, Tucker started talking, Then he couldn't seem to stop. At first Frank felt obligated to respond, but the hermit was talking to himself as much as to Frank. Sometimes it was as if Frank weren't even there. When the basso profundo muttering became too much, Frank would slip out into the glittering desert twilight and let the soft sounds of nocturnal stirrings take him into timeless realms. Tucker never seemed to notice; his deep murmurings rumbled on without regard.

For a while Frank thought that it was loneliness that drove the endless voice, but apparently that wasn't the case. Most of what Tucker said was a running commentary on the doings of his life and a list of things to attend to.

"Float valve's stuck again. Water all over the place."

"Damn foot's sore as hell."

"Be a while before we can hike up to Beverage, huh, Jack? Well, it ain't entirely your fault."

Jack-the-dog was addressed more frequently than Frank-the-human.

Frank fell in with the hermit's habits, came to be at ease with the muttering thunder, mixed occasionally with invective and

scripture. He could choose to respond or not. He found that especially liberating. Social amenities weren't required. In the mornings,
they'd get up and feed the chickens, the goats, and Pancho. Tucker
had named the rescued burro after Frank, citing scriptural reference to Balaam's donkey, who had had a few words to say. "The
Lord God spoke to Balaam through the mouth of a donkey. Maybe
one day something sensible will come out of your mouth, Ranger
Flynn," Tucker had added, not wanting to give too much ground.

Most days, they'd work the tailings of the old mine at the mouth
of the canyon, Frank hauling and shoveling, Tucker picking
through the ore, high-grading the good stuff, Frank running the rest
through the hand stamp. In the afternoons, when it was hot, they
washed the crushed rock in Tucker's old-fashioned wooden sluice
box. Then Frank would clean the black sand from the riffles and
rinse the matting in a bucket. Tucker showed Frank how to pan out
the color. When the sun dropped behind the Inyos, Frank would
hike up to the waterfall, peel off his clothes, and stand in the icy water. Frank and the muttering giant had fallen into an easy rhythm
that required no planning other than providing for the moment.

Frank was almost content.

They'd had visitors of late. Jesse Sierra and Greg Wilson, with
Eddie in tow, stopped their truck at the wire gate leading to
Tucker's dwelling and honked the horn. They'd roused the sleeping
giant from his nap. Tucker mumbled a welcome to the rangers and
greeted Eddie like a long-lost brother. They were strange ducks,
one crafty, one crazy, both honest as children.

Frank felt his face crease into an unaccustomed smile. He was
glad to see them. That night, he made tamale pie for dinner, Eddie's favorite. Tucker consumed two large bowls of the steaming
pie washed down with bottles of Mojave Red, courtesy of the visiting rangers. Eddie tucked away three bowls, scraping the last of
it out of the Dutch oven with his spoon. Frank hoped the dinner

would temper Tucker's monologue, but he muttered on, making the two rangers uneasy. Tucker's size always added an emphasis to his speech.

At first his former colleagues were tentative with Frank, but they were both too young to stay subdued. They told Frank about a new guy at the Joshua Tree Athletic Club. How he put the needle to that "meaner-than-a-snake Shaw" and how much they enjoyed it.

Sierra said, "Eddie popped some guy for giving Cece a bad time at the bar."

"You shoulda seen it, Frank." Greg picked the story up. "This big old boy's coming on to Cece and won't stop. So Eddie tells him to go sit down at one of the tables and mind his manners. Well, this guy looks at Eddie and starts cracking up. Calls him a rat-toothed runt."

"I'm not sure I want to hear this next part," Frank said.

"It turns out okay," Greg said. "Right, Eddie?"

Eddie grinned and nodded. "Not for him."

Sierra picked it up where Greg left off. "Eddie steps up to the dude and whacks him in the cojones, faster than anything. Then, as the guy is sagging, Eddie reaches up under the guy's armpit, grabs him by the back of the belt with his other hand, and frog-walks him to the door. 'Puke outside,' he says." Sierra grinned. His dark good looks and flashing eyes leant a satanic glee to his expression.

Frank pictured Linda tending bar and coming to her rescue. Silly stuff, he thought, but he was suddenly aware of his drifting isolation. Linda lived in a former world down in the valley, there and in his dreams. Sometimes she came to him as a seductress, vivid and erotic. Sometimes as a gentle presence, all mixed up with the warm valley winds and the sounds of Sage Creek singing near his caboose. He pushed the thoughts away. Thinking of Linda made him ache.

"They gave Shaw's leg a funeral," Wilson said.

"That's right. He kept complaining about it hurting and itching. This woman up at Janey's place told him that if he buried his leg, the pain and itch would go away," Eddie said.

Wilson shook his head. "What a bunch of bullshit. It was a hell of a party, though."

"Did it work?" Frank asked.

"He said it did for a while, but then he found out it wasn't his leg."

"Whose leg was it?"

"Don't know. Don't want to know. He says he wants to go back up to Janey's and get some more advice. He's a randy old devil." Sierra grinned.

●

Frank had arranged with the VA for Parker's burial, making sure a priest was on hand to give the last rites. Seth Parker had gone into the ground alone. His Silver Star, Bronze Star with two clusters, Combat Infantryman's Badge, and campaign ribbons were pinned to his uniform. He was thirty-six years old, boyish looking even in death. Frank wondered how he had lasted that long, the kid whose skill with a rifle was unmatched, a particularly cruel gift for one so tenderhearted. *What the hammer? What the chain? / In what furnace was thy brain?*

Half of the population of the Mojave Desert turned out for Dave Meecham's memorial service in Johannesburg. His wife had chosen the old Randsburg/Johannesburg Cemetery, where so many people of the desert rested. Dave's widow sought Frank out to thank him for being such a good friend to her husband. Frank had winced. He felt that he'd had a hand in Meecham's death. He couldn't get past it.

●

Zeke limped up the canyon, Eddie and Jack-the-dog in his wake. Eddie had said he wanted to take a shower up at the falls while he was here. Frank and the rangers sat on the porch in aluminum chairs with seats reconstructed of clothesline. The plastic straps had disintegrated in the sun long ago.

Greg wiggled around in his chair looking uncomfortable and then came to the point of the visit, without further preamble. "Brought Eddie up so you could come back for a while. There's people who wonder why the hell you are living up here with old shoot-your-ass-off Tucker and not even bothering to send out a word."

"He's a good conversationalist, Greg," Frank remarked, without cracking a smile.

The two rangers waited for Frank to continue, to see if he would agree to their proposal. They had made promises to bring him back.

"I guess it looks as though I don't give a damn about my friends," Frank said. He stared out into the Saline Valley. "The fact of the matter is I'm not sure what I'm coming back to or what's in store."

"We need you back in Ridgecrest," Greg said. "Carl Becker's filling in for Dave, and he's a piece of work."

Sierra grinned. "Becker's been chewing on Greg just for drill. He hardly has enough ass left to sit on."

Greg frowned at Sierra. "Yeah, and there's some people at a bar in Red Mountain waiting to see you, too," he added.

Frank knew hiding with a hermit wasn't going to be a lifetime occupation, but he didn't know what the hell he was going to do, either. Dave Meecham had taken his resignation with him. The first phase of investigation into the deaths of Parker and Gilman and the events at Sand Canyon was nearing completion, but there was more coming, lawyers and lawsuits, for sure. He knew he'd have to go back.

"Okay, I'll get my stuff."

Tucker and Eddie came out to the truck, Eddie pushing a wheelbarrow, laboring with the weight.

"This's gotta go to the Ophir mill in Randsburg. Get it to Pete Arnoldson. Okay?" Tucker hefted a burlap sack into the pickup, where it landed with a thud, and lifted another one from the arms of the struggling Eddie, who was trying to raise it over the side of the pickup.

"I think we can do that," Greg said, surreptitiously winking at Frank.

They climbed into the rangers' truck, said their good-byes, and started on the long haul back to pavement.

"How's Shaw doing?"

"One leg, one crutch, and one mean mouth. He's just fine."

As they lurched up the washboard portion of the Saline Valley Road, fast enough to make Frank cranky, Jesse Sierra said, "We found your truck."

"What?" Frank wasn't sure he heard right.

"It was below the fish hatchery, along Oak Creek. It must have been where Parker left it after he took it from Eddie. Started right up."

•

As they turned south onto Highway 395 toward Red Mountain, Frank felt uneasy. He didn't want a welcome home party. He didn't think he could deal with all the questions and noise.

"There's not a party, is there?"

"Who for?" Greg said. He turned and grinned at Frank. "Nope, but Mr. Collins and his pals are there. Cece's bettin' living with Tucker's turned your hair white."

Frank let out a deep breath. "What about Linda?"

"Who?"

"Come on, Greg. Will Linda be there?"

"Well, she's been pretty busy, in and out of town a lot, but I imagine so." Greg stared straight ahead.

Frank wanted to tell him to turn around, but he couldn't wait to see her. It was great having such a firm sense of purpose.

56

•

Frank was pleased to see his truck parked out in front of the Joshua Tree Athletic Club. Someone had washed it and given it a shine. The interior was clean as a whistle, and the blanket/seat cover had been washed. He opened the glovebox and rummaged around looking for his dad's brass switch keys, but he came up empty.

Right next to his Chevy was Jack's old International, bright, shiny, and dentless. That was an even bigger surprise. When they brought Jack's truck up from the mine shaft, the front part of the body had looked like an accordion, ready for the wrecking yard. Now it gleamed with the original two-tone paint job, fenders black, body blue.

Someone had poured a lot of money into bringing it back. He thought about how pleased he was to see his '53 Chevy five-window and realized he'd have done the same thing, providing he'd had the cash to spare. He just wished he had his dad's keys; one was to the caboose, damn it.

So far his return to civilization had been okay. People had greeted him warmly, Cece with a hug, the boys with crushing hand-shakes. They restrained their curiosity to the point that Frank had to ask questions to find out what had taken place in his absence. He sat at the bar, catching up on the news with Jack Collins and watch-ing the endless game of snooker.

Jack told him the boys were having difficulty with Shaw. He didn't want to go to the VA hospital over in Fresno to get fitted with a prosthesis. It turned out Jack was serious about getting a wooden leg. Worse yet, Eddie knew a one-legged guy up in Reno who could make him one.

Frank wondered if Eddie knew a guy with a glass eye.

Jack said he was afraid to speculate on Eddie's acquaintances and Shaw's proclivities. "If Ben thought he could have a wooden leg and an eye patch, he'd probably put out his own eye." They laughed. Frank was feeling the couple of beers he'd had swim over him. He'd been abstemious while he'd been with Tucker, and he was out of practice.

"Your truck looks really good, Jack. Must've cost you a bundle."

"Not really."

"Oh. How's that?" Frank said, not being able to help himself.

Collins pushed a rag around on the surface of the spotless bar. "Well, Eddie borrowed it, so he felt obliged to fix it up. Paid for the whole thing."

Frank was taken aback. "Wow! Who did the work?" *Where did Eddie get the money?* he wondered.

"He took it to a shop down in Pearsonville that specializes in restoration. Looks like new." He shook his head. "Now I'm tender about pounding it on the back roads. Ben's been riding me about being a candy-ass with a yuppie truck. Something else for him to bitch about."

"Where did Eddie come up with the money for something like that? If you don't mind me asking." Frank raised his eyebrows.

"Once a cop . . ." Jack let it hang; his eyes wandered around the room. "Well, it's like this. Eddie agreed to help out this man with a gold mine, up in the Saline Valley, who was temporarily crippled up. Then this other good fellow heard about the miner's plight, through Eddie, I might mention. So this Good Samaritan went out there and helped this man in his hour of need." Jack nodded at the wonder of it. "This good man worked like a dog, until the miner was almost healed from his injury."

Jack looked up, his face filled with innocence "Maybe you don't know about this part. When the miner's foot was injured, his toe was knocked right off. So he was brought right into the Lone Pine clinic. When Doc Robertson wanted to know where the severed toe was so he could reattach it, the miner cursed and swore and told the doc that his dog ate the toe before they thought to pick it up. Now the man was in a terrible plight. Temporarily estranged from his only friend, Jack-the-toe-eating-dog—I wish the dog had another name—and barely able to get around, much less take care of his place."

He raised his round face to Frank's. "That's when this Good Samaritan appeared." He interrupted his narrative. "I think you remember it was Eddie suggested you could stay with Tucker for a while and give him a hand." Jack continued speaking to Frank as if he were an audience far removed from the events. "This doubly afflicted man was so grateful to our Eddie for bringing his plight to the attention of this Samaritan that he agreed to bear the cost for restoring my truck to its original beauty before its visitation to the underworld. Oh, and he's paying for Eddie's new teeth in the bargain." He grinned at Frank. "Thanks, podner."

"You mean all that digging, hauling, and pounding I did was for Eddie?"

"No! No! It was to make an old truck new, to heal an old man's heart, and to keep our Shoshone brother on the path of righteousness. It was a good deed, Frank. A good deed is its own reward." Jack was grinning hugely.

"Jesus, Mary, and Joseph," Frank said, shaking his head. "With the amount of high-grade ore out in the truck, he could have a whole new set of gold teeth."

"I suppose so, but be careful what you say, brother Flynn. There are ears everywhere, and to tell you the truth, the idea of Eddie with gold choppers is unsettling."

"Well, here's one for you, Jack. That piece of threaded quartz you gave me probably fell out of Tucker's van."

Jack nodded knowingly.

"Tucker was carrying sacks of high-grade to the mill in Randsburg in his old van. The latch on the rear doors was faulty, so pieces of ore spilled out onto the road. Tucker remembers stopping and picking a lot of it up, but he must have missed some. That's probably what Linda picked up and tossed into Kevin's Jeep."

Jack looked thoughtful. "Follow the Yellow Brick Road. Hope no more of that stuff is lying around." He caught Frank's eye. "By the way, we think there's an original letter, maybe a map, too. So there might be another mine. We're thinking about the Lost Goler Mine, near Garlock. As a matter of fact, we're taking our old comrade Jefferson Lebeau for a looksee in a couple of days."

"The fellow that Shaw refers to as 'the man who died and went to Seattle'?"

"That's the one. He fancies himself a treasure hunter, among his many skills. He took one look at Cece's map and the reverend's letter, read some stuff on the Internet about prospecting, and declared that he was in possession of the mine's location, or at least in close approximation. Then he went into Ridgecrest and bought a GPS and announced that he is ready to show us the very spot—give or take a mile or two—of the New Hope Mine."

"That should keep you boys occupied for a while," Frank said, an easy smile creasing his face. Linda had yet to make an appearance, and Frank felt awkward about asking Jack where she was.

Shaw and his old nemesis of the green cloth Jefferson Lebeau were putting on a snooker show. Everyone's attention was captured by the hush of conversation that was preamble to a difficult shot. Lebeau had called the six-ball into the side pocket on a difficult cross-bank. He chalked his cue, bent down to sight, and then stood back up and gave the six an imperious stare. Shaw found this delay particularly annoying, and he gnawed around the edges of Lebeau's confidence without result. Lebeau sent the cue ball down the table for an impossibly thin slice into the cushion, driving the six into the right bank, where it rebounded so slowly that it crept across the table, balanced on the pocket's lip, and gently dropped in, giving Lebeau the game and Shaw the fits.

When the hell was someone going to mention Linda? His back was turned to the bar, so he didn't notice that she had taken her station behind it. When he turned, there she was, dark curls framing hazel eyes and generous mouth. She gave him a smile as she reached under the bar for a glass and drew a Sierra Nevada. "Hi, sailor, can I buy you a beer?"

"You bet you can." He grinned with relief and pleasure.

"We have a lot to talk about, Flynnman."

"Yes, we do." He wanted to ask her about the job but held back, knowing it wasn't the way to begin things.

"I'm so sorry about Dave. I know how much you'll miss him."

"Thanks. Sometimes I hear him. You know, in my head. He's joined the chorus of the departed."

"I thought you were a skeptic, a hard-nosed fact chaser."

"I am, but dreams are real. They're there in our minds, and Dad and Mom and others come and visit. And I'm glad to see them. Sometimes I don't even need to be asleep. I wanted Dave to come and forgive me for getting him killed, but he didn't. He wondered why I was letting life pass me by, letting you pass me by. I'm not going to do that if you give me half a chance."

"A whole one, Flynnman." She raised dark eyebrows. "I took the job with the *Times*."

"I thought you probably would. Uh, then, why are you here?

"To take care of Hobbes and 395, Ben's cat."

"Oh."

"The *Times* doesn't require my presence more than once a week, by the way, so I can still live in Red Mountain and give Dad a hand until Ben's stronger and they've worked out a schedule that doesn't include me every weekend." She frowned. "I guess I'll still have some time for the *Courier*, too. I'll be doing a column, but not the daily stuff. So it looks like there'll even be time for courtship. If I remember correctly, you like the idea of courting. So you better be thinking about it."

"You can count on it," Frank said.

"If you're headed out for the caboose, you'll need these." She dropped the brass keys on the bar. "I was checking to see the place wasn't a mess, since you might be having company." She grabbed him by the ears and kissed him, sending the boys into hoots and cheers.

EPILOGUE

•

The dirt road to the diversion point for the Los Angeles aqueduct was lined with cars. The road had been repeatedly wetted down so the participants and the observers wouldn't wind up choking in their own dust. Frank and Linda chose to walk to the site rather than take the bus shuttling people to and from the parked cars along the road to the pavilion where the ceremonies for the return of the waters would take place. The mayor of Los Angeles himself would throw the switch releasing the water into the dry-as-bone bed of the Owens River, where no water had flowed since 1913. It was an occasion.

Frank's mood was as sunny as the day. The winter sky was a deep blue, and the Sierra towered over the valley in snowcapped splendor. Here it was early December and people were peeling off their sweaters and jackets as they stood around waiting for the sluice gate to lower and the waters to flow.

Collective excitement electrified the air. After decades of strife, the water wars of the twenties and the endless litigation, the valley residents had won. The river would bring back life to the lower Owens Valley. People from the communities of Bishop, Big Pine, Independence, and Lone Pine and the surrounding ranches and mines; members of the Paiute and Shoshone bands scattered throughout the valley; citizens and cops—they had all gathered to bear witness to the returning of the waters.

Lieutenant Robert Dewey of the Inyo County Sheriff's Department stood apart holding court. Somehow he had managed to keep the dust off his brightly shined brogans, and the creases in his high-water khakis were knife sharp. Various cops came over to acknowledge his presence, Frank included.

"Good to see you here, Flynn." Dewey leaned forward as if to convey a confidence and boomed, "When the hell are you going to go back to work?" Frank looked uncomfortable. "Well, no matter." Dewey pounded him on the back. "Damn good to see you. You want to be a real cop, come on by and we'll talk."

"Thanks, Lieutenant," Frank said. He was thinking working for Dewey would mean a lifetime of earplugs.

The plan was that when the mayor and other speakers finished up, the mayor to throw a switch, the sluice gate would lower, and water would flow into the lower Owens River for the first time in almost a hundred years. Frank wandered over to the bridge fronting the gate holding back the river, where anxious reporters had gathered in expectation of the oncoming flood. Linda waited with the others, chatting with colleagues from the *Los Angeles Times* and other news organizations. Frank stood by himself, absorbing the atmosphere of anticipation.

"Hey, Flynn, don't get washed off the bridge." Jimmy Tall Horse and Eddie Laguna ambled in his direction. They were an odd pairing, mainly united by their penchant for trouble. Tall Horse was a towering Lakota Sioux who had married into the Big Pine Paiute band. Eddie was Eddie, small and wiry, the silver bell tied to his ponytail announcing his presence. "Hi, Frank." Eddie flashed a perfect smile. New white teeth framed a golden incisor. Alphonso Bedoya in *Treasure of the Sierra Madre*, Frank thought.

"So what do you think of my gold tooth?" Eddie's smile widened.

"Class, Eddie. An undertaker's wet dream."

Eddie's eyes opened wide, and the smile wavered. "I never thought of that." Then he relaxed. "Hey, that's okay. I'll give the tooth to my cousin Hector Goodwater. After I'm dead," he added. Frank wondered how he'd work that out.

Tall Horse leaned forward and lowered his voice. "I've been telling the reporters from Los Angeles about how Wovoka died up here in this valley and how his visions passed on to a secret Ghost Dance society that's still around." He grinned. "A lot of these reporters know about the Ghost Dance and who Wovoka was. So I've been telling them that some of the Ghost Dancers weakened the structure of this bridge and that we're all going to be swept away when the water's released." He laughed. "That would be okay, too. There's more white shitheads on the bridge than Native Americans. They act like they don't believe it, but see how they been moving away from the middle of the bridge? Now we've got a good place to stand, huh?"

As they were talking, there was a stir, and the mayor and several officials from the Department of Water and Power moved to the control platform operating the sluice gates. One of the Water and Power officials raised his voice and explained what was going to happen. Then the mayor pulled a toggle switch and there was a heavy vibration as the sluice gate inched slowly down and water began to pour over the edge. After a few inches it came to a stop.

"That's it?" Frank heard a disappointed television cameraman ask. There were more murmurs of disappointment from some of the reporters gathered on the bridge, especially from the television crowd. They had been expecting a roaring torrent, a great dramatic rushing of the waters. The water coursing over the gate into the holding pond raised a mild splashing at the end of a three-foot drop.

Frank had to admit that it hardy looked like the release of a mighty river. Tall Horse said something about getting the same effect by flushing six toilets at the same time.

Frank looked down from the bridge into the still water of the holding pond. A gentle current stirred the surface as the water began the long journey to the dry bed of Owens Lake. The Department of Water and Power hydrologists estimated it would take nineteen days for the water to reach the dry lake sixty-plus miles away at the south end of the valley. There newly installed pumps would recapture the water and return it to the aqueduct to quench the ever thirsty giant some 230 miles to the south.

Still, nothing could dim the moment for Frank. The water was coming back, not all of it by a long shot, but enough to restore some of the valley to the way his mother's people had known it. He squeezed Linda's hand in silent joy. Now maybe the ancient guardian up on the ridge could leave his stone prison and wander off with Coyote in search of mischief. He thought about the billboard across the highway from Ralph's Burritos, the picture of Jesus with the words SHALL FLOW RIVERS OF LIVING WATER. Who knew what things meant?

AN INVITATION TO THE READERS
OF THE DESERT SKY MYSTERIES

•

For those of you who belong to book clubs and discussion groups, I'd be pleased to join you in a discussion of this book or its predecessor, *Shadow of the Raven*. Both have thematic material of contemporary interest and both are set in the Owens River Valley, a place still remote and of great beauty. Let me add a thank you for reading this book. There's nothing like a good story. I hope this book has served that end.

David Sundstrand

Web site: http://www.davidsundstrand.com
E-mail: sundstrand@pyramid.net